ON EARTH AS IT IS IN HELL

THE OCULUS GATE SERIES

BOOK ONE: HEAVEN CAME DOWN
BOOK TWO: INVADING HELL
BOOK THREE: MY SOUL TO TAKE
BOOK FOUR: ON EARTH AS IT IS IN HELL

ON EARTH AS IT IS IN HELL

BOOK FOUR IN THE OCULUS GATE SERIES

BY

BRYAN DAVIS

On Earth as it is in Hell

Published by Mountain Brook Ink under the Mountain Brook Fire line
White Salmon, WA U.S.A.

All rights reserved. Except for brief excerpts for review purposes, no part of this book may be reproduced or used in any form without written permission from the publisher.

The website addresses shown in this book are not intended in any way to be or imply an endorsement on the part of Mountain Brook Ink, nor do we vouch for their content.

This story is a work of fiction. All characters and events are the product of the author's imagination. Any resemblance to any person, living or dead, is coincidental.

Scripture quotations are taken from the King James Version of the Bible. Public domain.

The Lord's prayer, traditional version in the public domain.

American Colony, and Horatio Gates Spafford. Draft manuscript copy of hymn "It is Well With My Soul" by Horatio Gates Spafford. to 1878, ca. 1873. Manuscript/Mixed Material. https://www.loc.gov/item/mamcol.016/.

ISBN 978-1-953957-28-3

Published in association with Cyle Young of Cyle Young Literary Elite.

© 2023 Bryan Davis

The Team: Miralee Ferrell, Alyssa Roat, Kristen Johnson, Cindy Jackson
Cover Design: Indie Cover Design, Lynnette Bonner

Mountain Brook Fire is an inspirational publisher offering worlds you can believe in.

Printed in the United States of America

Chapter One

Ben clutched the console's steering yoke as a gust slapped the hijacked transport pod. It careened to the side and flew toward a treetop, seconds away from collision. He jerked the yoke and dodged the limbs, missing the branches by inches. "Any ideas?" he asked, breathless.

At his side, Kat stood bracing herself with a tight grip on the back of Ben's seat as she studied the console's radar screen. "Veer to the right about ten degrees." Her words shook with the bucking pod. "A little less stormy that way ... I think."

Green lightning flashed, brightening the twilight sky for a moment. Clouds boiled above. From the left, a spinning funnel charged toward them with a deafening roar. "Tornado at nine o'clock! Making the turn." As he shifted the yoke, he glanced at Kat. "Picking up any radio signals? Signs of life?"

She blew her pageboy-style bangs out of her eyes. "This is Viridi, not Earth. I don't think any radio bases exist. And this transport pod doesn't have the infrared trackers. We have to rely on visual."

"And spot Leo in this storm? Impossible." Ben peered through the rain-spattered glass. "But Caligar's parachute might be big enough to see."

"He can't deploy a chute in this wind. It would be suicide."

"Suicide if he doesn't. He can't jump back through the portal." Ben glanced to the rear. The darker clouds appeared to be behind them now, though wind and rain still buffeted the pod. Before their portal jump from the Alaska tower site, Caligar mentioned that the season of storms had begun on Viridi, and the early ones were often monsters. "He knows his planet. Maybe he took a risk and dropped super quick. Deployed the chute at the last second. If he's already on the ground—"

"Parachute," Kat said, pointing. "Ten o'clock. Snagged in the treetop."

Ben swiveled in that direction. At the top of a windblown tree, a limb perforated an oversized parachute. Caligar held to the chute lines from below, swaying and bobbing with the limb's chaotic lurches. Time and again he pulled on the lines, apparently trying to climb to the limb and maybe catch hold, but with each effort, the wind slung him back. Of course, he could shrug off the pack, but since he hung about eighty feet in the air, he couldn't possibly survive a drop to the forest floor.

Kat touched the exit door's handle. "Get us under him and hold steady. I'll bring him in."

"Let me do it." Ben tried to rise, but the bullet wound in his foot sent a knifing stab up his leg, forcing him to sit again. "Give me a second and I'll—"

"You're benched, hero. Stay where you are."

Ben heaved a sigh. She was right … as usual. "Take something to cover your head and face. The rain is highly acidic here."

She pulled a cap from her back pocket and put it on, then lifted a neck scarf over her nose. "Don't worry. I got this."

"It's not your abilities I'm worried about." Ben steered the pod toward Caligar. "It'll take a miracle for me not to crash this flying tin can in this crazy storm. The driving propellers aren't exactly hurricane strength."

"Maybe so, but I believe in you." Kat opened the door. Wet air rushed in and swirled in the cabin. She whipped a knife from her belt and climbed out onto the pod's roof, leaving the door to bang against its frame as the windy assault continued.

Ben lowered the pod into the forest, barely fitting between Caligar's tree and the one next to it. As the beating door fanned stinging droplets against his cheeks, he settled under Caligar's bobbing legs. With each bob, his shoes struck the metal roof. Now he could safely shrug the pack off, especially with Kat's help, but only if the pod stayed close.

Kat's voice punched through the roof, muffled. "The lines are wrapped around his chest. I have to cut them off. Hold real steady."

"Easy for you to say." His hands white-knuckle tight around the yoke, Ben battled the gusts, forcing the pod to cut through the blasts. The boots continued drumming against the roof, a good sign, though nerve-racking.

A familiar roar penetrated the pod's cabin. Ben looked toward the source. The tornado ripped through the trees, tossing broken branches in all directions—maybe thirty seconds away. "Twister's coming! Hurry!"

Kat grunted. "Stay put. One more line to cut."

A branch slammed against the side of the pod. Glass shattered. New gusts punched through. The branch's jagged end butted Ben's shoulder like a sharp battering ram, throwing his hands from the yoke.

He slapped the branch away and regripped the yoke. The tornado spun closer and closer. Debris flew in a swirl, veiling nearly everything. The pod lurched, kicked, rocked. In seconds, they would be blown away. "Kat! Update!"

No voices responded. No shoes pounded the roof. Only the roar of the tornado filled the pod as it drew closer and closer.

"Kat!"

Something slapped the roof. "We're secure! Go!"

Ben shoved the throttle. The pod zoomed forward, angling toward the chaotic sky as the exit door banged again and again. The moment they broke into the clear, Ben reversed course, flew behind the tornado, and landed in its debris-strewn path.

He leaped out and looked at the pod's roof, blinking to see through the sheets of rain. Kat and Caligar sat on top, the parachute tied around their torsos as well as a roof antenna.

No longer wearing her cap, Kat pushed her hair back and smiled. "What a ride! I knew you could do it."

Caligar untied the chute and rose to his full ten-foot height, a large pack on his back. "It was, indeed, a harrowing ride. Although

I did not expect to see you here, I am grateful that you came. Releasing myself from the clutches of that tree would have been time consuming, perhaps impossible."

Ben nodded. "Especially with a tornado coming at you."

When Kat freed herself, she and Caligar made their way to ground level. The trio crowded into the pod, their hair and clothes dripping. Ben sat in the pilot's chair, Kat cross-legged on the floor next to him, and Caligar with his back to the rear cabin wall as he stripped water from his long braid, his parachute pack sitting next to him.

He blinked his huge eyes at Ben and Kat. "Why *are* you here? Have the plans changed?"

"Well ..." Ben glanced at Kat as she pulled her saturated shirt away from her skin. She gave him a resigned shrug. Caligar needed to know everything.

Ben focused on the giant's curious face. "Short version. Iona's in Alex's clutches in the angel cruiser, as planned, but Leo tried to save her by grabbing a landing runner. Alex flew through the Gate with Leo dangling below. We thought he might have fallen, but we're not sure, so we followed to see if we could rescue him. The storm squashed that mission."

Caligar nodded. "This has been a bad one, worse than any I ever saw on Earth, though I have seen a few like it here."

"I saw green lightning," Ben said. "Does Viridi get any other weather that we don't get on Earth?"

"Also red lightning, but I don't think there are any other material differences. Tornadoes are rarer on Viridi than on Earth. I have seen only one other here in my lifetime. It is highly unlikely that another will arise. We are safe here for the time being."

Ben glanced at the boiling sky. Getting an encouraging update from a native of this planet helped him breathe more easily. "Speaking of safe, are you concerned about your family? Do Winella and Bazrah know what to do when a storm like this comes?"

"I am concerned, but Winella is well versed in weather forecasting. I'm sure she and Bazrah hurried to our refuge when she realized this storm was brewing."

"Oh. A refuge. Not your observatory tower."

"Correct." Caligar set an elbow on his knee with his arm upright and waved it back and forth. "The tower is vulnerable in storms. High winds can force it into a sway, and it could topple. That's why I dug out a refuge in a cliff face within a half-hour's walk from the tower. The cave is not high in comfort level, but it is safe, dry, and well-supplied with food and technology. In fact, I installed a radio that receives and records a constant live audio feed from the tower. That way, I would know if any intruders are there while I am at the refuge."

"Good thinking," Ben said. "I suppose you'll want to check on them as soon as possible."

"At the proper time, but I am confident in Winella. She excels at watching over our … over Bazrah. All will be well." Caligar's shoulders drooped, and he let out a sigh.

"What's wrong?" Kat asked.

Caligar looked at her. "My own words are like a dagger. I almost said our children, but Alex killed Lacinda, my daughter, and she will not return to me. All will not be well."

Ben set a hand on Caligar's shoulder. "I'm sorry, my friend. I've been so focused on saving Earth from that evil witch, I haven't considered the catastrophe she inflicted on your family. Losing a daughter has to be devastating."

"It is, but you have no reason to apologize. Although I am glad that you consider me a friend, I have not earned that label. I betrayed you. I threw you into hell as a way to try to save Lacinda."

Ben compressed his shoulder. "I forgave you. You have proven your friendship—"

Caligar batted Ben's hand away. "I have proven nothing!"

Ben and Kat looked at each other, then again at Caligar. Kat spoke in a soft tone. "As you said, we're safe for now. We have some time. Tell us what's on your mind."

A tear trickled down his cheek. "I betrayed the most courageous man I have ever met, and for what? A promise from a witch in hell. Yes, I did it to save my daughter, but I am still guilty of a heinous act. I had no faith that Lacinda could be rescued without my treachery. In my wretched cowardice, I chose a foolish option based on fear, something that I know Benjamin or Katherine Garrison never would have done."

Silence descended except for the sound of wind whistling through the broken window. After a long moment, Ben spoke up. "I don't have a daughter. I can't imagine how difficult that decision must have been."

Caligar pointed a finger at him. "But you understood sacrifice. The second time you entered hell, you chose to go to rescue Iona. When I threw you in earlier, I had a similar choice, to go in myself to save Lacinda, but I opted to trust Alex instead." He rolled a hand into a fist. "There is no use trying to minimize the evil of my actions, and I cannot go back and undo my terrible choice. It's impossible." He withdrew a knife from a belt sheath. "But this I can do. I make an oath that I will never betray you again. I will never trust that witch again. I will reflect the courage and steadfastness that I see in you." He drew his braid in front. "Cutting off my braid and offering it to you in a handshake is the most solemn of vows on Viridi. I hope you will accept it."

As he set the knife to the braid, Ben raised a hand. "No, Caligar. Don't cut your braid."

Caligar paused. "Why not?"

"I don't need your solemn vow. I believe you without it. Save the vow for someone who wouldn't trust you otherwise."

Caligar stared at Ben for a long moment before sliding the knife back into its sheath. "I see the wisdom in this." He brushed a tear with a knuckle. "We should move on. The life of our friend Leo might be at stake. It is clear that, to you, he has been like family, and now he is to me as well. We must do all we can for family."

Ben gazed into the giant's mournful eyes. What could anyone say that would assuage his damaged conscience? Considering the circumstances, they shouldn't continue plowing unproductive ground. "You're right. For family. We'll focus on Leo."

"Yes," Kat said, her brow tight. "If Leo survived, we have another potential problem. He thinks Ben and I are dead. If he made it into the cruiser and told Iona, then she thinks so, too. Not sure what problems that might cause, but we need to be aware."

Ben pointed at her. "Exactly right. And Alex will use Iona's confusion against her."

Caligar opened his pack and looked inside. "Have you confirmed Alex's goal for coming here?"

Kat shook her head. "Not really. We're still pretty sure she wants Viridi for herself, but I think she's vindictive enough to try to destroy Earth. The devices her minions built under the Alaska tower looked more massive and complex than when the tower was just part of a conduit-generating network."

"Then we should move on." Caligar spread a hand toward the pod's control console. "May I suggest that we fly to my portal mirror on the mesa? Alex's only information about Viridi must have come from Dr. Harrid, and he might have told her how to use the mirror in ways about which I am unaware, perhaps with a destructive result for Earth. With the landscape so similar in most places, she could still have trouble finding it, especially in this storm. Perhaps we can arrive before she does."

Ben clenched his jaw. After all the talk about being *for family*, ending the search for Leo felt like abandoning a family member, giving up on a loyal friend and ally, but his chances of survival were almost nonexistent, and Iona was in Alex's clutches. Caligar's suggestion made sense. They had to choose to follow Iona's trail while they could.

He looked at Kat. "Can you track Iona's transmitter?"

"Maybe." She rose and tapped a finger on her chin as she studied the pod's controls and readouts. "The radio is less sophisticated than a SkySweep drone's, but it looks like it can scan for signals. Iona's tracker frequency is on the standard range."

"Then we can find Iona even if Alex isn't heading for the portal mirror."

Kat nodded firmly. "Yeah. I think so."

Ben mimicked her nod. With no leads to Leo's location, rescuing the fiery redhead from Alex was far more important. "Then let's brave the storm and get back in the air. We'll go to the mesa first, orient ourselves, and figure out what to do next."

Iona sat next to Leo in the luxury cruiser's passenger compartment while Alex piloted the craft in the cockpit, her hands tight on the steering column. With only her shoulder-length blonde hair and black leather jacket visible, Alex's eyes stayed out of view as she battled windswept rain and beating gusts. Completely focused on the storm, she was too busy to worry about what her two hostages might do.

Iona lowered her cloak's hood and gazed out her side window at the forest far below as she fingered the cross dangling at the end of its leather-cord necklace. She and Leo couldn't jump out. That would be suicide. And hijacking the cruiser was impossible because Alex had made herself the only pilot the computer would recognize. Only she could fly it, and only Kat could undo that command. Either escape attempt would end with a fatal crash to the ground.

Using a fingertip, Iona touched a tiny bulge in her camo pants pocket. The tracking transmitter Ben had given her lay inside. Since he and Kat were dead, it could never lead a rescuer to her location. But it held in its memory a mysterious tune that might be able to rescue everyone on two planets. All she had to do was play the tune in front of a special mirror and get Alex to touch the reflection. Then Alex would plunge through the mirror's portal and go straight to hell. At least that was the theory.

Iona let out a quiet sigh. Unfortunately, Alex had taken the mirror, a small square that Iona had hidden, but not well enough. Although she had managed to keep the transmitter out of sight, it wouldn't do any good without the mirror.

Her bladder pinched. It had been several hours since she had emptied it. At the moment, the storm had eased a bit. Maybe now was a good time to go.

Just as she unbuckled her seatbelt, a hefty gust shoved the cruiser hard to the right, tipping them to a sharp angle. The force tossed Iona against the window.

Leo grabbed her arm. "I've got you." As the cruiser regained its flying angle, he pulled her back to her seat.

"Why weren't you buckled?" Alex shouted from the cockpit, her silvery eyes glinting as she glared at them.

"I have to use the toilet." Iona fastened her belt. "It felt safe."

"It's not. Worse weather is ahead. You can wet yourself for all I care, but I don't want you getting thrown around the cruiser. Now stay buckled and hunker down until I say otherwise."

Iona folded hands on her knees and leaned forward. Leo bent low as well, his face only inches from hers. As they rode out the worsening bounces, she gazed at his rugged profile, his swarthy chin and cheeks covered by thick stubble and his mane of dark hair nearly touching his shoulders. With her red hair, fairer skin, and freckles, she looked nothing like him, no sign that they were biologically father and daughter. And with herself decked out in camo under a reddish Reaper's cloak and him in a black huntsman cloak, they didn't even look like they fought for the same team.

Even so, they were related, a fact revealed not so many hours earlier. And her mother was Charlie ... or Charlotte ... the Reaper she had met in hell, now dead because she sacrificed herself to open the gates of hell to let her newfound daughter escape.

Iona set the cloak's sleeve against her lips and kissed it. Charlie's soul also escaped hell, not physically, but as a disembodied spirit dwelling within these reddish-brown fibers. It seemed that she vanished after helping Iona reattach her own soul to her body. Being outside the fibers for a moment probably caused her to get whisked away to heaven. She gave up everything to save a daughter she barely knew.

Iona breathed a quiet sigh. At least she had the cloak. Earlier, Alex had taken the cloak to search the fibers, thinking Charlie's soul might be there, but when the search failed, Alex gave the cloak back to Iona, merely a keepsake now, but a treasured one.

A tear crept to Iona's eye. She brushed it away and grasped her cross. She couldn't let her mother die in vain. She had to keep fighting Alex in Charlie's name. And maybe now that she and Leo had an excuse to hunker low, it might be a good time to formulate a plan.

She whispered, "We've got to do something."

Leo looked at her with bloodshot eyes, probably a leftover symptom from having his soul stripped from his body and later restored in a violent manner. "Have you been mulling an escape option?"

"Nothing new. I've already told you everything I can think of."

"Which wasn't much."

"Tapping out a message in code is slow. I couldn't risk Alex listening."

Leo lowered his voice further. "I know. I know. But she's distracted now."

Iona lifted her brow. "Any ideas?"

"Well, I had some time to do a little mulling myself." The cruiser bounced hard, making them knock their heads together. Leo drew back and winced. "Jolts like that make my soul's reattachment points throb. At least I think that's what's happening. It's hard to keep my thoughts in a straight line. Maybe the genius ginger will brainstorm with me."

Iona rolled her eyes, but protesting the genius label would only give rise to another of Leo's nicknames for her. "Great. Let's do it."

He leaned closer, nearly nose to nose. "Alex has no direct use for me. I am a burden to her and, because of my size and skills, a potential danger. But she hasn't killed me, which means she'll probably try to use me as leverage against you."

Iona nodded. "Makes sense. Go on."

"And I think she's counting on that leverage to get you to meet with Satan."

Iona cringed. "So you know about that."

Smiling, Leo touched his nose. "You can't hide much from me."

"Your nose didn't tell you about a meeting with Satan."

"No. Damien did. But my nose leads me to the next part of my plan. When we land and the door opens, I will attack Alex and try to take the mirror from her. During the scuffle, you will escape into the storm. Run as fast and as far as you can. It doesn't matter where. I'll find you."

"Because of your nose."

He touched his nose again. "Exactly."

"Only if you can escape from Alex. That's a big *if*. And how will you take the mirror from her? Is it even on her right now?"

Leo nodded. "Jacket. Left pocket. I see her feeling it from time to time."

Iona scrunched her brow. Why would Alex check the mirror? Because of its truth-telling abilities? Was she able to listen in on their conversation even under these circumstances?

Iona whispered. "Back to tapping code. Just in case."

"Compromise. Tap out new information. Speak vaguely about what we've already decided."

Iona nodded and tapped a finger on her knee. *After you find me, what next? Ben and Kat are dead. We will be stranded on Viridi.*

Leo tapped on his own knee. *Jack and Trudy are alive. They will look for us.* His thick eyebrows bent low as he added out loud, "Eventually."

11

Another hard bounce rocked the cruiser, making them clutch their hand rests. Iona leaned even closer to Leo and whispered, "Alex might be a far better fighter than you think. She might kick your butt."

"Then my kicked butt ..." Leo tapped, *will at least give you time to get away. You have the tracker. If I don't find you, Jack and Trudy will.*

"Leo ... I mean, Dad ..."

He set his hand over hers. "Keep calling me Leo. That's what we're both used to."

"All right." Iona took a deep breath. "Leo, I didn't go on this mission to be *safe*." She tapped the rest of her message. *I came to send Alex to hell. Impossible without the mirror.*

His finger taps accelerated. Apparently his brain was working better now. *I realize that. One of us needs to take it from her. But even if we fail, there are other portal mirrors. Jack and Trudy know about them.* Leo settled back in his seat and mumbled, "Anyway, that's what I've been mulling."

Iona began tapping on his elbow. *I'm worried about you, taking all the risks while I'm running like a coward.*

"You're no coward." He tapped his finger next to hers. *We can't battle Alex if we're in her clutches. We have to escape.* He leaned close again, speaking with a firm whisper. "I caught hold of this ship's landing runner to save you, and that's exactly what I'm going to do."

When Iona opened her mouth to answer, Alex barked, "I see the portal mesa. We'll be landing in a minute. Hold on tight. This could be a rough descent."

Iona clutched Leo's hand and whispered, "It's show time."

Chapter Two

Trudy stripped off her bloodstained surgical gown, revealing camo pants and shirt—sweaty after the knee operation she had completed about an hour earlier. She wadded the gown, tossed it into a laundry bin, and walked to Jack's bed as he lay recovering. Except for a slight drop in blood pressure, his vitals seemed good. Most of the anesthesia had left his system. He could wake up now.

She compressed his shoulder. "Hey, Jack. You've been sleeping on the job long enough. We've got work to do."

His eyes darted under their lids, and he let out a soft moan. "My knee hurts."

"No kidding, genius. Someone shot you, and I put your kneecap back together. Six pieces. I painted a message on the biggest one. 'My sister rules.'"

"Very funny." He opened his eyes. "Where are we?"

"Temple bunker sleeping quarters. I had to rearrange it for surgery." She nodded toward the exit. "That door goes to the hallway leading to the computer room. Weapons cache is on the left as you go through the hall."

He nodded. "Got it. I'm oriented."

She touched a control button on the bed. "Want to try to sit up? I have a lot to tell you."

"Yeah. Sure."

She pushed two buttons, one to raise the head of the bed and the other to lift the support under his knees. As the segments moved into place, he grimaced. "What did you cut me open with? A chainsaw?"

Trudy smirked. "Pizza slicer. I couldn't find a chainsaw." She straightened the sheets and blankets. "I licked it clean, though."

"Thanks, Sis." He blinked at her, his eyes bleary. "Give me the scoop."

Trudy grasped the bed's rail with both hands. "I've been trying to contact Ben and Kat. The last I heard, they were in Alaska to sabotage the tower after Iona and Caligar got through the Oculus Gate. Our computer here shows no signals from the tower at all. Nothing."

"Maybe they succeeded with the sabotage, and they lost any way to communicate."

"Possible, but we have to go there to check it out. Not sure where we'll get transportation, but we'll find something. You're the pilot who can fly anything, so maybe—"

Something thudded in the computer room.

Jack angled his head to see past Trudy. "What was that?"

"I'll check." She walked toward the door.

"Hey, could you look in the weapons cache for a signal analyzer? I saw a Nova Seven in there earlier. It'll be perfect for checking out that chip Damien had in his neck. Give me something to do to take my mind off the pain."

"Copy that."

"And the chip. I'll need the chip."

She spun toward him. "I put it in a little plastic case. It's in your pocket. I knew you'd ask for it."

"Oh." He pushed a hand under his covers. "Got it. Thanks, Sis."

Trudy pivoted and strolled into the computer room. The huge display hung on the wall, dark and cracked. Only a desktop monitor on the table in front of the display gave evidence that the temple's massive system still operated. On the opposite side of the room, the vault's thick door stood closed, triple locked with Kat's personal security codes. Since no one else knew the long series of digits, the door would stay shut tight.

Trudy looked at the desktop monitor. It displayed a single box that requested the entry of a password, exactly as expected, but it might be a good idea to check the vault's security again. She typed in Kat's password. The display cleared, and security system windows appeared. She studied the settings. The vault door, still triple locked, revealed no entry attempts.

One window showed a facial-recognition program running in the background, an application she started a few hours ago to get an ID on the driver who delivered surgery supplies. So far, no results.

Everything seemed secure, no sign of where that thud came from. Maybe a change in temperature caused an air channel to expand and bend a metal panel. Relieved, she strode to the weapons cache, found the Nova Seven in a backpack, and carried it to Jack, a strap on her shoulder. She set the pack on his lap and turned toward the computer room. "You can play with that while I see what kind of transport I can scare up."

"No. Wait." He pointed toward the adjacent wall. "Help me get in the wheelchair. I'll go with you."

"No way. You're still soused with anesthesia, but I can wheel the bed out there."

He shook his head. "Quicker recovery if I can get in the chair. Pain will clear my head for analyzing the chip."

"Gotta be the macho man, don't you?" Trudy heaved a sigh and ambled toward the chair. "All right. But don't expect me to wipe your tears if your boo-boo makes you cry."

"Did you find anything that caused that noise?"

"Nope. It made me jumpy because of what happened when the surgery equipment arrived." Trudy grasped the chair's handles and began wheeling it toward Jack. "I used Kat's credentials to unlock the vault. No problem. After the delivery driver helped me haul the stuff in, I relocked the door with the same codes, but I heard something beeping, like it was echoing the codes in the door."

Jack's eyes narrowed. "Maybe that driver had a device to read the codes while the door accepted them."

Trudy parked the chair next to the bed and set its brake. "Exactly what I was thinking."

"No ordinary driver, then. It would take high-level hacking skills and intimate knowledge of the security system."

"Maybe one of Alex's hundred influencers. She was a woman, early thirties, about five seven. Physically fit. Wore a cap over short, dark hair."

"Did you get an image from the security camera and run a facial rec?"

"Yep. No hits yet. And right after surgery I tried to change the vault's locking codes, but the system asked for Kat's thumbprint. So the codes are the same as they were before, but the noise still bothers me." She nodded toward the hallway leading to the weapons cache. "We have enough firepower to repel a small army. Gas masks if they shoot a nerve agent in here. I think we're safe."

"Right. No use being paranoid." Jack lowered the bedrail and tried to get up, but Trudy pressed a hand on his shoulder. "Hold your horses, tough guy. Let me help you."

"Whatever you say, doctor." Jack extended his hands toward Trudy. "Ready when you are."

She lowered the bed as far as it would go and helped him into the wheelchair while keeping his injured leg as immobile as possible. With every movement, Jack winced. Only a few grunts escaped his lips as he settled in the chair, his leg propped on a padded chair extension. He looked at his clothes. "Did you dress me?"

"Sure did. Washed your camo threads, cut a big hole in the knee, and put them on you while you were knocked out. Less pain that way. Your boots are with your rifle in the weapons cache. Not that you'll need them, but we can get them on the way out in case you're up on crutches soon."

Another thud pulsed through the air, coming from the computer room. Jack narrowed his eyes. "That's the sound the vault door makes when it's being unlocked."

"I think you're right." Trudy rushed out, grabbed a rifle from the weapons cache, and hustled to the computer room.

The desktop computer beeped. The monitor showed the photo of the delivery woman next to its facial recognition match. Trudy whispered the caption. "Camilla Richert, Director of Technology at Cyber Wars Incorporated. Born in England. Age thirty-two."

Jack rolled in, pushing the wheels while holding a rifle, his boots, and a backpack in his lap. "Got some intel?"

"Yeah." She pointed at the screen. "The delivery woman was Camilla, Alex's toady. She put that death chip in Damien's neck. Obviously she didn't come here to help us."

"And no sign of her now."

"Nope, but I'll check the door." Trudy switched to the security screen and studied it. "The first two levels are open. Someone made four attempts to open the third using the wrong codes. It's holding." She sat in the desk chair. "I'll relock the other two, but I can't change the codes without Kat's thumbprint."

While Trudy worked on that task, Jack set the Nova Seven on his lap and opened a lid, revealing a control panel with dozens of dials and tiny LED displays. He showed Trudy the chip from Damien's neck, still lying in its tiny plastic case. "The theory is that this transmits a signal so that Alex can track down her comrades. Let's see if we can read the signal." He flipped a power toggle, making the device hum, and slid Damien's chip into a slot on the panel. A high-pitched note pierced the air. He turned the volume down and read a meter. "Okay. I got the frequency. But what we don't know is if everyone's chip emits the same signal. They might have varied them slightly for identification purposes."

"True, but I think they would all be close. A narrow range of frequencies."

"Most likely." Jack extended an antenna rod from the panel. "This will let us collect signals from a greater distance. No idea how far, though."

Trudy touched the edge of the Nova. "Now let's talk about the reason for analyzing the chip."

Jack lifted his brow. "The kill switch?"

"Right. Alex tried to activate the switch to kill Damien. If we can neutralize all the influencers with a kill-switch signal, we'd stop them in their tracks. That might be playing dirty, but all's fair, you know."

"Good point." Jack nodded toward the desktop computer monitor. "I'll look into that while you lock down a transport for us. Something that flies fast. The faster, the better."

"Not sure if a jet rental company is around, but I'll see what I can find." Trudy rolled the chair to the computer monitor and touched the screen, but nothing happened. She tapped it again, harder, but it stayed frozen. "I think I've been locked out."

"That's weird."

"Yeah. First time this has—"

"Not that." Jack squinted at the Nova's panel. "I mean, I'm getting another signal that's nearly identical to Damien's chip. Like another influencer is close by."

The vault door thudded, a lock disengaging.

"Camilla must be trying to get in," Trudy said. "She has the chip you're picking up."

Jack set the Nova on the desk and aimed his rifle at the door. "Get more weapons."

"On it." Trudy ran to the weapons cache, threw on a belt, and loaded it with ammo magazines. After grabbing two more automatic rifles, she hustled out. The moment she set a rifle on Jack's lap, another thud reverberated in the room. "That's level two."

"Let's give Camilla something to think about." Jack fired shot after shot at the floor inches in front of the door. The bullets strafed the concrete and clanked against the metal door. After about a dozen rounds, he glared at the entry. "Come on in, Camilla. I have something for you."

"Oh, so frightening!" The woman's voice came from the computer desk. "Is that how you welcome all visitors?"

Trudy spun that way. Camilla sat on the desk, still dressed in her delivery uniform, complete with gray coveralls and cap. Her legs dangled, casually kicking back and forth.

Jack wheeled his chair around and aimed his rifle at her. "How'd you get in here?"

Camilla chuckled. "I've been here for hours, ever since I delivered your surgery supplies." A third thud sounded. The vault door opened into the exterior corridor. No one stood on the other side. "As you can see, your security system is nothing more than a vapor to me. Laughable."

Trudy growled, "How did you do that?"

Camilla took her cap off and shook out her short curls, boyish in style, similar to Jack's. "An automated sequence I programmed while you were in surgery. Watching you type in the password before you began operating on Jack gave me all the access I needed."

Trudy set her rifle barrel against Camilla's head. "How did you get in, and why are you here?"

Camilla smiled without a hint of fear. "You let me in. You thought I left, but I decided to stick around awhile." Her face turned transparent, then her entire body. Within seconds, she was invisible, though her voice continued. "I have a Refector inside me. A Radiant." Her body shimmered from head to toe, briefly highlighting her features as the energy rippled—vague but recognizable.

Trudy lowered her rifle. "Stop putting on a glitter show and answer the second question. Why are you here?"

Camilla's light faded, and her body returned to normal. "I need your help." Rising anger spiced her tone as her brow bent low. "Your allies forced Alexandria to fly through the Oculus Gate prematurely, and they also damaged the Alaska tower to the point that the conduit network is inoperable. A specialized part has been damaged, and it will take weeks to replace it."

Jack shrugged. "Yeah. We gave that hellish witch the heave-ho. Mission accomplished."

"So you think." Camilla pushed herself off the desk and stood in front of Jack. "Alexandria is gone, but Iona is her hostage. I assume you want her to return safely."

Jack glared at her, his steely countenance unflinching. "As if you can do anything to prevent that."

"Such masculine bravado." Camilla set a hand on his repaired knee. "Shall we test how well you can keep that jaw firm?"

Trudy swung her rifle around and crashed the butt into Camilla's forehead. She staggered back, slammed a hip into the desk, and vanished to a light-filled silhouette, shimmering and sizzling. A lightning bolt shot out and slammed into Trudy's shoulder. She flew through the air, crashed to the floor, and slid nearly to the exit.

Her shoulder feeling aflame, Trudy sat up and struggled to her feet. Camilla, now visible, stood next to Jack with a hand on his chest. His eyes had closed, his head lolling to the side.

Camilla shouted, "I stopped his heart, Trudy. Agree to cooperate with me, and I will restart it."

Trudy lumbered toward them. "I can restart it, you gutless bug zapper."

A second bolt shot from Camilla's disembodied hand, grazing Trudy's ear. It burned like hellfire, but she refused to react as she staggered on.

Camilla raised her energized hand again. Radiance boiled in her palm. "One more step, and I'll cook his heart like pork sausage!"

Trudy halted. As she glared at Camilla, the room seemed to spin. Her shoulder burned. Numbness crept down her spine. In moments, she might collapse. Gasping, she breathed out, "Start his heart. I'll cooperate."

"Wise choice." Camilla pressed her hand against Jack's chest. His body jerked in a rocking spasm. When he settled in the wheelchair, his wounded leg hung haphazardly over the support. Camilla drew away, smiling like a satisfied tigress. "Perfect rhythm restored."

Trudy trudged on stiff legs to Jack's side and felt his wrist pulse. Yes, his heart thrummed in a normal cadence, though he was no longer conscious. She lifted his wounded leg and set it gently on the support. She looked at Camilla standing at the other side of the wheelchair. Surrendering to her felt like bowing to a demon. Every word of concession burned her lips like acid. "All right, Camilla. You win. For now. What do you want us to do?"

Camilla's smile turned sickeningly victorious. "My intel says that you were in Jerusalem only a few hours ago, and I know from the computer logs that you have been here most of that time, which means that somehow you instantly transported from Jerusalem to here. Is that true?"

Jack let out a low groan, his eyes blinking. He would probably wake up soon, most likely in a lot of pain. Trudy focused on Camilla. "Yes. It's true."

Camilla set a fist on her hip. "Don't make me ask for everything. Just spill what you know."

Trudy gave Jack another quick glance. He opened an eye, then shut it, awake and listening, apparently able to avoid cringing at whatever new pain he felt. Suffering through a heart stoppage had to be torture.

She locked her stare on Camilla. "Are you familiar with Alex's mirror in hell?"

Camilla squinted. "I have no idea what you're talking about."

"I see. She's been keeping secrets from you. Even Damien knew about the mirror."

Camilla's face turned semitransparent for a moment, pulsing with radiance, then returned to normal. "Alexandria informs people on a need-to-know basis. Obviously I didn't need to know about this mirror."

Trudy rolled her eyes. "Spoken like a true sycophant. Brainwashing complete."

Camilla growled, "I am not brainwashed."

"Oh? Then ask yourself why Alex wouldn't tell you about a special kind of mirror that can instantly transport you somewhere. You said yourself that your intel had us in Jerusalem. Well, we found such a mirror there, which is why we were able to get home in a flash." Camilla's cheeks flushed. It was time to drive the dagger deeper. "Alex told Damien about the mirror, to find one for her, and Damien was just a grunt she was ready to sacrifice when she finished using him. My guess is that you consider yourself higher on the food chain than Damien, but she didn't let you in on the secret."

Camilla scowled. "I know what you're doing, trying to drive a wedge between Alexandria and me. It won't work."

"I'm just laying out the facts. If you choose to ignore the obvious, that's up to you. But I know that Alex is for Alex, no one else. Her minions are simply useful tools … or fools. You'll learn that when she tosses you away when she's done with you."

Camilla's face faded again to transparency. Only blazing lights in her eyes remained visible. Sparks flew from her mouth as she spoke. "Do you have access to another of these mirrors?"

Jack cleared his throat. "Yes. At the Alaska tower. Why?"

Trudy spun toward him. He sat upright with both eyes open, his face pasty white. He was lying, off course, and she had to play along. "The one in Caligar's cave? In the silver frame?"

"That's the one, but the frame's not real silver. Wood painted with metallic paint."

"Yeah. I knew that." Trudy refocused on Camilla, who had returned to normal. "We have one. Why do you want it?"

Camilla's eyes glimmered in an unearthly manner. "So my comrades and I can join Alexandria on Viridi. This has been our plan all along. If you help me, you'll be rid of us forever."

"Gotta say, that's good motivation." Trudy crossed her arms. "Get us to Alaska. We'll be glad to use the mirror to send you and all Alex worshippers off this planet."

Camilla gave Trudy a long stare, as if searching for a hint of deceit. "I have a helicopter in the parking lot that will fly us to a jet. Can Jack endure a chopper ride in his condition?"

Trudy smiled. No need to ask him. "Of course. He's a trooper."

"Then pack a bag and meet me in the lot in fifteen minutes. No weapons. You will be searched." Camilla walked out the vault door at a casual pace and disappeared into the hallway.

Trudy rushed to Jack and lifted his shirt. His skin seemed to pulse with redness. "Does your chest hurt?"

"It burns." He pushed his shirt down. "What did she do to me?"

"Stopped your heart, then restarted it with her electric touch."

He set a hand over his heart. "I was wondering. I had an out-of-body experience. Not the first time that's happened."

"Yeah. I know. Did it scare you?"

"Not scared. Excited." A bright smile broke through the pain. "I thought I was going to heaven to be with Sophie and Alana." His smile wilted as a wince returned. "Waking up was pretty disappointing."

"I understand." Trudy ran a hand through his thick curls. "Any thoughts about Camilla? Do we go with this Alex ally? We can't take weapons."

"Without a doubt. Easy transportation to Alaska, and ..." He slid the Nova Seven into the backpack. "If I can figure out the kill switch, we won't need weapons. We know she has a chip."

"Since she was here so long, she must have heard us talking about the kill switch." Trudy stripped off her weapons belt and set it on the desk. "Maybe her chip doesn't have one, and she's not worried about it."

"Or she was *told* it doesn't have one. I had a good look at Damien's chip. It's old school, nothing Cyber Wars would come up with. I'm guessing Harrid made them for Alex."

Trudy nodded. "And he would've put the kill switch in all of them. Alex would lie to Camilla about that."

"Exactly. Camilla still has no clue that to Alex, she's just floor sweepings."

"Maybe I shouldn't push that idea. We'll let Camilla think she's a golden girl, Alex's number one, indispensable agent."

"Good strategy." Jack read the display on the Nova Seven. "Back to the kill switch. I already know Damien's chip emits a signal that tells us the frequency of the kill-switch signal, but I don't know what a kill message sent to the chip has to say to make it work. But since his chip was activated, I should be able to figure it out with a back trace."

"Suppose you can figure it out. Wouldn't it still take a while to work? Damien's activation was on a countdown timer. Four hours until it poisoned him with some kind of toxin. At least that's what Alex said."

"She's a liar. His chip has no timer, but it does have some kind of chemical inside. I don't know what it is yet, but you can bet it's toxic."

"So that means she planned to be in range four hours after her threat so she could send the kill-switch signal to his chip."

Jack nodded. "Or one of her minions could do it."

"Hello?" The new voice came from the vault door. Austin stood at the opening, his cloak's hood lowered to reveal his shaggy, over-the-ears hair. When he saw Trudy and Jack, he smiled. "I see I've come to the right place."

"Austin?" Trudy cocked her head. "Why are you here? I thought you were taking Charlotte's body to the crematorium and then the ashes to her family."

"That mission didn't go as expected." Austin averted his eyes as a tremor invaded his voice. "The crematorium was closed. Wouldn't open for two days. So I decided to try to transport her body as is. She has an uncle who lives a couple of hundred miles from here. I found a trucker with a refrigerated trailer who was willing to give me a ride there." Austin shoved his hands into his cloak pockets and looked directly at Jack and Trudy, tears glistening. "I felt terrible putting Charlotte in that refrigerator, but … you know."

As Trudy imagined the process, an icy sensation ran down her spine. She resisted the urge to shudder. "Of course, Austin. You had to do it."

"And I checked on my parents. They both died while I was in hell. The only relative I have left is an aunt who never liked me." He shrugged. "I didn't have anywhere else to go."

"You're more than welcome to join us." She waved a hand. "Come on in."

Austin ambled closer, his hands still deep in his cloak pockets. "Anyway, back to the first question. The trucker had a lot to say about what's been happening lately. Of course, I didn't tell him that I've been patrolling hell for the past four years and didn't know anything. I just let him rattle on."

"Can you give us a summary?" Jack asked.

Austin halted a couple of paces away, glancing around nervously as if uncomfortable with the surroundings. And no wonder. After so much time in hell, he needed time to adjust. "Apparently hundreds of millions of people headed toward the Arctic Circle because they were afraid of a contagion, and they were told that only a few thousand doses of a vaccine were available. So what did the people do? They started murdering each other so they could get the shots, and no one in charge tried to stop them."

"The angels probably planned for that to happen." Jack nodded. "Go on."

"So now the population of the Earth is way down. Less than a billion. And a lot of them are like zombies, wandering aimlessly. And some of them are violent. They try to kill anyone they come across."

Trudy let herself shudder this time. "The vaccine boosted with a violence payload did that. They have no souls."

Jack twirled a finger in the air. "Let's wrap this story up. We have to get going."

"Sure." Austin spoke more quickly. "When we arrived, her uncle removed her body from the trailer. I couldn't watch. I just turned around and hitchhiked my way back here."

"Must've been awful," Jack said. "I know what it feels like to lose someone close."

Austin withdrew his hands from his pockets and spread them. "Then you know why I want to help. Charlotte was the only friend I had in the world. We literally went through hell together."

"Of course," Trudy said. "But I'm not sure what you can do to help."

"Well, like all Reapers, I've been trained in the martial arts, so I can handle myself in a fight. And Alex is an Owl, a specialized Reaper." Austin touched his chest. "So am I. I know what she's capable of and how to weaken her."

"Like what, for example?"

"Well ... let's see ... one of her strengths is that she can resist wounds that aren't normally fatal. In other words, if you wing her, it won't slow her down much at all."

"And a weakness?" Jack asked.

"Owls rely on their vision. If you can somehow reduce her ability to see, she could become disoriented. But darkness won't help. We Owls see quite well in the dark."

"Sounds like you know what you're talking about." Jack extended a hand. "You're on the team."

Trudy nodded. "Any help we can get to stop Alex, I'm all for it."

Austin shook Jack's hand. "Great. Thanks."

"Ever been to Alaska?" Jack asked. "That's our next stop."

"Nope. Born and raised in Maine, though. Not as cold as Alaska, but close enough. I can handle it."

Trudy bent her brow. "We'll have to think of a good excuse to get Camilla to let him come along. It's her transport jet."

"Camilla needs us." Jack thumped a finger on the wheelchair's armrest. "We'll insist. If she balks, I'll come up with something."

"No need," Austin said. "As a Reaper, I can transform into what we call ghost mode. I can become like a disembodied soul, invisible to the eyes of a normal person."

Jack blinked hard. "Invisible? You're kidding, right?"

"Either invisible or semitransparent. Reapers have always been able to do that. In the radiation days, Reapers collected souls because a radioactive cloud surrounded Earth, keeping the souls grounded here. Reapers needed a special energy supply to transform, but, to make a long story short, it turned out that the energy created an addiction that caused them to be crippled without it. Reapers like me who never had the energy can transform without it. And as an Owl, I can transform super quick. Other Reapers are much slower."

"What about Alex?" Trudy asked. "Can she become invisible? From what I've heard, she was a Reaper during those radioactive days."

"Then she's crippled by exposure to the energy, but since she's an Owl, maybe she can. I'm not sure."

"No worries. We'll deal with the here and now." Trudy pointed at Austin. "You'll stowaway in ghost mode and get weapons for us from Caligar's lair. Then we'll take control of the tower site."

Austin lifted a finger. "One problem. When I've been in ghost mode for more than a few minutes, I need some adjustment time afterward. And the longer I've been in that mode, the longer the recovery time. After a flight to Alaska, I'll be dizzy and disoriented for quite a while, maybe half an hour."

"So when you get to Caligar's lair, come out of ghost mode, and we'll stall somehow till you show up with the weapons." Trudy strode toward the sleeping area. "I'll pack bags for all three of us—warm clothes, flashlights, food."

"And a ham radio," Jack said. "The relay station we set up is probably still working."

She halted and looked back. "Not a good idea. Camilla said they'll search us and your backpack, probably take it away."

"Same with the Nova Seven."

"Austin can pick up a ham radio in Caligar's lair. I know exactly where one is. Camilla probably won't object if I bring a medical bag, but we'll have to come up with a convincing lie for keeping the other stuff."

Jack grinned. "I leave the lying up to you. You're good at that."

Trudy bent over and set a hand on his knee. "I repaired this joint, I can break it again."

"Okay. Okay. I'll come up with a lie while you get our clothes." He nodded toward the doorway leading to the vault's sleeping quarters "Get plenty of layers. I'm not looking forward to another Arctic blast."

"You got it," Trudy said as she walked away. "It's time to go polar again."

Chapter Three

Iona held Leo's hand tightly as they sat side by side. The craft descended through gusts that blew it hard to the right, threatening to toss them out of their seats. After several shifts and bounces, the cruiser finally landed on the mesa's top. The hum of the engine died, though the whistle of wind and patter of raindrops continued.

Alex rose from the pilot's seat and stepped into the passenger compartment, her hair in disarray. "We will wait here for the storm to ease."

Leo whispered, "Now." He leaped up and lunged at Alex.

Sucking in a breath, Iona hustled to the side door and pressed the open button. When the door slid to the side, she looked back. Leo had Alex in a head lock from behind, both standing in the aisle. Iona rushed back, dug into Alex's jacket pocket, and yanked out the mirror. As Iona backed toward the open door and slid the mirror into her cloak's pocket, Alex closed her eyes and went limp, while at the same time pulling a knife from a belt sheath.

"Leo!" Iona shouted. "Watch out. She's got a knife."

Alex jerked away from Leo and slung the knife at Iona. The blade grazed her shoulder, tearing the cloak. Alex whipped around and kicked Leo in the face. He staggered into the cockpit and fell. From his back, he shouted, "Go!"

Iona jumped out of the cruiser into wind-driven rain and looked back as the acidic water stung her face. Alex stood at the doorway with a handgun. "Get back in here, you fool."

From behind Alex, Leo grabbed her wrist, thrust the gun downward, and pulled her deeper into the cruiser. Grunts and guttural shouts burst through the open door, but the fighters stayed out of view.

As furious gusts roared across the exposed mesa and blasted Iona with torrential rain, she clenched a fist. Of course she wanted to help Leo, but she had to follow the plan. Blinded by the rain, she brushed a hand across her eyes and scanned the area. The stairs lay to the left, the only way to safely get off the mesa.

She took a few steps that way, imagining the battle in the cruiser behind her. If Alex ended it quickly, Iona wouldn't be able to run very far. Alex could use the cruiser's infrared scanner in a small search zone to find her. But that threat could be ended here and now.

Her eyes half closed to see through the stinging rain, Iona staggered back to the cruiser's prow, removed the mooring cap, and stuffed it into a cloak pocket. She rushed to the mesa's stairs and descended, planting a foot on each slippery step with care.

When she reached the bottom, she looked at the narrow path leading around the mesa. Water cascaded down the mesa's sides and sloshed into rivulets that dug widening channels in the path, making it far more precarious than before. And to the left, the parallel-running river had risen to within a few feet of the path. Farther along the way, the path might be underwater, but she couldn't stay this close to Alex. She had to press on.

Sometimes walking on tiptoes and sometimes jumping over water-torn gaps, Iona traversed the path and arrived at the trail that led to Caligar's observatory. Ahead, the river ran across the trail from right to left in foamy torrents, a seemingly impassable flood. Beyond the water's far edge, the trail led upward to a higher elevation, but at least two hundred feet of rushing water lay between her and safety, water that would burn like acid.

She waded ankle deep into the flood. The water surged against her leg, pushing hard and making her reset her stance to keep from falling. From head to toe, the rainwater burned like harsh lye, already turning her hands bright red. If she didn't find shelter soon, she might turn into a boiled lobster, and Caligar's observatory stood as the only shelter that she knew about, though it would be the obvious place for Alex to search. Another option—a dense forest lay on the far side of the river to the left, a potentially good place to hide, but that would still require a river crossing.

She bit her lip hard. Every choice seemed potentially deadly, but the end result had to be getting somewhere far away from Alex, no matter where that might be. Leo could find her, assuming he survived, but trying to swim across this torrent was suicide. There had to be another way.

She backed out of the water and scanned the ground. A few broken tree trunks lay here and there, likely deposited by the river when it flowed at an even higher level. Obviously they were able to float or they would have sunk instead of being tossed to the side.

She chose the log closest to the water's edge and pushed it into the river, maintaining a firm grip on a short stub of a broken limb to keep it from being carried away. She walked it farther into the flood—knee-deep, thigh-deep, waist-deep. Then she let the surge sweep her and the log into its grasp. She swam with the flow, one arm battling the churning current as she rushed downstream and the other curled around the log. With every beat of her arms and kick of her legs, she pushed herself closer to the other side of the river.

Acid burned her cheeks, hands, and every inch of her body, like bees swarming, crawling, stinging. Ahead, a boulder protruded from the riverbed. Water blasted against it, sending splashes high, like liquid convulsions. She would crash into the rock in seconds.

She tried to steer the log away from the boulder, but the brutal current fought back. She released her grip on the log and let it go, then turned herself into a feet-first position. When her shoes struck the rocky surface, she let the impact bend her knees for a split second, then she tried to spring away from it at an angle, but the furious flow sent her upward, launching her through the air. When she splashed into the flow on the other side of the boulder, water rushed into her mouth. She swallowed some and spat out more, while the rest jetted into her lungs, then burst out again with a gush of burning bile.

Now no longer buoyed by a log, she battled the river with all four limbs, inching her way to the other side. After several minutes, her hand struck a narrow tree trunk. She hung on and fought to lift herself. Her feet pushed against the riverbed until she stood upright. The water rushed by at waist level, the shore only a few steps away. Beyond the water's edge, a dense forest rode a slope to a high hill—safety from the onslaught.

She looked at the narrow, leaf-bare sapling she held, a steady anchor at this spot. Could she let go and wade the rest of the way? That seemed to be the only option.

With the saturated cloak weighing her down, she set her feet firmly and released the sapling. She took a step toward the edge, checked her balance, and took another. The slow, deliberate slogging worked well, but her burning lungs and throat made her cough and wheeze, threatening to throw her off balance.

When she reached shallow water, she dropped to all fours and crawled the rest of the way to shore. She stopped on the muddy ground. Her head low, she coughed again and again, spitting bloody sputum. Wind battered her body. Rain beat across her back. Water dripped down her hair and mixed with the blood and mucus. After escaping the river, might she now drown in her own fluids?

Finally, the coughing eased, though the stinging pain in her throat and chest burned on. Setting a hand on the ground, she pushed herself upright, then trudged into the forest, both feet sliding in the mud. The rising slope battled her cramping legs, but it also provided hope that she would leave the flood far behind. At least she didn't have to worry about the pinch in her bladder any longer. The rough ride in the flood saw to that.

In the forest, huge trees with wide trunks towered all around. Head-high boulders lay here and there with no hint of their origins, maybe glacial deposits from long ago that the trees grew around in more recent years. In any case, thinking about these mysteries helped take her mind off the horrific pain.

Not far ahead, a large flat stone jutted out of a knoll, providing a sheltered spot underneath. After checking her cloak pockets and verifying that the mirror and mooring cap were safe, Iona hobbled to the stone and crawled underneath. Finally sheltered from the storm, she sat upright with her legs crossed to keep them out of the rain. The stone hung only an inch above her head as she rested her back against the knoll to the rear. Outside, wind howled, and rain poured in cascading white sheets that washed away any sign of footprints she had left behind. At least Alex would never find her here, but could Leo?

Iona sighed. Now to wait while drying off as much as possible and trying to ignore her burning skin. Unfortunately, she had nothing to dry off with. Only time would evaporate the stinging water, and with the humidity so high, that might take hours. At least she could get the saturated cloak off and wring it out.

When she drew her arm in from the cloak's sleeve, a whispered voice entered her ears.

"Iona, can you hear me now?"

"What?" She jerked the hood up over her head. "Charlie? I mean, Mother?"

"Call me Charlie. I've come to like that name. I've been trying to talk to you ever since you escaped from Alex. The surrounding noise has been deafening."

"It has." Tears welled in Iona's eyes, and her swollen throat roughened her voice. "I'm sorry I couldn't—"

"No apologies. I know what you went through. I've been in the cloak all along. Being a Reaper, I can see beyond the fibers, and, of course, I can literally hear the pain in your voice."

Iona sniffed. The burning pain continued, especially across her face. "Okay. Then you know what's going on."

"I do. I am so impressed with your courage. And Leo? Your father is truly heroic. He risked his life to make sure you could escape."

"He did, and I'm worried about him."

"You should be. Alex is formidable. Deadly. But Leo is relentless, as you well know. We should have hope that the light he follows will lead him to safety."

Iona narrowed her eyes. "About that. You've said you're not sure if Leo's in the light or in the dark. Since he risked his life for me, doesn't that mean he's in the light?"

"Perhaps. I am still contemplating that. His love for you is beautiful, a shining light, but something is still wrong. I can't put my finger on it. He is a mystery."

"True. And he is relentless, like you said." As Iona imagined Leo fighting for his life, a mental picture of his huntsman days arose, memories of him tracking her all night in an attempt to bring her back to the angels. He admitted that greed motivated him at the time, but when he met her, everything changed. "I do have hope."

Charlie spoke closer to Iona's ear. "I think Leo will—"

"Can we change the subject?"

"Uh ... yes. Of course. What do you want to talk about?"

A new sting pinched Iona's cheeks. The drying seemed to worsen the pain. "How about you? How did you stay in the cloak without Alex finding you?"

Charlie laughed. "Alex is crafty and is quite adept at searching through these fibers, but I know every twist, turn, and crevice in this cloak. Her senses whisked right past me several times, and she was too impatient to delve further. Her arrogance makes her believe that she would have easily found any Reaper in this cloak."

"I can believe that. She's arrogant to the max."

"Which means that we should figure out a way to exploit that fault. She is blind to how much her arrogance cripples her."

"I hope so." Iona's voice rasped. She cleared her throat, spiking the pain. "I think I need to rest."

"Of course. Take the cloak off, wring the water out, and spread it over your legs. Get some sleep. I'm sure you'll be safe here for a while."

"It'll be hard to sleep with my skin stinging from head to toe. Especially my face and throat."

"Very sensitive skin in those places, but maybe we can do something about it." Charlie hummed for a moment before continuing. "I would like to conduct a test, if you don't mind."

Iona lifted her brow. "A test? What kind of test?"

"A test of your powers."

"My powers? What do you mean?"

"We'll soon find out. And don't worry. You don't have to move a muscle." A sparkle rode down the cloak's left sleeve, then back up to the hood. "Did you see anything unusual?"

Iona blinked as she tried to focus on the wet fibers. "Just sparkles on the cloak."

"Good. Now close your eyes and concentrate on my voice. Let your mind meld with it. I want to try to take you on a journey."

"Okay." Iona leaned her head back against the knoll and closed her eyes. "I'm ready."

"When I'm not talking, I will be humming. Stay focused on the sound." Charlie's hum vibrated into Iona's ears, lovely and comforting. "Can you feel anything?"

A tingling sensation ran along Iona's face. "Tingles. Especially in my cheeks."

"Is it soothing? Is the pain going away?"

"Yes. It feels good." A sense of pressure drew her head to the side. "Is something pulling me?"

"Yes. I am pulling you. You might feel a little pain, but don't resist. It's all part of the test."

"Okay." Iona relaxed her muscles and allowed the sensation to take control. As the tension increased, she seemed to flow somewhere. But where? Impossible to guess, but the sound of wind and rain fading made it clear that she was leaving the storm behind.

After several seconds, Charlie whispered, "Open your eyes."

Iona did so. In the midst of blackness, a redheaded woman stood next to her, holding her hand. Her face lacked detail, but who else could she be? "Charlie?"

"Yes." She drew closer, her features clarifying as she caressed Iona's cheek. "How is the pain now?"

Iona touched her other cheek. "It's gone. I feel fine all over."

"Good. Then the test worked."

"What did you do?"

"Remember when we pulled Leo's soul from the Lake of Fire, how much pain he was in?"

"Yes. It was awful."

"Worse than awful. And the pain would have continued if I had not drawn him into my cloak. You see, hell provides physicality to a soul while it is in that realm. Not so in my cloak. The soul loses all physical properties and any pain associated with being physical. Souls experience healing there, and when they emerge from the cloak again, much of their pain is gone. I did the same for you."

"But I'm physical. How could you draw me in?"

"I wasn't sure I could, which is why I called it a test. It proves something that I suspected since the day we first met. You have Reaper powers. You are the daughter of a Reaper, so it's no surprise."

"But all souls can be drawn into a cloak," Iona said. "How is that a Reaper power?"

"The power is being able to transform into a spiritual state. We Reapers call it ghost mode. During the radioactive days on Earth, Reapers often used this skill to help guide wayward souls into their cloaks. It was safe for them at the time, because the radioactive shield covering the Earth kept them from being taken up, but it wouldn't be safe now. Here on Viridi, though, a soul stays put, at least that's what Ben told me. Apparently, he heard it from Dr. Harrid. In any case, once you transformed into a soulish state, I drew you in. Now you can rest without suffering the torture of the acidic water."

"Thank you." Iona ran her fingers along her cheek, now smooth and pain free. "I do feel much better. But will I heal here like the souls of dead people do?"

"I'm not sure. Maybe a little. I don't have any experience with doing this for living people. Once you revert to your physical form, we'll find out."

"I understand," Iona said. "Either way, transforming to ghost mode will come in handy when I need it. I'll have to practice."

"I don't think you'll have a problem. You see, my test proves that you're not only a Reaper, you are an extremely powerful one. Though you don't seem to possess an Owl's gifts, like Alex has, such as hyper-acute visual perception."

Iona shuddered. The word *Reaper* felt like the icy touch of a phantom. "What other powers can I expect to have?"

"For one, you will be drawn to the souls of the dead, to their feelings, like sadness, fear, desperation—the fruits of suffering. And any wandering soul will be visible to you even when not visible to others."

"What good would that do? Every soul has gone to heaven or hell, right? They're not wandering around as ghosts."

"Yes, I suppose you're right, but perhaps being able to detect the feelings will be helpful. You will sense them even among the living."

"That could be helpful." Iona pulled on her once-saturated shirt, now completely dry. "And I'm glad I'm escaping the pain now. Being a Reaper is pretty good so far."

"Yes, pain avoidance is a big benefit, but I can't let you stay in this state for very long. Otherwise the transition back to physicality will be difficult. Your brain will have a hard time adjusting. You will feel dizzy and disoriented, and the more time you spend here with me, the more time you will need to adjust when you return."

Iona nodded. "I understand."

"Then for now ..." Charlie sat on the black expanse, pulled Iona down with her, and drew her close, cheek to cheek. "Let's rest together. When you go into a deep enough sleep, I will send you back to your physical form. The pain will be minimal while you're asleep."

Iona nestled into her mother's arms and closed her eyes. Everything fell dark, and all sensations fled, except for Charlie's fingers running through her hair. Soon, she fell asleep, floating in the blackness—no pain, no worries. At least for now, she could rest and try to heal.

After several minutes, the sounds of the storm returned—whistling wind and pounding rain, background noise to lull her toward sleep. A dream began, Leo battling Alex in the cruiser. As fists flew, she winced at each blow he took to his face. At times he seemed to be holding his own, using his size to overwhelm her, but her speed and agility, combined with her martial arts skills, soon proved to be more than he could handle.

While still dreaming, Iona prayed, "God, please help Leo to be sharp-eyed, quick-minded, and strong. And even though their fight probably ended long ago, I hope my prayer does some good. Thank you for giving me a father who loves me more than he loves himself. Amen."

Chapter Four

Leo jerked Alex into the cruiser, knocked the gun from her hand, and threw her down the aisle toward the cockpit. She rolled into a somersault and leaped to her feet, facing Leo. The gun lay on the floor halfway between them.

Leo dove for it. As his face neared the floor, Alex charged and kicked him in the cheek. Something popped in his neck. Pain surged. Trying to stay conscious, he flailed for the gun. His fingers coiled around the barrel, but Alex pulled the handle in the other direction, the barrel pointing at him.

He turned the barrel just as the gun fired. The bullet zipped past and thudded into the cruiser's wall. He wrestled the gun away and aimed it at Alex. She kicked it out of his grasp, then thrust a foot into his gut, sending him to the floor in a reverse slide.

She scooped the gun, leaped at him, and landed in a sitting position on his chest. She set the barrel against his forehead. "Don't move a muscle."

Leo froze. One flinch, and she would likely blow his brains out.

She hissed, "You're a fool! You thought helping Iona escape would protect her, but you're wrong. This planet is unsafe. You've put her in danger."

Leo stared at her, still unflinching.

"Okay." Alex drew the gun back an inch. "You may explain yourself."

Leo cleared his throat. "*I* put her in danger? So says the greatest threat to both Earth and Viridi."

"Are you blind? Were you not watching as we flew? The storm is ferocious, and a raging river separates us from Caligar's observation tower, the most likely place for her to go. With her stubborn spirit, she won't let the danger of drowning stop her. You know that."

Leo imagined Iona pushing herself through a raging river, her eyes flashing with fierce determination. "I must admit that you're right. She would brave a flood."

"Then now you understand the foolishness of your rash actions."

"I didn't say that. I don't believe your plans for her are any less dangerous than a flood."

"You don't have to believe. I just need you to stay alive. You might be the only way I can get her cooperation." Alex rubbed the back of Leo's neck, applying something wet and warm. "And that should make you compliant until I find her."

Leo looked into her silvery eyes. With a gun aimed at his head, the only option might be to feign cooperation. "Maybe if you tell me more about your plans, I'll be motivated to help you."

Alex brushed her finger against her pant leg. "I don't need your help, only your presence as leverage. The cruiser's scanners will find her."

Tingling numbness spread across Leo's neck and down his spine. That witch's potion had started working. "Iona eluded me for days and had only a bicycle while I rode horses with two skilled helpers. She's cunning and clever."

"That much I already know." Alex rose to her feet. "Which is why I need her."

Leo pushed up to a sitting position in the aisle. His hands and fingers grew numb, and his legs would no longer move. "Why do you need her? Tell me. Maybe I can be persuaded to help."

"Not likely, but I don't mind telling you while we wait for the storm to settle." Alex closed the cruiser's side door and sat cross-legged in front of him. "Satan demanded to speak to her. She has gifts she doesn't even know about yet, and he wants to teach her how to use them in order to destroy hell."

"Destroy hell?" Leo blinked, his eyelids now drooping. "Why? And how could Iona do that?"

Alex took on the tone of a teacher. "The Lake of Fire was created for Satan and his minions. In the last days, God plans to deposit Satan there and leave him to suffer forever along with his followers. As you might expect, Satan wishes to avoid that eternity."

Barely able to move his lips, Leo spoke more slowly. "Okay. Fair enough. But what is Iona's role?"

Alex slid the gun into a belt holster. "The Arctic Circle towers on Earth are designed to create what my allies and I call a portal wheel, a massive revolving door that can lead to multiple destinations, one of which is a site where Iona must meet with Satan. I was going to take her there myself, but we had to leave Earth more quickly than I expected. Now I have to figure out a way to get her back there, perhaps by using Caligar's mirror, and then we'll use the portal wheel."

"And what does Satan want Iona to do?"

"Assemble a bomb that she will eventually place in hell. The bomb is similar to the missile Kat invented, the one that temporarily destroyed the conduit between Earth and the Oculus Gate. When the bomb explodes, the energy will rip hell into pieces."

"How do you know it will work?"

"Kat's missile was a test. It destroyed a temporary hell Satan created within the Oculus Gate. As you might know, he is a powerful archangel, or at least he was until God cast him out of heaven. He still had the power to fabricate the test."

Leo's throat numbed. He wouldn't be able to speak much longer. "Why Iona?"

"The bomb requires a human catalyst to set it off. The same was true for Katherine's missile. My understanding is that a brave woman volunteered to sacrifice herself to save the world."

"Yes. Chantal. But, again, why Iona? I would take the bomb myself if it meant Iona didn't have to."

"Of course you would. Any good father would sacrifice himself for the sake of his daughter. But this bomb won't kill Iona. Satan has known about her for years, that she has a special gift. As the daughter of a Reaper, she has gained Reaper powers, though she is not yet aware of them. She is endowed with the ability to transform into a ghost-like state and avoid the explosion. Then she will fly safely out of hell."

"Aren't you a Reaper?" Leo asked. "Couldn't you be the catalyst?"

"In theory, but my ability to transform has been crippled. I can partially transform but not fully. Perhaps being in the restoration box for so long has caused me to lose some of my power."

He smirked. "Or maybe you're a coward."

She punched him in the cheek. He fell to his back, unable to touch his face. The point of impact burned, though not as badly as expected. The numbness at least provided that benefit.

"Stay there." Alex rose and strode toward the cockpit. "The storm is letting up. We're going to find Iona."

Barely able to see her from his position, he focused on her gait, no longer a cocky strut. Losing Iona had taken away her swagger. Apparently she needed her badly. It seemed that having to answer to Satan had shaken her up.

Alex sat in the pilot's seat and pushed a button on the control panel.

The onboard computer responded with, "Cruiser is moored."

"What?" Alex shouted a string of profanities. "That wench took the mooring cap!"

Leo smiled. Good for Iona. Smart, as always.

Alex stormed back down the aisle, drew the gun, and aimed it at him. "Wipe that grin off your face."

He let his smile wilt. He couldn't have held it in place for much longer anyway.

"Much better." Alex slapped the door button. When it slid open, she pointed outside. "Now you and I will have to search for her on foot."

"May I …" Leo swallowed. "May I remind you that you paralyzed me?"

"The paralysis will wear off soon." Alex sat again on his chest and set the gun to his nose. "I will let you guide our hunt with your impeccable Iona finder. If you lead me astray, I will shoot you in the back."

"And lose your Iona finder?" Leo asked.

Alex's smile took on a know-it-all air. "You want to make sure she's safe. If I find her without your help, I can't guarantee that I wouldn't break a few of her bones."

Leo harrumphed. "I'm not letting her meet with Satan. That's a deal breaker."

"Perhaps there's a way around that meeting." Alex rose and extended a hand. "If I can pull that off, do we have a deal?"

Leo stared at her hand. Striking a deal with this devilish witch made no sense, especially considering that she was probably lying. But maybe he could pretend to cooperate, then lose her and find Iona on his own. He tried to lift his hand, but it wouldn't move. "Deal."

Alex grasped his hand and, with incredible strength, hauled him to his feet. His knees buckled, and he dropped to the floor, again in a sitting position.

"All right," Alex said, "you need a few more minutes to recover." She stalked to the rear of the cruiser and opened a tall cabinet, the top of the door as high as her head. "Let's see what we can find in here." She withdrew a rifle-like weapon with a wide barrel. "A grenade launcher. Rather unwieldy, but it will be far more intimidating than my handgun." She set it on the floor and again rummaged in the cabinet. "Hmmm. This looks like an audio recorder and player." She slid a tiny device from the shelf and pushed it into her pocket. "And what do we have here?" She pulled out a folded stack of plastic. "An inflatable lifeboat. We'll need this to cross the river."

"That'll help. I don't think I can swim yet." Feeling a bit stronger, Leo grabbed the back of a seat and hoisted himself up. "But I can walk now."

"Good." Alex set the folded lifeboat in his hands and picked up the grenade launcher. "Let's go. And remember, I'll be watching your every move."

Ben, with Kat standing next to him, piloted the pod toward the portal mesa, following Caligar's directions as he sat on the floor behind Ben. Although the storm had quieted to a gentle rain, the pod shook. Propellers squealed. The surrounding metal panels rattled, and wet air seeped in through widening gaps as rivets gave way. The entire craft might soon rip apart.

"The acid level in the rain is high," Caligar said in a loud tone to compete with the noise. "This pod was not designed to withstand a pummeling onslaught of acidic water."

"Good point." Ben scanned the ground as Caligar's observatory tower passed underneath, barely visible in the clouds. "Only a couple of miles to the mesa. Let's hope it holds together another few minutes."

Caligar rose to his knees and looked out the windshield. "I can no longer provide accurate guidance. The weather conditions are not allowing for a view of the mesa or anything else."

Ben looked ahead. Clouds raced across the view, veiling all landmarks on the ground. "You're right. We're blind up here. I'm going lower." When they broke through under the cloud bank, a stiff breeze assaulted the pod. It bounced like a wild horse. The surrounding walls creaked with every shift, and the rattles spiked. "C'mon, you bucket of bolts," Ben grumbled, "hold together."

Below, the river rushed in a foaming turmoil, three times wider than before. Raging water smashed broken limbs against boulders and tree trunks, then carried the shattered remains along in the foamy wash.

Beyond the rampage, the mesa stood in view. A vehicle sat atop the flat expanse, its size and shape unmistakable. Ben squinted at it before muttering, "The angel cruiser."

"Yep." Kat grasped the back of Ben's seat to brace herself. "Alex made it to Viridi."

Ben tried to look through the cruiser's windshield. No one moved within or anywhere on the mesa. "This pod doesn't have an infrared scanner. I won't be able to tell if anyone's on board."

Still on his knees, Caligar scooted closer to the dashboard and looked on. "Alex has no reason to leave the cruiser during a storm. The acid in the rain would keep her inside. We should assume she is there."

"Agreed." Ben slowed the pod and turned into an orbit that would take them around the mesa. "Let's get another look."

The squeal grew louder. The pod dropped. Ben pushed the lower props to max. Their plunge slowed but not enough. He shoved the forward throttle. The pod surged ahead and fell at an angle, maybe enough to slide into a safe landing. And maybe not.

He shouted, "Hang on!"

The pod slammed to the ground and skidded across the wet mesa top. Metal scraped against rock as they hurtled toward the edge. Five more seconds and they would topple over the cliff and plunge more than a hundred feet to the rocks below.

Ben lunged for the door and flung it open. "Jump!"

He and Kat leaped out together. Caligar followed, but the momentum sent the pod and him over the cliff. He grabbed the edge with both hands and held on. Ben and Kat rushed to him and hoisted him to the mesa's top.

Below, the pod tumbled down the sheer face, banging against the rocks several times before resting at the bottom, the body deeply dented and the lower props still spinning and squealing. Two seconds later, an explosion erupted from within. The windshield shattered, and fire spewed through the jagged hole.

Ben blew out a long breath. "That was close."

Kat hooked her arm around his. "Understatement of the year."

"One benefit," Caligar said as he rose to his feet, "is that the pod caused no damage to the portal mirror." He pointed toward the mirror embedded in the ground to the right of the pod only a stone's throw away. Although wet from the rain, it emitted no light or even a shimmer in the cloudy weather. "Breaking the mirror would have destroyed your ability to return home."

Kat nodded. "Thank God for small favors, but we were planning to use the pod's scanner to track Iona."

"Let's start with the cruiser," Ben said. "She might still be on board."

Caligar turned toward the mesa's access steps. "I will look for a trail right away. The lingering rain will make any remaining signs more difficult to follow."

"Sounds good." Kat strode toward the angel cruiser. "Ben and I will try to get some intel from the cruiser."

While Caligar hurried toward the steps with his long-legged strides, Ben hustled to join Kat, though his limp slowed his pace. The blasted foot wound still hurt like crazy. When they arrived together at the side of the cruiser, Kat touched a threaded hole on the fuselage. "The mooring cap's gone. The only reason for taking the cap is to secure the cruiser."

"Then no one's on board." Ben pulled a handle on the side door, but it wouldn't open. "Locked."

Kat called toward the cruiser, "Open the passenger access."

The door slid open. Kat climbed in, followed by Ben. Inside the vacant ship, everything seemed to be in place. "Any clues?" she asked.

Ben scanned the craft in his immediate area—the inner walls, the seats, and the floor. A spot of red marred the floor only a foot or so from the entry. He knelt and touched the spot, then examined the tacky smear on his finger. "Blood."

Kat pointed at another spot. "More over here." She stepped past the blood, strode to the cockpit, and sat in the pilot's seat. "Computer, replay the recording of the last fifteen minutes of voice activity before my arrival."

The cruiser's computer responded with, "Audio replay commencing."

Ben sat in the copilot's seat and listened to a raucous scuffle between Alex and Leo. It seemed that Iona escaped, and now Alex was forcing Leo to help find her. Leo's voice, though crippled by some kind of drug, sounded like music. He survived. A true miracle.

When the replay finished, Kat looked at Ben, her tight features a portrait of pensiveness. "Good news and bad news."

"Right. Leo's alive, and I'm guessing Iona's body and soul have been reunited. She wouldn't be so active otherwise. But the rest is pretty bad."

"Did you hear what I heard? A meeting with Satan?"

Ben nodded. "Sounds ominous, but with Alex, it's hard to know what's true and what's not. It could all be a lie."

"Either way, Iona's in the wind. Alone. We have to find her before Alex does."

"Caligar's on the hunt, and I think we can count on Leo to lead Alex astray."

Kat shook her head. "I'm not so sure. Alex will tighten the screws on Leo one way or another. Now that Leo knows he's Iona's father, he's more vulnerable than ever to Alex's threats."

"True. But he's also smart. Let's not sell him short."

"Fair enough." Kat's brow rose sharply upward. "Iona's transmitter! The cruiser might have a portable tracker." She jogged to the rear of the craft, flung open a cabinet door on the back wall, and rummaged through a cache of electronic devices. She snatched a handheld unit that looked like a primitive walkie-talkie and walked toward the cockpit, her eyes still on the unit. "This might do it." After turning a dial on the front, she flipped a switch and halted a couple of steps away from Ben. "Yep. I'm getting a signal from Iona's transmitter's frequency, but it doesn't give me a location. Only signal strength."

Ben rose and joined her. "Then we'll combine Caligar's tracking with monitoring the signal."

"Exactly." Kat hooked the unit to her belt. "I'm ready."

When they deboarded, Caligar quick marched toward them from the mesa's stairs, breathless. "The river is rampaging, extremely dangerous. I tracked Iona's footprints to the river's edge, and it is clear that she did not turn back. I tried to wade across, but the water was too deep and the current too strong. I had to abandon the effort."

"Let me take a look." Ben limped to the mesa's edge that overlooked the trail leading to Caligar's tower. The river's usual course crossed the trail about a half a mile away, then turned with the trail, flowed parallel to it, and streamed around the mesa. At the point it crossed the trail, it had forged a new channel that bypassed the turn and churned into a forest to the trail's left.

When Kat and Caligar joined him, Caligar pointed. "Based on the presence of several tree limbs on the closer shoreline and an impression made by a limb that is now gone, it's possible that she used that limb to try to swim across with help from its buoyancy. I couldn't see any footprints on the far side, though I can't be sure because of the distance. My guess is that she either exited the river well downstream or she drowned."

Ben winced. "Let's avoid talking about that option."

"I am merely being realistic. Iona is resourceful, but she is not invulnerable. The river's current would sweep me away, and I am twice her size."

"Is there a bridge? Some other way we can cross?"

Caligar shook his head. "My advice is to wait for the river to recede enough for me to wade across. I can carry you on my shoulders one at a time."

"Any idea how long it will take for the river to recede that much?"

"Based on similar floods during previous storm seasons, I would say three to four hours."

Kat looked up at the sky. "Unless another storm comes, right?"

"Correct, though the atmospheric conditions are not portending one now."

Ben stared at the river as it sped from right to left—churning, foaming, and heaving with white caps. Apparently Iona waded right into that chaos to escape from Alex's clutches, a decision made in desperation.

He clenched his teeth. How could he stay put and wait for the flood to ebb? He had to find her. To help her. To—

"Hey, hero man." Kat slid an arm around his and pulled him close. "I know what you're thinking."

He gazed into her probing eyes. "You do?"

"Of course." She rose to tiptoes and kissed his cheek. "You taught me not to underestimate Iona. Now it's my turn to remind you. She is an amazing girl."

Ben drew in a long breath and let it out slowly. "You're right. Good reminder."

"And also remember this. God is on our side. Too many amazing coincidences have happened to us to think otherwise."

Ben's cheeks warmed. Getting a dose of reality jolted his brain back to sanity, but the medicine burned going down. "You're right, of course, but a lot of good people have died—Commander Barks, Doc, Summer, everyone else in our rebel squad, and in other squads. I'm worried that Iona might join them."

"I can't blame you for that." Kat patted his chest. "You have a good heart, Ben. Filled with love."

The warmth spread across the rest of his face. "Thanks. I appreciate the boost."

"While we're waiting …" She turned toward the mirror portal's control panel near the mesa's opposite edge. "Caligar, can we try to call Jack and Trudy using the ham radio frequency?"

"I will check." He strode in that direction and called back. "I keep a bow and arrow hidden in my control panel. We might have need of it."

Ben reached around to his waistband at the back and touched the handgun he had picked up in Alaska—still in place. Its full mag and Caligar's bow should be enough to fend off Alex.

Kat pivoted toward Ben and extended an arm. "Can you walk?"

"That far, sure." He took her hand, and the two walked together toward the control panel. Ben released a silent sigh. Her presence felt so good. He had to focus on her and what he could do, not on the young redhead and what he couldn't do. And let God take care of the rest.

Chapter Five

Iona awoke to a burning sensation on her face, but the reason seemed elusive, lost in a fog. Then, memories flooded in. She had swum in that acidic river to escape from Alex, and now she lay ... somewhere.

She opened her eyes. Still on her back under the rocky shelf, she glanced around. Rain continued, though now only a light drizzle. She shifted to a sitting position. Her cloak, camo pants, and shirt, still quite wet with acidic water, chaffed her tender skin. The pain would continue unless she could build a fire and dry off, but where could she find anything burnable in this saturated land or a way to ignite it? Maybe Charlie had an idea.

Iona pulled her hood up. "Charlie? Are you listening?"

"Yes. I am here."

"Any ideas on how to get dry? The wetness stings all over."

"Not unless you can find someone's abode."

Caligar's observation tower flashed to mind. It couldn't be far away. "I thought of a possible hideout, and I can follow the river upstream to find it, but it's probably the first place Alex will look for me."

"Perhaps she already has, and it's safe now. Or you could go in ghost mode, that is, the state you were in when I drew you into the cloak." Charlie paused. "No. That won't work. Alex could see you since she's a Reaper."

"Did you ever switch to ghost mode when the hell cats chased you?"

"I did once, but I learned that my state made no difference in hell. The cats could see and attack anyone in either mode."

"Okay, so back to the point. Since ghost mode won't help, how can I sneak into Caligar's observatory? The path to get there is out in the open. No forest to hide in."

"You took the mooring cap, so Alex will have to search on foot. And she'll probably take Leo with her. He's sure to detect where you are before Alex can. I think you can count on him to lead her astray."

"If she hasn't killed him." Iona heaved a sigh. "Okay. I'll take the risk. Better than burning up in an acid suit all day." She crawled out from under the protective rock and stood in the light drizzle, again raising a stinging sensation on her hands. Down the slope, the river raged on, still dangerous, though it provided a path toward her destination.

Trying to ignore the sting, she strode upstream while staying several paces away from the river. She dodged trees and boulders, tromped into and out of shallow ravines that channeled rainwater toward the river, and trudged through sludge—mud mixed with debris tossed to the ground by storm-shaken trees.

After twenty minutes or so, she arrived at the edge of the forest and halted. About thirty paces ahead, a trail led to her left and climbed a steep slope in the distance, switching back and forth until it reached a ledge. Above that, Caligar's tower probably still loomed, but the rainclouds veiled its presence. To the right, the river crossed the trail, still churning in a foamy froth, though not as violently as before.

Iona scanned the open area in all directions. No one walked anywhere in sight. "Looks clear, Charlie. I'm going to hoof it as fast as I can." Just as she lifted a foot to take a step, an odd sensation seeped in, like a pull in the opposite direction. She set her foot down and spun a one-eighty. Something moved behind a tree about fifty paces back. The object vaguely resembled a human form. She whispered, "Charlie, did you see that?"

"I can tell that you're looking back into the forest. That's about it."

"I think someone's there. But it's like I felt the person before I saw him or her."

"Interesting. Close your eyes and check if you can still feel it."

Iona did so. The same pulling sensation returned, like strings drawing her toward the movement, as weak and fragile as spider webs but still noticeable. She opened her eyes and drew a line that followed the sensation to a tree with a wide trunk. That had to be where the person hid. "I can feel it again. I know where it's coming from."

"You're feeling the presence of a disembodied soul. A living human wouldn't give you that sensation."

Iona scrunched her brow. "A ghost? Here on Viridi?"

"I assume so. Ben said it was only a theory that disembodied souls stay put here, but maybe now we'll have proof."

Iona called out, "Who's there? Show yourself."

A woman stepped out from behind the tree. Standing about five-foot-nine and wearing jeans and a long-sleeved button-down beige shirt over her narrow frame, she looked like a normal human from Earth. She pushed dark bangs from her eyes and squinted. "You can see me?"

Iona nodded. "My name is Iona. What's yours?"

"Quinn. Dr. Quinn Harrid."

Iona bit her lip. Carson Harrid's wife. She did look like the woman in the mirror's image who transported to Viridi, where she was eaten by the bestial giants. At this point, it might be better to feign ignorance about her identity and get her to spill as much information as possible. "Well, Quinn, I get the impression that you're surprised that I can see you. Why is that?"

Quinn scowled, bending her features as her tone turned bitter. "Because no one else can see me. Not the giants. Not even my own husband, whom I saw not many days ago. I figured out that I'm not on Earth, but why I'm invisible to everyone but you is a mystery." Her scowl deepened further. "But I doubt that a girl your age can help me figure it out. In your saturated condition, you look like you don't know enough to come in out of the rain."

Iona resisted the urge to shoot back with a barb of her own. She laughed in an amiable way. "I got caught in the storm, and the swollen river nearly drowned me. I'm lucky to be alive."

Quinn closed the gap and looked Iona over. "Since you can see me, I thought maybe you and I are in the same state here. If so, why is it that the rain makes you wet, but it doesn't affect me at all?"

"Because it's not so. You're a disembodied soul, and I'm not. I'm alive, and you're dead."

Quinn slapped at Iona's face, but her hand passed through, making Iona's cheek tingle as it swept by. Quinn drew the same hand into a fist and shook it as she raged. "I can walk on the ground. I can climb the trees. I can sit on the rocks. But I can't touch the people I see here. Nothing makes sense."

Charlie whispered, "Disembodied souls adapt to their surroundings so that they can achieve a semblance of physicality with them. But they cannot make bodily contact with living forms. It's a mystery that I don't understand."

Iona touched the tingling spot and smiled. "Well, Quinn, I, for one, am glad you can't touch me. That slap would've hurt like the dickens."

Quinn shook her fist at Iona. "I'd do worse if I could. You're obviously mocking me."

"You could reap her," Charlie said. "Send her into the cloak. I'll teach her a lesson in manners."

Iona rolled her eyes. As if she knew how to reap a soul. "Listen, Quinn, I know you're angry, but there's no use taking it out on me. I'll be glad to tell you what's going on."

Quinn crossed her arms. "Okay. Let's hear it."

Ignoring the persistent stinging wetness, Iona told the story of Quinn's transport to Viridi, her death at the hands of the giants, and her presence on Viridi as a wandering, disembodied soul.

During the explanation, Quinn's scowl deepened further, though near the end, every feature softened. Finally, she uncrossed her arms. "Do you know where my husband is? His name is Carson."

Iona gazed at her expectant eyes. She hoped for good news, but there was so little to give. Ben mentioned that Carson, that is, Dr. Harrid, murdered the remaining bestial giants, and Caligar skewered him with an arrow through the heart on top of the mesa, but his body wasn't around when they landed there in the angel cruiser. "I don't know where your husband is now, but I do know that he was trying to avenge your death. He killed the giants that killed you. Every last one of them."

"Killed all the giants?" A hint of a smile bent Quinn's lips. "Good. For all his faults, Carson was always loyal to me, even when I treated him like dirt."

Iona opened her mouth to ask why she treated him that way but thought better of it. "Listen. Maybe we can help each other. I have an idea where to look for Carson, but first I need to get to the observation tower. Have you seen it?"

Quinn nodded. "Inside and out. No one's been there in a while, as far as I can tell."

"No surprise, but I'm hoping to do something about these wet clothes. The acid in the water is scalding my skin. I need to get to the tower without a certain person seeing me. Her name is Alex, a tall blonde wearing black leather. Looks like a member of a motorcycle gang. Anyway, she'll be able to see you, so if you go out in the open and she's around, she might follow you. If you can lead her away from the tower, I can get inside and meet you there later. If not, we'll go to the tower together."

Quinn crossed her arms again. "So I'm your bait, huh? What do I do if she catches me?"

"She's after me, not you. Just tell her you haven't seen me. Or even better, you saw me leaving the tower."

"Lie for you?" Quinn let out a tsking sound. "So you're a lying schemer. If I lie to this Alex person to literally save your skin, you're going to owe me big time."

Several more well-deserved barbs rushed to mind, but Iona swept them aside. "True. And if I find Carson for you, that'll make us even."

"Fair enough. I'll see you at the tower." Quinn walked out of the woods and straight toward the trail with a quick, confident stride.

Seconds later, Alex emerged from the forest about a hundred yards upslope to Iona's left, followed by Leo. She jogged toward Quinn. She would catch up in a few seconds.

With Alex's back to her, Iona stepped out into the open. Leo looked back and spotted her. He gave her a sharp nod and waved a hand behind his back, signaling her to ascend the slope out of sight.

Iona nodded in return and, staying in the forest, climbed parallel to the trail while constantly keeping Leo, Alex, and Quinn in view. Now, even if Quinn pulled a double cross, she wouldn't know where Alex's quarry had gone.

Standing on the trail that led to Caligar's observation tower, Leo studied Alex's tight facial expression—serious, no-nonsense, perfectly sane, no sign that talking to an invisible person could be unusual in the slightest. Even the acidic drizzle did nothing to alter her countenance.

Alex set a fist on her hip. "All right, then, *Doctor* Quinn Harrid, I am addressing you as you requested. Have you seen a female teenager with red hair, wearing military camouflage and a reddish cloak? Her name is Iona."

While Alex continued standing in her stern pose with her back to the tower, apparently listening to Quinn's answer, Leo brushed stinging water from his face and sneaked a glance behind Alex. Midway up a steep cliff, Iona hurried along its switchback path.

If Alex happened to turn, she would see Iona, especially with her enhanced Owl vision.

"Where did you see her?" Alex asked, her stare still fixed on empty air. "If you tell me, I'll take you to Carson."

Hoping to keep Alex from turning toward the tower, Leo began pacing in front of her, sniffing the air in an exaggerated way.

Alex squinted toward the forest to her right. "Which tree? ... Yes. I see it." She shifted her gaze to Leo. "What does your talented nose tell us?"

He inhaled deeply one more time. "I do detect Iona's scent. It is the strongest in the direction you last looked."

Alex gave him a stern glare, then let it fade. "Oh. That's right. You couldn't see where Quinn pointed." She extended a hand as if setting it behind someone's head. "It would be helpful if you could become visible and audible to normal humans. Since you're a level-three ghost, that's well within your abilities." Alex leaned forward. "Look at me and concentrate. Make yourself appear in my eyes. This has worked for other ghosts. I'm sure it can work for someone with your mental abilities. ... No, I'm not patronizing you. I am simply stating facts. ... Okay. Whatever. Your obscenities mean nothing to me."

Alex extended her other hand. It faded and disappeared along with half of her forearm. "Do as I say, or I will enter your spiritual world and break your miserable neck, you obstinate, egotistical shrew." Her upper arm tightened. "Do I make myself clear?"

After a tense few seconds, her muscles relaxed. As she withdrew her hand, it rematerialized. "Good." She leaned forward again. "Now concentrate."

Silence descended. Even the patter of raindrops ceased. Only the slightest rustle from wind in the nearby trees interrupted the tense quiet. A few seconds later, the slightest wisp of a human form appeared in front of Alex. As it grew clearer, its slender feminine shape became obvious. Wearing denim pants and a long-sleeved shirt, she soon became fully visible, no trace of transparency as she stared at Alex.

Quinn stepped back, blew dark bangs out of her eyes, and glared at Alex. "Satisfied?"

"For now." A sinister grin dressed Alex's face in evil. "I can believe that you would play the traitor to Iona. You have a devilish air about you."

Quinn spat toward Alex's face, but the spittle vanished before it could reach its target. "Listen, witch. I finked on Iona because you promised to reunite me with my husband. So drop your uppity charade and pay up."

"In due time." Alex turned toward the forest, then the tower.

Leo followed her line of sight. Fortunately, Iona had finished climbing the switchback trail and was probably in the tunnel by now.

"The tower was my first guess," Alex said, "the obvious place to go, an excellent observation point. Dry. Likely plenty of food. But it's too obvious. And maybe Iona was worried about walking in the open to get there." She pivoted again toward the forest. "Let's go."

After taking two long strides, she halted. "Wait." She pushed a hand into a pocket and withdrew a flat, square device that fit in the palm of her hand. She studied a display on its face for a moment, then cursed.

"What's wrong?" Quinn asked.

"He's here." Alex pivoted in place, her Owl eyes searching in every direction before stopping and staring toward the mesa. "He must be close. On Earth, the chip's signal gets amplified by nearby transmitters, but not here. I'm picking up a direct signal from him."

Quinn looked in the same direction. "Who?"

"Someone you don't know. But it's all good. I need him here to complete my modified plans." Alex spun to Leo and jabbed a finger toward the forest. "Lead the way. And hurry."

Chapter Six

Iona halted near the top of the switchback trail and looked back. Alex stopped Quinn and stood in front of her. As the two conversed, Leo began sniffing the air in dramatic fashion, then pointed in the direction Iona had been moments ago. Smart move. This way, if Quinn corroborated Leo's sniffer, Alex would be convinced.

Iona continued scaling the slope. Whether or not Quinn ratted no longer mattered. Leo would make sure Alex stayed in the forest and out of sight.

When Iona reached the ledge, she stopped and rested for a moment as she surveyed the scene before her. Directly ahead, a rope ladder led up to a precipice at the edge of a forested promontory. Water from a swollen stream poured over the ledge and beat against the ladder, making it bounce and sway. The cascade struck the ledge a few steps in front of Iona's feet and poured over her ledge to the right, missing the switchback trail.

To the promontory's left and farther back, the observation tower stood atop a slope that ran downward from the base of the tower, to the top of the arched entrance, to a tunnel that led underneath the tower.

After catching her breath, Iona hustled into the tunnel. Remembering that the floor held no tripping obstacles, she jogged into the darkness and arrived at the end, where light from the hole in the ceiling painted a glowing circle on the floor.

The remains of the rope ladder she had cut dangled from above. She grasped it with both hands and, setting her feet on the wall, climbed, shifting her grip to the knots where the rungs used to be. Sweat poured, partially easing the sting as it diluted the acidic water. She grunted with the effort. The going proved to be tough and tiring, but being able to see the surrounding area from the high elevation would be worth it.

When she reached the top and climbed through the hole to the observatory's telescope room, she reeled in the rope and set the coil on the floor by the rope's anchor—a metal ring embedded in the floor next to the hole. Now, even if Alex figured out what had happened, it would be nearly impossible for her to climb up.

New sweat mixed with acid water trickled into her eyes, stinging them harshly. She strode into the adjacent room where she had once eaten a snack of fried eyeballs with Leo, Bazrah, and Melinda, Caligar's android. She ventured beyond that room to another chamber where two thick mats lay, one big and one small, probably the bedroom for the family of giants. Blankets lay scattered across the mats, along with a stack of three towels abutting a wall.

On the other side of the bedroom, she peeked through an open door that led to a bathing area that included a chamber-pot-style toilet and a tub with a diffusing spigot protruding from the wall, maybe fed by a cistern somewhere above. Since any gravity-fed water collected during a storm would be just as acidic as the water in her clothes, it wouldn't do any good to wash herself or her clothing here.

A memory flashed—Melinda dropping a pill into water to make it drinkable for people from Earth. A supply of those pills could be around somewhere. Iona snatched a towel from the top of the pile and bustled around the observatory until she found a food-preparation room. She rummaged through drawers and cabinets and found a fig-like dried fruit and a quart-sized glass bottle bearing a label written in an indecipherable language. The pellets within looked exactly like the pill Melinda used.

Iona grabbed the bottle and fruit and hurried back to the tub while munching on the fruit. It tasted sort of like a fig, though mealy and bland. No matter. Her stomach welcomed it gladly.

After emptying her cloak and pants pockets and setting the transmitter, mooring cap, and mirror on a counter with the towel, she pulled the cloak's hood over her head and spoke into the fibers.

"Charlie, will it bother you if I give the cloak a bath? I want to rinse out the acid."

"It won't bother me, and I would like to try something. Since we know for certain now that I would not be taken up to eternity while in this world, I could leave the cloak. That way I can be with you in visible form."

"That would be great. Any way I can help?"

"Just put the cloak into the bath. Since I have never done this before, I am hoping the wetness will act as buoyant force to help push me out."

"Okay. Let's hope." Iona set the cloak in the tub and turned the spigot on. As water sprayed, she dropped several pellets into the growing pool and swished it with her hand to make them dissolve. The mixture stung at first, but soon it felt like cool bathwater on Earth. Cupping with her hand, she slurped several mouthfuls and swallowed slowly, letting the water bathe her raw throat. It helped, but some soreness remained.

"Charlie," she said as she eyed the cloak, "if you can hear me, I don't see you coming out yet. I'm going to go ahead and rinse myself."

Still holding the bottle of pellets, she turned the spigot off, stepped into the tub, and sat near the back while the cloak continued to soak near her feet. She set the bottle on the side of the tub and, using both hands, splashed the doctored water over her face, back of her neck, and scalp until the stinging sensation eased. Then, bending her knees, she slid down and let the water cover her torso and saturate her shirt. As the acid leached into the water, she added more pellets. After a few minutes, the water had soothed every burning spot on her skin.

She rose, grabbed the towel, and stepped out of the tub. After drying off as much as possible without shedding the wet clothes, she again looked at the cloak, still in the water. "Keep trying, Charlie. I'll be right back."

As she unbuttoned her outer shirt, she hustled to the telescope room. There, she tied the loose end of the rope to a wooden dowel that protruded from the telescope's pedestal, making an angled clothesline, low to the floor but usable. She took her camo shirt off, revealing a black T-shirt that adhered closely to her wet torso, her cross necklace dangling in front. After caressing the cross for a quick moment, she pulled her shoes and socks off and hung them and the shirt over the line.

Her bare feet slapping the hard tiles, she hurried back to the tub. Charlie stood in the room, her body completely dry as she smiled. "Well, that wasn't easy. It was probably easier for you to go in and out because you're alive, and I'm not." She wrapped her arms around Iona, though they couldn't really embrace physically. "I'm so glad to see you."

"Same here." When they drew apart, Iona reached into the tub, withdrew the cloak, and wrung it out, her smile so wide, her cheeks hurt. "Come with me."

After plucking the transmitter, mirror, and mooring cap from the counter, she slid them into a cloak pocket and hurried toward the domed room, looking back every few seconds. It seemed impossible, but the ghost of her mother followed, looking completely solid now, her red hair flowing out the sides of her cloak's hood, the same way she appeared when they first met.

When they arrived, Iona draped the cloak over her makeshift clothesline, careful to keep the items in the pocket from falling out. She gestured toward the telescope, angled so that it pointed toward the curved ceiling. "I'm thinking that since this is an observation tower, there has to be a way to see the surrounding area, not just the sky. Caligar, the giant who lives here, would've seen to that."

Charlie walked around the telescope in a slow orbit, touching the surface with a finger. "I agree. What is in its view now?"

"I'll check." Because of the telescope's angle, the eyepiece stood at a low position, making it easy for Iona to access. She peered through it. The Oculus Gate loomed above like an evil eye, as if watching and waiting for a chance to draw someone through its portal. "The Oculus Gate. It looks the same as always."

Charlie stopped and crossed her arms as she scanned the room. "I don't see any other viewing devices."

"You're right." Iona backed away from the telescope and looked around. The walls below the lower edge of the dome looked like moveable panels with handles that might make them slide downward to open. She grasped one of the handles and pulled, but the panel wouldn't budge. "No use. Maybe there's a switch somewhere."

At the side of the room farthest from the entry hole, a darkened laptop computer sat on a desk that abutted the curved perimeter. She stepped to the desk and pressed one of the laptop's keys. The screen flashed to life, showing a menu on a bar at the top. One of the items read, "Window Controls."

"I think I got it." She tapped a finger on that selection. The menu dropped down and showed two options—Open Windows and Close Windows.

She tapped on Open Windows. Clicks sounded all around. The panels slid down into the lower part of the wall, fully opening the windows to the outside—no glass or screen, just air filled with dense fog.

Iona walked to the opposite side of the room and looked out the window toward the portal mesa. A damp breeze blew in, making her blink. Fortunately, the rain had stopped. "I can't see the ground. If this fog doesn't clear, the windows won't do us much good."

Charlie joined her. "Are you warm enough dressed like that? You're still pretty wet, and your undershirt doesn't have sleeves."

Iona shrugged. "I'm fine. It feels kind of tropical here on Viridi."

"Sorry. I can't feel if the air is cold or warm. I'm too ghostly, you know."

"No worries. You're just being my mother." Iona grinned. "Ghost Mom."

"I like that label." Charlie took a step closer to the window and looked out. "The mist is moving. Maybe it will clear soon."

As they watched, a gap in the fog passed by, providing a brief glimpse of the trail Iona had recently climbed. When the fog again enveloped the view, she waited through the pause. Soon, another gap drifted by, a bigger one that allowed her to study the distant forest. After spotting the place where she had spoken to Quinn, she extended a pointing finger. "See that tree with the forked top? The tall one at the edge."

Charlie looked that way. "Yes. I see it."

"Leo led Alex into the forest there, trying to keep her away from me."

"What do you think will happen when they don't find you?"

"I suppose they'll come back. If Quinn rats on me, Alex will find us, but maybe Leo will tell her the scent leads somewhere else. I'm worried she'll believe Quinn and not Leo."

"Actually, you're in good shape here," Charlie said, her voice calm and reassuring. "The tower is veiled by the fog and suspended high where she can't get to you."

"True. I pulled the rope ladder up. It's my clothesline now."

Charlie laughed. "Good thinking."

"But I should try to find a weapon. I'd feel better if I could shoot an intruder."

"Like Alexandria? Shoot to kill?"

Iona imagined shooting a bullet through Alex's heart. It would feel good to put her down like a rabid dog, but that would release her soul and maybe make it harder to send her to hell. "I think I'd try to wing her. Incapacitate her. Keep her body and soul together."

"Again, good thinking."

Iona scanned the dome room. Drawer handles protruded from panels under four of the windows. She hustled to one, pulled the drawer, and rummaged through an assortment of electronic devices but found no weapons, not even a knife. After searching with no success in the three other drawers, she jogged to the family bedroom and opened a closet. Behind some hanging clothes, an archery bow and a quiver of arrows leaned against a rear corner.

She grabbed both, hurried back to Charlie, and set them on the floor next to the dome room's wall.

"So you're an archer?" Charlie asked, nodding toward the bow.

"Not really. Crossbow mostly. But if Alex gets within fifty yards, I could probably put an arrow in a painful spot."

Charlie rubbed her hands together. "Ah, that would be a delightful sight. Insult and injury at the same time."

"Right, but I need to focus on what I came here to do." Iona retrieved the transmitter, mooring cap, and mirror from the cloak pocket and showed the transmitter to Charlie. "Supposedly, *The Eternity Psalm* is recorded on this device. It's my only hope to send that witch back to hell forever. I need to check to make sure it works. After all that acid water, maybe it won't."

"Then let's check it together." Charlie sat cross-legged, her back to the wall, the top of her head at the lower edge of one of the windows. "I saw the sheet only briefly, but maybe I can detect if there are any gaps in the music."

"Sounds good." Iona set the mirror and the mooring cap on the floor and sat next to Charlie. "Ready?"

"Ready."

Iona flipped the transmitter on. "Here goes."

Chapter Seven

Trudy helped Jack down from the helicopter. When he reached ground level, he stood on one foot while Trudy retrieved her medical bag and a pair of crutches from the chopper's passenger compartment. Both wearing parkas with furry hoods raised, they surveyed the Alaska site while Austin, if he followed their earlier instructions, headed toward Caligar's lair in ghost mode, invisible to everyone.

Back at the vault, he, too, wore a parka, and it vanished with him. He had explained that some things would change to a ghostly state along with a Reaper, especially smaller items and clothing, and some would not. Even after the explanation, watching it happen still made Trudy shudder. Ever since Jack told her six-year-old self a tale about a guillotined woman who carried her head while haunting an old mansion, any mention of ghosts raised chilling memories of hiding under a blanket until she could fall asleep.

She shook off the newest chill, then yawned as she gave the crutches to Jack. After a speedy ride on a supersonic jet to an Alaskan military airstrip, they had transferred to a helicopter for a quick hop to the tower site, but they couldn't be sure that Austin had made the transfer. He never said a word. Maybe the invisibility made him inaudible as well.

Now Trudy and Jack stood about fifty feet from the partially destroyed tower. Although wintertime darkness shrouded much of the region, several spotlights at the tower's base aimed their beams at a dozen or so workers laboring to repair the structure. A few other spotlights focused here and there, illuminating the surrounding area, including several all-terrain vehicles with deeply treaded, oversized tires.

The small outpost building stood twenty or so paces from the tower. Whether or not it still provided underground access to the tower's machinery remained to be seen. In any case, with an armed guard standing next to the building's only door, access wouldn't be easy, and with at least six other armed guards stationed at various points around the tower base, any attack on the tower might be impossible.

Accompanied by a rifle-bearing guard, Camilla deboarded the helicopter and joined them, her parka open to reveal a lab coat over loosely fitting jeans. She hoisted Jack's backpack's strap over her shoulder. "Let's not waste time. Take me to the transporting mirror." She fastened her parka and raised the hood. "Now."

Trudy set the medical bag on the ground. "Listen, Voltage Vamp, we're here to help you leave the planet. You're not in charge."

Jack snickered. "*Voltage Vamp* is good, but *not in charge* is even better."

Trudy suppressed a grin and kept her glare on Camilla. The not-in-charge pun was unintended, but Jack didn't need to know that. "So I'm in charge. You got it?"

Camilla offered an exaggerated bow. "Forgive me, humans whom I could fry with a simple touch. I would very much appreciate it if you would kindly lead me to the mirror."

Trudy crossed her arms. "No."

"No?" Camilla half closed an eye. "You said you would get it for me."

"And we will, but I'm not taking you to Caligar's lair. Its location is a secret. I'll get the mirror and bring it back to you."

"Why so secretive about a Viridi giant's hideout?"

Trudy gestured toward the backpack. "We use the radio receiver device you found in there to open a door at Caligar's lair. If anyone else is with us, the computer inside will detect it and lock us out. Then no one will be able to get in."

While Camilla absorbed the explanation, Trudy kept her stare fixed on her adversary, who now stood in a skeptical pose, gloved hands on hips and eyes narrowed. That pack of lies Jack had come up with sounded ridiculous. Camilla wasn't buying it.

She mimicked Trudy's arms-crossed pose. "Do you really expect me to believe that absurd fable?"

"Well ..." Trudy gave Jack a stern look. They needed another story, something more believable, and they needed it fast.

"We lied," Jack said. "The receiver device we brought *is* the transport device. We don't have to go to Caligar's lair at all."

Camilla offered a knowing nod. "No wonder you insisted on bringing it. You could have simply told the truth and kept to yourself how the device works. You would have had all the leverage you needed to stay alive."

"Yeah." Jack let out a resigned sigh. "I guess you're right."

"To prove your new story is the truth ..." Camilla lowered the backpack from her shoulder. "Give me a demonstration."

"Sure." Jack crutched to the chopper, turned his back to it, and, after leaning the crutches against the fuselage, used both hands to boost himself to the chopper's floor. "Put it right here." He patted his thigh.

Camilla retrieved the Nova Seven from the backpack and set it on his lap. While he fiddled with the various dials on the unit and Camilla looked on, Trudy kept a straight face. The only way Jack's lie-confession gambit could work would be for them to sell it, even though the device would never do anything remotely connected to transporting anywhere. They had to stall while Jack tried to figure out how to trigger Camilla's chip's kill switch.

"How long does it take?" Camilla asked.

"Not sure." Jack squinted at the display. "But usually not long at all."

"Cold weather?" Trudy asked. "We always used it at room temperature."

"That could be it." Jack turned a dial. "I've got the right frequency and encoded message now. I'm just not sure about the timing mechanism."

Trudy nodded. Jack's cryptic words meant that he had figured out the kill switch signal and could send it to Camilla's chip, assuming her chip had the kill technology encoded, but he needed to know if doing it now made sense. In short, should he kill her right away or try to get more information from her first?

She eyed Camilla closely as she stood in rapt attention, strangely content to stand and watch Jack. The alien life form in her brain likely made her unusually curious about this odd technology. A normal human might not be so patient.

Trudy scanned the surrounding snow and ice, hoping to catch of glimpse of Austin returning from Caligar's lair, though he hadn't yet had time to recover from his transformation out of ghost mode. If they decided not to kill Camilla right away, they needed firepower, which meant they had to extend the delay. "Camilla, since you're planning to leave for Viridi using our device, what's the point of all the work going on at the tower?"

"We are completing a project for Alexandria before we leave. On the way over here, my foreman radioed me. They should finish soon. Maybe they already have." She cupped her hands around her mouth and called toward the tower where several men and women scurried about. "Foreman, do you have a report?"

A burly, bearded man broke out of the group and strode toward her, his lips firmly pressing a cigarette that sent smoke into the parka hood encircling his face. "Yes, Dr. Prentiss." When he arrived, he took a long drag on the cigarette and flipped the butt to the ground. "The bomb did a lot of damage to the transport engine, too much to repair in a few days—"

"I know. I know." She scowled at him. "You're not the foreman I spoke with by radio."

"No, ma'am. New shift. He's sleeping in the barracks." He pointed toward a newly constructed steel building, maybe twenty feet long and ten feet wide, barely visible at the outer edge of the spotlights' range. "Twelve hours is a long shift, especially in this weather."

"Without a doubt, but you haven't been informed that I don't care about the transport engine anymore."

"Really?" He lit another cigarette and took a long drag, then blew the smoke as he talked. "What about traveling to Viridi? We're all hoping to go when—"

"Quiet." She coughed and batted the smoke out of her eyes. "We will all transport in another way. For now, I want a report on Dr. Harrid's portal wheel. The foreman from the previous shift told me that repairs were nearly finished."

The foreman dropped the cigarette on the ground and mashed it with a shoe. "They're finished. The wheel software is online here and at the other three towers. We can test it whenever you're ready."

"I am ready. I want to make sure it's operational and fully engaged before we leave for Viridi."

The foreman gave her a firm nod. "I will engage the engine and tell the operators at the other towers to do the same." He pivoted and jogged toward the outpost building, coughing into a gloved fist. When he entered, Trudy imagined his progress through the underground tunnel leading toward the tower base. Obviously that passage could still be used.

Camilla sat next to Jack and looked on as he continued working. "How long will your demonstration take? Once the portal wheel is operational, I will need your device to leave this planet."

"Soon." He pointed at a display on the Nova Seven. "I'm getting interference from other sources of energy. I almost have this one isolated."

Trudy eyed the display, unable to decipher it, but Jack's words were easy enough to interpret. He was getting chip signals from people other than Camilla and needed to isolate hers. Trudy touched Camilla's shoulder. "What does the portal wheel do? Maybe you could explain it to me while Jack works."

"In mere moments, I can show you exactly what it does." Camilla rose and walked toward the tower, gesturing for Trudy to follow. "Come."

Trudy glanced at Jack. He waved her on without looking up, apparently confident that he could send the correct kill-switch signal soon. If he managed to dispatch that alien-possessed zombie, maybe they could finally complete a mission without somehow botching it.

She broke into a quick jog, caught up with Camilla near the base of the tower, and refastened her parka, shivering. "I'm here. Let's see it."

"One moment." Camilla fixed her gaze high on the tower. The workers had repaired the transmitter, and a bright light strobed at the top of a rod at the tower's highest point. About six or seven workers climbed down a makeshift ladder. They would reach ground in a few seconds. "They're finished. The operation should begin at any moment."

A loud hum emanated from below, and the ground began shaking, sending vibrations into Trudy's feet and up her legs. "Is an earthquake starting?"

Camilla nodded. "It won't last long. No harm will come."

At the center of the ground area at the base, a metal plate the size of a manhole cover slid to the side, revealing an opening into darkness. The foreman climbed out and stood under the tower, facing Camilla. "Everything is working," he called. "We should see the portal wheel soon."

She raised her voice to compete with the various noises. "Good. Make sure everyone has come down from the tower."

The foreman looked up at the ladder and shouted, "Is everyone down, Joan?"

A woman wearing a thick sweatshirt and jeans leaped from the lowest ladder rung to the ground. "I'm the last one, Smokey."

A new shiver ran through Trudy's body, blending with the quake tremors. How could Joan stand the bitter cold dressed like that? Maybe she had a Refector inside with Radiant power to warm her body.

The foreman waved an arm as he walked toward Camilla. "Let's all move at least ten steps away from the tower. Better safe than—" He halted and stared, then crumpled to the snowy ground.

Camilla and Joan both ran to him. Trudy spun toward Jack. Glancing at her for a moment, he shrugged, then began fiddling with the controls of the Nova Seven again. Apparently, he chose the wrong signal and killed the foreman. How many more signals did he have to choose from?

She pivoted back. Camilla sat on the foreman's stomach, performing chest compressions while Joan knelt nearby, shouting to the other workers, "Let's get him away from the tower!"

Two men ran to the fallen foreman and helped Camilla and Joan carry him, but before they could take three steps, Joan tripped and fell on her face, unable to even thrust her arms out to break her fall. With the loss of balance, the two others toppled over and dropped the foreman.

Camilla rose with the two others, brushed snow from her pants, and shoved Joan with a foot. "Get up! We have to move Smokey!"

Joan lay motionless, apparently as dead as Smokey.

Trudy again glanced toward Jack. He shrugged once more and went back to work.

"What's going on?" Camilla shouted as she glared at Trudy. "Are you doing this?"

Trudy raised her gloved hands. "What kind of power do you think I have?"

One of the helpers toppled, then the other. An armed guard ran toward them from the outpost building, but he, too, dropped dead.

"Then it's Jack." Camilla stormed toward him while shedding her parka. Her head and hands had already transformed into flashes of energy. In seconds she would be on him, and he couldn't defend himself or even run away.

Trudy sprinted after her, but what would she do when she caught up? Camilla could easily win a battle using her electrically charged body.

A gunshot rang out. Camilla fell forward and writhed on the frozen ground, only a few steps away from Jack. He set the Nova Seven to the side in the chopper, grabbed his crutches, and hobbled to her, though he could do nothing but stand and stare.

When Trudy arrived, she crouched, grabbed Camilla's arm, and rolled her out of a pool of blood. More blood spurted from a small hole in her chest, apparently shooting from a severed artery. Obviously she hadn't transformed in time to avoid the wound.

She spoke with a bloody gurgle. "You will not defeat Alexandria. The Queen of Hell will bring hell to Earth, and you will all die."

She lifted a small box and pushed a red button on its side. An explosion erupted in the barracks and another from the outpost building. As the buildings burned, more bombs detonated in the all-terrain vehicles and the helicopter. The concussive wave from the chopper slammed into Jack and Trudy, flattening them over Camilla.

The spotlights blinked out one by one, leaving the raging fires as the only sources of light. When heat from the blast lessened to a tolerable level, Trudy rose to her knees and checked Camilla's neck pulse—no heartbeat. Flames shot out from the chopper, and the Nova Seven lay nearby in the snow, smoke curling from its molten ruins.

She helped Jack up and gave him the crutches. "Are you all right?"

"Snow in my face, but …" He nodded. "Yeah. I'm good."

She searched for the source of the gunshot, scanning everything within the glow of the fires. It seemed that everyone had died. And no one stirred at the burning barracks. The explosion had probably killed everyone inside. "Should we check on the victims?" she asked.

"You can if you want. But I'm in no hurry to pull bad guys out of an inferno while a shooter's lurking."

"Did you see the shooter?"

"No." Jack pointed away from the tower. "But the shot came from that direction. I saw the flash."

"I shot her." Austin walked into the dim light, a rifle in one hand and a duffle bag in the other, the hood of his cloak drawn back. "Looks like I recovered from ghost mode just in time."

Jack whistled, though his chapped lips shattered the musical note. "A shot to the heart from that distance? In the dark?"

"And while Camilla was moving," Trudy added. "You're as good as Iona."

Austin set the duffle down next to the medical bag Trudy had deposited earlier. It flopped open, revealing another rifle, several ammo magazines, a crossbow with three bolts, and a portable ham radio. "Actually, Iona and I talked about marksmanship while we were in hell. That and music. I was a musician in school. Anyway, we've both been shooting since we were little. She said she was pretty good with a crossbow, too." He set the rifle to his shoulder as if aiming. "This has a scope and a laser targeting beam. Made my shot a lot easier."

"Still a super hit." Trudy nudged Camilla's corpse with a foot. "Why would she sabotage the operation and kill her comrades?"

Jack leaned over and pried the detonator from Camilla's stiffening fingers. "Maybe a suicide pact. We squashed their plan, so they wanted to die instead of living without their queen."

"Total devotion to that witch," Trudy said. "The vaccine payload really scrambled their brains. But what she said explains more."

"Right. 'The Queen of Hell will bring hell to Earth, and you will all die.'" Jack dropped the detonator. "Pretty chilling. Alex's toadies wanted to avoid whatever she planned to do to Earth."

"Exactly. So we have to figure out what the plan is and how to stop her." Trudy turned toward the burning chopper. "Since Camilla blew all the vehicles sky high, we'll need an exit strategy. Maybe the portal wheel she mentioned will give us one. She was about to show it to us." Trudy eyed Camilla's parka, separated from her body a couple of steps behind her. "Know what's weird? She took off her parka as she was transforming into electricity. The last time we saw her do it, her clothes transformed with her."

"Check the pockets," Jack said. "Maybe she was protecting something she didn't want to zap with her electrified body."

Trudy crouched again, slid a hand into the outer pocket of Camilla's parka, and withdrew a metallic sphere about twice the size of a billiard ball. Covered with at least fifty black square buttons, it looked like nothing she had ever seen before. "What in the world is this?"

"No clue." Jack scrunched his brow. "I'm wondering if it interfered with me getting a fix on her chip. The moment she got shot, I looked at the Nova Seven. One close-by chip was still active, hers, I assume. Several others were farther away, probably in the barracks. I guess they're all dead now."

A loud tone sounded from the top of the tower. The light now emitted a steady bright beam of sky blue that shot upward at an angle to the Oculus Gate. Three beams joined it, separated from each other at ninety-degree intervals.

One of the buttons on the sphere depressed on its own, as if responding to the tower's new activity. The ground quaked, sending Trudy toppling off her haunches to her side. Jack staggered back and braced himself with the crutches to keep from falling, while Austin spread his feet and balanced against the tremor.

After pushing the sphere into her parka pocket, Trudy took one of the rifles and a magazine from the bag, climbed to her feet, and popped the mag into the rifle. She pointed a finger at Jack. "Stay here and man the radio Austin brought." She shifted her finger toward Austin. "Come with me."

Battling the shaking ground, she jogged toward the tower, Austin at her side. A lone man stood bracing a hand on one of the tower's supports, staring at them as they approached, apparently unarmed. White beard and eyebrows indicated at least sixty years of age.

When they arrived, Trudy set the rifle at her hip, aimed it at the man, and raised her voice to overcome the tower's clamor. "Tell me what's going on."

He gasped and raised his hands, then nearly fell and grabbed the support again. "Don't shoot. Please." Streams of vapor blew out with his words. "I'm not one of them."

"Them?" Trudy repeated. "What do you mean?"

"Those Reflectors. Or Refractors." He shook his head hard. "Or whatever they're called. Aliens. I'm not one of them."

The tone from the tower diminished, as did the tremor, allowing them to speak normally. "Then who are you?" Trudy asked. "And what are you doing here?"

He exhaled and released the support. "I am Lemuel Kovaleski, but you may call me Lem. I am the conductor of the BSO, the Boston Symphony Orchestra."

"The BSO? Never heard of it." She glanced at Austin. "You?"

Austin raised his hood over his reddening ears. "Nope."

Lem's shoulders sagged. "It's not well-known now, but it was once world renowned. In any case, because of my knowledge of music, the aliens kidnapped me to help them with this contraption. The scientist who designed it told them that musical notes combined with certain light beams could create what they called a portal wheel, and it would give them access to worlds beyond."

Trudy lowered the rifle. "Is the scientist Dr. Harrid?"

"Yes, yes. That's his name." Lem's eyes darted as he looked at the surrounding corpses. "But now they're all dead."

Jack's voice intruded. "That's because ..." He puffed as he labored on crutches through the snow and ice. "I sent the kill switch signal to every chip. Except Camilla's, of course. She died before I could zap her."

"Jack!" Trudy propped her rifle against her shoulder. "I told you to stay put."

"Who promoted you to supreme commander, Sis? Anyway, I got a call on the radio. Ben, Kat, and Caligar made it to Viridi. So did Leo. Somehow he got on board the angel cruiser. Since Iona took off on her own, Ben's assuming her body and soul are back together. And when she escaped, she took the mooring cap. That grounded the cruiser, and a storm crashed the pod Ben and Kat and Caligar were in. Now everyone's searching for Iona on foot, and the only weapons they have are a handgun Ben picked up in Alaska and Caligar's bow and arrow."

"Sounds like they need us," Austin said. "How can we get there?"

"Maybe the portal wheel." Trudy faced Lem. "What were you supposed to do to get it going?"

He set his gloved hands in a cradle as if holding something delicate. "It was my job to use a device called the symphony sphere."

Trudy set her rifle on the ground and retrieved the sphere from her pocket. "Do you mean this?"

"Yes." He waved a hand frantically. "Be careful with it. It is not as sturdy as it appears to be."

She touched the button that was already depressed. "This one's lower than the others."

"The tower sent a signal to the sphere that indicated its readiness to create the wheel. That signal triggered the depression of the button, which, in effect, turned the sphere on. It is ready to be used. If we are to complete the portal wheel creation process, I need to continue to the next notes in sequence. Unfortunately, I am the only one who can operate it. The remaining buttons will not work without my thumbprint."

"Where will the portal wheel lead?"

"I have no idea. Not being one of them, I was left in the dark about that detail. My goal was to survive. They constantly threatened to kill me if I didn't cooperate."

"The ultimate leverage." Trudy looked at Jack. "Should we try to create the portal wheel, or shouldn't we? Your call."

Jack pointed at himself. "My call? A minute ago I was a lowly pawn. Are you trying to dodge the blame if we botch another mission?"

"Yep." She set a hand on his shoulder. "I'll let these broad shoulders carry the guilt."

Jack let out an exasperated sigh. "All right. Let's do it. It's the only way to see what Alex planned, and we're marooned here if we don't."

"Agreed." She extended the sphere toward Lem. "Now, either enter the rest of the notes, or freeze with us. I hear it's a slow, painful death."

"Since you put it that way …" He removed his gloves and stuffed them into his parka pocket. "I will do my best. I do know what the next note is, but I won't know the following ones until I listen to the echoes from the Oculus Gate. From what they told me, the Gate will provide each note as we continue. I hope it works."

She set the sphere in his cupped hands and retrieved her rifle from the ground. "Do you know how many notes it'll take to create the portal wheel?"

Lem shook his head, no longer as visible as before in the light of the ebbing fires. "I have no idea. I suppose we'll know when the wheel forms."

"Where will it form, and what will it look like?"

"Again, no idea. Camilla and the other aliens told me very little."

"Okay." Trudy gave him a nod. "Press the next note."

Chapter Eight

Avoiding the bow on Caligar's shoulder, Ben slid down the giant's back onto dry ground a few paces from the river behind them. Kat, who had ridden the giant's back several minutes earlier, patted his shoulder. "How's your foot?"

"Wet. My feet dangled in the water. Couldn't be helped. The acid did a number on my bullet wound. Hurts like hellfire."

She pointed at the ground. "Sit. I'll have a look."

Ben lowered himself and gingerly untied his shoe. When Kat slipped it off and looked at the shoe, she creased her brow. "What's this?" She pinched something off the heel and showed it to Ben—a metallic square the size of a pinhead with two tiny prongs on one side. She drew it close to her eyes. "It has circuits of some kind, but I'll bet the acid fried them."

She set the square in Ben's palm, slid his bloody sock off, and looked at the gash across his heel. She smiled and winked. "We need a bandage for your boo-boo."

"Yeah. Laugh it up." Ben eyed the twin prongs on the piece of metal. Bearing tiny barbs, they were designed to penetrate and hang on. Did someone intentionally push them into his shoe?

His fight with Alex flashed to mind. As he replayed the moves, a particular moment sped by, a brief second that Alex's hands moved out of his view. Yes, she could have planted this in his shoe during that moment. If it had the same locator technology as the chips she implanted in her minions, she could track him, maybe even here on Viridi.

Caligar crouched close. "I have a fully supplied first-aid kit in my observatory. We could go there first."

"Maybe." Ben threw the locator into the river. "Alex's work. It's a good bet she knows I'm here. If we go to the tower, we might be sitting ducks."

"Why?" Kat asked. "What could she do?"

"We don't know what weapons she might've taken from the angel cruiser. If she can topple the tower, then we'd be—"

"Stop it, Ben. You're letting her get into your head. She's probably not anywhere close, and we'll only be in the tower a minute to get you a bandage."

Heat rose into Ben's cheeks. She was right. Too much paranoia. He couldn't let Alex have a free parking space in his brain. "Okay. We'll go to the tower. If Alex shows up, she'll wish she hadn't."

"That's the spirit." Kat put his sock back on, rolling the sides up his leg, then slid his shoe over it, tied the laces, and helped him rise. "Let's head to the tower."

"Wait a moment, please," Caligar said as he studied the ground close to the river. "I noticed the remnants of Iona's footprints on the other side, but there are none here. As I suspected earlier, she did not exit the river anywhere close."

Ben limped to him. "Are you sure?"

"I am quite certain. The river has receded recently, which means that the flow would not have washed away her footprints. Her prints on the other side prove that, especially since the consistency of the mud here is the same." He lifted a foot, revealing a four-inch-deep impression, illustrating his point. "I think my earlier theory is accurate. She dragged a limb into the flow and used it to help her cross."

Ben scanned the shoreline for any sign of prints but saw none. "So she came ashore somewhere farther downstream."

Kat looked at the tracking device, her brow furrowed. She took several steps downstream, then returned. "The signal doesn't get stronger that way. If anything, it gets weaker. Hard to be sure."

"Because she might not be in that direction anymore," Ben said. "She came ashore somewhere in that direction, then headed elsewhere."

Caligar strode along the river's edge downstream, calling back. "Then we should be able to find her exit point and track her from there."

When he walked out of earshot, Kat turned toward Ben, her nose wrinkled in a way that meant Caligar's decision annoyed her. "I think we should follow the signal. That's where she actually is, not where she was."

"I agree, but Caligar's on his home turf. He's our guide. We can't go one direction while he goes another."

"Yes, we can. And we should. Like I said, we need to go where she is, not where—"

"Where she was. I know." Ben looked downstream. Caligar had stopped about fifty yards away and now stood motionless, looking back at them. It made no sense to delay any longer, but it also made no sense to plow ahead without Kat's approval. "The signal doesn't tell us where Iona is. It tells us where the transmitter is. The two places might not be the same. But Iona's footprints will take us where *she* is. Besides, the transmitter signal could bounce, amplify, or degrade for countless reasons. We might wander aimlessly for hours."

Kat sighed. "Okay. Okay. Good points. But I'm going to keep monitoring the signal."

"As you should." Ben set a hand on her back. "Let's go."

They jogged together, Ben with a hobbled gait, until they caught up with Caligar, then the trio strode at a brisk pace as Caligar studied the shoreline. They entered a dense forest, forcing them to stay close to the river, often sloshing into its shallows, again irritating Ben's wound.

After several minutes, Caligar pointed at the mud. "Someone left the water here." His finger shifted toward an upward slope leading deeper into the forest. "And walked up there with struggling, dragging steps. It won't be hard to follow the trail."

Ben studied the pair of ruts in the mud. Obviously something with two feet trudged here, someone who traveled alone, exhausted from the river crossing. Since Alex and Leo probably traveled together, this had to be Iona's trail. "Lead the way, Caligar."

While the giant marched up the slope, followed by Ben and Kat, Kat checked the tracking device but said nothing, though her taut face meant that the signal had dropped too low for her liking.

Soon, they came to a protruding flat rock that created a shallow cave of sorts. Caligar leaned low and looked into the recess. "Someone lay here. Not long ago, I think. The ground is relatively dry within, and it hasn't absorbed a number of small puddles that were likely deposited by a wet traveler."

"A solo traveler?" Ben asked.

Caligar nodded. "Judging from the impression the traveler's body made, I am confident that the traveler is Iona." He pointed at the ground. "And she went this way when she left." Caligar set off again, this time in the direction they had come, though at a considerable distance upslope from the river.

While they navigated through the forest obstacles, Kat checked the tracker again. "We're getting closer now."

"Because we're heading back the way we came." He rubbed her shoulder. "Thanks for not saying 'I told you so.'"

She grinned. "Not yet, at least. I'm keeping it in the bank for later."

After a few minutes, Caligar halted, whipped an arrow from his quiver, and nocked it to the bowstring. When Ben and Kat stopped close behind him, he whispered, "I saw someone hide behind a tree about thirty paces ahead."

"Not Iona, I assume," Ben said, also whispering. "Since you're ready to shoot."

Caligar shook his head. "I am fairly certain the mystery person is a man and absolutely certain that he is taller than Iona."

Ben withdrew the handgun and called out, "Whoever is there, show yourself."

A man stepped from behind a tree, his hands over his face. He returned Ben's call. "If I show myself fully, I wonder if you will have a heart attack. I know what it's like to lose heart function. It's not a picnic."

The familiar voice registered. Dr. Harrid? Impossible. Caligar killed him with an arrow through the heart.

The man, wearing loose jeans, a green T-shirt, and dark sneakers, walked closer and halted about five paces away. He lowered his hands, revealing his identity. Yes, he was, indeed, Dr. Harrid.

"Speechless?" Harrid's tone turned condescending. "I shouldn't wonder. After all, how often does an executioner see his innocent prey return to accuse him of murder?"

Kat whispered, "What in the world is he babbling about?"

"I disposed of your body myself," Caligar said as he drew the arrow back. "I burned it and tossed your bones and ashes into a sewage trench, exactly where they belong."

"Surprise, surprise!" Harrid tilted his head in a cocky manner. "I've come back from the dead to finish the job. Three more giants to kill—a father, a mother, and a child."

Caligar released the arrow. It zipped away and passed directly through Harrid's chest without harm. A triumphant grin spread across his face, as if he expected this result, or maybe planned it, knowing what would happen if he goaded Caligar with his ridiculous taunts.

"Ha! You see? I am invulnerable. There are drawbacks, of course, to being a ghost, but the benefits are many. I need no food or sleep, and I can pass through most objects here on Viridi. And, best of all, I don't have to worry about that silly heaven-or-hell nonsense. I am free to explore this world at my pleasure."

Ben let out a tsking sound. "Pretty pathetic, if you ask me."

Harrid furrowed his brow. "Why is that?"

"Alone in a ghostly realm. Doomed to wander with no friends. No love. No purpose. Sounds like hell to me."

Harrid stabbed a finger at Ben. "Stop playing mind games, you hypocrite. You believe yourself to be so moral and upright, but you let me think you were Alexandria in disguise. You led me to my death at the hands of this ten-foot-tall ape you call a friend."

Caligar growled but said nothing.

Ben eyed Harrid's flustered expression. Maybe playing to his ego would get him to spill some information. "Okay. You got me. I was playing mind games. I should've known better than to cross mental swords with you. I hope you'll forgive me. But for now I have to continue searching for someone and leave you to your exploration of this world." Ben waved a hand toward Kat and Caligar. "Let's go." They walked past Harrid without looking back.

"Wait," Harrid called. "Who are you looking for? Maybe I can help."

Ben halted and pivoted toward him. "Why would you want to help? And what could you do?"

"Well, I know you and Alexandria are enemies, and I figured out that she is behind every evil that has happened lately, including inciting the barbaric giants to kill and eat my wife. I would be more than happy to exact some revenge." Harrid glanced around, as if fearing who might be listening. "As to how I can help you, I learned how to become visible or invisible to living creatures here. I could easily spy on Alexandria for you. I heard her voice not long ago, and I tried to follow it, but then your voices led me in a different direction. I'm confident that I could find her."

"We think she's with Leo, a tall huntsman with thick dark hair. The best way to help would be to get word to him that we're on Viridi. Last we heard, he thinks Kat and I are dead."

"Should I tell him where you're going so he can meet you?"

Ben shook his head. "Leo will take it from there. With his nose, he'll catch our scent and find us."

Harrid gave an exaggerated nod. "I get it. You don't trust me. That's why you won't tell me where you're going."

"Whether or not I trust you isn't the issue. I don't want you to know in case Alex captures you. With her Reaper powers, she might be able to torture a ghost and get the information out of you."

Harrid half closed an eye. "No, I think your lack of trust in me *is* the issue." He shrugged. "But I understand your suspicion. After I prove myself by getting your huntsman up to speed, maybe you'll change your mind." He turned upslope and strode away, fading to invisibility.

Kat crossed her arms in front. "He's right about one thing. We don't trust him."

"Exactly why I didn't tell him where we're going."

"Okay. Where *are* we going?"

Ben nodded forward. "We'll keep following Iona's trail, whether by Caligar's keen eye or by the transmitter signal. Either way, my bet is that she went to the observatory tower, guessing that Alex might think it's too obvious."

"It is a good strategy." Caligar gestured with his hands, moving them as if he were drawing in a fishing line. "Iona would have pulled the remains of the rope ladder up to the observatory. No enemy in her right mind would attempt climbing up there knowing that the occupant could shoot the intruder long before she could get to the top."

"Do you have weapons in the tower?" Kat asked.

"A bow and plenty of arrows in a closet but no rifles or handguns."

"Let's follow the trail and see where it goes. We can keep talking on the way."

With Caligar in the lead, scanning the forest floor, Ben walked as fast as his gimpy foot would allow, Kat at his side.

Soon, Caligar slowed, then halted and pointed at the ground. "I no longer see evidence of a trail. The ground is rocky, so it does not allow for footprints, and the prevalent tree species here does not shed its foliage, even in violent storms. Therefore, there is no debris for a walker to disturb."

Kat held up her tracker and eyed the display. "The signal's stronger than before. We're going in the right direction."

"Then we head for the tower," Ben said as he marched on, trying to avoid limping. When the others caught up, he spoke while grimacing with each step. "We assume Leo and Alex left the cruiser together, but we can't be sure they stayed together, so we can't count on Leo's help to lead Alex in the wrong direction. Even if he tries, she's too smart to be fooled for long. And if she finds Iona, she'll figure out a way to threaten her and force her to surrender." He glanced at Kat. "Or am I being paranoid again?"

Kat kept her stare forward, staying quiet for a moment before answering. "No. I think you're right. Iona is in danger. I just remembered that the angel cruiser weapons cache used to have a grenade launcher and several grenades. When I picked up the tracker, that compartment was empty. I didn't put two and two together until just now. I was in a hurry. Way too distracted."

"And a grenade launcher could easily send a grenade up to the tower. It could do a lot of damage."

"Not necessarily," Caligar said. "I left the window panels closed. They are made of a reinforced wood that is extremely strong. A powerful explosion could perhaps punch a hole through it, but very little harm would come to the inside. A greater danger would come from an assault on the tower's foundation. I mentioned earlier that toppling is a risk in a violent storm. The same instability could be exploited by grenades."

Ben blew out a long breath. "Maybe I'm being paranoid again, but Alex is smart enough to figure that out. We'll assume the worst and hope for the best."

"But we also don't want to give her too much credit," Kat said.

"Maybe, but Bart told Iona that Alex has never been outwitted. She died at the hand of a person who overpowered her rather than mentally outmaneuvered her."

Kat patted Ben's shoulder. "Well, Mr. Master Planner, do you have a plan to break Alex's unbeaten streak?"

Ben smiled. "Working on it. For now, let's just get to the tower as fast as we can."

In the midst of the forest, Leo halted and sniffed the air once more. Iona's scent had long since departed, but now Caligar's seemed to waft in the air. Not being as familiar with the giant's smell, it was difficult to be sure. In any case, he had to continue deceiving the wicked witch. Keeping her away from Iona was all that mattered.

"Well?" Alex stood with arms crossed, tapping a foot. "Which way to Iona now?"

"Deeper into the woods."

When Leo took a step in that direction, Alex grabbed his arm. "Wait. I sense something."

Leo pivoted toward her, trying his best to keep a straight face. "What?"

"A ghost. A disembodied soul."

"Of course you do." Leo gestured with a hand. "Quinn is standing right next to you."

"No, you idiot. A different ghost." Alex peered to their left, her eyes like glittering silver. She called out, "It's no use hiding. I know you're there."

A man spoke from a leafy bush. "But I'm invisible."

"Not to me. I am a Reaper." Alex gestured with a thumb toward Leo. "For his sake, kindly become visible, and we'll talk."

A man emerged from behind the bush, his identity instantly obvious—Dr. Harrid.

"Carson!" Quinn dashed to him, her arms outstretched. They embraced and kissed passionately.

"There," Alex said. "I told you I would find Carson for you."

Leo scowled. This reunion was purely an accident. Alex had no intention of keeping her word.

Quinn drew away from Harrid and looked at Alex. "Yes, you did." She glanced at Leo and took a deep breath. "Now I have a confession to make."

Leo concealed a cringe. This specious specter intended to give away Iona's location, and there was nothing he could do to keep her quiet. But he could cause a distraction.

He shouted into the woods, "Caligar, can you hear me?"

Alex jerked her head toward him. "How dare you call for him!"

"Caligar!"

Alex lunged at Leo. He dodged and ran into the woods, darting from tree to tree in a zigzagging path. Once he was sure he had lost Alex, he crept back toward them, tossing stones and branches as far as he could, hoping the distant noise would conceal his location and movements.

Soon, he came within viewing distance of Alex. She stood motionless, craning her neck, apparently listening. She sighed and shook her head. "It's useless. Leo is an expert huntsman. I'll never be able to track him down." She turned toward Quinn. "Now what is this confession you're talking about?"

Quinn grasped Harrid's hand and faced Alex. "I lied to you. Iona didn't go into the forest. She's in the tower. I told her I would lead you away from her."

"Really?" Alex let out a derisive laugh. "Well, you treacherous little beast, now you've betrayed both me and Iona. It's no surprise that Leo would deceive me, but you?" She laughed again. "Congratulations on being the slimiest eel I've ever met."

"But I'm on your side now. You found Carson for me."

Dr. Harrid shook his head. "No, dear. I found you. This woman is the vilest liar on any planet."

Quinn balled her fists. "If I could go physical for just five minutes, I would scalp you and hang that blonde mop from a yardarm."

"A yardarm. How amusingly odd." Alex took a deep breath and sighed. "Well, it seems that I'm on my own now, so I'll be going.

Iona awaits in the tower." She stalked in that direction, her pace faster than a quick march.

Leo's heart pounded. He inhaled deeply to settle his body. He had to get to the tower before she could without giving away his location. But how?

When she passed out of sight, Harrid called with a whisper-shout, "Leo, I talked to Ben and Kat. They want you to know they're alive. They're here on Viridi and looking for Iona."

Leo stifled a gasp. Ben and Kat alive? How could that be?

"No need to answer me, of course," Harrid continued. "But I thought you'd like to know so you can find them and join forces. They're heading in the tower's direction, too."

Leo walked out of his hiding place and faced the two ghoulish ghosts. "Why should I believe anything you liars say?" He pointed at Quinn. "This one just betrayed my daughter to the Queen of Hell."

"Your daughter?" Quinn huffed. "I couldn't possibly have known that."

"Either way, you betrayed her, and I have to stop Alex and save Iona."

"Wait a moment," Harrid said, a hand raised. "To make up for our lapse in judgment, I should tell you something."

Leo nodded. "Make it quick."

"I invented an engine that I call a portal wheel. Well, a prototype, not a working model. In any case, I drew up schematics and wrote detailed instructions so that Alex and her scientists could fabricate it themselves at the Alaska tower."

"Why would she need a portal?" Leo asked. "The towers can send her through the Oculus Gate."

"I did not design my wheel for traveling to Viridi. Well, I suppose it might open a door to come here, but Alex wanted to send someone into the Oculus Gate itself, to a small pocket that acts as the locus for all the worlds. That is, the worlds for which portals have been recently opened—Earth, Viridi, heaven, and hell. You see, the wheel provides access to certain areas because of weaknesses created in the space continuum due to portals being forced open. That, combined with—"

"I don't need to know the physics," Leo said, waving a hand. "Just give me the bottom line."

"Well, the wheel isn't based on physics alone. It also involves metaphysics. Spiritual forces can alter the portal destinations. In any case, my point is that Alex will soon have, or perhaps already has, a way to open a portal to the central point of all recent cosmic rifts, that is, the Oculus Gate itself. From there, a person can easily pass back and forth between the realities that have recently been visited. Alex's purpose is to force Iona to go to the central point—the Oculus Gate—and take a bomb from there to hell in order to destroy that place forever. In theory, Iona should be able to escape the blast."

"*Should* be able to? Alex said the same thing, and I don't trust a word she says."

"Your wariness is valid. All of this is based on theory, though Alex is quite certain of Iona's ability to survive. Still, Alex will need two things to succeed." Harrid raised a finger with each point. "One is to capture Iona herself. And two is to find a way to send her back to Earth where the portal wheel is. Yet, since she has no idea how to use my mirror portal here on Viridi, she will have to conjure another plan. A difficult obstacle, but I wouldn't underestimate her ability to overcome it."

"Nor would I." Leo looked in the direction Alex had gone. She had a huge head start, but he could still track her. "Okay. Another question. This portal wheel. You're the inventor. Is there any weaknesses in the design?"

Harrid again raised a finger. "Perhaps one. As I mentioned, metaphysical forces can alter the portals in various ways—their exact destinations, the ease of passing through, even the method of passing through. My wheel cannot counter those forces. In fact, it might even enhance them, become a tool for the forces to use."

"Metaphysical forces." Leo narrowed his eyes. "Do you mean God?"

"Yes, of course—God's hand actuated by the prayers of his followers. I considered such ideas nonsense until I appeared here in spiritual form. And before that, I aided Alex in her quest to destroy hell because I was … hedging my bets, you might say. Now that I am safe here on Viridi, I don't care if she fails."

"I understand. Now one last question. Where did you see Ben and Kat?"

Harrid pointed deeper into the forest. "In that general direction. Maybe a few hundred yards. With your skills, I'm sure you can locate them."

"I'm sure I could, but they're able to fend for themselves for now." Leo jogged in pursuit of Alex. With her head start, she would easily get to the tower before he could, even considering his quick pace. And when he finally arrived, what then? With her weapons and superb fighting skills, that hellish harridan could drub him again, and this time refuse to spare his life. She was coming within striking distance of what she wanted and didn't need a human hound any longer.

He blew a hefty sigh and accelerated. Of course he had to fight her anyway, though it might be insane to try again. Within a couple of minutes, he would know who the victor would be—the wicked witch or the hysterical huntsman.

Chapter Nine

With Kat close at his side, Ben limped through the forest. Caligar continued leading the way, knocking down low branches with powerful blows from his swatting hands as he warned about protruding roots and prickly bushes.

Sweat dampened Ben's shirt. Since his pants had been drenched by the river when he rode Caligar's back across it, wetness now covered most of his clothes. Acid from the river water stung his legs and feet, shooting more pain into his wound. Every stab felt like a dagger plunging into his heel. He couldn't keep this up much longer.

"Caligar," he said, trying not to let the pain shred his voice, "any idea how much farther?"

"To the edge of the forest, about half a mile by Earth measurements. Two miles to my tower."

"Two miles." Ben's foot caught on a root, but only for a second. "I'm slowing you down. Maybe you should go on ahead. I'll get there eventually."

"Not a chance," Kat said as she grasped his wrist. "Put your arm around me. I'll help you."

Just as he complied, two people stepped out from behind a tree about twenty paces ahead—Dr. Harrid and an unfamiliar woman.

Caligar raised a hand, signaling a halt. "Harrid, why are you stalking us? And who is this woman? I have seen her before, but my memory fails."

"You should remember her." Harrid touched the woman's shoulder. "This is my wife, Quinn. She was murdered here and is also a ghost. We ran ahead so we could cut you off and provide you with information. Your friend Leo has gone to the tower to try to rescue Iona from Alex. Since he is much faster than you, he will arrive long before you do, but he is obviously not at full strength. Against Alex, he will be at a great disadvantage. Quinn, here, was a medical doctor, and, based on external observation of his manner and gait, she thinks he has some kind of brain injury, perhaps a concussion, or maybe he suffered a stroke."

"That's possible," Kat said. "He lost his soul and had it restored. Lots of brain trauma involved."

Harrid blinked. "Oh. Well. I suppose that would explain his malady. In any case, I expect that Alex's minions on Earth will create and activate a portal wheel that I invented. Alex's goal is to open a safe-passage door to hell so she can destroy it, but her boot-licking morons will probably try to use it to come to Viridi. Such is their misguided loyalty to her."

When he paused, Quinn nudged him with an elbow. "You didn't give him our advice."

"Oh, yes." Harrid refocused on Ben. "We think you should allow Alex to proceed with her plan. She hopes to set up a meeting between Iona and Satan, who will teach Iona how to use a special bomb that will destroy hell. Apparently only she is capable of completing the mission, though I'm not sure why."

Ben huffed. "Let Alex proceed? Are you out of your mind?"

"I meant allow her to proceed only for a short time. Alex will be most vulnerable when she thinks she is succeeding. When my portal wheel is activated, one of the portals will open here on Viridi, and Alex will take Iona to Earth through it and then use another portal on the wheel to usher her to Satan. You should wait until the moment Iona is ready to enter the portal leading back to Earth, then launch a surprise attack. Until that time, Alex will not leave anything to chance. She will be wary and guarded. And please understand my motivations. I hate Alex. She's the ultimate reason for our deaths."

"Where will the portal appear?"

"If it works as designed, it should appear at the top of the mesa. But ..." Harrid narrowed his eyes, as if unsure. "Maybe not."

"Do you mean it might appear somewhere else?"

"Yes. Since the portal is metaphysical, it can be moved by metaphysical forces, such as great need and … well … prayer. But I see no reason why that would take place. Alex certainly isn't going to pray for the portal to move, and even if she did, a benevolent deity probably wouldn't listen to anything that spews from her vile mouth."

"True," Ben said, "but it would be best if we could simply neutralize the portal wheel. Is that possible?"

"Of course. I always include a backdoor to my inventions in case I need to shut them down."

"All right. How do we use that door?"

Harrid took on a professorial tone, as if giving a lecture. "The portal wheel runs on the music inherent in the cosmos, and the notes are manually entered into a translator on a device called a Symphony Sphere. A certain combination of musical notes will cause the wheel to stop and eventually disappear, though the portals that are active at the time of the wheel's demise will stay open for about a minute."

"Okay," Kat said. "What are the musical notes?"

"F-seven, G-one, and B-eight. If the Symphony Sphere sends those notes to the towers in that order, the portal wheel will immediately stop and eventually vanish."

Kat whispered the notes quietly, probably memorizing them.

Ben gave him a genial nod. "Thank you, Dr. Harrid. You've been very helpful."

"You are very welcome, but there is one more issue you need to consider. Although Alex states that she wants to destroy hell, be certain that she will use that bomb or some other means to also destroy Earth. Otherwise, she wouldn't be content to stay on Viridi. And whatever her plan is, she always has a backup plan. If Earth survives her scheme and the Oculus Gate continues to loom in the sky, she can still contact the towers on Earth by using the mirror portal here on Viridi. What could the towers do? I can't be sure. But we know they can cause earthquakes, and perhaps she could trigger a massive cataclysm that will wipe out every life on the planet."

Without another word, Harrid set a hand on his wife's back, and the two walked away, slowly disappearing.

Kat let out a quiet, "Whew."

"Yeah. Pretty dismal outlook. But I think he's right. We have to keep a possible backup plan in mind." Ben waved for Kat and Caligar to join him. When they huddled, Ben whispered, "The ghosts might stay close and listen, so let's stay quiet. Caligar, do you have any other weapons, maybe at the mesa or in your weather refuge?"

"A knife and a few small bombs that are similar to your Earth hand grenades, though they explode instantly on contact. They have no pin or timer. Therefore, they are more volatile. But a simple jostling won't set them off."

"Understood. Can you get them for me and bring them to the tower? Maybe in a backpack?"

Caligar nodded. "Lacinda's pack should fit you. It's in the refuge. I wanted to check on my family anyway."

Ben patted Caligar's arm. "Then go, my friend. I'll see you at the tower."

"Should I destroy the mirror in case Alex wishes to use it?"

Ben shook his head. "Not yet. It might be our only way to get home. But we'll keep that option in mind."

"Agreed." Caligar hustled away, his heavy steps thrumming the ground.

Ben draped an arm around Kat's shoulders. "You didn't know I'd be such a burden, did you?"

She straightened, giving him support, a hand on his back and on his chest. "Not a problem. But we'll be slow."

"Slow is okay." They began walking at a normal pace, Ben favoring his wounded foot. "Like Harrid said, we'll give Alex some leeway, let her think she's in charge. Then we'll drop the hammer."

"And that hammer is?"

"Still working on it. The plan is coming together."

She patted his chest. "Let's brainstorm. It might take both of our brains to bring that hellcat down."

Iona held the transmitter device on her palm while Charlie sat at her side. A woman's voice emanated from the tiny speaker. "No camera. Not allowed."

Jack's voice followed. "I'm running a translation program so I can understand the lyrics. I don't know Italian."

"Okay. But no camera." The woman began singing in an unfamiliar language, apparently Italian.

Charlie whispered into Iona's ear, "The melody perfectly matches Vivaldi's composition, at least the first measure. That's all I had time to commit to memory."

"It's so quiet," Iona whispered in return. "Jack must not've been close to the singer." She picked up the mirror and set it on her other palm. The reflection showed only her perplexed face. "The mirror's not changing."

"Even if Jack were close enough, that little speaker probably doesn't have the power to do anything."

Iona let her shoulders sag. "Then we're sunk."

"Unless we sing it ourselves."

"In Italian? I can't make heads or tails out of those words."

"True. I know a little Italian, but not enough to figure out what she's singing, and she's not enunciating clearly. I don't think I can mimic her."

When the song ended, the woman added, "You like?"

"It was truly heavenly," Jack said.

A click followed, then silence.

Iona flipped the switch off and looked at the mirror. It remained unchanged. "Think we could hum it?"

"We could try." Charlie nodded toward the receiver. "Can you play it through again?"

"Let me see." The device had the usual play/pause, restart, and fast-forward buttons. She turned it back on and pressed restart.

As the woman sang again, Charlie hummed along with her, her voice much louder than the woman's. Iona joined in. She caught on quickly, but, as before, the reflection stayed the same.

Iona pressed the pause button. "Any other ideas?"

"Maybe we do have to sing the lyrics. Vivaldi included them for a reason."

"That makes sense."

Charlie drummed her fingers on her thigh. "If we were on Earth, we could use a translation app. Even if the app couldn't decipher all the words, we could probably fill in the gaps."

"You're right, but that's like wishing to find iced tea in the desert. It ain't gonna happen." Iona probed her brain for a clue. The plan called for Jack and Trudy to send *The Eternity Psalm* to the receiver, and they succeeded, but didn't a second transmission come in, signaled by a vibration she felt while the receiver was in her pocket? "Let me check something."

She pushed the pause button again. After a few seconds of silence, a new recording played.

"Iona, this is Kat. I have critical new information. In order for *The Eternity Psalm* to work, it must be sung in a language you know, not in Italian, unless, of course, you know Italian. Anyway, it has to come from your heart, you know, sung with passion. In short, you have to really mean it. To help you, I translated the lyrics into English, but I didn't have time to reproduce the rhyme and meter that Vivaldi included in the original. I hope it's good enough."

Kat cleared her throat. "When the tempest blows my ship at sea, I call to my rock from my soul. Hear my cry and protect my life from the snares they set. Give me an escape for my soul." She paused, then added, "I suppose you could substitute *storm* for *tempest* or whatever synonyms you're comfortable with. My guess is that as long as the lyrics mean the same as the original and it comes from your heart, it should work. I'm not sure what sparked the museum worker's passion, but I could hear it in her voice, and it worked then.

Maybe turmoil at home, her own personal tempest. Anyway, that's all I have. I hope you can figure it out."

The recording ended with another click. Iona waited to see if a third message had come through, but only silence followed. She turned the device off. Hearing Kat's voice stabbed her heart. She and Ben were dead because of Alex, and now that witch lusted for more deaths, more spilled blood. She had to be stopped.

Grief narrowed Iona's raw throat, making it sting worse than ever, but she managed to whisper, "Sounds like you were right. We do have to sing it."

"That shouldn't be a problem for you. You have a lovely voice."

"Not anymore. The acid in the water burned my throat. It hurts to talk. Singing would be worse."

"I could sing it, I suppose, but it might not work for a ghost like me to do it."

"All right. I understand. I guess I'll have to give it my best shot." Iona firmed her jaw. "Let's give it a whirl."

"Let me think." Charlie stared straight ahead, her lips silently moving. After nearly a minute, she looked at Iona. "The lyrics Kat provided don't quite work. The syllables don't match the melody. I'm trying to come up with syllables that do match."

"Maybe that doesn't matter. Like Kat said, it's all about the passion. The heart."

"Vivaldi strove for both—perfection in musical technique and in heart. He never gave his second-best effort in either category."

"Okay. I get that. What should we do?"

Charlie again nodded toward the transmitter. "Play both parts again. I almost have the tune memorized, and I need to hear the translation one more time."

Iona complied, listening carefully and trying to embed both the melody and the lyrics in her brain. When the recording finished, Charlie sat staring with her mouth hanging open. "What's up?" Iona asked.

"The song. One of the lines is so much like 'It Is Well with My Soul,' the one we sang together. Remember 'when sorrows like sea billows roll'? That's like 'when the tempest blows my ship at sea.'"

"Okay. Why did that make your jaw drop open?"

"Those lyrics fit the first part of the melody perfectly. We can use it instead of the original. They mean the same thing."

Iona quietly sang the new lyrics in sync with the tune. They really did fit perfectly.

"And the next line has the same meter, and it already rhymes. 'When sorrows like sea billows roll, I call to my rock from my soul.'"

"You're right. But the third line doesn't rhyme. 'O hear my cry and protect.'"

"It sort of rhymes with the fourth line. 'My life from the snares they set.' But the meter's off in both lines. We have to add another syllable in each, like this in line three. 'O hear my lament and protect.' *Lament* is a good synonym for *cry*."

Iona let both lines run through her mind. "So the added syllable we need in line four has to go between *snares* and *set*."

"Exactly. Now you're getting it."

"Then all we have to do is add *that*. 'My life from the snares that they set.'"

"Yes. Yes. That should do fine."

"And the last line?"

Charlie tapped her chin with a finger. "It already rhymes with the first line, like coming back full circle, a common poetic technique, but the meter is off right away. The emphasis is on the first syllable, but it should be on the second, so we need a two-syllable synonym for *give* that has the accent on the second syllable."

"Provide?"

Charlie clapped her hands. "Yes!"

"Then it's 'Provide an escape for my soul.' That sounds right."

"Okay. Let's sing the whole song. Together now."

Iona and Charlie sang the lyrics with the melody, though with halting phrases, not always able to remember the words quickly enough. Iona's throat stung, feeling like someone was scrubbing the inside of her throat with steel wool. When they finished, the mirror hadn't changed at all.

"I'm sorry," Iona said as she massaged her throat. "I sound like a grunting pig."

"Not that bad, but let me sing solo while you rest your voice. At least that will help you memorize it. Then the next time you try, you won't have to hesitate."

While Iona sat and listened, her hands folded and tense, Charlie sang. Her mesmerizing alto sounded angelic as her supple voice caressed each word.

"When sorrows like sea billows roll,
I call to my rock from my soul.
O hear my lament and protect
My life from the snares that they set.
Provide an escape for my soul."

As before, the mirror stayed the same, reflecting only Iona's face and the observatory room. Charlie sang the psalm three more times to no avail.

Iona leaned her head back against the wall. "Well, at least I've got it memorized now. I can try again."

"Rest a bit more." Charlie pulled her legs close and wrapped her arms around them. "I'll keep thinking about the lyrics. Maybe we changed them too much."

"Speaking of changing, I'm going to see if my shirt's dry enough to put on." Iona slid the transmitter and mirror into her pocket and walked to the line. She retrieved the shirt and felt the sleeves—damp, but not too bad. With all the fog outside and the windows open, it probably wouldn't get much drier anytime soon. After putting the shirt on, she returned and sat next to Charlie again. "Still thinking about the lyrics?"

She nodded. "But I can't come up with anything better than what we already tried."

"Maybe the passion is missing." Iona pulled her necklace cord and drew the cross up, then set it in front of her shirt. "While we sing, we should try thinking about the message—"

"Iona!"

The call came from outside.

Iona turned and straightened slowly until her eyes rose above the lower edge of the window. A gap in the passing clouds revealed Alex standing on the ledge at the summit of the switchback trail.

Chapter Ten

"Iona," Alex said as she strolled closer to the tower's access tunnel. "I know you're in there. As a Reaper, I can sense a nearby disembodied soul. I'm assuming your mother is with you, no longer stashed in her cloak. I admit that your ploy was ingenious, and I congratulate you on your cleverness, but I'm afraid you've been too clever for your own good."

Iona ached to ask, *Why is that?* But giving away her presence couldn't be a good idea. Alex might be fishing for her with a lie and a tantalizing question—good bait for the gullible.

She whispered to Charlie, "Can she really sense you?"

Charlie nodded. "Without a doubt. She's an Owl. Her senses are likely better than mine ever were."

"Well," Alex continued, "since you're not answering, I can assume it's safe for me to send explosives into that tower. Obviously no one will be hurt if it's vacant."

Iona peeked out again. Alex entered the tunnel for a moment and returned carrying a rifle-like weapon with a wide barrel. As she lifted the butt to her shoulder, she shouted again. "Have you ever seen one of these before? Perhaps when you were spying for the angels in the rebel camp?"

Iona thrust herself back down. "Alex has a grenade launcher! She's getting ready to shoot it."

Charlie grasped Iona's wrist, though her phantom hand passed through. "She's not bluffing. You'd better believe that."

"I'll close the window panels." Iona ran across the room to the laptop and tapped the proper icons. Just as the panels started rising, a grenade flew into the window directly over Charlie's head and rolled along the floor to Iona's feet. She lunged toward Charlie, dove headfirst, and slid against the wall next to her.

The moment she rolled into a ball and shielded her face with her arms, the grenade exploded with an ear-splitting boom. Sharp objects pelted her arms and legs, stinging like hornets, and something bigger slammed into her ribs.

She grunted, resisting a gut-wrenching shout. Pain roared up and down her side. She looked at the wound. A spear of wood protruded a couple of inches. As thick as a thumb, it penetrated deeply, probably at least as far as it stuck out. And it hurt. A lot. Like a hot poker constantly jabbing. But she couldn't pull it out, not without risking a lot of bleeding or maybe tearing something important inside.

"Iona," Charlie whispered, "are you all right?"

"Not really." Iona blinked through hot tears. The laptop lay next to her, its screen smashed. The window panels had stopped moving, now covering only the lower ten percent of the openings. A new five-foot-wide crater marred the floor where the grenade exploded, and the telescope lay in it, half of its cylindrical tube protruding upward. She reached into her pocket and felt the mirror. It seemed to be intact.

"Iona!" Alex called again. "I have five more grenades. I trust that they can finish what the first one started. Shall I launch the second one, or will you surrender?"

Wincing, Iona whispered again to Charlie. "She knows I'm here. I might as well talk to her. Maybe I can find out where Leo is."

Charlie nodded. "Agreed."

They rose together. Iona looked out the window, the top of the panel at chest level, and spoke as loudly as her sore throat would allow. "I'm here, Alex."

"Ah!" Alex lowered the grenade launcher and smiled in a triumphant manner. "A little explosive persuasion brought you to your senses, I see."

Iona felt the wound in her side. Warm wetness trickled down to her waist. As new pain spiked, a stream of shouted insults begged to spew, but she swallowed them back. "You demanded that I surrender. Do you still plan to take me to Satan?"

A cloud drifted by, blocking Iona's view but not Alex's voice. "My plans are not a topic of discussion. I demand unconditional surrender. You are not in a position to negotiate."

When the cloud passed, Alex's brow lifted. "Charlotte, how good to see you again. You're looking very well for a dead woman."

Charlie offered a mechanical smile. "And you're looking halfway decent for your age. How old are you now? About two hundred? You don't look a day over one hundred."

Alex's smile tightened. "Charlotte, your wit is as sharp as a wooden spoon. I think you should—"

"Hush, you two. You can trade insults later." Iona glanced at the bow and quiver on the floor where they lay next to the mooring cap. Since the mirror failed to work, killing Alex might be the only way to defeat her.

Her hands out of Alex's view, Iona picked up the bow, selected an arrow, and nocked it to the string. From this distance, nailing Alex with an arrow would be pretty easy if not for the breeze left behind by the storm. Even a slight gust would nudge it astray.

Iona searched the trail leading to the river. The flow still raged but not as swollen as before. Leo was nowhere in sight. She called, "Tell me where Leo is."

"Not that I am obligated to tell you," Alex said, "but he abandoned me. I have no idea where he is now. I assume he will continue searching for you, but I was lucky enough to find you first."

Iona felt the mirror in her pocket. It didn't react to Alex's words. She must've been telling the truth. Iona heaved a pretend sigh. "All right, I'll surrender. Better than getting blown up." She whispered to Charlie without looking at her, "Keep Alex distracted." Iona then called again to Alex. "I have to get my shoes on. I'll be down in a minute." She backed away a few steps.

Charlie shouted through the window, "Alexandria, do you want to know how I opened the gates of hell to help Iona and Leo escape?"

"Not especially, but I suppose you'll tell me anyway."

While the two conversed, Iona tuned them out and shifted to the next window, far enough back from the opening to stay out of Alex's view. When another cloud came by, she scooted closer. With the point of the arrow extending through the window, she drew the string back to her ear. Now to wait for the cloud to move past. She needed less than a second to take aim.

Her ribs throbbed, forcing her to ease the tension on the string. Not good. She would have to draw it back again at the last second to get enough power. If she could skewer Alex's heart, the fight would be over. If she missed, Alex would be furious and likely to launch more grenades. But what other option existed? Ben and Kat were dead, and Leo still hadn't shown up. For all practical purposes, she was alone.

The moment the cloud thinned enough to allow a view of Alex, Iona drew the string back and fired. The arrow zipped through the air, but a gust pushed it lower. It plunged into Alex's stomach instead of her heart.

The grenade launcher thudded to the ground. Alex grasped the arrow's shaft, bent over, and groaned through a string of obscenities as blood dripped from the wound to the ground.

"Great shot," Charlie said.

Iona smiled. "I was aiming for her heart, but I guess close enough is better than a miss."

Alex's eyes glittered, a silvery sheen obvious even from a distance. With a loud grunt, she snapped the arrow shaft, leaving only an inch or two protruding from her gut. She slammed the rest of the shaft to the ground and shouted, "You fool! You will pay for your stupidity!"

Iona gulped. How could she possibly have the strength to stand, much less snap the arrow?

"She's an Owl," Charlie said, as if reading Iona's mind. "She can tolerate a lot of blows."

Alex picked up the launcher and set the butt to her shoulder. "Lucifer will just have to wait for another person to do his bidding. I'm going to kill you here and now."

Iona snatched another arrow from the quiver, nocked it, and fired again without taking aim. Alex launched a grenade at the same moment. Iona's arrow slashed Alex's shoulder, ripping her shirt and drawing blood. The grenade zipped into the window and rolled along the floor until it dropped into the crater the other one had blasted.

Bracing for an explosion, Iona nocked a third arrow. This time, she took careful aim while Charlie watched, breathless. Unfortunately, the grenade launcher covered Alex's heart as she appeared to be checking for a jam in the weapon's feeder.

A muffled boom sounded below. The tower shuddered, then swayed. Iona kept her eye close to the bowstring, but hitting Alex now seemed impossible.

Alex readied the launcher once more. When the tower paused in its sway for a split second, Iona fired again. The arrow clanked against the gun's body and bounced off at an angle.

Charlie winced. "Better get down."

A third grenade rocketed out of the launcher and zipped toward Iona. She ducked into a low crouch. The grenade struck the top of the window panel and exploded on contact. The concussive wave knocked the bow loose and sent her into a reverse somersault. As she rolled, she covered her face with her hands. Sharp panel fragments sliced into her arms and torso.

She stopped only inches from the crater and rose to her hands and knees. The floor bent, ready to give way. She crawled slowly toward the wall, begging the floor to stay intact. Shards protruded from her sleeved arms. Blood trickled down her skin to her wrists, and warm streams flowed along her back and chest—maybe blood, maybe sweat, maybe both. And her side ached most of all, bleeding worse than all of the other wounds.

At the wall, Charlie crouched below the window, tight worry lines in her brow. She whispered, "Oh, Iona! You look awful."

"I feel awful." When Iona arrived at the wall, she lay on her side in a curl. "What's Alex doing now?"

Charlie peeked over the window's lower edge. "She's staring at the tower, like she's waiting to see what's going to happen."

"Maybe it's about to topple over. I feel it swaying."

Charlie smiled. "At least we're harder to hit now."

Iona tried to smile but could only grimace. "You're so funny."

"Okay, I'll be serious. Listen, Alex won't wait long. If this tower doesn't fall, she'll shoot another grenade up here. I don't think you or the tower can survive another hit. The way I see it, we have to try singing *The Eternity Psalm* again."

"Iona!" Alex shouted. "In mere moments, your tower will collapse. You have only one way to survive. Transform into ghost mode. Charlotte can show you how."

"Or that," Charlotte said.

Iona narrowed her eyes. "No surprise that Alex knows about me since she's Satan's lapdog, but she should guess that her telling me to go ghost is more likely to make me *not* do it."

"True, but she thinks you have no choice. For some reason, she's testing your abilities."

"If I go to ghost mode, Alex can still see me and catch me, right?"

Charlie nodded. "Right."

"And if the song works, what do we do, throw the mirror at her? That's a terrible option."

"No, but the psalm is a cry to God for help. It's a prayer for rescue. And now that we're really in trouble, our singing will truly be from the heart."

The tower's sway worsened, nearly enough to make Iona slide on the floor. "Okay. I'll sing the best I can." She withdrew the mirror from her pocket and set it on her palm where Charlie could see it. "You start. I'll join you."

"Very well." Charlie began the song in her usual alto. "When sorrows like sea billows roll …"

Iona sang along, starting at the beginning and catching up. Although pain throttled her voice and made it sound more like a table saw than a human, she managed to struggle through it. The mirror, however, never altered in the slightest.

"No, no, no," Charlie said, interrupting Iona after the second phrase. "You're singing by rote, not from the heart."

"I don't think that's the problem." Iona winced at the pain in her throat. "Besides, I'm doing the best I can. I'm bleeding from about twenty holes."

"I know. You look like a pincushion." Charlie peeked out the window again. "Alex is taking aim. She's moving the gun back and forth like she's measuring the tower's sway. She'll probably fire at any second."

Iona bit her lip hard but said nothing. Although Alex would have to make a nearly impossible shot, it seemed like a bad idea to bet against her.

Charlie gasped but kept her voice low. "I see Leo."

"What?"

"He's on the trail. Sneaking up to Alex from behind."

Iona struggled to her knees and peeked out the window. As Charlie had said, Leo crept up the final portion of the switchback trail leading to the ledge where Alex stood. But what would he do when he arrived? He appeared to be unarmed, while Alex stood armed to the hilt. He needed a distraction.

Iona shouted, "Alex! Wait!"

Alex lowered the grenade launcher. "For what? You lost your chance to surrender."

"Please give me another chance. I thought I could escape, but now I know I can't. I'm injured. I can't walk. I can barely crawl." Iona lifted an arm. The torn sleeve revealed multiple bloody gashes with a half dozen embedded wooden spears, some protruding more than an inch. With Alex's vision, surely she could see them, though they were tiny compared to the one embedded in her side. "I'm riddled with shards all over my body. If I pull them out, I'm afraid I'll bleed to death."

Alex stared for a moment before answering. "I believe you. A ruse with that much self-inflicted injury is too over-the-top, even for you."

"Then can I still surrender?"

"You're too eager." Alex glanced around. Fortunately, Leo now crouched behind a nearby boulder, out of her view. "What's your game?"

"No game. I just don't want to die. But I'm too injured to climb down."

"So you want me to risk my own life and come up there to help you? Step into an ambush?" Alex laughed. "What kind of fool do you think I am?"

Charlie whispered, "Can I answer that question?"

"No," Iona said with a hiss. "I'll handle her."

"I would be better off," Alex continued, "if I blasted you again and picked through the tower's rubble to see if you survived. If not, no big loss. Lucifer would be disappointed, perhaps even vengeful, but he has no power to harm me here on Viridi."

Charlie set a hand on the window panel and poked her head out. "Then why were you doing his bidding, since you were already safe from hell here on Viridi?"

"Ah, the ghost speaks." Alex set a fist on her hip. "I was doing him a favor in trade for him doing one for me. A business transaction, you might say."

Iona felt the mirror. The surface tingled. Alex was lying.

"What favor is he doing for you?" Charlie called.

Alex sneered. "That is not your concern."

"Listen, Alex," Iona said, "you don't have to come up here. I'll try to climb down the rope, but I need you at the bottom to catch me if I fall. You'll see that I'm too injured to ambush you."

"Oh, very well." Alex pivoted toward the tunnel and pointed. "I assume the bottom of your exit shaft is in there."

"Yes. It's dark inside, but there aren't any obstacles."

"I'm not worried about obstacles." Alex strode to the tunnel and disappeared inside. The moment she left, Leo rose from behind the boulder and skulked toward the tunnel entrance.

Iona stiffened and looked at Charlie. "Alex can see in the dark."

"Right. That's why she said she's not worried about obstacles. She's an Owl, so—" Charlie sucked in a breath. "We have to warn Leo!"

Iona pushed her torso as far out the window as she could, pain stabbing her all over. "Leo," she whisper-shouted. "Wait."

He glanced at the top of the tower, gave a two-fingered salute, and crept inside the tunnel.

Iona pulled back into the tower. "I guess he couldn't hear me." Prickly heat coursed up her back and down her arms. Fear. Pure fear. "I don't like this, Charlie. Leo's in big trouble. And now I'm wondering if Alex guessed I was plotting something. She's the one planning an ambush, not me."

"I know what you mean. She gave in too easily. It was all part of a scheme. She probably saw Leo before she agreed to come."

"And now all we can do is wait." Iona plucked one of the more painful spears from the back of her hand and threw it to the side. Blood oozed from the hole, adding to a trickle from a wound on her wrist. The blood dripped to the floor in a slow cadence, making a tiny splash, like a doomsday timepiece counting the seconds.

After nearly a minute, Alex's call came from the hole leading down to the tunnel. "Iona, where are you?"

Iona tensed. What happened to Leo? Would Alex sound so cavalier if she had just ambushed him? "I'm coming. Sorry I can't move very fast." She grabbed the mooring cap, stuffed it into her pocket, and crawled to the rope where it lay severed from the telescope. The cloak had fallen to the floor close by. She grabbed the rope and tossed it into the hole.

Charlie sat at the edge of the hole, her legs dangling. "I'm going first to see what she's up to. I'll let you know if it's safe."

"But she's a Reaper. She can see you. Catch you."

"I'm also a Reaper. I know what to do to avoid her." Charlie slid off the edge and descended out of sight.

Iona crawled to the hole and looked down. Charlie floated like a human-shaped balloon toward the bottom. Alex waited for her there, her irises sparkling with a silvery sheen and her right hand extended, as if ready to catch Charlie.

When Charlie came within reach, Alex grabbed her by the throat. Charlie's body thinned, and she slipped down through Alex's grip, then leaped away, out of Iona's sight.

"Iona," Charlie shouted. "Alex has Leo. He's lying on the ground. I think he's out cold."

Iona cupped her hands around her mouth and called down. "What did you do to Leo?"

Alex spoke in a matter-of-fact tone. "I hid in the darkness and waited for him to try to ambush me. He never saw my kick to the face coming. It landed square on the jaw, instantly knocking him unconscious. He likely suffered a concussion … or worse."

"Alex," Iona growled, "if Leo dies, I'll—"

"You'll what?" Alex hummed through a laugh. "Dear Iona, I hold all the cards. Except for that pitiful bow and arrow, you have no weapons, while I have a grenade launcher with three more grenades, and those are infused with a fire accelerant. You're badly injured, and I am not. Yes, I have a wound that you likely thought would cripple me, but you didn't realize that Owls are far more resilient than any other Reapers. It takes a lot more than a puncture wound to the abdomen to stop me. And now I have your father. You thought I didn't realize that he was tracking me, but I knew he would eventually show up, being the expert huntsman that he is, so I was ready, and I saw right through your transparent ruse."

Iona curled her hands into fists. Rage burned from head to toe. Her voice trembled as she barked a response. "So now what, you cowardly swine?"

"First, cool your anger. I will do no further harm to your father if you cooperate. Second, climb down the rope. I will catch you if need be, as you suggested. Third, you will agree to meet with—"

"Hush, witch!" Charlie leaped into view and shinnied up the rope with incredible speed. When she arrived at the top, she whispered, "Leo woke up and sneaked away into darkness. I don't think Alex knows yet."

"Then let's give him some cover."

"What do you have in mind?" Charlie asked.

"I'm going to try to even the visual odds." Iona looked down through the hole again. "Okay, Alex, I guess I have no choice. Give me a minute. I still don't have my shoes on." She shuffled on hands and knees to the bow, grabbed it and an arrow, and crawled back. After finding her socks and shoes, she put them on as well as the cloak, then, keeping the bow out of Alex's view, she sat with her legs dangling through the hole. "Are you ready to catch me?"

Alex's eyes glimmered silver again. "What kind of trick are you trying to pull?"

"No trick. You said I had to—"

"You should know by now that you can't fool me." Alex's head swiveled as she swept her gaze across the area.

Charlie whispered, "She's distracted. Do it. Now."

"Right." Iona nocked the arrow and pulled the string back. Hitting an eye from this distance and angle while in so much pain might be impossible. Her timing and aim had to be perfect.

"Oh, I see," Alex said. "Your father's gone. His head must be tougher than I thought." She looked up again, her eyes now looking like fiery steel. "He has signed your death warrant."

Iona released the arrow. The point glanced off Alex's left eye socket, ripping the skin in a spray of blood. She reeled back, out of sight. A stream of obscene curses flew up the shaft, feeling almost physical as they shot into the room.

Alex appeared again, blood flowing from her eye socket over her cheek. She aimed the rocket launcher upward. Iona dove out of the way, curled against the wall, and covered her face with her hands, a gap between her fingers.

A loud *phoom* shot up from the hole. A grenade zipped in, struck the domed ceiling, and ricocheted at an angle. When it hit the floor and rolled to the wall at the far side of the room, Leo shouted from below, "Iona. I have her." Grunts peppered his words. "Get down here."

More curses erupted from both Leo and Alex. Charlotte stood at the hole, looking down. "They're fighting."

The grenade exploded, blasting a hole in the wall across the room. Fire splashed across the ceiling and floor. Shards shot toward Iona. She tucked her head under her arms. Again, knifelike stabs pelted her body. New pain roared across nearly every inch of skin.

The tower's sway grew worse. The structure creaked and groaned. Iona risked a peek. Flames crawled along the ceiling, the floor, and the curved wall, burning everything in sight. Even if the tower managed to stay upright, the fire would consume her as well. She breathed a whispered, "God, help me."

Charlie rushed to Iona and knelt at her side. "You have to get out of here."

"I know." Iona tried to roll up to her knees, but every move pushed embedded shards deeper into her skin. Pain shot into her skull, making her head pound. Her muscles gave way, and she flopped back to the floor. "I can't."

"You have to."

Smoke wafted into her side of the room—noxious and choking. She coughed, making more pain spike. "Leo." She coughed again. "Call him. Maybe he can help me."

Charlie looked out the window. "Oh, no!"

"What is it?"

"Alex is standing out there with a foot on Leo's head. He's not moving a muscle. And she's staring at the tower like a vulture waiting for roadkill."

"That's what I'll be in less than a minute." The wind shifted, sending the smoke back toward the fire. Flames now engulfed half of the room, and the breeze stoked their fury. Iona heaved a sigh. "Maybe it's all for the better. I'll be a ghost like you, and we'll be together forever."

"Then go to ghost mode. You'll be a living ghost instead of a dead one."

"But I've never done it before. And with so much pain, I don't think I can."

"It does take complete concentration." Charlie paced in front of Iona. "God is our only hope."

"Do you mean we should pray? I've been doing that. A little, anyway."

Charlie halted. "Yes, pray, but let's sing our prayer. *The Eternity Psalm*. It's a cry for help. But let's sing it with more passion this time. Like we really mean it."

"That won't be a problem, but I still think it's not going to work." Iona plucked a few painful shards from her arm and pushed to a sitting position with her back to the wall. Charlie was right. With Leo in a helpless state, Ben and Kat dead, and Jack and Trudy stuck on Earth, only God could help her now. She withdrew the mirror from her pocket, set it on the floor at her side, and began singing without waiting for Charlie. "When sorrows like sea billows roll …"

Charlie sat at Iona's side and joined in.

"I call to my rock from my soul."

Only a few steps away, flames inched closer and closer, sending heat and smoke in a smothering blanket. As in the song, the flames looked like billows, but not from the sea—from hell.

Trying not to cough, Iona sang on. With each phrase, her voice strengthened. Warmth flooded her mind, though the pain roared on. The mirror's reflection rippled, and the image of an open door appeared. Light streamed out from it, a glorious radiance filled with glittering specks.

"O hear my lament and protect."

"Iona," Charlie said, breathless. "The mirror is showing heaven. You can escape there. Maybe both of us can."

Iona glowered at her, hoping to communicate a silent message—*shut up and keep singing.*

Charlie nodded. "Right. It might not work until we finish." She rejoined the song.

"My life from the snares that they set. Provide an escape for my soul."

Iona gazed at the mirror. The radiant door remained—brilliant and inviting. All she had to do was touch the surface, and all of her troubles would be over. Forever. No more fighting. No more pain. No more Alex.

She whispered, "Alex."

"What?" Charlie asked.

"I can't go to heaven. I have to stop Alex. Help Leo."

Charlie heaved a sigh. "You're right. We can't abandon our allies now, but if we're going to survive, our only hope is an answered prayer. We asked God to save us now, and we meant it. Now we just have to keep believing."

Chapter Eleven

Lemuel pushed a button on the symphony sphere. The light at the top of the tower brightened and emitted a pale orange beam along with a lower musical tone. The ground trembled once more, forcing him to brace himself on the tower support again.

Jack struggled to stay upright on his crutches. Trudy set her feet, dropped her rifle, and held Jack's arm on one side while Austin held the other.

Lem stared upward. Trudy followed his line of sight. Clouds obscured the Oculus Gate. Beams from the other three towers joined the first and shone in the gate's direction, each with its own color, though the musical notes couldn't reach this far. "I know the next note," Lem said, focusing on Trudy and Jack. "Should I go on?"

Jack nodded. "Let's see it through, unless the tremors make it too dangerous."

"Very well." Lem pushed another button. The musical note changed again, higher this time, and the light beam altered to dark purple. As Lem continued pushing buttons, much more quickly now, the colors shuffled through dozens of hues, and the tones knitted into a melody that sounded like a dark dirge—dire and foreboding. The tremors continued, neither strengthening nor abating, not enough to knock them off their feet.

At the Oculus Gate, the beams melded from four directions and created a nearly flat multicolored cylinder high in the sky—a three-dimensional chamber that rotated slowly on a vertical axis like a glowing, upside-down, deep-dish pie plate.

After several minutes, Lem exhaled heavily. "I think the portal wheel is finished. I hear no more notes to press." He set the sphere on the ground. "And this ball is getting too warm too hold."

The icy snow under the ball melted. The buttons depressed on their own, and the melody and array of lights continued shifting, faster now. Trudy eyed the scene, nearly mesmerized. The chamber rotated more quickly as well, resembling a revolving door with flashing panels, though it spun opposite the direction she had seen similar doors rotate.

The tremors spiked. Trudy tightened her grip on Jack's arm, keeping both of them from toppling. The tower swayed, though its light beam stayed locked on the spinning door. As the door slowly descended and expanded in size, the tower looked like a fishing rod bending back and forth while pulling its catch closer and closer.

Trudy's legs flexed, unbidden. The urge to turn and run seemed overwhelming, but she had to see this through, no matter what.

The rotating wheel landed on the ground with a gentle thud, the outer edge of the floor only about a hundred feet away and extending to the east and west as far as the eye could see. The impact sent a muted rumble through the frigid air, like thunder during a snowstorm. Then, the floor of the wheel lifted a few inches off the ground and hovered in place, floating aloft as if supported by jets of air beneath.

The tremors ceased, though the musical tones continued, quieter now, interrupted only by the revolving door as each panel drew close from the right, then passed by to the left with a whoosh that sent a gust of warm wind across their bodies. But whether the panels moved, or the floor moved and carried the panels along, seemed impossible to tell.

As a panel approached, it displayed multicolored lights on the front, then darkness on the back when it whisked by. The lights on the front painted shapeless silhouettes, like colorful shadows undulating on a drawn shade. Radiance from the wheel illuminated everything nearby, providing plenty of light to augment the lesser glow from the dwindling fires.

When one of the whooshes faded, Trudy released Jack's arm. "What in the world is that thing?"

"Or what *on* the world. It looks like it's hovering on top of the earth, covering the entire Arctic. If that's true, then it's about three thousand miles wide."

"How tall are those partitions? Maybe a thousand feet?" Trudy looked at the sky. A central axle extended into the Oculus Gate, as if a huge giant beyond the Gate were spinning the wheel with a twist of his fingers. "And the connection to the Gate has to be hundreds of miles taller."

"If it's a portal wheel," Austin said, "then if you walk into a gap between the door panels, will it whisk you away somewhere?"

"I assume so." Trudy gave the contraption a skeptical stare. "But I'm not taking the plunge until I know where I would go, and it could be that one of the gaps between those upright walls—panels, partitions, whatever—could send you one place, and another could lead somewhere completely different."

Jack looked at Lem. "Did Camilla drop any clues about where the portal wheel leads?"

Lem shrugged while trembling, maybe cold, maybe fearful. "None that I can remember."

"Think," Trudy said. "Any clue at all might help."

Lem put his gloves back on and picked up the sphere. "All I know is that Camilla wanted herself and her alien cohort to join Alexandria on a planet called Viridi, but she said that isn't what the portal wheel is for. She claimed that she didn't know where it would lead, only that she was supposed to generate it."

Jack crutched closer to Lem and set a hand on his shoulder. "Tell us exactly what Camilla said, word for word."

"All right. I'll try." Lem's eyes rolled upward for a moment. "She said something like, 'Alexandria is calling for all of her elite followers to join her on Viridi, but the portal wheel that you will help us create is not for that purpose. Those destinations are not yet known, except for one, and that one is not Viridi.'"

"Those destinations," Jack repeated. "Plural."

"Correct. I am certain of that."

"And one of them is known. That might be helpful information."

"I also heard," Lem said, "that the wheel sends someone to a destination when it stops, though I have no idea how the stoppage actuates the transport."

"Then you must know how to stop it," Trudy said.

"I do. A combination of five specific notes."

Trudy pointed at the sphere. "Then punch them in. Since we're not actually on the wheel, I'm thinking we'll stay put. Maybe when it stops, we'll be able to check it out more closely."

"As you wish." Lem pressed a button, waited for the tower to respond with a tone that interrupted the ongoing song, then pressed four more buttons, waiting again between each press. After all five notes sounded and died away, a new panel whooshed by at a lower speed than the others before it. The deceleration continued until the wheel stopped rotating, and everything silenced.

A panel stood in view, the next one that would have passed if not for the stoppage. The floor that the panels swept across glowed orange, with sparkling red dots throughout that pulsed like tiny LEDs.

Trudy picked up her rifle and strode closer, calling back, "Everyone come. Austin, help Jack if he needs it." She halted within a few paces of the outer edge of the enormous wheel. The panel stood on the wheel's floor about fifty feet to her east and even taller than she had estimated earlier, too tall to even guess. "Some kind of image is taking shape on that panel's surface. Maybe it'll give us a clue to where the portal leads."

"How would you use it?" Jack asked as he arrived. "Walk through the panel? Stand in front of it?"

Austin, with Lem at his side, peered at the image. In the light of the portal wheel, his steely eyes seemed to shimmer with a metallic sheen. "I see a man sitting with his hands folded on an odd-looking table. At least I think it's a table, sort of round with rough edges. And it looks like a tree is growing out of the center. Not sure, though. It's kind of fuzzy. Just the man, table, and three chairs in a gray void."

"Is it like a still shot, or is he moving?" Trudy asked.

"He's moving. Nervous twitches, I think."

"Weird." Trudy turned toward Jack. "What do you make of it?"

He shrugged. "Sounds like we don't need to go there, if that's what you mean."

"Yeah. Pretty much. Let's see if there are other destinations." She spun toward Lem. "Do you remember the tune that conjured this portal wheel?"

He nodded. "It played through several times. I'm quite sure I know the notes."

"Then try pushing the buttons to play it. I'm betting that it'll make the wheel spin again."

"As you wish." Lem removed his gloves, returned them to his pocket, and retrieved the sphere. He pressed buttons in a rapid fashion. With each press, a musical note emanated from the top of the tower, along with its corresponding light beam.

The portal wheel began moving again. When the panel with the man at the table swept past and another panel came into view in the distance, Trudy called out, "Stop."

Lem pressed the halt-code buttons. The five notes sounded, and again the wheel decelerated. The new panel drew closer and eased to a stop about a hundred feet to the east.

"Okay, Owl eyes," Trudy said to Austin, "it's farther away this time, but can you see into this portal?"

Austin squinted again. "That's an easy one. It's hell. A view of the Lake of Fire and the gates beyond it."

"Hard pass. We're not going there." Trudy nodded at Lem. "Give it another twirl."

Lem pushed the start-code buttons. Again, the wheel began rotating, and Lem stopped the movement on Trudy's command. This time the next panel came to rest almost directly in front of them, only slightly to the east.

Trudy and the others trudged a few paces to the west to get a better look at the entire panel. A brilliant light shone through it, bathing them in radiance and warmth.

Jack spread an arm and basked in the glow. "I know what this is. A portal to heaven. I saw a doorway like this when I flew to the Never-ending Highway as a disembodied soul. After Summer blew the highway up, she and my wife and daughter went through the door." He lowered his arm and looked at Trudy. "I'm looking forward to going through that door to see them again, but I have to stick around to keep you out of trouble for a few more years."

Trudy flapped her lips. "I hear you, Mr. Broken Kneecap."

Lem lifted the symphony sphere. "I assume you want to check the next one."

"Yep." Trudy twirled a finger in the air. "Let 'er rip."

Once more, Lem pressed the buttons, restarted the rotation, and stopped it again. This time, the next panel came to rest about twenty paces to the east.

Austin took a few steps closer and peered at the images on the panel's front. "This is interesting. I see a telescope in a circular room with a domed ceiling."

"An observatory," Jack said.

"I think so. And beyond the telescope, two females are looking out a window. I see their backs. Both are wearing a Reaper's cloak, and one of them is Charlotte. I'd know her anywhere, even from behind. And the other is shorter. Another redhead. I'm guessing she's Iona."

Trudy blinked hard, but the image stayed fuzzy for her. "You see Charlotte? How is that possible? She's dead."

"Caligar's observatory is on Viridi," Jack said. "They must be there. But that doesn't answer how Charlotte could be alive."

"Hold it." Austin squinted. "Something flew in through the window." A flash of light illuminated the panel for a brief second. "That's not good. An explosion. Debris is flying everywhere. Some hit Iona, but other pieces passed right through Charlotte and smacked against the wall or flew out the window. She must be a ghost. A disembodied soul."

Trudy took Jack's hand and held it tightly. A lump swelled in her throat, forcing her to swallow. "Is Iona okay?"

"Sort of. She's standing now, but she's wincing. I see a dark splotch on her shirt at the side, maybe blood. She's prepping a bow and arrow. Looks like she's going to shoot out the window."

"They must be under attack." Trudy popped out her rifle's ammo magazine and checked the bullets, a full load. She slapped the mag back into place. "I'm going in." Jack grabbed her wrist, but she jerked away. "Don't try to stop me."

"I'm not. You should go. But how? Trying to walk through the door? We don't know if it would send you there or vaporize you."

"Don't worry. I'll test it first." She jogged to Camilla's corpse, snatched up the medical bag she had left nearby, and hurried back to the portal wheel, slowing as she neared the edge of its floor. She touched it with the barrel of her rifle. No sparks flew. She tossed the medical bag onto the floor's surface. It slid to a stop without harm.

Lifting her foot about eight inches, she carefully set her boot on the glittering floor. No sparks, no shock, no pain at all. She pressed her weight down and vaulted the other foot to the surface. Again, no response. She turned toward Jack and Austin. "Safe so far."

Austin continued staring at the panel. "Iona shot the arrow, but now she looks tense, maybe scared. I think you'd better hurry."

"I'm on it." Trudy scooped her medical bag, rushed to the panel, and touched it with the rifle. The end of the barrel passed through. She drew it back and examined the metal in the surrounding glow. It appeared to be fine. Steeling herself, she pushed a hand through. A tingling sensation crawled up her arm, but no pain. She pushed her head in and looked around. Only the portal floor on the other side of the panel lay in view.

She walked the rest of the way through and turned toward the rear side of the barrier, a solid black wall. She touched it with a hand—solid. She walked around it to the floor's outer edge, hopped off, and hoofed it back to Jack and Austin, the rifle and bag still in hand. "Update on Iona and Charlotte?"

Austin squinted once more. "It's hard to be sure, but it looks like they're ... singing?"

"Singing?"

"Yeah. While looking at a square object in Iona's hand."

"The mirror," Jack said. "Maybe they're trying to open a portal with *The Eternity Psalm*. Iona got the message we sent."

"Trying to escape to heaven?" Trudy asked.

Jack shrugged. "Who knows? I'm just guessing."

Trudy pivoted back to the portal and scanned the enormous panel. If this contraption really worked like a revolving door, maybe she was going about it completely wrong. To pass through a revolving door, a person had to walk with the rotation as it moved. She stepped onto the portal floor and pivoted back to the others. "Lem, get this merry-go-round started again."

"Very well." Lem began pushing the sphere's buttons once more.

Trudy walked farther onto the floor. Musical notes descended from above, one tone after another. Here, the notes seemed physical, dropping on the top of her head like a gentle shower of featherweight leaves. When the door panel began moving toward her from the east, she walked westward at the same pace, carrying the rifle and medical bag.

She nodded at Jack and Austin as she drew away from them. "Keep watching. Maybe Austin will see what happens to me."

Jack set a hand to the side of his mouth and called, "How will we know when to stop the door?"

"You won't. I guess if this doesn't work, I'll show up again coming from the east."

"But it's nearly ten thousand miles around the Arctic Circle."

"Then I'll be tired, won't I?" Now nearly out of voice range, she continued walking while craning her neck to look back as she shouted, "I don't know how long. Just guess. Maybe ten minutes."

Radiance from the door washed out her view of the tower. She focused ahead and marched onward to the rhythm of the music. The notes seemed to envelop her in a cocoon of sound. The outside world to her left, completely dark now, looked like a black blur. A summerlike breeze filtered warmth through her parka, a welcome relief from the polar chill.

After about ten minutes, the music stopped. The door panel behind her slowed to a halt. As if carried by momentum, the light emanating from the panel continued forward and stretched out over Trudy with a tingly wash. She shuddered, casting off the tingles, though the light around her remained.

She looked toward the floor's outer edge. Beyond it, where darkness, snow, and ice had dominated the landscape, now ambiguous objects took shape—first, a telescope lying in a hole on a floor, then, two human figures, both sitting. Bright light undulated, like flames scattered along the ground—blurry and indistinct.

Trudy continued staring at the new scene, bathed in the glow from the revolving door. In seconds, if she were to walk into that light, she might find herself on Viridi with Iona. The scene could also be a mirage, ready to disperse and disappear, leaving her alone in the Alaskan winter darkness without a clue as to what to do next.

In any case, the air had grown extremely warm, as if she were standing directly in front of a bonfire. She set the rifle and medical bag down, shed her parka, dropped it, then picked up her other items again, one in each hand. After taking a deep breath, she whispered, "No time like the present," and marched straight into the light.

Chapter Twelve

Wincing with every step, Ben finally limped out of the forest, Kat supporting him at his side. With the observation tower now in view, he squinted at the ledge perched over the switchback trail about a mile away. Someone stood there looking at the tower as it swayed, apparently ready to topple.

Something shot into one of the tower's open windows, maybe fired by the person on the ground. Seconds later, the sound of an explosion rumbled like thunder. Smoke billowed from the far side of the tower and rose toward the sky—fire in the observatory. "The tower's under attack."

Kat nodded. "Probably Alex firing the grenade launcher."

"Let's go." Steeling himself, he jogged toward the trail.

When Kat caught up, she breathed easily as they jogged abreast. "With that switchback slope and your injury, it'll take at least twenty minutes to get there. And based on the smoke and the way the tower's tipping, I don't think we have twenty minutes. I can make it by myself in less than ten."

"Then go." Ben withdrew the gun from his waistband and handed it to her. "I'll catch up as soon as I can."

"See you there." She slid the gun behind her belt and took off at a sprint.

As she shrank in the distance, Ben focused on the ledge and imagined a battle strategy, a way to stop Alex once and for all. Maybe these extra few minutes by himself would give him a chance to put all the facts together and come up with the ultimate plan, a way to finally send that witch back to hell where she belonged.

Iona sat against the tower's wall, riding its terrifying sway. The mirror still showed an apparent doorway to heaven, maybe a last resort if the worst happened, one she might have to take. No way would she ever voluntarily go to a meeting with Satan, not even on the threat of death.

A bright light flashed near the center of the room. A radiant sphere hovered in midair over the hole in the floor. It expanded in all directions, brightening as it seemed to absorb the surrounding flames. Soon, the light filled the far half of the observatory. At the center of the light, a dark silhouette took shape—a slender woman carrying a long-barreled gun in one hand and some kind of bag in the other.

Iona gulped. Who could this be? Another ghost? Not wanting this intruder to see the mirror, Iona picked it up and slid it into her pocket, careful to avoid touching the reflection.

"No more chances, Iona," Alex called through the window. "You'd better go to ghost mode now. Otherwise, you're dead."

The launcher emitted another *phoom*. A grenade sailed through the window and rolled toward the center of the floor. The woman within the radiance stepped out and dropped her bag and rifle. She dove headfirst to the grenade, scooped it up while sliding through the debris, and threw it out the window in one sweeping motion. Outside, an explosion pierced the air, far enough away to do no damage to the tower.

The woman climbed to her feet, finally showing her face, though the radiance behind her blinded Iona's eyes for a moment.

She gasped. "Trudy? Is that you?"

"In the flesh." She dusted herself off and looked at Iona, blinking. "Girl, you're a mess!"

"Yeah. I know." Iona spoke rapid fire. "The woman next to me is Charlotte, my mother. She's a ghost. I know that's a shock, but disembodied souls on Viridi stay here. They don't go to heaven or hell." While the two women nodded at each other, Iona went on.

"I've got a lot of shards jabbing me and a big one in my side. I didn't want to take them out because—"

"You thought you'd bleed worse." Trudy picked up her bag and set it next to Iona. "Explain everything while I have a look at you."

The tower swayed, forcing Trudy to spread her feet to keep from falling. "What in the world?"

"Alex is out there shooting grenades at us." Iona touched the bow at her side. "I hit her eye with an arrow, but that only made her mad. She's out there with Leo. He's unconscious."

"Let's chase her with something a bit more persuasive than an arrow." Trudy retrieved her rifle and knelt at the window.

As the tower continued swaying, Iona struggled up to her knees and watched. Alex still stood on the ledge, her foot no longer on Leo as she set the launcher at her shoulder. "You won't be so lucky this time, Iona. Transform to ghost mode or die."

Trudy set her rifle barrel on the sill and took aim. "Tough shot with all the movement." She and Alex fired at the same time. Blood splashed from Alex's chest just below her shoulder, and she dropped to her knees. The grenade zipped in through a different window, rolled into the radiance, and dropped through the hole in the floor, out of sight.

"Where's the exit?" Trudy asked.

"This way." Charlie ran to the exit hole and pointed. "Down there."

"We have to bolt." Trudy threw the medical bag. It slid to the exit hole and dropped through. She then scooped Iona up, hoisted her over her shoulders, and grabbed her rifle, holding Iona in place with one hand. "Hang on tight. I'll need both hands."

Iona obeyed, clutching Trudy's shirt. "You can let go."

The grenade exploded. Fire spewed from the hole in the floor. The tower rocked and tilted farther to the side than ever. Trudy, her feet set wide apart, rode out the initial jolt, then trudged to the hole with Iona on board.

When she reached the hole, Charlie jumped into it, calling, "I'll watch to see if Alex shows up." She disappeared below.

Trudy dropped the rifle into the hole, grabbed the rope, and began climbing down, her feet pressed against the shaft's inner wall, a tight squeeze. As she descended, she spoke with grunts interrupting her words. "Is the pressure ... pushing any of the shards ... deeper?"

"No. They're mostly in my arms and legs. A couple in my back. And the big one in my side."

"Okay ... how'd you ... get so wet?"

"Long story. The short version is we had a flood I had to swim through."

Above, a crash sounded. Rocks and dirt cascaded through the shaft, pelting their bodies. Trudy slid down the rope the rest of the way, falling with the raining debris. When her feet touched down, Charlie shouted, "Over here!"

Trudy grabbed the medical bag and dove with Iona away from the shaft. They rolled along the tunnel floor and came to a stop next to Charlie's feet. Dust followed in a wave that blew across them before settling to the ground.

Iona rocked to a sitting position and looked back. A lantern flame flickered near the tunnel wall, illuminating a huge pile of rocks that blocked the access hole in the ceiling. "The tower must've fallen, but this tunnel isn't part of the tower."

"Good thing." Trudy walked to the pile and kicked a small stone. "But not all good. My rifle's under there somewhere."

"Near the center," Charlie said. "I watched the rocks bury it. It would probably take an hour to unearth, if it's possible at all."

Iona struggled to her feet and picked up the lantern. "Who put this here? Alex can see in the dark."

"Interesting." Charlie eyed the lantern. "Maybe her Owl abilities are more handicapped than she led us to believe."

Iona set the lantern down and looked at Trudy. "This tunnel leads to the ledge where Leo is. You can go see about him. I'll be all right."

"Alex isn't handicapped enough for my liking." Trudy set the medical bag next to Iona. "She's armed, and we're not."

"But she's wounded," Iona said. "Pretty badly. In the chest."

"I know." Trudy withdrew surgical gloves, an ointment tube, and several wrapped packages of gauze from the medical bag. "Bullet went high. Missed her heart. Not a kill shot. Blasted tower wouldn't keep still. I imagine she can still pull that launcher's trigger."

"Then we're stuck here? While Leo's out there? Maybe dying?"

"For the time being." Trudy slipped the gloves over her hands. "At least until we know what's what outside."

Charlie raised a hand. "I can go and see how badly she's hurt. If she's incapacitated, it'll be safe for you to check on Leo."

"Sounds good." Trudy lifted Iona's shirt at the side and grimaced. "I'll be busy here for a while. This wound will need minor surgery and stitches."

While Trudy pulled out a few smaller spears, Iona averted her eyes. "Charlie, you're a Reaper. What would you do if you got hurt as badly as Alex did?"

"Ghost mode. She's an Owl, so she can transform pretty fast. Or at least she used to be able to. Before she died, I mean. But if she does transform, it'll be to our advantage, at least for a while. Although she'll heal somewhat in ghost mode, she'll come out dizzy and disoriented." Charlie nodded toward Trudy. "I'm mentioning that for your sake, Trudy. Iona already knows about ghost mode."

"Weirder and weirder." Trudy tore the seal on one of the gauze packages. "Either way, let's hope Alex thinks we're either dead in the tower's rubble or armed inside this tunnel."

Charlie walked toward the pile of rocks blocking the tower entrance hole. "I'll see what I can do to make her think you're dead in the rubble." She passed through the pile and disappeared.

Trudy held a hypodermic needle close to Iona's side. "Is it strange that getting introduced to a ghost and watching her vanish barely registers at all on the 'that's creepy' meter? Oh, and get ready for a tiny sting. I'm going to deaden this a bit." She pushed the needle in.

Iona winced. "I know what you mean. When you showed up out of nowhere and when I turned into a ghost myself, it didn't shake me up much at all."

Trudy's eyes shot wide open. "Okay. You broke my meter just now. Hearing about Alex's ghost mode was creepy enough, but *you* turned into a ghost?"

"Um … yeah. Kind of. It's a long story."

"It's going to take a while to patch you up, so go ahead and spill it, then I'll tell you how I got here. That might break *your* meter."

With Austin at his side and Lem trailing, Jack crutched to the edge of the portal, no longer revolving as it hovered inches above the ground. Jack climbed to its floor. Since several of the partitions had passed by after Trudy vanished, it would take far too long to hobble to where she probably ended up, if it was possible at all in these cold, dark conditions.

Jack waved a hand toward the others. "Join me. Not so cold here."

Austin hopped up to the wheel, then reached down, grasped Lem's wrist, and hoisted him. Trembling as his eyes darted, Lem cradled the sphere with both hands as if it were the world itself. "You're right. It is warmer. Thank you for the suggestion."

"Austin." Jack pointed at the next partition. "What do you see in this one?"

Austin gazed at the wall. "I see Alexandria. I mean, Alex. I should get used to calling her that. Anyway, she's wounded badly. Bleeding from her chest, her abdomen, and one eye. She's holding some kind of weapon. I know my guns, but I'm not sure what it is. If I had to guess, I'd say it's a grenade launcher."

"Anything else?"

Austin squinted. "In the distance, a woman is running closer, with a man trailing pretty far behind. Alex doesn't seem to notice."

"Let's hope that's Kat and Ben. When they called, they mentioned that Ben's hurt. That's probably why he's lagging behind."

Austin turned toward Jack. "Should we try to go through the portal and help?"

Jack shook his head. "No. Let it play out. They might need us here, and it sounds like they might get the jump on Alex. We'll stand down unless you see our team getting pummeled."

"Stand here and do nothing while they're in danger? We have a duty to—"

"You're not doing nothing, and, like it or not, in my condition I can't do much more than set up camp here. Since the other fires are about to go out, I'll start a new one and see if I can rustle up some food. Maybe they stored something outside to keep it frozen. And Caligar's cave probably has some stores." He grinned. "And I'll find a bucket so the Owl-eyed sentry can stay on duty even if his bladder insists on relief."

Austin rolled his eyes. "You're so funny."

"I thought so."

Slowed by his crutches and aching knee, Jack managed the short hop back to ground level. Once there, he gathered a small stack of wood from the debris tossed about by the various explosions. Checking the prevailing wind for the best spot to keep smoke from blowing over Austin, Jack piled the wood several steps away from the portal wheel floor. He started a decent blaze, but it wouldn't last long. He needed lots more fuel.

He scanned the area. Debris from an earlier tower collapse lay scattered across the snowy field, but most of it was metallic. The bodies of the Refectors and several giants looked like snow-capped lumps disturbing the flat landscape. Even though they were now frozen, they would burn. It would be hard to roll them to the fire, but Austin could help if he could stand to leave his post for a minute or two.

Jack crutched to Camilla's body. She would be a good one to start with—much lighter than the giants. As he stood next to her, he imagined the laborious process of carrying her to the fire, even though it burned only about thirty feet away. With crutches bedeviling him every step, it might be impossible.

Cupping his hands around his mouth, he called, "Austin, I need your help getting fire fuel. You can go back to your post after each load."

"Coming."

While Austin trudged, Jack looked at the portal wheel and breathed a sigh. It would be great to charge into the fray with Trudy and the others, but he had to do his part here, sidelined and far from the action. But that was okay. The front-line soldiers would never survive without the behind-the-lines supporters. At least that's what he had to tell himself. He huffed a laugh and smiled as he mumbled, "You'll have to get it done without me, Ben. Good luck with that."

Chapter Thirteen

When Ben arrived at the top of the switchback trail, he skulked onto the ledge and stopped next to Kat behind a boulder. On a higher plateau, the tower was now no more than a heap of rubble that sloped down over the tunnel entrance, blocking more than half of the opening. A huge, shining window, maybe fifty feet high and wide, had taken the tower's place, maybe something to do with the portal wheel Harrid mentioned.

A few paces away from the base of the rubble, Alex pivoted in place as if searching for an enemy while plotting her next move. She held a grenade launcher loosely, its barrel pointed toward the ground. Blood streamed from her left eye, and a splotch of blood matted her white T-shirt against her chest, visible through her open leather jacket. Leo lay on his stomach a step or two from her, motionless, maybe not even breathing.

Kat whispered, "Alex has been standing there ever since I got here. Obviously waiting for something. No sign of Iona. I've been watching for an opening to check on Leo, but no luck so far."

Ben's throat tightened. "Maybe Alex saw Iona escape from the tower before it collapsed, and now she's looking for her."

"Could be. I can't think of any other reason she'd be rotating there like the ugliest music box ballerina in history."

Ben slid the gun from Kat's belt. "I'm taking her out."

Just as he flexed to run at Alex, Charlotte appeared out of nowhere, walking down the side of the tower's hill, seeming to float as she descended. When she arrived on the ledge, she stopped in front of Alex just out of reach. "I've come to check on Leo."

Alex glanced at him, pure callousness in her expression. "He's alive. Unconscious. With all the head trauma, I wouldn't be surprised if he's suffering a brain bleed."

"Then he needs medical care right away."

"Of course he does. And as long as I hold him, Iona is more likely to do what I ask."

Charlie looked Alex over. "You're badly wounded yourself."

Alex sneered. "Don't you think I know that?"

"You're a Reaper. You know what to do in situations like this."

"Better than you do." Alex set the grenade launcher down. "I've been trying to transform my weapon with me, but it's too big. I don't want to lose it while in ghost mode."

"Good point, but no one will take it. I certainly can't."

Alex stared intently at Charlotte, as if her vision could penetrate her rival's brain. "The fact that you're out here without a hint of grief means that Iona did not die in the collapse. The only safe refuge is in the tunnel." She drew a knife from a belt sheath and stalked toward the tunnel entrance, her back toward Ben and company.

Ben whispered to Kat, "We have to move. Check on Leo." He sneaked out from behind the boulder and jogged toward Alex, keeping his footfalls quiet, though his limp made the effort a chore. He passed Charlotte and Leo without a word, as well as the grenade launcher, not wanting to risk making a sound by picking it up.

When he drew close enough to Alex, he leaped at her, his hands aiming for her neck, but instead of grabbing hold, he passed right through. He dropped hard on his wounded foot. Pain shot up his leg, and his knee buckled, sending him tumbling to the ground.

He looked up. Alex stood over him, one foot on each side and a knife in hand. Her eye no longer bled, and her chest wound had vanished. "So we meet again, Benjamin Garrison. If I remember correctly, I guaranteed that we would do battle before this was all over. But, alas, it is not to be at this time. I have a feisty redhead to persuade at the edge of a knife."

While Ben struggled to his feet, Alex stalked past him and closed in on the tunnel entrance. Charlotte ran ahead and blocked Alex's way. With her arms crossed and her cloak expanded, Charlotte looked like an immovable sentry. "You'll have to get past me to get to Iona, and you know that your injured body is healing while you're in ghost mode, draining your energy. You don't stand a chance against a mama bear like me."

Alex halted and copied Charlotte's pose. "Well, Mama Bear, I can deduce quite a bit from your stance. Iona is definitely in there, and she's hurt. Otherwise she would be out here checking on Leo. While it's true that a battle between the two of us would be skewed toward your side, I do have other ways to persuade Iona's compliance."

Ben pivoted toward Leo, obviously the leverage Alex was talking about. Kat knelt next to him, her fingers at his neck as she looked at Ben. "I've been monitoring his pulse. His heartbeat's erratic."

Alex walked toward Leo with a swagger in her gait. "Of course his heart is erratic. His soul's attachment likely hangs by a thread. I reattached it myself, and it took all of my skill to make it work even at this capacity, a poor connection at best. Since that time, I had to defend myself against his attacks. My defensive kicks to his head surely worsened his condition. In short, he is likely dying as we speak."

Iona's voice pierced the air. "Leo's dying?"

Ben pivoted toward her. Trudy stood at the tunnel entrance with Iona at her side, the hood of her cloak pulled back. Several gauze patches adhered to her face, neck, and hands, some tinged with blood.

"Trudy?" Ben squinted. "How did you get here? And where's Jack?"

Trudy sighed. "I just finished telling Iona, but here's the short version. That door up where the tower used to be is a portal, and …" She shook her head. "Never mind. Tell you later."

Iona limped toward Leo, Trudy trailing. "He's losing his soul?"

"Yes." Alex knelt across from Kat and set a hand over Leo's forehead. "But I can help him. While I am in ghost mode, I can enter his body fully and strengthen his soul's attachment. Earlier, I entered with only a hand."

Iona looked at Charlotte. "Can't *you* do that?"

A doubtful expression sagged her features. "I can have a look and verify if Alex is right. If so, I can try to help him, but I don't have Alex's skill or experience. If I don't do it exactly right, I could kill him."

"Verify," Ben said as he hobbled toward Leo. "Then report to us."

Charlotte joined Ben and the others and knocked Alex's hand away from Leo's forehead. "Back off, witch."

"Of course," Alex said in a sarcastic tone as she rose and stepped away. "I wouldn't want to interfere with your examination, especially considering my inadequate skills."

"You're not fooling anyone." Charlotte laid a hand over Leo's eyes and pushed her fingers through them. Her arm followed, then the rest of her body as if his eyes were sucking her in.

Everyone stared in silence. Leo flinched once, his eyelids tightening. He breathed in halting gasps, then his face relaxed as his respiration calmed.

"A neural jolt," Alex said. "You have to soothe the raw nerves to give the soul a chance to make a stronger connection."

"How do you do that?" Iona asked.

Alex crossed her arms. "I will keep that to myself. Leo is the only leverage I have left to get you to comply." Her expression turned sincere. "But hear this, Iona. The meeting with Lucifer is not as foreboding as you imagine. He told me that any request he makes of you is exactly that, a request. You will be free to turn him down and leave after you hear him out."

"How can we trust your word?" Ben asked. "Or Lucifer's?"

"The portal she will go through to reach Lucifer will remain active during the meeting. She should continue watching it. If it warps at all, that is a sign that it will soon close. She can leap through it and escape before it does."

Iona leaned close to Ben and whispered, "She's telling the truth. The mirror says so."

He looked at her. She kept a hand in her cloak's pocket, probably where the mirror lay. Its lie-detecting ability was coming in handy.

Just as Ben opened his mouth to respond to Alex, Charlotte's head flowed out of Leo's eyes, followed by the rest of her body. Soon, she stood upright and looked at Ben. "Alex is right. His soul is holding to his brain by two threads. I barely touched one of the connection points, and it caused him a lot of pain." A tear trickled down her cheek and vanished as it dripped from her chin. "Ben, Leo's dying. Probably only minutes left. Not hours. He won't last long."

"Ben ..." Iona slid her hand into his, pulled him close, and whispered, "I'll go with Alex. I have to. For Leo's sake."

Ben glanced at Alex. She appeared to be trying to listen. He looked at Charlotte and flicked his head toward the trail. Charlotte grasped Alex's arm and guided her behind the boulder, Alex muttering something too quiet to hear as she left.

When Ben turned his attention back to Iona, he kept his voice low. "Knowing you can leave isn't good enough. Once you're with Satan, you never know what tricks he'll pull to get you to do what he wants. And I met with Harrid's ghost. He said Satan wants you to destroy hell."

Iona blinked hard. "Destroy hell? How is that possible?"

"Something about a special bomb. But that doesn't matter. It would be a bad move to agree to meet with Satan."

Iona's tone turned plaintive. "But Leo will die. I can't let that happen."

"Leo would choose to die to keep you from doing Satan's bidding."

"But I won't. I mean, I'll listen to him, but I won't actually do anything wrong. I can always say no and leave, like Alex said."

"Satan is an archangel. Far more powerful than Alex. And craftier. He'll confuse right and wrong."

Iona raised her voice. "I'm not stupid. I know right from wrong. Not even Satan can change that."

Ben lifted a hand in a calming manner and kept his own voice even keeled. "I know you're not stupid. But it's not how smart you are that matters. It's how experienced you are with the tangled webs that Satan spins. Since you're just a—"

"Don't say it." Iona's face hardened, turning red as she shouted, "I know I'm *just* a girl. But so was Summer. And she had a demonic alien in her brain." Her voice dropped to a simmering growl. "But that *girl* defeated the alien and saved the entire planet."

Ben lowered his hand. What a huge mistake. His old bigotry against female warriors had sneaked back in to bite him in the backside. He had to get off his high horse and appeal to Iona on a different level. He took a step closer to her and bowed his head. "You got me. I shouldn't have said that. Or even thought it. And I was dead wrong. You and Kat and Trudy are three of the bravest and most capable soldiers I have ever seen, male or female."

Iona brushed a tear from her eye and spoke barely above a whisper. "Thank you."

"But I hope you understand that I wouldn't want anyone, man or woman, to face Satan. I would never go against him myself, unless I had to."

Her lamenting tone returned. "But don't you see? I *do* have to, and I'm the only one who can."

As Ben gazed into her glimmering eyes, a recent conversation with Caligar returned to mind. The gentle giant lamented over the death of Lacinda, his only daughter. *My pride in my daughter's warrior abilities blinded me to the fact that she was still vulnerable to attacks she had never faced. I wish with all my heart that I could go back and alter my approach. Instead of being a proud teacher of warrior tactics and sending her on journeys without limits, I needed to decide her boundaries for her, make the difficult decisions to limit her forays, even if it meant facing her wrath. In short, I needed to be her father, and I rue my foolish pride with every fiber of my being.*

Ben's own tears welled. Now Iona begged to go beyond all reasonable boundaries, a mistake that got Lacinda killed. How could he allow her to walk directly into grave danger with a set of Reaper skills he didn't even understand? On the other hand, how could he let her father die?

"Ben?" Iona's whisper interrupted his thoughts. "Leo's time is running out."

"Yes, yes, you're right." He took a deep breath. "Listen, Iona, I know I'm not your father, but I think you should—"

"You're right." Iona squared her shoulders and spoke with a confident tone. "You're not my father. Leo is." Then a hint of shakiness rattled in her voice. "But you are still my commander, and … and I'll do what you say."

Warmth coursed through his body. Even though her heart said to do anything to save her father, she was willing to submit as a good soldier. Still, if he forbade her from going to the meeting and Leo died as a result, she could be shattered for life, and she, rightly or wrongly, might blame Benjamin Garrison because he wouldn't give her a chance to save her father's life, a tantalizing carrot that Satan and Alex dangled in front of her.

Ben closed the gap between them and caressed her freckled cheek, brushing a tear away with his thumb. "Do you think you're ready?"

A new tear trickled down her other cheek and into one of the gauze patches near her chin. "I … I think so. I mean, I don't know." She strengthened her voice. "But does that matter?"

Ben glanced at Leo's face—pale and expressionless. Whatever he was thinking, there was no way he would ever let Iona go on this dangerous journey, at least not without him, and he definitely would object to her going to save his life. But maybe there was another way. "You're right. You have to go. But we'll make sure Leo's not about to die before you do. I don't want you to bear that burden."

Ben turned toward the boulder. Now it was time to get Alex to act, to give up her leverage willingly, though that might be impossible. He waved for Charlotte to bring Alex back. When they arrived, he stared directly into Alex's eyes. "I want to make a deal with you."

Her brow lifted. "Oh? Do tell."

Ben gestured toward Leo. "Repair his soul connections the best you can, and I'll let Iona meet with Satan."

"Well, this is an interesting turn of events." Alex let out a series of tsks. "But I would lose all of my leverage, Benjamin. What kind of fool do you take me for?"

"I give you my word. Isn't that good enough for you?"

She met his stare with her piercing eyes. As her pupils pulsed, she continued staring for a long moment, then backed away a step. "Your word is good enough."

"Then Iona will go to meet Satan. But that's as far as she will comply. If she doesn't like what he has to say, she won't go any further. As you mentioned, she can leave through the portal whenever she chooses."

"Agreed. I will help Leo if I can. A delicate operation like this is never without danger. Every soul attachment is different. If I stabilize him and keep him from dying, will that be sufficient? Charlotte can check my work."

Ben nodded. "That will be sufficient."

"Then we have a deal."

While Alex strode toward Leo, Ben looked at Iona. A hand in her pocket, she gave him a nod. Alex was telling the truth.

Alex knelt close to Leo's head. Copying Charlotte's moves, she set a hand over his eyes and flowed into his body.

Charlotte knelt on Leo's other side and set an ear close to his face. "Alex is talking to Leo, mimicking Iona's voice. Trying to keep him calm, I assume." She glanced up at Ben and company. "Actually, she's quite convincing."

"That sounds promising," Ben said. "Can you tell what else she's doing?"

Charlotte shook her head. "I could if I went in there and joined them, but I'm afraid Alex wouldn't like that. I'll just keep listening." She leaned closer. "She told Leo in Iona's voice that she loves him, and if he loves her, he'll work with Alex to strengthen his soul's connection to his brain."

Leo's lips moved, maybe trying to answer Alex, but no sound came out. Seconds later, he grimaced tightly, then groaned through clenched teeth.

Ben grimaced with him. The pain had to be immense, but it seemed that Alex was keeping her word. She had no reason to pretend to be Iona unless she truly intended to try to heal him.

After a few tense moments, Alex's body flowed out of Leo and stood upright, her arms crossed as she looked down at him. "I reestablished the two remaining connections, but they're still relatively weak. He can't take much more trauma. The other connections were too callused to work with."

"Do you think he'll wake up soon?" Iona asked.

"He's already awake. It will take him a few moments to regain his motor control. When he does, you will see that I did exactly what I said I would do. When he heals further, I can try again, which I will be glad to do if you successfully complete your quest, which means doing what Lucifer requests of you, not merely meeting with him."

As if on command, Leo's eyes fluttered open, then darted around as he took in his surroundings. When he spotted Iona, he smiled and spoke with a rumbling rasp. "You look as bad as I feel."

"Leo!" Iona dropped to her knees next to him and wrapped her arms around his neck. "You made it! Thank God, you made it!"

Warmth again surged through Ben's body. Getting Leo back felt wonderful. But that meant Iona would have to meet Satan. No way out of it. And Alex still kept a measure of leverage with her pledge to heal him further if Iona destroyed hell. Maybe the partial healing was merely a ploy. She patched Leo up enough to prove her ability but left something undone on purpose.

Staying on her knees, Iona drew back and grasped Leo's wrist. "Want to try to get up?"

"Not yet. My head's swimming like a bowl full of jellyfish."

"We should go," Alex said. "I don't want to keep—"

"Then go." Iona rose and limped back to Ben as she glared at Alex. "Don't let us stop you."

Ben read Iona's expression. Apparently she didn't want Leo to hear that she was planning to leave with Alex. Good idea. But he would figure it out eventually.

Alex narrowed her eyes, first looking at Iona, then at Ben. After a few seconds, she nodded. "Very well. But don't believe any foolish notion that any secretive scheming will avail you. You have no idea what you're about to face." She walked toward the tunnel. Pausing at Ben's side, she whispered loudly enough for Iona to hear, "Both of you meet me at the portal in ten minutes. Iona, practice going into ghost mode. You'll heal faster, and you need to learn to transform quickly if you're going to complete the quest."

When Alex had climbed the slope of rubble far enough to be out of earshot, Ben whispered to Iona, "Ghost mode?"

"I'll explain later." She smiled at Leo and spoke in a cheery tone. "I have to leave for a while, but you're in good hands with Trudy."

"Whatever you say, my perky pumpkin." Leo reached a hand up. "I think I'll try to stand now."

Trudy grabbed his wrist and pulled while Kat hoisted him from the other side. When he stood upright, he wavered for a moment before settling, then blinked several times. "Does someone want to tell me what's going on?"

"I will." Trudy looped an arm around Leo's. "There's a good sitting rock just inside the tunnel. You can rest there while I look you over."

As the two walked slowly, Caligar appeared from around the boulder, a backpack in hand. After glancing at Alex, who now stood in front of the portal, he passed the pack to Ben and spoke at a low volume. "I have returned with the items you requested, as well as four mackataws. They are a vegetable Winella grows. They will enhance your endurance."

Ben looked inside. Next to a sheathed knife, two short pipes rested at the bottom, unlike any grenades he had ever seen, but it probably wouldn't be hard to figure out how to use them. The four mackataws, the size and shape of apples, though gray instead of red, lay with the grenades. He took the sheath, attached it to his belt, and put the backpack on, a perfect fit. "We need a family brainstorming session."

"I'll get Trudy." Kat jogged toward the tunnel.

When she and Trudy returned, they huddled next to Ben, as did Iona and Caligar. "Okay," he said in a low whisper, "I've been working on a plan ever since we got here. The first step will require stealth skills, Iona's specialty, but since she's going to meet with Satan, I'll need someone else who's good at deception."

Caligar shook his head. "I would be the worst choice. My deception skills are practically nonexistent."

"Which is why you're such a critical part of the plan. Alex won't respect you. Her arrogance will make her think she's superior to you in every way, especially mentally. But more on that later. For now, I need you to go with Kat to fetch the cruiser."

"Wait." Iona fished the mooring cap out of her pocket and gave it to Kat. "You'll need this."

When Kat took it, Iona withdrew her mirror from her cloak and showed it to Ben. "It works. I mean, the reflection changed when Charlie and I sang *The Eternity Psalm*, but it's back to normal now. And I don't see how we could ever fool Alex into touching it if we change it again."

"Perfect." Ben took the mirror and looked it over. "Exactly what I was hoping for. But let's get back to the stealth job. I need someone to fool Alex into going through the portal back to Alaska. Since she wants to destroy Earth, let's put her in danger. Get her to make a mistake. And she'll do whatever it takes to halt Earth's destruction while she's there."

Trudy rolled her eyes. "You want me to do it, right?"

"I think you're the only candidate left."

"Fine. I'm a brute-force gal, but I'll give it a shot."

Charlotte raised a hand. "If I may ask a favor."

Ben nodded. "Go ahead."

She ran a ghostly hand along Iona's hood. "If you would put the cloak on Leo, I could go into the fibers and speak to him. Comfort him. I could also more easily check on Alex's brain surgery."

"Sure." Iona shook the cloak down her arms. "Should I put it on him now?"

Ben waved a hand. "Yes. Both of you go ahead. And Trudy, too. Check on our huntsman's health."

"All right." Trudy pointed straight at Ben's nose. "But don't leave until I have a look at your foot. I see a bloody sock."

"Will do."

The trio walked toward the tunnel, Iona's limp no longer evident. Charlotte stopped and raised a finger as she spoke quietly to the other two. Then she faded and turned invisible.

Ben eyed them as they continued toward the tunnel. If Charlotte had decided to do something in addition to checking on Leo, she had informed Trudy and Iona about it. Good enough. He turned toward Caligar. "You visited your family. Can you tell me if you checked on the device that records audio from the tower?"

"I did. Winella was quite animated about the recording. She was even singing a song that Iona and Charlotte sang while they were in the tower."

"Excellent. Everything's falling into place." He draped an arm around both Kat and Caligar and drew them closer. "Here's the rest of the plan."

Chapter Fourteen

The moment Ben finished explaining the plan, he drew away from the huddle, and Caligar took off down the switchback trail. Kat hooked her arm around Ben's and walked with him toward the tunnel, where Iona and Trudy stood waiting, a medical bag at Trudy's feet and Iona no longer wearing Charlotte's cloak. Alex continued her perch at the top of the rubble slope, her arms crossed as she stared at them like an expectant vulture.

When Ben and Kat arrived at the tunnel, Ben sat on the ground and shrugged the backpack down. Kat and Iona joined him, one on each side. Trudy knelt, took Ben's shoe and sock off, and began cleaning the wound.

"Kat," Ben whispered, "You decide how much to tell Leo. I'll help Iona get up to the portal."

"Think Alex will let you escort Iona?" Kat asked.

Ben winced as Trudy injected his heel with something, maybe lidocaine. "That's the plan. We need Alex to stay behind for Trudy to do her part. I think she'll comply, and I'll force the issue if she doesn't. I don't want Satan and Alex ganging up on you during the meeting."

"I'm sure you'll figure it out." Kat kissed him on the lips, then kissed Trudy and Iona on the cheek. "I love you all." She hurried into the tunnel and called back, "I'll get the cruiser after I finish talking to Leo."

Trudy applied a bandage to Ben's heel. "Three stitches. It should hold pretty well. Just don't do anything dangerous."

"Yeah, well, you know me."

"I do know you," Iona said. "You'll probably do something dangerous in the next five minutes."

"More like one and a half." Trudy put his sock and shoe back on and tied the laces. "Okay, you two. Better get going before Alex loses her cool."

With Trudy's help, Ben climbed to his feet. After retrieving the backpack, he and Iona climbed the sloping rubble toward the portal. The bandage on his heel seemed to be holding up well, and the anesthetic had deadened the pain. "I saw Charlotte disappear. Did she go somewhere besides the cloak?"

Iona pressed a hand against her injured side. "She saw the Harrids spying on us. She said she'd chase them off and come right back to the cloak."

"Okay. Good. And now another question. What did Alex mean by ghost mode?"

"I'll try to show you." Iona halted several steps from the top, pulled away from him, and closed her eyes tightly. After a few seconds, she began fading—first semitransparent, then fully transparent with only a dim outline of light. Finally, she turned completely invisible.

Prickles ran up and down Ben's back. "So, I guess you're a ghost now. I can't see you."

"Iona," Alex called from the portal, "focus on your skin. It should be tingling. Concentrate on making the tingle stop. That should bring you back to visibility while in ghost mode. Ben can't see or hear you until you do."

Ben trained his eyes on Iona's previous location. Her outline reappeared and slowly filled in. Soon, she stood as before except without the gauze patches or the wrapped ankle. "I assume you're healed in ghost mode."

"Yep." She bounced on her toes. "Good as new."

"Then you should walk the rest of the way in ghost mode and change back when we get to the portal."

"Charlie said the longer I'm in ghost mode, the dizzier I'll be when I change back, so I'd better do it as soon as we get there."

They climbed together, much faster now. When they reached the shimmering window, Alex nodded toward it. "This should take you two back to Alaska."

Ben pointed at himself and Iona. "Us two? You mean—"

Alex set a hand on her hip. "Benjamin, did you honestly think that I don't know you would never let Iona go without you?"

"Well, I guess I didn't consider—"

"Then stop guessing and realize that I am always a step ahead of you. Whatever you're planning, I have already anticipated it and devised a counter plan. Get used to the idea."

The words *we'll see about that* begged to erupt, but Ben kept the retort in check. No use giving her any hint that she needed to watch out for his *own* counter plan.

"Once you arrive at the tower," Alex continued, "ask Lemuel to start the portal revolving. When you see a man sitting at a table in one of the portal partitions, stop the process. You will enter the portal at that time. The man will tell you what you need to know."

"Okay." Iona stretched out the word. "Sounds pretty crazy, like a fairy tale."

"Everything will become clear when you arrive in Alaska. If you have questions, Lemuel will explain."

"This Lemuel person," Ben said. "Is he one of your hundred influencers?"

"He is, indeed. A musician and an actor. Quite proficient at both, which is why I chose him."

"How do you know he's there?"

"I know because the portal wheel would not be operational without him. Trudy's presence proves that it works."

"Okay. That makes sense."

"Yeah," Iona said. "That part does, but why were you trying to kill me if you wanted me to go on this mission?"

Alex laughed. "Oh, I was never going to kill you. That was a ruse to gain your cooperation."

Iona crossed her arms tightly. "Well, you sure fooled me. I could've died several times."

Alex raised a pair of fingers. "I had two reasons. The first was to encourage you to learn how to change to ghost mode. The second was to bring the portal here instead of to the mesa where we originally planned to put it. You see, placing you in danger caused you to pray for help. I could hear you and Charlotte singing a prayer from where I stood."

Her tone turned sarcastic as she continued. "God, in his infinite wisdom, moved the portal here so Trudy could rescue you, a relocation that Dr. Harrid told me was quite possible." She rolled her eyes. "God and his followers are so predictable, just as Lucifer has said to me many times."

"Cut the theater," Iona said. "You're making me gag."

"Well, we wouldn't want that." Alex focused on Iona, her tone turning serious. "You'll need to transform back to your physical body. If you go to Earth as a ghost, you will immediately be taken into the afterlife."

"I guessed that." Iona closed her eyes again. After several seconds, the gauze patches took shape on her face, as if growing on her skin. When she opened her eyes, she winced. "Looks like I'm back. And so is the pain."

Alex crossed her arms. "Have you healed at all?"

Iona pressed a hand against her side. "Maybe a little, but I'm pretty dizzy."

"Disorientation is normal. From what I understand about your quest, you will have other safe opportunities to transform to ghost mode to aid your healing. And you'll need to make the change more quickly. Five seconds, not twenty seconds. Practicing will be helpful."

"Okay. I guess I'll find out what all that means soon enough." Iona took Ben's hand. "Ready?"

"Ready." They marched toward the portal hand in hand.

The moment they passed into the radiance, snowflakes pelted their faces, and swirling air caressed their cheeks, not as cold as expected.

Now on a radiant floor with a tall, glowing partition at her side, Iona picked up a parka. "Trudy must've dropped this. She wasn't wearing a coat when she showed up in the tower."

"Because it's warmer here than out in the snow," Ben said.

"Still pretty cold compared to Viridi." Iona put the parka on. "And I'm still kind of wet. But at least the chill will help snap me out of the dizzy spell. I already feel better."

Ben scanned the glowing contraption around them. "What is this thing we're on?"

"A portal wheel. Trudy told me about it. Don't know much else, though. Only that she had to walk for about ten minutes to get here. We might have to hoof it back that far to the tower. Austin and Jack should be there."

"Austin? I thought he was supposed to take Charlotte's body to—"

"I already did that." Austin leaped onto the portal-wheel floor. "I'll tell you the story later, but first, have you seen Trudy? Jack sent me here to hunt for her."

Ben nodded. "She's safe on Viridi."

"Then let's go." Austin strode to the partition and passed right through it, raising a splash of light.

Ben blinked at the radiant sparkles. "Okay. I didn't expect that."

"Time's a wastin'." Iona took Ben's hand and pulled him with her through the partition. Their own splash tingled painlessly. When they emerged on the other side, they walked on, Austin several paces ahead. "We'd better get it in gear. He doesn't know you have an injured foot. Besides, he's younger than you."

"Oh?" Ben broke into a quicker stride, keeping abreast with her. "Are you saying that I'm old?"

"Yep. But I'll keep your secret. I mean, when you came along, the wheel was already invented, right? So you're not all that old."

Ben nudged her arm with an elbow. "You're as funny as a harpoon to the side. And you know exactly how that feels, right?"

"Oooh, now that's fighting dirty, Methuselah. I take it all back. You're older than the hills. Than the dirt *in* the hills. You lived before color came around, and I'm not talking about photos. I mean color itself."

For the next few minutes, the two exchanged verbal jabs and gentle shoves, all the while keeping Austin in sight as he hustled through more partitions. Soon, Jack came into view, propped by crutches and standing in front of another partition. An older man, maybe Lemuel, stood next to him.

When Ben and Iona arrived, Jack hugged them in turn. "I built a fire, but we've been warm enough standing here. I guess you might call it a partition pocket in this glorified revolving door."

"Good thing," Ben said. "Winter's got an icy handshake." He scanned the area. The damaged tower loomed about twenty paces away, some of its lights still blinking. Heavy snow swirled through the pocket, floating on constant eddies that blew in and out of their partial shelter. "I'm supposed to ask someone named Lemuel to restart the rotation, and stop it when we see a man sitting at a table. Don't ask why. The story's way too long."

"Sure thing, Bro. We've seen the table, so we know it's possible."

"I am Lemuel," the older man said as he withdrew a fist-sized sphere from his pocket. Covered with buttons, it looked like a child's toy ball. "We'll have to step off this portal floor before I restart it." He hopped down and looked back. "Let's not tarry long in this weather."

Austin, now clad in a Reaper cloak, gave Ben his parka. "Go ahead. I'll get it back from you when it's time for you to go."

"Yeah," Iona said, grinning. "Let the old man warm his fossilized bones."

Austin drew his head back. "Did she just say—"

"Never mind her." Ben took the parka and put it on over his backpack. "She's about as funny as a cactus."

"Whatever you say." Austin turned and helped Jack climb down. Wind gusts pummeled them, making everyone lean into the storm to keep from being blown over.

While Lemuel took off his gloves, Ben sidled close to Jack. "Has Lemuel given you any trouble? Alex said he's one of her influencers."

Jack's brow shot upward. "He is?"

"Yeah. She said he's a musician and an actor."

"I can believe the acting part. He had me fooled." Jack tightened his lips and nodded. "It makes sense, though. I saw more chip signals on the reader before it got fried."

"Okay. I'm not sure what you mean about chip signals, but we have to watch him. He's not on our side."

"Got it."

Lemuel pressed a button on the sphere with a thumb. A tone emanated from the tower, muffled by the falling snow. The partition began moving. As Jack had said, the portal wheel resembled an enormous revolving door, though completely silent as it swept along its arcing path.

Soon, another partition came into view, purplish and partially veiled by the cascading flakes. Austin stepped closer and leaned toward it, his legs nearly touching the spinning floor as he spoke with a loud voice to overcome the wind. "I see hell, so this isn't the one."

"I don't see anything," Ben said. "Just shadows."

Jack nodded. "Austin's Owl eyes. They're coming in handy."

"Alex didn't mention needing Owl eyes. She seemed to think we would be able to see through the partitions."

"Maybe someone told her that *she'd* be able to see through the partitions, which means she doesn't know everything about them."

"Good point."

When the partition zipped past, Austin drew back to keep it from hitting his head, then leaned forward again. Within several seconds, another partition approached, this one brighter than the one before—orange and yellow instead of purple. "This is it," Austin called. "Lemuel, stop the wheel."

Lemuel pressed five buttons in quick succession. When the tones sounded, the tower fell silent, and the revolving door slowed to a stop.

Austin boosted Ben and Iona to the floor. As they walked to the partition, Ben shed his parka and tossed it to Austin. Iona did the same.

They stood together in front of the partition and gazed at the glowing scene, too fuzzy to make anything out. "So what do we do now?" Ben asked Iona.

"Trudy told me a person has to be standing near a partition when the revolving door stops, then it kind of sucks you in. But we have to walk in front of the partition while it's moving."

"So Lemuel has to restart it and stop it again." Ben looked at him. "Do you mind?"

"Not at all. The last time, I waited ten minutes before stopping the wheel, but now that we know how it works, there is no need to wait so long." Lemuel pushed a button on the sphere.

As before, the tower cast a musical tone through the falling snow, and the carousel swept into motion. Ben and Iona leaped into a brisk walk to stay in front of it. Ben looked back and gave Jack a brief wave, but snow and darkness covered any return wave he might have offered. Soon, only the tower's blinking lights lay in view as it receded into the night.

About two minutes later, the stopping tones emanated from the tower. The portal wheel slowed, and Ben and Iona slowed their pace to match. When the partition halted, its glow expanded toward them. As the radiance washed over them, the table and the man appeared where the Alaskan landscape used to be, the white snow replaced by vague grayness with no walls or ceiling.

Ben and Iona walked into the scene and stopped next to the table. It appeared to be a sawed-off stump with a tree growing out of the center and bearing sycamore-shaped leaves, though twice the usual size. Shimmering with gemlike radiance, the leaves dazzled the senses. More than beautiful, they looked like sparkling silk, silver interwoven with pure light energy.

They hung throughout the branches, some extending out of sight above and others dangling within reach of the seated man. His head low, he sat in one of three chairs that stood at equidistant intervals. High backed with ornate carvings in the wood, they appeared to be antiques from days long ago. The man wore denim overalls, a forest-green flannel shirt, and a baseball-style cap with gray hair protruding at the sides and back.

Staying quiet, Ben ran a hand along the table. Thin, shallow channels etched the smooth surface, drawing a pattern that looked like a map of veins in a human body, or maybe branches in a tree that forked into dozens of smaller branches and twigs. The systems of branches appeared to emanate from three fist-sized holes in the table, one in front of each of the three chairs.

Three tall black candles stood within an inch of the trunk, their brass holders in line with the holes in the table's surface. The flames burned without a hint of air to disturb them.

Ben shrugged the backpack off, set it on the floor, and looked back the way they had come. A bright window hovered a few steps away, its bottom edge a few inches off the floor, easily accessible. The portal wheel lay within it. A quick hop would take them out of this place.

He turned back toward the seated man and breathed an intentional, "Ahem."

The man jerked his head up and refastened a clasp on his overalls. Thin-faced with white whisker stubble dressing his cheeks and chin, he looked like a sixty-something farmer who recently came in from plowing a field. "Oh," he said, a tremor in his voice. "You're here."

Iona gasped. "Papa?"

Chapter Fifteen

"Yes." The man smiled as he looked at Ben. "I am Horace Macklin, Iona's adoptive father. And you are?"

"Ben Garrison. Iona's ... friend." After the two shook hands, Ben drew his hand back. His skin tingled slightly, maybe a sign that Horace was not as physical as he appeared to be. Ben sat in the remaining empty chair. If this man really was Iona's adoptive father, he needed to let them talk without interference. But if Horace was Satan in disguise, he had to be watched carefully. His allure might knock her off balance.

Horace set his gaze on Iona. "I'm glad you recognize me. It's been a few years since I died."

"It has." Iona sat in one of the chairs, her eyes narrowed, obviously skeptical. "Why are you here? I thought you'd be in heaven."

"I hoped I might go there, but I didn't. I went to hell."

Iona set her hands in her lap and straightened her body, apparently trying to keep her composure. "Okay. I've been there, and I got out, though it was really difficult. How did you manage to leave?"

He smiled in a sad sort of way. "You remember that story Mama read sometimes about Satan talking to God about Job?"

Iona nodded. "Sounds familiar."

"Well, something like that happened again recently, and Satan asked God to remove me from hell for a short time so I could talk to you here."

Iona shook her head hard. "This doesn't make sense. I was supposed to come here to talk to Satan, and you're supposed to be in heaven. I know you weren't religious, but you were a good man. Honest. Trustworthy. Didn't any of that matter?"

Horace sighed. "Apparently not."

"What about Mama? Is she in hell?"

He brushed a tear from his cheek. "No. At least I didn't see her there. I can't be sure. Hell is a big place."

"What about Little Brother?"

"I didn't see any souls of babies in hell. Not even children. Only adults. Well, maybe a teenager or two. But who knows how a baby's soul appears in the afterlife anyway? They might not look young at all."

Iona sniffed, her eyes glimmering. "Okay. I get that. But did Satan tell you why he wanted you to come here to meet me?"

"Yes." Horace slid an open hand across the table. Hesitating at first, she laid her hand in his, and they closed the clasp gently. "To convince you to destroy hell. If you do, the souls of the damned will be released to the sky. They won't be welcomed into heaven, of course, and they can't be on Earth because of God's edicts, but they will be free to explore the universe."

Iona narrowed her eyes at him. "How can I be sure you are who you say you are?"

"I don't know." Horace drew his hands back. "What could I possibly do to prove myself?"

"You would have to tell me something that Satan couldn't possibly know." Iona tapped a finger on her chin and looked upward. "Let me think."

Ben glanced between the two. What could she come up with? While Satan was neither omniscient nor omnipresent, who could know what one of his minions might learn and secretly report to him?

"Maybe this will work." Iona focused on him with a stern stare. "You know how we sometimes squeezed each other's hand to send a message?"

"Of course. Three squeezes means, 'I love you.' Four in return means, 'I love you, too.'" Horace smiled. "And five means, 'I want to go home.'"

"Right. And Satan could know that. But there was one time we were holding hands, and I squeezed yours three times, but ..." Her face reddened. She swallowed hard before continuing. "And you didn't respond with four." She inhaled deeply and brushed a new tear from her eye. "Do you remember?"

Horace's mouth dropped open. Ben felt his own jaw loosen as well. Iona's question was brilliant. Satan couldn't know the answer. And if the man made up an answer, Iona would know he was lying.

"Iona ..." Horace cleared his throat. "I remember it like it was yesterday. We were at a funeral for Timothy Floyd, the young teenager who died in a car crash. Same age as you at the time. One of your best friends." He smiled, the glimmer in his eyes matching hers. "Remember how you and he and his twin sister, Lynette, used to throw acorns at me from your treehouse?"

Iona let out laugh that sounded like a stifled sob. "I remember. You always pretended to get mad and throw them back at us. We called it acorn artillery."

"That's right. I had forgotten about that cute name you gave them. Anyway, at the funeral, the preacher was talking about how Timmy and Lynette used to come to the church altar every morning and pray together. Although it was Lynette's idea, Timmy would go along just to be with her. After all, they were inseparable. And the preacher said now they're together for all time, because Lynette had died only a few days earlier during one of the plagues."

Iona nodded, now fully crying. "I remember."

"And I'll never forget the preacher's closing words. Rather poetic, I thought at the time. 'Hand in hand, they walked this soil, now hand in hand they'll never toil. Forever clasped, no longer masked. They've broken free from mortal coil.'" Horace exhaled in a mournful way. "That's when you squeezed my hand three times and I never responded."

Ben's throat tightened. That story was far too detailed to be a lie. Was he really her adoptive father after all?

Iona bit her lip, her face now redder than ever. Tears dripped from her chin to the table. She took a halting breath, not bothering to brush her tears away. "Why didn't you respond?"

"I ..." Horace sniffed, his voice breaking. "I am too ashamed to explain." He covered his face with his hands and sobbed. "Iona, I know I'm not perfect. Far from it. But it's so awful in hell. No one deserves to be there. No one."

"Papa ..." Iona rose, scurried about the table, and hugged him from the side. She pressed her cheek against his, and they wept together, both heads bobbing in rhythmic spasms.

Ben flexed his legs to rise and join them, but something kept him planted in his chair. A niggling doubt? A feeling that it would be inappropriate? Maybe both. This time of grief was theirs alone, but something still felt wrong. Very wrong.

"Horace Macklin," a new voice boomed. "It is time for you to return to your rightful place."

Ben searched the vast grayness behind Horace's chair, but, so far, nothing appeared. Iona stepped back from Horace and searched as well. Soon, a beam of light broke through, and a bright silhouette took shape—a tall man with wings spread behind him. Seconds later, the man stepped close and clarified.

Iona gasped. "Azrael?"

Azrael nodded. "God granted your adoptive father's session here with you, and the allotted time has expired. He must now return to his eternal dwelling place."

Iona's expression tightened into an angry mask. "You mean hell, right?"

"Correct." Azrael wrapped his huge, glowing hand around Horace's neck and lifted him from his seat, his legs dangling. He offered no resistance as he hung limply and continued crying.

"But, Azrael!" Iona hugged Horace's legs. "He doesn't deserve hell. He's not a bad person."

Ben rose and reached for Iona to pull her away, but a quick shake of the head from Azrael made him step back.

"I will tell you," Azrael said to Iona, "what I have told every Reaper who has served me in hell. God is a perfect judge. The Almighty sent your father to hell. Who are you to say otherwise?"

Iona released Horace's legs and glared at Azrael, her fists tight at her sides. "Plenty of other glowing wing flappers have told me to shut up and stop asking questions. Well, I'm sick of it. This is my Papa we're talking about, and I want answers."

"I have no answers for you. My duty is simply to do as God commands, and I must return this soul to the abyss."

"And sometime later he'll go to the Lake of Fire, right?"

"As will all souls in the abyss. Your father is not a special case."

Iona's voice nearly squeaked. "What about a second chance? He'll do better. I know he will."

"A lifetime is filled with second chances. Horace threw them all away."

Iona clenched her fists and beat them against Azrael's hip. "No, no, no! You can't take him to hell!"

Unaffected by the blows, Azrael looked at Ben again, this time giving him a nod. He stepped in, wrapped his arms around Iona from behind, and pulled her away. She dropped to her knees and sobbed.

Azrael walked slowly into the grayness, then halted and looked back, partially veiled by the haze. "I have seen Austin peering into the portal. I assume you have been with him."

"We have," Ben replied, nodding.

"Kindly tell him for me that I miss his and Charlotte's presence and their excellent service. He would be interested to learn that quite recently I found a wayward person in hell whom I had to collect, both body and soul, and transport to Earth. A most unusual case. I am still trying to decide what to do with her."

"Her?"

"Yes, but her identity is not your concern at this time." Azrael stared at Ben with fiery eyes. "Come closer. I have a message for you alone."

Ben trembled, but he steeled himself and stepped quickly to the angel. "I'm ready to hear it."

Azrael spoke softly, and it seemed that his voice penetrated Ben's mind instead of traveling through the air. "The Almighty is aware of your motivations in joining Iona. Your instinct to protect her is right and good, though you have doubts that are reasonable and need careful consideration."

Ben whispered, "Would it have been better to let Leo die?"

"Better for some, not better for others, but the point is that Iona is wavering. Her heart told her that she could investigate Satan's quest and reject it if the quest's morality failed to match her internal code of ethics, a code that aligns quite well with those of the Almighty."

"Then should I put a stop to it? Force her to give up on this quest?"

Azrael shook his head. "Iona will do what she thinks is right regardless of what you say, and emotional upheavals that are sure to come might skew her perspective. You must continue your role as her protector no matter what she decides. But know this. As long as you follow the light that is in you, you will do well, though the end result could include great pain and heartache. Still, no matter where you go, God will be with you. Just be sure to take care of Iona's heart, demonstrate love to her at every turn, and she will be able to see the right choice. Even so, she must be allowed to choose, even if her final choice is the wrong one."

Ben nodded. "I understand."

"Good. And I have more advice to convey. This you may pass along to Iona. You and she will eventually have an audience with Satan, but God is protecting you even in this. Satan has been bound to tell you only the truth. As much as he wishes to follow his corrupt nature and lie in order to bring about his desires, his words will be true. You may have confidence in that."

"Thank you. That will help. But I need to know if Alex can heal Leo. Did she only partly heal him on purpose? Can she help him any further?"

"Ah. You're wondering if her leverage is real or fabricated." Azrael's face dimmed a shade. "That witch tells the truth when it suits her, and in this case, she has. She healed him to the best of her ability at the time, and she could very well heal him further at a later time."

"Is Leo in danger of dying without that further healing?"

"Without a doubt. Alexandria's leverage is authentic. Leo's life might very well hang on the decision Iona makes here."

"Should I tell her? I mean, would her knowing all this put more pressure on her to destroy hell?"

"You should tell her. And the pressure would increase. But she must make her decision in the light of truth. Without that light, her decision would not be fully informed."

"I understand. At least, I think I do."

"My words will become clearer as the journey progresses, and at that time you must also consider two more truths. One is that the deadliest fruit is borne of hidden poison, for it disguises itself as revelation. The other is that a father's betrayal is the source of that poison, and only a father's sacrifice can heal a heart that has been infected by it. I know that you cannot fully understand these truths now, but I trust that you will remember them."

"Understand fully? I don't understand them at all."

"No, but you will at the proper time if you seek the light in the midst of darkness."

Ben took a deep breath. "All right. Thank you again."

"You are welcome." Azrael continued into the grayness, still holding Horace above the floor. Within seconds, they faded out of sight.

Iona leaped to her feet, rushed to Ben, and hugged him around the waist, her head against his chest. Not saying a word, she sobbed with fitful spasms.

Ben set a hand behind her head and rubbed her back with the other. This startling revelation had torn a hole in her heart. Doubts flared from the bottom of her soul, dredging up age-old questions that never found satisfying answers. Every believer on Earth had to be content with the idea that God knew what he was doing, bury those questions, and keep them underground until they could see the judge face to face and finally understand.

He gazed at the faint glow in Azrael's wake. How strange that he began to leave before turning and providing such important information, as if he received a message from on high at the last moment. If so, that could mean that God was actively watching over them, intimately involved. A good sign.

After a few moments, Iona drew back and looked up at Ben with tear-filled eyes. "So what now?"

Ben brushed a tear from one of her cheeks. "We haven't seen Satan yet, so let's sit and wait a little while. My guess is that he set up that meeting to weaken your resolve."

"Weaken?" Offering a trembling smile, she brushed a tear from her other cheek. "My resolve got flattened, run over by a steamroller. It's a pancake."

"Let's sit." Ben guided her to a chair and sat in another, leaving the one Horace used empty. He reached a hand toward her, and she gladly took it. As they held hands, the practice of signaling with hand squeezes came to mind, but doing that now would probably tear open the wound yet again—best to just be there for her.

He looked again at the portal—no sign of warping. It would be safe to continue waiting.

After a few quiet moments, Iona took in a deep breath, wiped her cheeks with a sleeve, and gave Ben a firm nod. "I'm all right now. I can do this."

"I believe you. The way you questioned your father was ingenious. Brilliance under pressure. I loved it."

She smiled. "Thanks, but I have a feeling that was just a warm-up. It only gets harder from now on."

"You're probably right." Ben took a deep breath. "I need to tell you something Azrael said. Alex told the truth about Leo. She healed him the best that she could, and later she might be able to heal him more. His life is definitely in danger unless she does more."

"So he might die if I don't blow up hell."

"Might. Not definitely. Azrael said you need to know the truth so you can weigh the options."

Iona nodded. "I'm glad *he* thinks I can. I'm not sure *I* do."

A leaf fell from the tree and floated in a zigzag pattern to the table. Ben picked it up and looked at its silvery, veined surface. Other than its color, it appeared to be normal, nothing dangerous.

"Ben." Iona pointed. "Something's on the other side."

"Oh?" He turned it over. Words written with beautiful black calligraphy ran across the leaf. He read them out loud. "I, Lucifer the archangel, will speak to you through this tree's fallen leaves."

"Weird." Iona searched the table and floor. "There aren't any other fallen leaves."

Three more leaves dropped from the tree and settled to the table. Iona picked one up and read the underside. "There are more leaves now."

"Do all three say that?" Ben picked up another leaf and spoke its message. "No, only the leaf Iona read says that."

Iona scrunched her brow. "How could the leaves possibly know which one we were going to pick up?" She grabbed the final leaf and read it. "Because humans are so predictable." She pounded the table with a fist. "Stop playing games with us!"

The impact sent dozens of leaves falling from the tree, though none came close to the candle flames. As Iona scanned the top sides, void of any words, she mumbled, "How are we supposed to know which one to pick up next?"

Ben grabbed a leaf and read it. "It doesn't matter. Whichever leaf you choose will be the correct one."

Iona clutched two fistfuls of her hair. "How is that possible?"

"Maybe Satan is making text appear the split second after we choose a leaf. He's trying to look powerful and clever."

She released her hair and scowled. "So he's a cheap trickster. It's all smoke and mirrors."

"Exactly my thinking." Ben looked up into the tree's branches. Although he had already heard what Satan had in mind, it might be best to get him to state the matter plainly. "All right, Satan, or Lucifer, or whatever name you'll answer to. We're here. Tell us why you wanted us to come."

"I'll start." Iona turned a leaf over and read. "I understand that you can transform into a nonphysical state." She spoke her reply toward the tree. "Yes. I'm a Reaper."

When Ben touched another leaf, Iona reached over and grasped his wrist. "Let me. This part is my gig."

He nodded. "Sure."

Iona selected a different leaf and read the underside. "Stored in a compartment that will eventually be revealed is a special kind of bomb that can destroy an entire realm. You will need to access it."

"How do we do that?" She turned another leaf over. "Four seeds planted in the soils of suffering will yield four trees, and their fruit will fuel the cells in the bomb and make it accessible."

"The soils of suffering?" Iona asked. "What does that mean, and where are the seeds?"

Lights flashed from each of the three holes in the table. Iona peered into the hole closest to her. "A little red ball, like a marble. One of the seeds, I guess."

Ben looked into the hole in front of him. "Blue one here." He rose and stretched himself over the table to look into the third hole. "Yellow. I wonder where the fourth one is."

"Here." Iona pushed a finger into a hole at the base of the tree's trunk. "A black seed." She withdrew her finger. "I wonder why it's inside the tree. And this hole's smaller than the others."

"Let's see what else we can learn." Ben touched a leaf. "Mind if I pick one?"

Iona nodded. "Go ahead."

He turned the leaf over. "If you wish to proceed, take one seed and walk in the direction you came from. The Reaper will know where to plant it. The tree will grow to maturity and bear fruit instantly. Return with a fruit from the tree."

"Okay. What's the next step?" Iona grabbed another leaf. "Put the fruit in the seed's hole, the black one last of all. Then you will be able to access the bomb that you will carry to hell in order to destroy that realm. Take note—once you embark on the quest, you cannot leave for good without detonating the bomb. Once you detonate it, you will be sent to where you started on Earth."

Iona frowned. "So if we start, we have to finish."

"Right." Ben said. "Our portal home will probably close if you decide to go through with this."

Her head drooped. "Yeah."

"Let's get more intel before you decide." Ben looked up at the tree. "How do we detonate the bomb? And put as much info as you can on one leaf. This is getting really tedious." He turned a leaf over and squinted at the tiny print. "Three buttons must be pressed in a certain order, as on your Liberty warhead. Once the red button is pressed, the human touch will begin the chain reaction to detonate the bomb, a process that takes five seconds, which means Iona will have five seconds to transform to ghost mode. She must keep a physical fingertip on the button until the final microsecond. When the bomb explodes, she will not be harmed except perhaps for the loss of a fingertip, and the force of the blast will send her dematerialized body out of hell and back to Earth's realm."

"What about Ben?" Iona asked the tree. "What will happen to him?" She read another leaf. "The bomb's explosion will kill any physical person who is in its current realm, including Ben."

"What if he stays here and doesn't go with me to hell?" She reached up, plucked an unfallen leaf, and read it. "If Ben stays in the Oculus Gate when the bomb explodes in hell, he will be safe. These walls are impenetrable to the force the bomb will create. The continuum will be broken, and he, like you, will automatically be deposited at his entry point."

Ben mentally replayed Satan's words. He had given away a vital piece of information. They were actually sitting within the Oculus Gate at this moment, and his earlier explanation that the bomb would destroy any realm meant that it could destroy this one as well. "Interesting."

He looked in the direction they came from. The portal window still glowed, perfectly formed. "What do you want to do? We fulfilled our promise to Alex to meet with Satan."

Iona stared straight ahead for a long moment before focusing on him. "When we were with Alex, I was thinking, 'No way am I going to do what she tells me.' But now I know she might be able to save Leo's life. And after seeing my Papa, I *want* to get the job done as soon as we can." Her lower lip quivered. "Ben, hell is an awful place. I felt just a few drops of the Lake of Fire. Worst pain in my life. I can't imagine how horrific it must be for the souls flailing in it."

As she paused, Ben gazed into her tortured eyes. How could he possibly counter her claim? She was right about the pain. Completely right.

"I don't understand," she continued. "Why does God torture souls forever? Maybe they did some bad things on Earth. Maybe even Papa did. But forever? And that much pain? Why?"

She paused again. This time her sad eyes seemed to expect an answer, but he had nothing satisfying to give. "I don't know, Iona. I've thought about it for years, and I always came up empty. But I trust God. He's a lot wiser than I am."

Her chin firmed. "Then the way I see it, I'm moving forward. All the way. If God wants to put hell back together after I destroy it, that's up to him. But I love Leo. I want to save his life. And I love Papa, and I want to get him out of that place."

Ben nodded. "Love motivates you. I never doubted that. I don't agree with your decision, but I understand. I won't try to stop you."

"Thank you." Iona reached for another leaf as she called out, "Is there anything else we need to know?" She flipped the leaf over and read it. "With each journey, you will stay for a maximum of one hour and return here automatically, or you can leave sooner if, while touching the fruit, you stand where you appeared on Earth. The soil, perhaps not literal soil, will be less than a mile away."

Iona squared her shoulders. "Ready?"

"As ready as I'll ever be." Ben withdrew the blue seed from its hole. "This one can be first."

"Fine with me." She took the seed from him and pushed it into her pocket.

A door slid open on the tree trunk, revealing a stopwatch. Ben took it and looked it over. "For timing our hour, I guess." After retrieving the backpack and putting it on, he started the watch, slid it into his pocket, and reached for Iona. "Let's go." When she grasped his hand, they turned toward the direction they had come, bypassed the portal, and walked into the gray expanse.

Chapter Sixteen

Trudy sat next to Leo on a flat rock a few steps inside the tunnel. She flashed a penlight into his eye once more, then flicked the beam away. The pupil responded perfectly this time. After checking the other eye, she set the light back into the medical bag. "How do you feel?"

"Besides the hammering headache, not too bad, but I think my memory took a hit." He lifted an arm. "Did I ask you why I'm wearing Charlotte's cloak?"

"Nope. First time. Iona brought it. Charlotte asked us to put it on you." Trudy rose to her feet and extended a hand. "Do you want to try to walk around?"

"I was hoping you would ask that." He grasped her wrist and rode her pull. When he balanced himself, she let go, though she kept a hand near his back, just in case.

She walked with him out of the tunnel toward the boulder at the top of the trail, all the while watching his steady gait. "Not bad, Leo. Not bad at all."

"Thank you, but merely being able to walk isn't good enough."

"No worries. Kat and Caligar should be back soon with the cruiser. We can fly wherever you need to go."

"That I doubt."

They stopped at the boulder, turned around, and walked toward the tunnel. "What do you mean?"

"I heard some of the conversations that went on while I was trying to come out of my postsurgical stupor. I gathered that Iona has gone with Ben on a dangerous mission to hell. The cruiser can't go there, as far as I know."

"True. But you were in no shape to go."

They arrived at the tunnel and turned back again. "I realize that, but now that I am mobile, I would like to try to help. After all, Iona is my daughter. It's my responsibility to protect her."

"I understand, but based on my knowledge of the portal wheel, if you go through the portal to Earth, it probably won't take you where you want to go. By now it's spun around quite a bit, and the chances of you appearing within walking distance of the Alaska tower are almost zero."

"And I assume I would need to be at the tower to follow Ben and Iona."

"Right. You'll need Austin to see through the portals. He tells us what's on the other side." She motioned with her hands to try to draw a picture in the air. "It's like a revolving door with vertical partitions. Each partition leads to one of the worlds—heaven, hell, Earth, Viridi, and maybe others. And the one Ben and Iona were planning to go through leads to a table and chairs where she's supposed to meet with Satan. You would need Austin's eyes to know which one that is."

"But if I were to go to one place and discovered it's the wrong one, couldn't I merely go back to Alaska and try another door?"

Trudy shrugged. "I don't know. I guess it depends on the environment you find yourself in. The doorway to heaven looks like a brilliant light in outer space. If you go there, you might not be able to come back at all. But I guess that wouldn't be so bad, right?"

"Maybe not for you. I'm not entirely sure heaven would have me. But you're right. I would need the Ocular Owl to help me find the right portal." Leo stroked his chin as he picked up the pace. "So in your estimation, what is the farthest distance from the tower I might show up?"

"Hard to guess. Maybe several miles. Maybe only a couple. That is, if there aren't multiple exits. Worst case, going back could lead to one of a hundred different partitions scattered around the portal engine."

Leo slowed as they turned again. "Two or three miles is doable."

"Weren't you listening to the part about scattered portals? You could come out a thousand miles from the tower."

"I was listening, but I'm not a believer in worst-case scenarios. The portals are more likely to be static than to be jumping around like caffeinated rabbits. I choose to believe that I would come out within two or three miles of the tower. Like I said, that's doable."

"In the cold and darkness? Without a parka, and in your condition? Are you serious?"

He touched the cloak's sleeve. "This is quite warm. I can survive a few miles in it."

"You're dreaming. Not in Alaska."

"My huntsman training will come through." Leo halted and smiled. "Dr. Garrison, are you saying that I shouldn't go?"

"As your doctor, that's exactly what I'm saying."

He looked her in the eye. "What about as my friend?"

Trudy gazed at him, taking in his solemn, serious expression. His bloodshot eyes and multi-day beard growth told a story all their own. He would be a passionate hunter, a tireless bloodhound. Somehow, he would find Ben and Iona, and he would help them in any way he could. But with a severe concussion and his soul hanging on by a thread, could he handle the stress? She grasped his hand. "Look. You're a dad. First timer. I get that. But it's a crapshoot. You have no idea what you'll be walking into."

His eyes seemed to twinkle as he smiled. "And your answer?"

After staring at him for another moment, she heaved a deep sigh. "You have to go."

His smile widened. "I knew you'd see it my way."

"Yeah, well, good thing Kat's not here. She'd sit you on your butt and get Caligar to guard you like a prisoner. She'd say, 'Ben's got this. Trust him and take a seat.'"

"What do you think? Has Ben got this?"

"I trust him, if that's what you mean. He's the best warrior we've got."

Leo touched his nose. "My well-trained proboscis smells a *but* coming."

She laughed. "*But* if I had a choice, I'd rather have two papa bears on this mission, watching over each other as well as over Iona."

"My thoughts exactly." Leo nodded toward the still-glowing portal at the top of the tower rubble. "Will you help me get up there?"

Trudy rolled her eyes. "The hero father is ready to battle the demons of hell, but he needs help climbing a pile of dirt." She waved a hand. "Don't answer. Just come with me before I regain my sanity and change my mind."

Again arm in arm, they walked up the tower debris. Leo glanced around as he grimaced with each step. "I didn't see where Charlotte or Alex went."

"Alex probably tried to follow Kat and Caligar. Getting the cruiser's a big deal. But I'm sure they can handle her if she shows up."

"Without a doubt. And Charlotte?"

"She saw the Harrids and took off after them. I haven't seen her since, but she and Alex can disappear whenever they want, so …" Trudy shrugged. "They might both be staring at us right now."

Leo shuddered, then quickly stilled the tremor. "That wasn't from fear. I was practicing a shiver for the upcoming cold."

"And I believe you." Trudy bumped his hip with hers. "Now we've both told a whopper."

When they reached the portal, Leo gave Trudy a two-finger salute. "Thank you for your help and your medical care." He took a step toward the glow.

"Wait." Trudy grabbed his sleeve and pulled him into an embrace, patting him on the back as she whispered, "You're a good dad, Leo. And a good friend." She kissed his cheek and drew away. "Take care of yourself. I don't want to lose you."

Leo opened his mouth as if to reply, then merely nodded. He turned again, walked through the portal, and vanished in a splash of light.

"Trudy!" a woman called.

Trudy looked down from her perch. On the ledge near the boulder, Alex stood in her physical form, blood oozing from a closed, swollen eyelid and two swatches of blood on her otherwise white T-shirt. Still, her erect posture and squared shoulders proved that she had plenty of strength in spite of her injuries. Or she was faking it.

Hoping to display a strong stance of her own, Trudy straightened and crossed her arms. "What do you want?"

"I have a proposal." Alex waved a hand. "Kindly come down, and I will explain."

Trudy glanced at the portal. Could this be her chance to implement Ben's plan? A bit of deception instead of brute force? Although Alex seemed to be injured, tangling with her in hand-to-hand combat might be biting off more than a non-Owl could chew. Deception was the way to go. "I have to guard the portal, Alex. You come up. I'll listen."

Alex gave the rocky path a doubtful stare. Apparently she wondered whether or not the climb would expose her real condition. She let out a sigh and nodded. "I'll come up."

Chapter Seventeen

As the grayness dispersed, Ben blinked, trying to clear his vision, but dense fog persisted. He and Iona stood in an alley between two brick buildings, a blank wall to the rear and an exit straight ahead that led to a street with a car parked at each corner. Beyond that, the fog veiled his view.

A few feet within the alley, a group of six plastic garbage bins stood against one wall, and a seventh lay on its side, its contents partially spilled on the pothole-scarred pavement. A trio of rats chewed on stripped chicken bones from a torn box next to the capsized bin.

Iona released Ben's hand and pinched her nose. "What's that awful smell?"

Ben took a short whiff. The odor of rotting flesh oozed in. "Something dead nearby."

They pivoted slowly and scanned the trash-strewn scene. Near the back wall, more rats had gathered around a dark form about six paces away. The sounds of munching and scolding chitters drifted past. "Stay here." As he drew the gun from his waistband, he walked to the form and kicked into the feasting rats. They scattered, revealing a human hand protruding from a rip in a burlap sack, the flesh stripped from the fingers—feminine, if the red polish on a thumbnail meant anything.

Ben expected an eruption of bile, but it didn't come. With so many deaths recently, desensitization had set in. He crouched and set a finger on her wrist. No pulse. She had probably died quite some time ago. Her soul was likely long gone.

"What did you find?" Iona asked.

"A dead woman. Don't come closer. It's an awful sight."

"I think I need to see it. Feel the evil here. You know, the soils of suffering. It might be the only way to find the right place to plant the seed."

"Agreed." Ben gestured for her to join him. "This poor woman was left here as rat food, maybe murdered, maybe overdosed. But either way, evil was behind it. So go ahead and have a look. See if you can sense something."

"Yeah. Won't be easy." Iona padded softly to the burlap bag, stooped next to it, and untied the top. She pulled the material down, revealing a young woman with an ashen face and dark hair. As Iona pushed a tress from the woman's eyes, her voice cracked. "She's not much older than me. Maybe eighteen or nineteen."

Ben bit his lip. Now the bile was starting to boil.

Iona laid a hand over the woman's eyes and closed her own. After a few seconds of silence, she whispered, "Her soul's not here, but I do sense something, like a sad person crying. No hope. No one to help her escape her prison." She opened her eyes and rose. "Let's see if I can follow the feeling. Maybe it'll get stronger."

As Iona walked past Ben, he gazed at the dead woman for another moment. Maybe they should call local law enforcement to investigate, to bring the perpetrator to justice. Then again, having police around might complicate their search and scatter the vermin, so to speak. The poor woman was dead. It wouldn't do her any harm to investigate her death themselves, at least for now.

Iona shrieked. Ben spun toward her. A huge man with beefy arms held her from behind with a pistol to her head. "Drop your gun. Now. Or I'll shoot her."

"Okay. Okay." As Ben leaned over to set the gun down, he looked at Iona. Her hands and feet had already turned transparent. She would escape from this goon's clutches soon, but maybe not soon enough. He released the gun and raised his hands.

"And the backpack."

Ben slid the straps down and set the pack on the ground. "What do you want?"

"A replacement for Judy." He nodded toward the back of the alley. "I saw you gawking at her. And now you'll let me walk away with this cute little ginger if you know what's good for you."

Ben narrowed his eyes. Iona's transition had migrated to her elbows and up past her knees. This cockroach would notice the weight change before she could pull free. He had to act now. He dove to the ground, snatched the gun, and fired. His bullet zipped through Iona's ghostly legs and ripped into her captor's.

At the same moment, Iona slid upward through his arms and into the air. Ben fired twice more, piercing the man's chest with bullets. He crumpled to the ground and twitched in death throes.

Ben scrambled to his feet and looked up, but Iona was nowhere in sight. Since they had come to Earth, going to ghost mode meant that she would be taken to heaven. Did that fact slip her mind? She was too smart to forget something so important.

His body trembling, he cupped a hand around his mouth and called, "Iona!"

"Drop your weapon!" A man dressed in a dark uniform with a badge stood at the entry, a gun in hand.

"Sure, officer. Of course." As Ben again leaned over to lay the gun down, Iona crashed into the officer from above. His gun flew from his hand and skidded to the side.

Iona leaped off the prostrate officer and massaged her ribs, wincing. "That hurt more than I thought it would."

Ben slid his gun away and hurried to the officer. "Sorry about this, but you have no idea what's really going on here." He took the officer's handcuffs, fastened his wrists behind him, and hoisted him to his feet. "Are you all right?"

Groggy and blinking, he spoke with a slur. "Not really."

"Then have a seat." Ben guided him to the wall and helped him sit with his back against the bricks.

Iona picked up the officer's gun and sat at the wall across from him, the gun in her lap. "Gotta recover. I'm pretty dizzy."

"We'll take some time here. We have an hour." Ben crouched in front of the officer and took in his features—crow's feet around his bloodshot eyes, short white hair, a deep cleft in his shaven chin, and loose skin covering his jowls, apparently from a recent loss of weight. "Have you been sick recently?" Ben read his badge—Atlanta Police. Then his nametag. "Officer Pete Pataski?"

Pete winced. "Second plague. Barely survived. Why?"

"You're back on the beat, but you look retirement age. You must have a passion for law and order."

"This is my home. My city. It might be a fool's errand, but someone's got to do something about the crime." He struggled against the cuffs, then blew out a tired breath. "Not that I've made much of a dent recently."

"I get the impression that this is a prostitution area."

"The worst. And drugs. Took a twelve-year-old off the street just yesterday. High as a kite and turning tricks. Buyers were lining up for her. Makes me sick."

Ben laid a hand on Pete's shoulder. "Believe it or not, I'm on your side." He pointed toward the thug. "I shot that pimp. I think he killed the woman at the back of the alley. He called her Judy, and he was trying to kidnap Iona to take Judy's place."

Pete glanced at Iona. "When did she show up?"

"Like I said, you have no idea what's going on here, and I want to keep it that way." Ben looked him over. "Where do you keep the key to your handcuffs?"

"Why? Are you going to unlock me?"

Ben nodded. "But only if you'll let the girl and me go about our business. I can't leave you here as gang bait."

Pete gazed at him for a moment. "No guarantees. I have a sworn duty. I can't ignore a shooting."

"Then you can think about it for a while." Ben rose and turned toward Iona. "Feeling better?"

"Yeah. I think so. My side's pretty sore, though."

"No wonder." He grasped her wrist and pulled her to her feet. "How far did you fall?"

She tucked her cross necklace behind her shirt and the gun behind her waistband in back. "Not sure. As soon as I figured out that I was heading for heaven, I changed back to physical, and I landed on top of that building." She pointed. "Five stories, maybe? But I fell slowly at first, so it wasn't so bad. Then I jumped on Pete to save you. That was faster."

"Thanks. Good thing Pete broke your fall."

"You got that right, but we'd better scoot before I try to track anything."

"One second." Ben dug into the officer's pants pocket and withdrew a key ring. A small handcuff key dangled among other larger ones. He reached the ring behind the officer and set it in his hand. "Unlock yourself. That'll give us a head start. And if you're smart, you'll call in Judy's death and leave us alone. We have world-saving business to take care of." Ben grabbed the backpack and put it on. "Ready."

When Iona took off at a trot, he followed her along a sidewalk littered with trash, especially empty glass bottles—beer, rum, vodka, and others. To the left on a four-lane road, a dairy truck whizzed by from one direction and a bakery truck from the other. To the right, a pawn shop stood dark, as did a plasma donation center and a title loan company. Apparently early morning had arrived in this part of Atlanta, and the city dwellers hadn't yet risen.

At the first intersection, a traffic light flashed yellow. Iona turned right and, now out of Officer Pete's view, slowed her pace. After passing a bar, she slowed at a strip joint and peered through its tinted glass door.

Ben caught up and looked as well, his head higher than hers. "I don't see anything in there," he said. "Too dark."

"Right, but what I sensed from Judy is super strong here." She turned toward the street, walked to the curb, and pointed. "Or maybe over there."

Ben scanned the other side of the street. An old, one-story motel with boarded windows stood at the back of a weed-infested parking lot, vacant except for a lone, rusted pickup truck. "Looks like it's closed down. Abandoned."

"Yeah, but I feel the suffering." Iona checked the street for traffic and jogged across.

Ben hopped into a sprint. His wounded heel sent a sting up his leg, but Trudy's patch job seemed to be holding together.

When he caught up to Iona, they walked across the crumbling pavement, both with their guns hidden. He let his eyes dart as he watched the area for movement. Under a portico, a light flickered beyond the lobby door, the only unboarded glass at the front of the building. "Did you see that?" he asked.

"Yep. Signs of life."

"Front door might be guarded. Let's check the back for a way in." They jogged side by side around the motel and into a rear parking lot. A metallic back door stood near the center of the building with several room windows to each side. A card reader hung on the wall next to the door, complete with a number pad.

Iona tried the door, but it wouldn't budge. "No use guessing the number. Just trying a code might alert someone."

"Right." Ben crept to the window to the left of the door and peered through it. The curtains inside hung partially open, providing a narrow view of the room. No one lay on the stained mattress, completely stripped of coverings. A mini refrigerator lay on its side, and a cracked mirror dangled from a wire, ready to fall into a sink where a faucet dripped at a steady rhythm. "This one's vacant, but the water's turned on. Good sign that someone's around."

When Iona joined him, he withdrew his gun and jabbed the glass with the butt, making a jagged hole. He reached through, unlocked the window, and pushed the sash up. After sliding the gun away, he climbed in over a wall-mounted AC/heating unit and helped Iona crawl in as well.

"Okay. Quiet, now." Ben opened the door to the hallway and peeked outside—no one in sight on the ratty, stained carpet. They walked together toward the lobby, silently checking two rooms along the way—locked and quiet.

When they reached the lobby, Ben drew his gun again, stepped in, and looked around the spacious, musty room. An unshaded lamp with a flickering bulb stood behind the curved service counter, where half of a cigarette lay on a brass ashtray, still smoking. A can of beer stood next to it, condensation on the outside.

Ben strode back to the hallway and continued on with Iona. After they had checked three more rooms, a humming sound reached his ears, maybe a heating unit. When he found the door leading to the sound—the entry to a room facing the rear of the motel—he tried the knob. Locked, as expected.

Ben lifted his brow at Iona and whispered, "Sense anything?"

She nodded. "Super strong. We need to go in."

He lifted a backpack strap. "I have grenades, but they'd be too loud."

"I can switch to ghost mode to pass through the door and switch back before I go flying through the ceiling. I'm a lot faster at switching back."

"If you're sure."

"Not sure at all, but I'm going." She faded to transparency, then disappeared. A few seconds later, something thumped inside the room, probably Iona landing on the floor.

While Ben waited, he looked down the hall toward the lobby. Footsteps sounded in that direction, but they didn't seem to be getting closer. The seconds ticked by. Other sounds drifted through the air—a can getting crushed, a man laughing, a phone chiming, then conversation, the words impossible to distinguish, likely a foreign language.

Soon, Iona opened the door from the inside, her cheeks aflame as she held the door ajar. "A girl my age is in there, chained to the bed by the wrist. She's wearing a nightgown, and I told her to put her pants and shoes on. That we're getting her out of here."

"Is she hurt at all?"

"Not that I can tell, but she's drugged. Spaced out. I think she believed me, though. She's getting dressed. Her name's Candy." Iona opened the door a bit wider, squeezed out into the hall, and pulled it partially closed again. "I found the place to plant the seed. On her mattress. I'm sure of it. We were told it might not be literal soil."

"Did you plant it?"

"Not yet."

"Okay, you stay with Candy, and I'll go around back. We can take her out the window. Less risk that someone will hear us."

Iona shook her head. "Bars on the window."

A voice down the hall drifted in, growing louder. "You'll like her," a man said, his accent foreign, maybe Russian. "She's young and pretty. She won't give you any trouble." Two men rounded the corner from the lobby, one of medium height and build, the other shorter and plump. When they saw Ben and Iona, the taller one grabbed the other man by the arm, and they scrambled back to the lobby.

"Let's move." Ben pushed the door open and hustled inside, Iona at his heels. The girl sat on the bed, dressed in jeans under a frilly white nightgown, one shoe on and the other somewhere unseen.

She blinked at him, obviously dazed. "Who are you?"

"Ben. I'm getting you out of here." He aimed his gun at a manacle latched around the bedpost at floor level. "Cover your ears, Candy."

When she did, Ben blasted the manacle, shredding the metal, and jerked the chain free. "Iona, plant the seed and cover me."

"On it." She pulled the blue seed from her pocket and set it on the mattress, then drew her gun. "Ready."

Ben slid his gun away and scooped Candy into his arms. She clung to his neck, her hands cold and clammy. With Iona leading the way, her gun extended, he walked out to the hallway and looked toward the lobby, his foot holding the room's door open. So far, no one stood in sight, but that could change in a hurry.

A cracking sound erupted from the room. Inside, a tree of blue ice sprouted from the bed, its central shoot growing straight up and its rigid roots knifing through the mattress. Its limbs punched into the ceiling and ripped a hole through the roof. As ice particles rained, the lower branches spread from one end of the room to the other. Crystalline buds formed at the pointed ends and crackled open, looking like perfectly shaped roses, though blue instead of red. Some of the roses transformed into frosty blue fruit the size of a plum while others remained in a partially open state.

Then the growth stopped. All sound died away, except for the tinkling of ice dropping to the floor. At least fifty of the fruit hung throughout the branches, several within reach, and about the same number of blossoms remained.

Iona pocketed her gun, tiptoed in, and reached for a fruit. One of the blossoms turned toward her and shot an icicle spear that pierced her forearm. As more blossoms shifted her way, Ben called, "Watch out!"

Iona ducked under a barrage of icicles, then leaped up, plucked a fruit, and ran back, tossing it from hand to hand, gasping, "Cold. Cold. Cold."

When she cleared the door, Ben closed it behind her. Seconds later, the fruit's frosty coat faded. She pushed it into her pocket with a loud sigh. "Okay. That's done."

"Now we have to scat."

"Where are we going to take her?" Iona whispered as she drew her gun again and aimed it down the corridor.

"To Officer Pete, if we can find him." Ben shifted Candy in his arms. "All right. Let's go out the back exit."

Again leading the way, Iona strode quickly down the corridor, a hand brushing the wall, maybe to keep her balance since she had recently been in ghost mode. Ben followed. Candy stayed quiet, though her fingers squeezed his neck tightly.

When they reached the back door, Iona flung it open. The rusty pickup truck roared around the corner and skidded to a stop several paces away, the driver side toward her. Three men scrambled out the passenger door, all armed with handheld machine guns.

Iona fired, nailing one, then slammed the door and dove to the side. Bullets clanked against the metal. Some broke through and thudded into the wall on the other side of the corridor.

Iona vaulted to her feet and waved her gun. "Front door. Hurry." She and Ben ran through the lobby and out to the front portico. The truck zoomed into view again, this time with a man in the rear bed, his machine gun aimed at them over the top of the cab. Bullets sprayed all around as the gunman bounced with the speeding truck on the pockmarked lot.

Ben ducked back inside with Candy, while Iona returned fire. She shattered the windshield and struck the driver in the face. The truck careened, throwing the gunman out of the bed. When he stopped rolling, he lay on his stomach like a sniper and opened fire with a hail of bullets.

Iona rushed inside, blood dripping from her right hand. Ben shouted, "Take cover!" He carried Candy behind the service counter, laid her on the floor, and stayed low as he drew his gun and peered over the counter.

Iona joined them. Holding her gun in her left hand, she breathed heavily as she copied Ben's pose. "Flesh wound. Heel of my hand. Not too bad, but I can't shoot with it. I'm decent with my left, though."

"Understood. We're in pretty good shape two against one, but we're handicapped." He motioned with his eyes toward Candy, who now sat upright, still dazed. "And that guy knows it."

"The longer we wait, the more time he has to get reinforcements. After I made a run for it, I looked out the window and saw him pull a phone from his pocket."

"Then it's better to force a confrontation now while we have better numbers." He sidled close to her and whispered, "Outside where we won't put Candy in danger."

"Leave her here?" Iona whispered in return. "She's drugged. She might wander off."

"Then stay with her and back me up. I'll try to lead him in here. Maybe he'll think I'm alone."

"Got it."

Bending low, Ben sneaked around the counter and skulked to the front door, now just a metal frame with shattered glass. The pickup still sat in the parking lot, fumes puffing from its tailpipe and the driver leaning his bloodied head against the window, but the gunman was nowhere in sight. Ben glanced back toward the rear of the motel—no one in that direction.

A door closed somewhere down the corridor. Thumping footsteps approached, then a voice blended into the clamor. "I got another girl here, whoever you are." The gunman appeared at the opening to the hallway, a young woman in his clutches and the machine gun barrel pressed against her head. Pale, blonde, and wearing only a camisole and short pajama bottoms, she trembled, her eyes wide with fear. "Put the gun down," the man growled, "or I'll blow her brains out."

Ben kept his focus on the man, careful not to glance at Iona's hideaway. Normally, with her skill, she could put this guy down without hitting the girl, but maybe not left-handed. "That girl's a money maker for you," Ben said. "Why would you kill her?"

"Chloe's a dime a dozen. I could put out some crack bait and get five more like her in an hour. But Candy's younger. More valuable. I want her back." He nodded toward the floor. "Like I said, put the gun down."

"If I do, you'll just shoot me. We're at a stale—"

A shot rang out. Blood splashed from a hole in the gunman's head. He crumpled in a heap, his arms sliding away from Chloe. She dropped to a crouch and shivered.

Iona rushed out from behind the counter, knelt beside Chloe, and laid an arm around her shoulders, whispering into her ear.

Ben gave Iona a smile. "Great shot."

She looked up at him. "I didn't shoot him."

"What?" Ben glanced all around. "Then who—"

"I did." Officer Pete walked in from the hall, a rifle in hand. "And our team rounded up a couple of others in the gang who were heading this way."

Ben slid his gun behind his waistband. "Another girl, Candy, is behind the counter. She was chained in one of the rooms. We didn't check them all."

"My team is doing that now."

A lanky female officer walked in from the hall, wearing a bulletproof vest. "The other rooms are clean."

"Good. Take this girl and another behind the counter to the station and call the shelter."

"Will do." She set a hand under Chloe's arm and coaxed her up, then guided her toward the counter.

Iona rose as well, blood still oozing from her hand wound.

Officer Pete grasped her wrist and examined her hand. "I'll have one of my officers patch you up. First-aid kit's in the squad car."

"No, thanks." Iona pulled free. "I've had lots worse."

"Really?" Officer Pete looked at Ben. "Are you two some kind of vigilante team? Rescuing trafficked girls?"

"You could say that." Ben gave Iona a stealthy wink. "At least we are today."

"Mind explaining what that tree is all about?"

Ben and Iona looked at each other, then at Officer Pete. They shrugged at the same time. "Beats me," Ben said. "Never saw anything like it in my life."

"Why do I get the feeling that you're not telling me everything you know?" Officer Pete exhaled heavily. "Well, just so I don't have to deal with all the paperwork ..." He flicked his head toward the rear door. "If you'll promise to stop out back and see to her wound, I'll send you two on your way."

"Sounds good, Officer." Ben extended a hand toward Iona's left side. She took his hand, and the two walked together into the hall and out the door.

In the rear lot, two police cars sat with strobe lights flashing, each with a man in the backseat, probably the gunman's reinforcements. A bearded officer bearing a shotgun stood nearby guarding the vehicles, though he kept glancing at the huge tree that protruded from Candy's room.

Officer Pete called from the motel door. "Hawkins, get the first-aid kit and see to this girl's hand."

The officer retrieved the kit from one of the patrol cars. While he cleaned Iona's wound, Ben walked closer to Candy's room. Tree branches protruded between the bars in the shattered window and through the roof like blue icicle spears, some adorned with blossoms and fruit. But were the blossoms still dangerous now that Iona had reaped her harvest?

He padded closer and halted about ten paces away. One of the blossoms shot an icicle toward him. He jumped to the side. The spear struck the pavement and broke into glittering fragments. He backpedaled, turned, and jogged back to Iona.

The officer fastened a bandage around Iona's hand. "That should do it."

"Thank you," Iona and Ben said at the same time.

As they walked back the way they had come, now with rays of sun shining through diminishing clouds, Ben withdrew the stopwatch and checked the time—ten minutes to go. No problem.

Iona kept her head low, saying nothing. As she walked, her shirt rode up at the side, exposing a gun at her waist—Officer Pete's gun. He knew she had it, but he didn't ask her for it.

She let out a sigh, her head still drooping. Ben slid the stopwatch back into his pocket. Obviously something heavy weighed on her mind. But did she want to talk about it? Her silence said no, but her sigh said yes.

He let out a sigh of his own. No experience as a father was proving to be a huge handicap.

"Something bothering you?" Iona asked, looking at him.

"Just wondering if something's bothering *you*. Not sure if I should pry."

She focused straight ahead. "You can. Always. I'll tell you anything."

"Okay ..." He lengthened the word. "What's on your mind?"

"A couple of things. Those traffickers are the worst of the worst. How could anyone possibly think they have a right to sell those girls' bodies? It's pure evil."

"They don't care about good or evil. No God, no morality. The biggest dog wins. It's as simple as that."

"Yeah. It's sickening. If anyone deserves to go to hell, they do. And that customer who came shopping for a girl. I guess he took off like a scared rabbit. Disgusting coward."

"You're right. The traffickers and customers are all guilty."

After a quiet moment, she glanced at Ben again. "I'm glad there are still good people around. Like Officer Pete and his team. Good move to give him the handcuffs key. He saved our butts."

"Thanks. And you're right. There are still good people in this world."

When they turned into the alley together and stopped at the spot where they appeared from the portal, she pulled the fruit from her pocket. As she stared at it, she spoke in a low tone. "I decided to go ahead with the quest because I wanted to help Leo and Papa. I wasn't thinking about rats like those traffickers and how much they deserve to be there."

Ben focused on the fruit. Any expression of agreement might sound like *I told you so*. Better to stay quiet.

"Anyway, I'm still going forward." She looked at him. "What if God actually *wants* us to do this? I mean, we did something really good here. We saved two girls and put down some rabid dogs. Maybe we can do something good at all four places, you know, stop the suffering wherever we go. At least put a dent in it. Then when I set off the bomb so we can go home, God can rebuild hell, like I said before. At least maybe he'll let Papa stay out of it. He's powerful enough to do all that." As before, her expectant eyes seemed to hope for a response.

Ben nodded slowly. "I agree that we should keep going. I'm all for trying to help people. But I'm still against trying to destroy hell. Like you said, God is powerful. I think he'll show us another way to go home."

"At least we're agreed on the next step." Iona extended the fruit toward Ben. Its blue glow washed over her bandaged hand. "Let's go find fruit number two."

Chapter Eighteen

Leo hopped down from the portal wheel to the snow-covered ground. Except for the glowing portal itself, darkness covered everything beyond the range of its aura. He inhaled deeply through his nose. Only the aroma of evergreens entered—no human scents at all. With nothing to orient himself after his leap from Viridi to Earth, how could he hope to find the tower? Was Trudy right? Had he exited a thousand miles away instead of two or three? In these conditions, who could tell?

He pivoted and eyed the wheel. As Trudy had said, it could resemble a huge revolving door, though its massive size made that perspective true only in the imagination. Looking along its edge in either direction revealed only the slightest curve, which made sense for a device that encompassed the entire Arctic Circle.

In any case, since such doors usually rotated from left to right, the portal he just came through probably originated somewhere to the left. The tower, therefore, likely also stood to the left, and since the wind blew from that direction, he should be able to detect Jack's scent relatively soon. For a huntsman, that would provide more information than a clear, sunny day ever could.

He strode to the left into a stiff breeze that blew across a field of white. Snowflakes pelted his face, prompting him to raise the cloak's hood and draw the front low over his brow. So far, the material seemed warm enough, but that wouldn't last.

Hoping to allow his eyes to adjust, he angled away from the portal and searched the area ahead for tower lights, but only darkness stretched across the sky. The snowstorm likely shrouded the tower in clouds, or, again, it might be a thousand miles away.

In any case, he had to trudge on. Iona needed him. So did Ben. Those two had changed his life forever, and helping them meant everything.

As he walked, he shivered at the bitter wind, muttering, "So, here you are, Leo, supposedly one of the best trackers in the world, hopelessly lost in an Arctic apocalypse. Of course you had good intentions, but you know what they say about the road to hell being paved with them. You just have to—"

"Leo, don't be so hard on yourself." The woman's voice came from the cloak's hood.

He shifted his eyes upward. "Charlotte?"

"I'm glad you recognized me. I didn't know how muffled my voice would be coming through the fibers."

Her ghostly presence radiated an unexpected warmth, the way she once made him feel so long ago. "Is that why you asked Iona to give me your cloak? Because you wanted to talk to me?"

"Yes, Leo. I wanted to keep you company during your recovery and enter your brain more easily if need be. I don't trust Alex. She might not have done all she could to heal you properly."

"You're right. I don't trust her either. But your kindness has turned into a bad situation for you. I'm back in Alaska on a path to nowhere. If you come out of the cloak, you'll go straight to the afterlife. Heaven, I'm sure."

"Yes, I am aware, and I'm glad to accompany you on this ... how would you, my alliterative ally, put it? Arctic adventure?"

Leo chuckled. "You always knew how to make me laugh."

"Not always, Leo. And that leads me to another topic. I finally have a chance to make a full apology for my past actions."

He waved a hand. "No need, Charlotte. You expressed your regret already, and I forgave you. I have no ill feelings toward you whatsoever."

"Even if it will make me feel better? I have a ten-ton burden on my heart."

Leo blew a vapor-filled sigh. "Of course. If it will make you feel better. Tell me what's on your mind."

"Okay. Here goes." The sound of her inhaling came through the hood. "As I told Iona while we were in hell, I sense darkness in your soul. I thought it might be the result of the sins we committed together, and maybe you have not been cleansed, but now I understand that you have found redemption. Your soul is clean."

"I think so. I've asked for forgiveness a hundred times. I'm definitely not the same person I was then."

"And I was foolish to think otherwise. Yet, the darkness persists, and I have since learned that I am the reason for it, not you."

Leo lifted his brow. "You're the reason for darkness in me?"

"Yes. I'm sure of it."

He shook his head. "I don't understand."

"You will soon. Let me take you back to the day we met. You had three days off from huntsman training, and you drove into town to eat at a restaurant with a fellow huntsman in training. Do you remember?"

"Of course. Aquila and I went to the pasta place next to the pancake restaurant."

"Yes. Donatello's. I had heard from a friend that you two were coming, and I went there with the sole purpose of meeting you."

"Oh? I didn't know. I thought it was a chance meeting."

"Which is what I intended. You were nineteen, and I was twenty-six, though I told you I was thirty, thinking it would be flattering that a woman my age would show interest in you. Anyway, I actually introduced myself to you on a bet. My friend at the time, a woman whom I now find contemptible, dared me to try to corrupt a huntsman. The huntsman moral code is as high as it gets, though few follow it the rest of their lives. But those in training are true believers, and we thought it would be fun to draw a pair of huntsmen into our web and corrupt them."

Warmth flooded Leo's ears. Reopening this old wound burned, but if it helped Charlotte, he could keep listening. "I understand. Go on."

"Well, once I had you eating out of my hand, so to speak, with romantic meetings in the forest and excursions in the canoe across the lake, I knew you were mine. I had won the bet. And, as you might expect, my so-called friend refused to pay up, a mere hour's wages. I was furious. Such a trifling amount. That's when the guilt bomb hit me. I was so upset that she wouldn't pay such a small bet, but I was toying with your heart over the same amount. My sins were far worse than hers."

"Charlotte, there's no need to—"

"Yes, there is." Her voice took on a lamenting tone. "Please, I must continue."

"Very well. I'm listening."

"Thank you. You see, the shame of my hypocrisy made me unable to face you again. I didn't love you, so why should I keep stringing you along? I said goodbye in the most awful way, hoping that you would hate me and never try to see me again. Putting a woman like me behind you would be best for both of us."

Charlotte paused for a moment, giving Leo another chance to reply. "It's true that you said goodbye in an awful way, but I got over it. I survived."

"I know you survived physically, and since my heart grew even darker afterward, you really were better off without me, but did you survive emotionally? You never married. You became a loner. You stayed a huntsman longer than most do, thereby cementing your solitary ways. Knowing how much you once enjoyed the company of others, I have to believe that the change is the result of darkness that I instilled in you."

Tears welled in Leo's eyes, and a shiver erupted. She was right. Her betrayal did darken his soul. No use mincing words at this point. "It's true. All of it. What you did punched a hole in my heart. But it's all good. It helped me as a huntsman. I experienced how much pain one person can inflict on another, and I avoided doing that to anyone at all costs."

"That's no surprise. Steadfast men like you can find a silver lining in any dark cloud. But the cloud still remains, and it cripples you. I believe the only way to purge the remaining darkness is for me to confess everything, that I was the demonic vixen who intentionally tore you down. I broke your heart, devastated your confidence, and made you cast suspicion on anything good in the world."

"Until I met Iona."

"Until you met Iona. You were drawn to her because of the light you saw in her. But the darkness still persisted because she isn't able to purge it. Only I can do that, because I put it there. I am the one who ripped your heart out of your chest and stomped on it with spiked shoes."

Leo allowed himself a half smile. "That's a vivid picture."

"And a true one." Charlotte sighed. "Oh, Leo, don't you see? Your forgiveness of my sins against you was only partial, because you didn't know the extent of them. My cruelty wounded you more deeply than you knew. Memories of my hateful rejection stabbed you with words of condemnation, lies that you were inadequate. You thought I forsook you because of an imagined lack of manliness. But that wasn't true at all. I forsook you because of the wickedness in me."

Leo's throat tightened. Heat coursed along his skin in spite of the cold. Charlotte was right. He had let her betrayal change his perspective on himself and the world. He had been a crippled loner ever since.

"What I did to you was wrong, Leo, and every atom of blame falls on me. You were all the man you needed to be. Let the light of that truth flow into your mind. Let it purge the darkness from your soul. Let it strengthen your good, good heart to be the hero that God called you to be. And …" A sob rattled her voice. "And I hope, now that you know the extent of my evil folly, that you will forgive me. I am so, so sorry, Leo. So, so sorry."

Charlotte wept, and the sounds of her grief filled the cloak's hood. Leo halted and cried as well. The wind whipped his hood back, and frigid wind beat his hair into a frenzy. But that was all right. It felt like a cleansing breath, a bath of ice, as if it absorbed his own coldness and carried it away.

After a few moments, he pulled the hood up and cleared his throat. "Charlotte, you're right. I needed to hear that. Thank you. And I forgive you for all of it. One hundred percent. There is nothing left to forgive."

"Thank you, Leo, and I need to tell you one more thing. Over the years after I left you, I remembered your kindness and your gentle spirit. I fell in love with you, at least my memory of you, and between that and God's love for me, I was able to endure my duties in hell. Then when I saw you again, love rekindled, and I nearly squealed with joy. But I knew I had to let you lead the way and reveal our secrets in your time. Then I learned who Iona is, and my heart felt like it might burst. You and her showing up together. I couldn't believe it. I know God orchestrated the meeting. Although we deserved condemnation, especially me, he used our actions for good and gave the world Iona. And through her, God might very well save the world from Alex and her destructive schemes."

"You're right." New tears streamed down Leo's cheeks. "Like he used Chantal. Two young women cut from the same cloth. Courageous and sacrificial to the end."

Her voice spiked with energy. "Yes, Leo. A thousand times yes. And God is the one who made them both to be that way. His faithfulness is fully intact, no matter how painful our journeys have been."

"But I don't want Iona to sacrifice herself. She has to survive and continue blessing the world with her courage, her light. She's …" Leo's throat caught. "She's so precious. I can't stand the thought of her dying. She's everything good in this world. She has to live. I have to help her survive."

"Of course you do, but I don't see how you're going to from this Arctic wilderness. What were you thinking when you decided to come here?"

Leo huffed a laugh. "I guess you could say it was a leap of faith. Maybe a last-ditch cry for help, that God could put me in the right place at the right time." He lowered his head. "A stupid choice, I suppose."

"Maybe. Maybe not." Charlotte's voice steadied. "Leo, is your mind clear?"

"Never been clearer. You've been a breath of fresh air."

"Are you stronger and more confident?"

"That's hard to say. My brain connections aren't fully intact."

"Well, if it helps, I believe in you. May God help us both."

"Indeed. We'll need it." Just as Leo took a step, the wind shifted, now at his back. He took another deep breath. A foul odor entered—the stench of burning flesh and clothing. But it smelled different from other burning corpses. Maybe the giants that died during the battle at the tower?

Leo pivoted and walked that way. How far would he have to go? Hard to tell. But now a strong odor would guide him.

"I've picked up a scent, Charlotte." He strode at a faster pace. "Let's find our daughter."

Chapter Nineteen

"The matter is simple." Now standing near the portal with Trudy, Alex set a fist on her hip in a confident posture, though a wince revealed her pain. "Since events have not unfolded completely to my liking, I have to take what I can get. If you and your allies will return to Earth through the portal and leave me here, I will not accost you in any way, and I will give up my effort to destroy Earth."

Trudy feigned surprise with a short gasp. "Destroy Earth? How could you do that?"

Alex paused for a moment, still staring, maybe trying to concoct another lie. "My influencers were going to do it for me by generating massive quakes with the tower network, but because you showed up here by using the portal wheel, I deduce that they have lost control of the situation, and that objective is now impossible."

Trudy shook her head. "Sorry. You'll have to do better than that. Your lying prowess is sinking fast, like a boat full of holes."

Alex scowled. "And your verbal jabs are counterproductive. We're talking about the fate of Earth."

"Okay. I'll back off if you'll admit you were lying just now. Tell me the truth."

Alex rolled her eyes. "As if you would believe me now."

"Good point. But give it a shot. You have the stage."

"Very well." Alex took a deep breath. "Earth's destruction was part of my plan, but I no longer have control over it. And I hope to live on Viridi in peace, so whether or not Earth survives isn't critical for me."

Trudy nodded. "Okay. I'll buy that, but what about Caligar? Viridi is his home. He won't want you here."

"I will strike a truce with him. A treaty. Half of Viridi for him, and half for me."

"I don't think Caligar would ever trust you, and he would claim that he has no reason to give you the corner of a cave, much less half of Viridi. But let's say the impossible happens, and he agrees. What would you do with yourself on Viridi? I mean, with no other humans around, won't you get bored?"

Alex smirked. "Are you worried about my comfort, Trudy Garrison?"

"No, I'm worried that you'll cause trouble. If you can escape hell and get restored to your body after a couple of centuries, I think you can cook up some mischief here."

"Perhaps I can, but I won't. Since I will live the rest of my days here and explore this world as a ghost when I die, I will be content. Staying out of hell is enough for me."

Trudy half closed an eye. "Your ship of lies is sinking again. I don't believe a word you say."

"Suit yourself." Alex shrugged. "I made a peace offering. At least give it some thought. It's not like you have any other reasonable options."

"Okay. Give me a minute." Trudy looked out over the Viridian landscape—a wide variety, from forests to rivers to mesas. Taking this time to ponder felt wasteful, but she had to sell the idea that she was really thinking about the offer. Soften Alex up. Get her to lower her defense radar.

Alex turned toward the slope leading to the ledge. "I'll give you some time alone to ponder further."

"No. Wait." Trudy grasped Alex's wrist and turned her back. "I know what we should do."

Alex smiled. "Good. Tell me."

"If we're to leave Viridi …" Trudy pivoted toward the portal and waved a hand across it. "Do you think it's big enough for the angel cruiser to go through?"

Alex stepped closer and crossed her arms as she studied the shimmering panel. "I think so, and from what Harrid told me, the exit on the other side is even bigger—"

Now. Trudy grabbed Alex from behind and wrestled her toward the portal. Alex snatched Trudy's hair and pulled. Pain ripped through Trudy's scalp. Her feet slipping as she inched her way closer to the opening, she released Alex with one hand and clawed at her face, managing to clutch of fistful of blonde locks. With a final lunge and a loud grunt, Trudy heaved Alex through the portal and tumbled with her to the glowing floor of the portal wheel. Trudy vaulted up and faced a partition that stood a few steps away.

Alex scrambled to her feet. Her hair in disarray and eyes glistening silver, she hissed, "You fool!"

"Maybe so, but at least now you won't destroy Earth while you're here. Unless you want to die with it."

"You're an idiot." Alex ran through the partition and disappeared in a splash of light. Unable to resist a smirk, Trudy crossed her arms and waited. A few seconds later, Alex shouted, "I'm still in Alaska!"

Trudy walked through the partition. Alex stood on the portal floor, slowly pivoting in place and looking at the sky. She spun toward Trudy and glared at her. "The wheel has to turn to create a portal I can pass through, correct?"

Trudy snorted a laugh and spoke with more than a hint of sarcasm. "You mean you don't know how it works? I'm amazed. I thought you were the smartest woman in the world."

"Mockery suits your detestable character." Alex walked to the wheel's edge and looked both ways. "Assuming that you might have a change of heart and answer my question with civility, how far are we from the tower?"

"I don't know. Maybe a few miles. Maybe a hundred miles. It depends on how much it turned."

Alex growled, "We'll freeze before we can get to the tower and tell Lemuel to restart the engine."

"Or we could stay here. It's not so cold inside the portal wheel."

"That's not an option."

Trudy eyed Alex as she surveyed the scene with both fists on her hips, a furious pose. Obviously, she hated being out of control of the situation. Keeping her off balance might be the best strategy to get her to spill more intel. "I guess being on Earth is kind of shocking, right? Especially if you're still planning to destroy it."

"I'm not the one who will destroy it." Alex stalked back to Trudy and shoved her with both hands.

Trudy stumbled to the back of the partition and slammed into it. She bounced off and set her feet and fists for battle. "C'mon, witch. Let's see what you're made of."

Alex scoffed. "It's not worth bothering with the likes of you."

"Shove me when I'm not ready and then beg off? Not happening, honey." Trudy charged.

With lightning-fast reflexes, Alex stepped to the side and tripped her. Trudy tumbled to the floor and rolled to a sitting position.

"Stay there," Alex said, pointing. "You won't get another warning."

Trudy blew a lock of hair from her eyes. "If you weren't looking for a fight, then why did you push me?"

"To check the portal wall in a way that's safe for me. It's solid from this side. Now I remember how this contraption works." Alex jogged away from the partition.

Trudy leaped to her feet and followed. Alex's cryptic words about not being the one who was going to destroy Earth pounded at her brain. If not Alex, then who? Obviously Alex wanted to get off this planet before her plan could come to fruition. Maybe she would spill the information before too much longer.

Soon, Alex came to another partition and passed through it. Trudy again followed. Going to the tower this way would keep them warm enough, but it might take hours to get there, if they could get there at all.

At the next partition, Alex halted and stared at it. When Trudy caught up, she halted a few steps out of Alex's reach. On the surface, an undulating dark blob intermixed with the partition's glow, but Alex's eyes, having the same Owl powers as Austin's, might be able to figure out what lay beyond, even with one eye injured.

"What do you see?" Trudy asked.

Alex kept her gaze fixed. "A possible solution."

"For you to tuck tail and escape to Viridi? Save your worthless hide?"

Alex stabbed a finger at Trudy. "You have no idea what's going on, so keep your impudent mouth shut."

Trudy crossed her arms. "Then inform me, O high and mighty Queen of Hell. Fill my ignorant brain with your wisdom of the ages."

"All right, but only because I need you to help me save this planet from your stupidity." Alex took a deep breath and spoke in a clear, rapid cadence. "I'm concerned that something is wrong at the tower. Lemuel has not followed my instructions properly, which means that he might be dead or incapacitated. And we need him so we can use the wheel to save Earth."

"Okay, so tell me how to use it. I'm sure I can get there faster than you can. You're hurt."

"Very well." Alex took another deep breath. "Lemuel uses a spherical device to make the tower play the necessary musical notes to start and stop the wheel. The buttons on the device are not labeled, so I have to teach you how they are arranged. But first, I will explain how Earth will be destroyed." She pointed at the partition. "The Oculus Gate is through there. Iona is using it as a depot, of sorts, to build a bomb by collecting the necessary fuel from places of suffering on Earth. At each location, she plants a tree that produces fruit."

"And the fruit is the fuel?"

"Exactly. What she doesn't know is that the trees create connections between hell and Earth, in effect sewing them together. So when she takes the bomb to hell and sets it off—"

"She'll destroy Earth and hell together," Trudy finished.

"Correct. That has been the real plan all along."

Prickles ran along Trudy's spine, like hot stabbing needles. "Why are you telling me now?"

"So we can work together to stop it in case I'm unable to return to Viridi."

Trudy raised a finger. "Okay. This is the new plan. You tell me how to use Lemuel's device to restart and then stop the engine, but before I do, I need to get someone to stand in front of a partition leading to Iona's depot. That person will transport there and warn Iona that destroying hell also destroys Earth. Right?"

"Right. Lucifer will be furious, but that won't be my problem." Alex pointed at the partition. "I'm going past this portal to look for one that will take me back to Viridi. When the engine restarts and stops, I'll know you were successful and that you have your person in place to warn Iona."

"And I'm supposed to believe you because you're not sure you can escape Earth. You're spilling your guts to save your own hide."

Alex copied Trudy's earlier sarcastic tone. "Your ability to summarize what we've already discussed is extraordinary."

Trudy's hand tightened, as if wanting to form a fist, but she resisted. "Does mockery somehow suit my character but not yours?"

"Touché, and well struck. I see that you might be quick-witted enough to do your part." Alex pushed a hand into her pocket and withdrew a folded sheet of paper. "Harrid gave me this map of Lemuel's device in case something happened to Lemuel. Each button is labeled with a sound frequency that matches a musical note in a legend at the bottom, but only Harrid and Lemuel knew which combination of notes stops the wheel."

Trudy took the paper. "How can I figure out the right combination of notes?"

"If Lemuel is still available, you need not worry. If not, then maybe whoever disabled him will have heard the combination, giving you a starting point for guessing." Alex walked toward the floor's outer edge. "I wish you luck."

"Where are you going?"

Alex halted at the outer rim. "Away from you. I don't want you or any of your clan to know what became of me." She hopped to the ground.

Trudy stuffed the paper into her pocket and ran to the edge in time to see Alex dashing into the deepening shadows. Trudy jumped down and jogged in that direction, but both Alex and her footprints were nowhere in sight.

Trudy stopped at the outer limits of the portal wheel's glow. A gust of frigid wind tipped her to the side and bit through her shirt. She shivered hard. Since Alex had only a leather jacket covering her arms and torso, she wouldn't last long out there, and she could easily double back and find a portal to Viridi with her Owl vision. It was useless to follow her and way too cold.

Sighing, Trudy tromped to the portal floor and vaulted back on. As she walked toward the next partition, she withdrew the paper from her pocket, unfolded it, and studied the hand-drawn map—a messy combination of drawings, letters, and numbers, more complicated than Alex had indicated. How could anyone decipher this chicken-scratch code and run toward the tower at the same time? Impossible.

Maybe the best option would be to walk while reading, and as soon as she figured it all out, she could run the rest of the way, however far that might be.

Chapter Twenty

Both still touching the fruit, Ben and Iona reappeared in the Oculus Gate, the table only a few steps away. The candles continued to burn, though they stood only about three quarters as tall as before. Ben searched for the portal leading back to Alaska, but, as expected, it had vanished.

Iona hustled to the hole from which Ben had plucked the blue seed and dropped the fruit inside. Its azure glow bled into the artery-like paths on the table's surface and branched into narrower and narrower vessels that covered about a third of the area, like blue-water tributaries running through a brown expanse.

"Which seed next?" Ben asked.

Iona took the red one from its hole. "Let's go with red."

"How's your hand?"

Iona held her gun with her right hand and aimed it away from Ben. "Kind of shaky. Not sure I can pull the trigger without spoiling my aim. Probably better with my left for now."

"Let's hope we won't need it." Ben shook his backpack down and retrieved one of the mackataws Caligar had provided. "Hungry?"

"Starved."

He handed her the mackataw and withdrew another. They bit into them at the same time. The flesh tasted more salty than sweet, and the flavor raised reminders of stewed cabbage. Since it had no core or seeds, they were able to eat every bit of it.

When they finished, Ben put the pack on, reached into his pocket, and restarted the watch. "Shall we?" He presented an elbow.

Iona put her gun away and hooked her arm through his. "Let's do it."

They strode into the grayness again. This time, they emerged in what appeared to be the lobby of a doctor's office. Ben whispered, "Your gun is showing."

Iona flipped the hem of her shirt over her gun. Beyond the glass exit door, a male security guard with a sidearm walked through a paved parking lot, looking at car license plates.

A woman behind a window slid the transparent divider to the side. "Oh, hello. I didn't see you come in." She smiled at Iona. "Are you here for a pregnancy test? Or do you already know?"

Iona folded her hands behind her back. "Um ... I already know."

"When was your last period?"

"Not sure. Maybe two months ago."

"No worries." She typed on a computer and studied the screen. "I can fit you in for an exam, and we can schedule a follow-up for Thursday next week at ..." She tapped on a few more keys. "Is eight fifteen all right?"

Iona bit her lip. "Yeah. I think so." She looked up at Ben. "Okay with you?"

Ben concealed his gritted teeth. "Yeah. Fine."

The woman handed Iona a clipboard and pointed at the chairs in the lobby. "Fill out the forms, and I'll need your insurance card when you're ready. You shouldn't have to wait long." She smiled again. "I like your camo clothes. Very cool."

"Yeah ... um ... thanks." Iona hurried to a two-person bench and slid a pen from the clipboard's clasp. Ben sat next to her and looked around the room. Another teenaged girl sat to his left, an older guy in the next seat, and a twenty-something woman sat to Iona's right, apparently here alone.

Iona leaned close to Ben and whispered, "The next evil. Baby killers disguised as doctors. Definitely soils of suffering."

"Right. Must be a new business. The angels outlawed abortion. Even murderous aliens know you don't kill your own children."

"Yeah. It didn't take these creeps long to start it up again."

"Do you sense anything?"

Iona shuddered. "Pure evil. It's coming from that door." She nodded toward a door next to the receptionist's window. "Got a plan?"

Ben glanced around again. "I don't see a restroom anywhere. Probably in the hall. Ask the receptionist if you can use it and see if you can get a better read on where to plant the seed. Then when you come back, we'll come up with the next step."

"Got it." Iona rose, set the clipboard on her seat, and walked to the window. When the woman slid the divider again, they carried on a whispered conversation. The woman pointed at the door and pushed a button. When the door emitted a buzz, Iona pulled it open and walked inside. It closed with a loud click.

Ben flinched at the sound. Of course, Iona could handle herself, but letting her go alone felt wrong. At least for a few moments, he had to suppress his fatherly instincts.

After about a minute, Iona returned, grabbed the clipboard, and sat next to Ben again. She whispered, "I think I found it. Looks like a surgery room. I opened it a crack to peek inside. It felt like a wave of grief pouring through the gap. It's gotta be in there."

"Was anyone in the room?"

She nodded. "A man and a woman in scrubs. A girl was on a table with her feet in stirrups. They were talking to her, so I guess she's awake."

"Could it be just an exam?"

"I don't think so. A nurse was hanging an IV bag."

"Then we need to make our move before they put her under." Ben rose and reached for his gun.

Iona grabbed his arm. "But she's here voluntarily. Not chained."

"She's still a victim." Ben whipped the gun out. "And so is her baby."

Iona kept a firm grip on his arm and covered the gun with her free hand as she whispered, "I know how you feel, like you have to stop a murder, no matter what. I'm normally a shoot-first kind of person, myself. But we have a mission—to plant a seed, not shoot up this place. Let me try something."

Taking a deep breath to slow his racing heart, Ben nodded and stealthily put the gun away. "Sorry. Impulse got the best of me."

"No worries." Iona stepped over to the receptionist and tapped on the divider with a knuckle. "All right if my dad sees the exam room? He's really nervous about all of this."

The receptionist smiled. "Dads are like that, aren't they?"

"He's a good guy. Really supportive. But ..." Iona shrugged. "You know."

"Room three is open. You can take him in there for a couple of minutes." She pushed the button.

When the door buzzed, Iona opened it and gestured for Ben. They walked into the hallway together and closed the door. She glanced around and whispered, "So far, so good."

"Right. But we need to hurry. I'll come up with something to clear the place out."

"This way." Iona rushed down the hall. Ben followed at her heels. She ran to a closed door on the left and nodded toward it. Ben touched the knob. "Doctor," he called, adding breathless fear to his tone, "we have an emergency. An armed intruder came in, one of those anti-abortion freaks. He's demanding to see you."

"Did you call the police?" a woman said from inside.

"They're on the way."

"Who are you? I don't recognize your voice."

"Security guard. I was outside and came in the back door. You and whoever is in there with you can get out that way."

"All right. But we'll need a wheelchair for our patient."

"I'll find that," Iona said as she jogged away.

Hoping those inside wouldn't question his camo outfit, Ben opened the door. A woman in blue scrubs peeled off surgical gloves while a man in scrubs stood at a window, looking out, maybe watching for the intruder. A gowned teenaged girl lay on a surgical bed, her feet resting near a pair of stirrups. Based on their apparent ages, the woman was probably the doctor and the man, the nurse.

"Can she sit up?" Ben asked.

The woman nodded. "She's just groggy from the sedative. We hadn't started yet."

When Iona rushed in with a wheelchair, Ben withdrew his gun. "Get her in the chair. I'll watch for the intruder."

Once the doctor and nurse had seated the girl, Ben pointed down the hall toward the rear exit. "Take her outside until you hear it's safe to come back." The two wheeled the girl out in a rush.

Ben slid the gun behind his waistband. "Do you think the soil's in here?"

"Definitely." Iona winced. "The feeling's like a trash compactor. It's crushing my skull."

"The surgery table?"

"Maybe." She touched the top of the padded table near the center, then bent over double and clutched her stomach. "I'm ... I'm getting sick."

Ben extended a hand. "Give me the seed."

"No. I want to do it." She straightened and dug the red seed from her pocket. Grimacing tightly, she placed it on the table. The moment the seed touched the paper lining, it melted into the whiteness and spread to all sides, as if the pad were bleeding.

A tree trunk shot from the top of the table. Roots knifed in all directions. The limbs swelled into dragon-like monsters that curled their necks back, then snapped their heads forward, their gaping maws spewing fire at the walls. Each time a mouth opened, the monster revealed a red fruit sitting on its tongue.

Ben grabbed Iona's collar. "Let's go."

"Wait!" She lunged at one of the dragons, jammed a hand into its mouth, and jerked out the fruit. The moment she drew back, it reared with its woody neck as if ready to spew fire. Ben grabbed Iona by the arm, leaped with her into the hall, and slammed the door. Leaning his back against it, he gasped for breath.

Iona flopped to the floor on the other side of the hall and set the fruit next to her. "Are you all right?" Ben asked.

"Not really." She grimaced as she blew on her reddened hand. "I got scalded."

"How bad is it?"

She turned her hand over and back again. "No blisters. At least not yet. But it stings like crazy."

"But you got the fruit."

"Yeah." A smile broke her grimace as she pushed the fruit into her pocket. "I got it."

"Great work." Ben rose and helped her up. "Now we have to—"

The receptionist burst into the hallway and shouted, "What are you two doing?"

Ben released Iona's hand and set his shoulder against the door. "Making sure the dragons stay inside."

"You're insane." Her eyes grew wide. "You have a gun!"

Ben flipped his shirt tail over his exposed gun. "I assure you, I'm not going to—"

"A gun!" She threw her office door open, screaming. "Everyone hurry out. A madman is on the loose with a gun."

Shouts flew through the air. Doors slammed. Then, silence ensued.

Ben set a finger to his lips and whispered, "Let's see what we're up against."

They crept to the waiting room. Ben opened the door a few inches and looked through the gap. Other than a toppled chair, the vacant area seemed normal.

A siren whined in the distance, then another, much closer. "Police are on their way. We'd better hurry."

Iona raised the fruit in her palm. "Should we go to the spot where we appeared and touch it at the same time?"

"Maybe. The problem is—"

A loud crack sounded at the door to the surgery room. A hole broke open, and a dragon head poked through. When it saw Ben and Iona, it roared, its mouth now without its fruit.

"You want the fruit back?" Ben asked as he shook the backpack off. "I'll give you something better."

The vine swelled, shattering the surgery-room door. The dragon blasted a ball of fire. Ben dove over Iona and pressed her against the carpet as the sizzling spheres flew over their heads. Ben rolled off Iona, opened the pack's flap, and withdrew a grenade. He slung it at the dragon's mouth, then took Iona's hand, hoisted her up, and leaped with her into the waiting room.

The second he slammed the door, an explosion boomed in the hallway. The door rattled, and smoke poured through the gaps. Then silence ensued again.

Ben opened the door a crack and peeked out. In the midst of smoke and blackened walls, the vine whipped back into the surgery room while a dragon head lay severed and wriggling on the floor. Another dragon head shot out. When it caught sight of Ben, roared and spewed fire.

Ben slammed the door again and stood with Iona in the smoky waiting room. Several sirens wailed in the parking lot and tires screeched. "With the explosion and smoke, they'll think we're terrorists. If we get close to the window, we could be targets."

"Then let's see if the fruit works where we're standing." When Iona pulled the red fruit out, Ben touched it. Nothing happened. They still stood in the clinic waiting room.

"I guess we have to go to the exact spot in front of the exit door," Ben said, "but we have to be careful."

A thin red laser beam flashed into the room—a sniper's targeting light. After wavering for a few seconds, it settled on Iona's chest. Ben grabbed her and dove with her toward the exit. His shoulder thumped on the floor, and Iona fell on top of him. When they slid to a stop, everything turned black.

Ben looked around. As the blackness faded to gray, the tree table took shape nearby. Now the candles stood at about half their original size, still burning without interruption. Yet, no melted wax had built up around the holders.

Iona climbed to her feet and staggered toward the table. Ben rose and followed, the shoulder that took the impact aching. With a hefty thrust, she jammed the red fruit into its hole. As with the blue one, the color bled into the network until scarlet filled the arteries in another third of the tabletop.

Iona set her hands on the edge of the table and exhaled. "Two down and two to go."

"Ready to go to number three? Stop some more suffering?"

She spun, tears once again in her eyes. "Did we stop the suffering that time? Won't that girl just try to kill her baby again?"

"Not there. It won't open for weeks."

"Right. I get that. But I'll bet other abortion places are springing up now. She'll just go to one of those."

"Maybe. We can't be sure. We have to do what we can and let God take it from there. A lot of girls who come to places like this are scared. Coerced. Feel like they don't have a choice. All we did here was destroy the villains' slaughterhouse. We have to trust God to take care of the victims."

Iona sighed. "All right. I can't argue with that. But next time, I want to do something more permanent for the victims, not just throw a grenade in a building and leave without making a lasting change."

"You're right. We should. But we can't plan anything until we see where seed number three leads us."

Iona shuddered. "The quest is getting harder. It jumped from spear-shooting blossoms to fire-breathing dragons. I can't imagine how terrible the next one's going to be."

"Maybe it won't get worse. We're choosing the colors at random."

"Like we chose the leaves at random?" Iona laughed under her breath. "It'll get worse. Trust me. And the black seed will be the worst of all. Satan made sure to tell us to take it last."

"Well, we could stop. Ask God for another way to escape."

She shook her head. "I'm going. The bomb's a separate decision, and I'll make it later. For now, I want to do whatever I can to help more people, like I said, more permanently." She looked at him, every muscle in her face tense with determination. "Are you still with me?"

He tousled her hair, scattering debris fragments. "You know my answer already, don't you?"

"I do." She grasped his hand. "Let's get the yellow seed."

Chapter Twenty-One

Kat guided the cruiser over the tower's rubble and searched the area. No one stood or lay anywhere around. Had they all gone into the tunnel for some reason?

A gust shifted the cruiser. When Kat righted the ship and flew again over the site, she gazed at the horizon. Dark clouds boiled, maybe ten miles away. Caligar had warned of another storm approaching, and he hurried back to his refuge to check on Winella and Bazrah. He wouldn't be available to help, at least for a while, maybe after this new storm blew by.

She spoke toward the dashboard. "Is there enough room to land on the ledge directly below us?"

The computer responded with a mechanical, "Affirmative, but one wing will extend over the edge. The safety factor is suitable unless a gust of wind pushes the craft. Considering the current wind speed and gusts, I suggest a ground anchor."

"Good idea. Calculate a landing plan and put us on the ledge."

"The wind is unpredictable. I suggest a pilot-guided landing."

"You're probably right." Kat grasped the yoke and pushed the throttle. In spite of several strong gusts, she set the cruiser down without much trouble. As the computer had calculated, the ledge had enough room, though one runner sat close to a precipitous drop.

A new gust lifted a wing and pushed the cruiser a few inches toward the edge before letting it settle again. Kat spoke again toward the control panel. "Deploy the ground anchor."

"Ground anchor damaged. It cannot deploy."

"Why didn't you tell me that before?"

"The damage was not detectable until I made an attempt to deploy it."

"All right. Fair enough." Kat rose from the pilot's seat, pressed the side-door button, and exited. As wind blew her hair and clothes, she hurried to the tunnel and looked inside. "Hello? Is anyone in there?"

A faint echo returned her call.

She climbed the rubble to the portal and peered at the ground in front of it. Scuff marks marred the stones, and two of the bigger rocks pinched several hairs between them, some brown and some blonde. A fight had taken place, probably Trudy and Alex, judging by the length of the hair. Apparently Trudy decided to opt for brute force over deception.

Kat gazed at the portal. If the two tumbled into the portal, that would explain why they were gone, but where was Leo? Trudy wouldn't risk fighting Alex so close to the portal if she could help it. As a doctor, she needed to stay with her patient, unless Leo had already gone through.

Kat nodded. That had to be it. Leo would do anything to help Iona, and transporting to Earth was his only way to get to her. But in his condition, could he survive the trek?

As she scrambled down the rubble, she scanned the area again. Charlotte was nowhere in sight. Of course, she might be invisible, but would she try to go with Leo? That wouldn't make sense. She would just get snatched up into heaven, unable to help him at all.

Kat halted at the door to the cruiser. Either way, she had to travel to Earth to help Leo and Trudy. With a new storm coming and no ground anchor to secure the craft, she couldn't stay here.

She leaped into the cruiser, strapped into her seat, and lifted off. When she steered the ship in front of the portal, she spoke to the computer once more. "Is the expanse of light ahead large enough for us to pass through?"

"No light expanse detected."

Kat waved a hand at it. "Are you blind? It's right in front of us."

"No light expanse detected."

"Aren't you equipped to detect any kind of heat or light?"

"I have access to a thermal scanner and a white light detector. Not all spectra are detectable."

Thunder rumbled. A gust threw the cruiser back a few feet and tilted it to the side. When Kat righted the ship, she hovered in front of the portal again. Since the curtain of light stood immediately in front of a rock face, if she tried to fly through it and the portal wasn't big enough, she would crash.

She set her hand on the throttle and whispered, "For family," then accelerated toward the portal.

Holding Iona's hand at his side, Ben blinked at the brightness as warm sunlight beat down from above. They stood at the center of a village square surrounded by humble one-story buildings—some dilapidated with walls of tin ready to topple over, some with mud walls and thatched roofs, and a few more modern structures bearing stucco-covered walls, windows with glass panes, and wooden shutters.

Well beyond the most distant houses, tall trees loomed in a long line, maybe a sign that a river watered the area, but the trees blocked a view of any water.

Ben checked his pocket for the yellow seed. It lay next to the ticking stopwatch. Everything, including his backpack, now carrying only two mackataws, seemed to be in order.

A dark-haired boy wearing dark shorts and a ratty yellow T-shirt led a saddled mule over the road's hard-packed dirt to a hand-pumped spigot that dripped water into a trough. While the mule drank, the boy, probably about eight years old, filled a metal pot from the trough and smiled at Ben and Iona. He waved and said something in an unfamiliar language, his gleaming smile much whiter than his nut-brown skin.

Ben and Iona waved in return, offering smiles of their own. Iona dug into Ben's backpack, retrieved one of the mackataws, and pinched off a hunk. She popped it into her mouth and chewed while rubbing her stomach. "Yum." She extended the rest of the mackataw toward the boy. "For you."

His gaze skeptical, he walked slowly toward her, then snatched the mackataw, backed away, and took a big bite. While chewing, he broke into another smile and rubbed his stomach. "Yum."

Iona laughed. "All right if I give him yours, Ben?"

"Of course."

She pulled the last mackataw from the pack. When she handed it to the boy, he ran to his mule, slid it into a saddle pack, and led the mule away, smiling and waving as he left.

"I think you made a friend." Ben searched for any sign of evil. With the other two seeds, the evil slapped them in the face. Here it probably lay hidden somewhere. "Do you sense anything?"

Iona wrinkled her nose. "Only a stench. Do you smell it?"

He inhaled and took in a foul odor. "Something dead?"

"Yeah. And it's close. I hope it's a dead animal and not another Judy."

"Agreed. We'd better mark our spot. Apparently whatever takes us back to the Gate demands precision." Ben hammered his heels against the packed road and made a couple of shallow dents. "That should do it. Let's follow the scent of death. It might be a clue."

As they walked toward one of the modern buildings, several people, both young and old, emerged from the humbler dwellings and stared at them. All appeared to be thin, but not painfully so. The males wore short-sleeved, button-down shirts of varying colors along with non-denim work pants. Long skirts dressed most of the females, though a few wore capri-style pants. Frilly white tops with poofed-out short sleeves seemed popular among the adult women, while the girls most often opted for T-shirts.

Ben looked at a field between the houses and the tree line—nothing but cracked clay and wiry grass. Maybe a drought had afflicted the area, not enough rain to grow crops, but if a river lay beyond the trees, some kind of irrigation had to be possible.

A man approached—shirtless, and shoeless. His ribs protruded from his narrow torso, and the rope strung through his belt loops barely kept his pants above his scant waist. He scratched his scalp through matted hair and spoke in a strange language that sounded similar to French with a hint of Spanish.

Ben and Iona glanced at each other, both unfamiliar with the words.

"English?" Ben asked.

The man raised a finger, limped to a door three huts down a side street, and disappeared inside. A few moments later, he walked back with an old woman who hobbled with the aid of a makeshift cane. Nearly as thin, she wore a long black skirt and a tattered yellow T-shirt.

When she arrived, she smiled. "I am Mary. I speak English."

Ben pointed at himself. "Ben." He shifted his finger to Iona. "And Iona." He waved a hand. "Where are we? What is this place?"

Her smile thinned. "It is our village."

"I mean, what country are we in?"

"Country?" She narrowed her eyes. "How do you not know this?"

"Okay. Never mind that. Could you tell me what the bad smell is?"

Her skeptical expression deepened. "That is a strange question, but I will show you." She walked toward her hut. "Follow, please."

While Ben and Iona trailed Mary by a few paces, a few of the villagers tagged along. Mary stopped in front of a nearby hut where a man sat on the ground with a small boy curled on the ground in front of him. When Ben and Iona drew within a couple of steps they stopped. Ben nearly gagged at the odor. Flies buzzed around the boy's head. A few had settled on the foam oozing between his cracked lips. His distended belly seemed ready to burst as it protruded through the gap in his unbuttoned shirt.

The man gazed at them with blank, bloodshot eyes, his leathery face sagging, maybe from grief, maybe from exhaustion. Mary set a hand on the man's shoulder and said something in their language. He nodded, rose to his feet, and walked toward the village square.

"Did he die of starvation?" Ben asked.

Mary shook her head. "A parasite that makes a person waste away. We have medicine, but it is not working for many of the children."

"What kind of medicine?"

Mary glanced from side to side. A quiver invaded in her voice. "A doctor comes once each week. He changes the medicine to try to find a cure. But nothing works for the younger ones. I know so little about it, I cannot help you with that."

Ben looked into Mary's fearful eyes. Since the seed led them here, it made sense to interpret the happenings with a dark filter. Something nefarious was going on. "Is the doctor from a nearby village? One of your people?"

Her eyes darted. "No. He is from a foreign country. And I was expecting him to come this morning. He is late."

"Does he give you and your people physical exams?"

"Sometimes. Usually he just takes the dead children and changes the medicine when he needs to."

Ben searched the area for whatever might be making her nervous, but nothing obvious came into view. He gave her a head bow. "Thank you for your help."

"You are welcome." She smiled, apparently relieved that the questions ended. "Would you like something to eat or drink?"

"That won't be—"

The sound of an engine interrupted. As it drew closer, a rattle joined the noise. A pickup truck drove around a corner and onto their street, two men inside. They stopped near the dead boy, a few steps from Ben and Iona.

The driver, a thirty-something man sporting a short, scraggly beard, got out. Wearing jeans and a dirty T-shirt, he looked at the boy. "How many today?" he asked Mary.

"Two. This boy, and ..." She pointed toward the village square. "A girl at the far end of this road."

"Better than last week." The man walked to the bed of the pickup and grabbed a pitchfork. He set it in front of his body with the tines down and leaned on it with both hands. "Doc, I think you'd better have a look at this one. He's got the signs."

A tall, fifty-ish man, presumably Doc, stepped out of the truck's passenger side. Wearing a white lab coat and carrying a medical bag, he walked around the front of the truck and looked at the boy. "Reeking of parasitic excretions. Distended belly. Pretty typical of what we're looking for." Doc set the bag down, fished a pair of surgical gloves from it, and put them on. "The foaming at the mouth is the giveaway." Kneeling, he used a cotton swab to push some of the foam into a collection vial. "If he tests positive, then maybe it means we're finally making some progress."

"Progress?" Ben asked. "How can a death be a sign of progress?"

Doc looked up at him, a skeptical frown bending his features. "And who might you be?"

"A concerned visitor."

"Well, if you must know, he received a medication that helps his body fight a parasite that we are working on eliminating. Now that he is dead, we will conduct an autopsy to figure out how our treatment failed."

Iona huffed. "Whole lotta good the treatment did."

Doc glared at her. "Are you a physician? A scientist?"

"No." Iona crossed her arms. "But I know *dead* when I see it. And dead translates to failure. Epic failure."

"Failure is merely a steppingstone toward success. What we learn from his body will eventually help other children fight the parasite." Doc rose and gestured toward the boy. "Load him up, Rick, and let's move on."

Rick lifted the pitchfork and stepped toward the boy, then halted and looked at Ben and Iona. Grumbling under his breath, he tossed the pitchfork into the back of the truck and pulled a mask and surgical gloves from the medical bag.

While he moved the boy to the truck's bed, Iona glared at Doc. "How many dead kids are in your *eventually* timeline?"

Doc sneered. "None of your business, you impudent—"

"Wait." Ben held up a hand and turned toward Mary. "How many of these deaths did you have before this doctor arrived?"

Her eyes shifted toward Doc before locking on Ben. "None. And we have had more than thirty since then. But we didn't have a choice. The irrigation systems broke down, and we don't have the money or equipment to repair them, so our farms are too dry for crops. And the food trucks don't come through here anymore, either from the government or the missionaries. The doctor gives us food, but only if we'll take the medicines."

Ben scowled at Doc. "Does the food come with a hidden parasite? Is this village your personal petri dish?" His cheeks flamed hot as he continued. "And you coerced these people. Submit or starve. You treated them like lab rats."

Doc stalked toward the pickup. "I don't have to listen to this."

"Yes, you do." Ben lunged, grabbed Doc's shoulder, and spun him back. "Did you cause the irrigation breakdown? Are you blockading the food relief?"

"I am trying to save people from a ravaging parasite that is spreading throughout this region. The fact that the people of this village never suffered from the parasite made it a perfect testing ground for various medications. Since we control the food and water supply as well as the infections, we have a real-world laboratory. Isolating them allowed us to control all aspects of the experiment, including the introduction of the parasite. I make no apologies for that." Doc offered a conciliatory nod. "Yes, some people die, but we are doing this for the greater good."

"The greater good?" Ben balled his hand into a fist. Slugging this quack would feel like the greater good, but it wouldn't help these people. He clutched Doc's shirt tightly in front. Keeping his voice calm, he spoke slowly. "Listen to me. You and anyone you work with will leave this village, this country, and never come back. Is that clear?"

"Perfectly clear." Doc nodded toward Rick. "You know what to do."

Rick reached into the truck's bed and whipped out a rifle with an extended mag. He chambered a round and aimed the rifle at Iona. "Let Doc go."

Ben released Doc's shirt and backed toward Iona, his hands raised. "Okay. Okay. No need for—"

"We can't let them report our activities," Doc said. "Kill them."

Rick pulled the trigger. Ben dove toward Iona, his hands outstretched. The bullet smacked into his wrist only inches in front of her face. He dropped to the ground and writhed on his stomach, pain roaring.

Two more shots rang out. Mary screamed. Amidst the murmurings of the gathered crowd, Ben rolled to his back and bumped into Iona's legs. She stood straddling him like a guardian soldier, her gun aimed toward the truck, smoke rising from the barrel. Doc and Rick lay in front of the truck, motionless. "Are you all right?" she asked, her stare riveted on the bodies.

Ben looked at his wrist. Blood streamed down his arm to his elbow. Apparently the bullet struck the outer edge of his wrist bone, maybe cracking it. "Pretty much all right. I guess I tried to catch the bullet and missed."

"You deflected it. I think it would've nailed me between the eyes." Iona lowered the gun and extended her left hand. "Need help?"

"Sure." He grasped her hand with his own and rode her pull to his feet. He showed her his damaged wrist. "I guess we both needed a war wound."

"Let's keep it to one each." Iona stalked to the medical bag, grabbed it, and brought it back to Ben. "I'll try to patch you up."

Iona and Ben knelt together. While Iona bandaged his wrist, Mary directed two men to pull the dead boy out of the truck and lay him where he was before. Four other men dragged Doc and Rick to a dilapidated building across the street.

Iona sniffed and brushed a tear with her sleeve. "Thanks for what you did."

"You mean deflecting the bullet?"

"That ..." She tucked the end of the bandage and set her hands on her thighs as she looked at him. "And for standing up to that freak doctor and his lackey. They were monsters."

"I'm afraid they're not the only ones. A researcher like that works for a team. They'll send someone else to continue the project. Someone got a grant, and they'll want to keep the money spigot flowing."

"Then we have to figure out how to keep those vermin away. Like I said before, we need to make a change that lasts." Iona swiveled her head toward Mary. "Do you have a phone?"

"Let me get the phone some of us use. We'll see if it works out here." She hobbled toward the village square, again aided by her cane.

Iona rose and walked the three steps to where the dead boy lay. She sat at his side and took him into her arms. Although she wept openly, a hint of a smile broke through as she gazed at his cherubic face. Humming softly, she laid a hand over his eyes and closed her own. She whispered something, too quiet to hear. After a few seconds, she smiled fully and looked up to the sky, as if following a bird in flight.

Ben climbed to his feet and walked to her side. "What are you doing?"

She looked up at him. "I'm going to use their phone to contact some people who can protect the villagers here."

"No. I mean ..." He nodded toward the boy. "With him."

"Oh." She focused on him again. "He reminds me of the baby my mother had. We called him Little Brother. Same nose and chin. I loved him so much."

New warmth flowed into Ben's cheeks. Iona's heart couldn't be any more beautiful. "Handsome kid. That's for sure."

"He is, and I was singing him a lullaby. I tried using my Reaper powers to see if his soul was still inside his body."

"And?"

"It was. He was lonely. Scared. Confused. That's why I started singing to him. Then I coaxed him out, and he flew into the air, happy and free, like a dove escaping from a cage."

A sob tried to erupt from Ben's gut, but he swallowed it down. "That's great, Iona. Really great. You gave him comfort and courage."

"I hope so. And I hope Pablo wakes up in a better place."

"Pablo?"

She nodded. "The name I gave him. Pablo Hermano. Hermano is Spanish for brother, and Pablo is related to *little*. So he's Little Brother. Anyway, I think the people here might be Hispanic. Maybe Dominican or Haitian. But it didn't sound like they were speaking Spanish."

Ben crouched and set a hand on her shoulder. "Well, I'm sure Pablo will wake up in a better place."

She jerked her head toward him. "How can you be sure? Did he believe what he's supposed to believe? Faith and all that? You can't possibly know."

"I know Pablo's a child. He's innocent. Sending him to hell would be a monstrous injustice, and God is no monster."

"Yeah, I know. God's a perfect judge. Never makes a mistake." She heaved a sigh. "Ben, I don't know what to think. We don't know who's going to heaven and who's going to hell. We don't know why God chooses one or the other. I only know that my adoptive father is in hell. That's a fact I can do something about. Like I said before, I'm going to see this through, and now I'm leaning toward destroying hell with the bomb."

"I guessed as much." Ben withdrew the yellow seed from his pocket. "Do you know where to plant it?"

Iona touched the ground. "Right here where we found Pablo. The soils of suffering. It's almost like it's crying out to me."

With Ben's help, she rose with Pablo in her arms. "Mind if I keep holding him while you plant the seed?"

"Not at all, but you'd better move. No telling what weapons this tree will have."

Iona backed away with Pablo and shouted warnings to everyone to keep their distance. Although they probably couldn't understand her words, they seemed to recognize the urgency in her voice, and they eased farther from the planting site.

Ben knelt and touched the dry, sunbaked earth—too hard to dig into. He slid Caligar's knife from its sheath and used it to chop up the ground. When he had broken through a few inches, he dropped the seed into the hole, covered it, and rose while stepping back.

The ground began to tremble, and a rumbling sound filled the air. A yellow shoot sprouted and shot upward. Within seconds, it expanded into a thick trunk and divided into dozens of limbs and even more branches. Velvety leaves sprang forth, like elephant ears in size, cupped, as if ready to carry something on top.

On each leaf, a golden fruit took shape, the size and shape of a lemon. As the tree grew in height to about forty feet and in breadth to about thirty, the fruit elevated from the leaf, supported by a human figure holding it in the palm of a hand.

After nearly a full minute, the process ended. At least forty children sat within the foliage, each atop a leaf, carrying a fruit. Clothed in garb similar to the people of the village, they gazed straight ahead, saying nothing.

While everyone stared, Ben took a step closer. If this tree was like the others, this manifestation of children had to be darker and more dangerous than it seemed.

A woman cried out, "Isadora!" and ran toward the tree.

Ben shouted, "No! Wait!"

She ignored him and reached up toward a little girl who perched on a leaf over her head. The girl leaned down as if offering her fruit to the woman.

Ben dashed toward the woman but couldn't reach her in time. When she took the fruit, she collapsed to the ground and twitched. Most of the other villagers ran away, some screaming. Iona handed Pablo to Mary, took a phone from her, and ran toward the tree.

Ben kicked the fruit out of the woman's hand and looked up at the little girl. She cocked her head and stared back, as if confused.

From within the tree's foliage, the other children leaned toward Ben and extended their fruit, all with imploring eyes as they whispered in different languages—some Spanish, some Russian, some French, and one in English.

"Take this from me." The little boy, maybe six years old, widened his sad eyes. "I can't go to heaven unless you do."

Ben looked down at the woman who had taken fruit from Isabel. She lay on her back, Iona now kneeling next to her. "She's alive," Iona said. "Her breathing sounds fine."

"Good. I think the fruit is toxic to the touch, like it infuses the skin with poison."

Iona used her sleeve to mop sweat from the woman's brow. "You must've kicked it away from her in time."

"But that girl is probably the woman's daughter, or some other relative. Why would she offer her poisonous fruit?"

"No clue." Iona rose and slid the phone into her pocket. "And if it's poisonous to the touch, how are we going to take one and get it back to the table? Wearing gloves?"

"Or I could use my sleeve. It didn't hurt me when I kicked it with my shoe." Ben searched the ground for the fruit. It lay a few steps away, now black instead of yellow. "It changed color. Probably no good to us anymore."

"Most likely." Iona helped the woman to her feet. She staggered toward Mary, sobbing. "Maybe when we're ready to go, we can take a fresh one and hurry back to the table."

"That won't work. We have to touch the fruit to get sent back before the hour is over. We'll have to wait till the last minute and grab one with a sleeve."

"Then we'll wait. I have something I wanted to do anyway." Iona held the phone up and looked at the screen. "No signal. Mary said it worked in their church's steeple, but I can climb the tree instead. Give me a boost to the first limb."

Ben took the backpack off and crouched. "Climb aboard. Just be sure to dodge the fruit givers."

"No problem." She pushed the phone into her pocket, scrambled onto his back, and straddled his shoulders. "Ready."

When he straightened, she set her feet on his shoulders and stepped onto a limb. The moment she balanced on both feet, several of the children began walking toward her from their perches, extending their fruit as they closed in.

"They're on the move," Ben called. "Hop back to my shoulders."

"No. I got this." Iona set her back against the trunk and closed her eyes. The English-speaking boy walked toward her on the limb, and several other children inched her way from surrounding limbs, both at her level and from above. Their fruits pulsed with yellow light, drawing closer and closer. The glow washed over Iona, turning her face sallow, as if she were jaundiced.

"Iona, they're almost on you." Ben held his arms out. "Jump. I'll catch you."

Her body turned semitransparent, and her feet lifted from the limb and out of reach of the groping hands. She rose through the foliage, passing through branches along the way. When she cleared the top, she stopped and hovered for a moment, then dropped. She caught hold of the central shoot and hung on, making it sway. With her free hand, she withdrew the phone and punched in numbers with her thumb.

Ben averted his eyes. It would be best not to let the children know where Iona went.

Mary crept closer, her head low as she waved her cane like a weapon. "Is it safe?"

Ben nodded. "Just don't touch the fruit. I think the children will stay in the tree."

"What is she doing?" Mary asked as she watched Iona.

Ben touched her back and guided her away. "Knowing her, probably trying to get help for your village."

"She can do that?"

"I'm learning that she can do just about anything."

Mary looked at Pablo's body as it lay on the ground nearby "I will get someone to take him." She hobbled away, once again supporting herself with her cane.

While Iona continued whatever she was doing on the phone, Ben scanned the nearby huts. Several villagers, young and old, had reassembled across the road and stared at the tree, their mouths and eyes wide.

Soon, Mary returned with a man who carried Pablo away in his arms. Mary stayed behind and watched from a distance. Ben stood near the tree alone, the children now back on their leaves, staring at him. Hoping to keep their attention, he put the backpack on and paced under a limb, staying quiet.

After several minutes, Iona climbed down, too fast for the children to react. She ran to Ben and showed him the phone screen. "I logged in to Kat's Queen Laramel account and funneled some money to a mechanic in the area who'll repair the irrigation system. I had to use a translation app to text with him, but it's all set up. He said he would get here pronto. And a Christian relief agency is sending a truckload of food today. More are scheduled. One per week until the crops come in."

He gave her a high five. "That's fantastic. How much money did all that take?"

"Just a second." Iona ran the phone to Mary and hustled back. "I left a note on the screen telling her everything I did."

"Perfect."

Iona smiled. "Now to answer your question. It took a lot of money. Apparently the angel queen hoarded quite a bit. Good thing, too. I had to send a big bribe to the local police so they would arrest any other researchers that show up." She rubbed her thumb and finger together. "A little grease to lubricate the wheels of justice, if you know what I mean."

Ben laughed under his breath. "Unfortunately, I do."

"And here's another weird thing. When I entered Kat's password, the bank's system said it would email me an authentication message to make sure I was who I said I was. But I didn't know how to get into Kat's email to intercept the message and verify myself. I waited quite a while, not knowing what to do next, but then it let me in, like it ignored its own security check."

"That is weird. You would think Queen Laramel's account would be more secure than that."

"Exactly what I was thinking." Iona shrugged. "Anyway, it worked. And these people should be a lot better off real soon. Long-term help. Just like we hoped for."

Ben pointed at her. "Because of you."

She prodded his chest with a finger. "And you. Another team effort."

"I suppose so." Ben pulled the stopwatch out and checked the time. "Only five minutes left." He put the stopwatch away. "Let's see if we can get a fruit."

They walked together and looked up at the English-speaking boy. He sat once again on his leaf, his hand extended. "Take this. Please."

Ben pulled his sleeve over his hand. When he reached up, the boy jerked the fruit away. "No. You must touch it. I will not let you have it unless you do."

Ben drew his hand back. "You do realize that it's poison, don't you?"

The boy's tongue darted out, then back in, forked and green. "Yes." His voice sounded like a hiss. "Poison." He extended the fruit again. "If you want it, you must touch it."

Ben eyed the boy's narrow arm—scaly, as if covered with snakeskin. He whipped his knife out and whacked down on the boy's wrist. The blade sliced through, severing his hand. Ben caught the hand and backed away. The fruit stayed put on the palm.

The boy screamed and cursed. "How could you do this to me?"

"With a sharp blade, you spawn of Satan." Ben shrugged the backpack off and carefully laid the severed hand and fruit inside. It remained yellow, still glowing. "I'm guessing less than a minute left."

"Sounds right." She took the backpack strap. "One more to go."

"Right. One more." Seconds later, light flashed all around. When it faded, they stood next to the table. The candles, now at about a quarter of their original height, continued to provide enough illumination.

Iona lifted the hand out of the pack, rolled the yellow fruit into its hole, and threw the hand on the floor, where it shattered and crumbled to dust. The fruit's golden hue filtered into the wood's veins and spread across the final third of the surface, ending at the borders separating it from the other colors.

"Now the last one." She set the empty pack on the table and plucked the black seed from the hole in the tree trunk. "No time like the present."

When Iona took a step, Ben grasped her wrist and pulled her back. "Wait."

She looked at him, her eyes expectant. "What?"

"Just a feeling. You mentioned that the quest is getting harder. Since Satan told us to take the black seed last, I'm sure it'll be the hardest of all."

She huffed. "I know I said that, but we're getting through it. We've kicked butt every time."

He pointed at her. "I mean harder on you. Maybe mentally or emotionally. You were selected for a reason, and I doubt that it's just because you have Reaper powers. Something's cooking, and it smells pretty foul."

"Okay. Maybe so. But why the wait?"

"To pray for the strength to get through this. We shouldn't go on the fourth quest thinking we're invincible just because we survived the other three without too much trouble."

"Without too much trouble?" She shook her head. "We dodged icicle spears, dragon fire, and demonic fruit peddlers. That's not too much trouble?"

Ben laughed. "You win. We had loads of trouble, but I still feel like we're in the calm before the storm."

"If you're right, I guess the black seed will give birth to the storm." Iona slid the black seed into her pocket. "Okay. Let's pray, but nothing real specific about our plans." She glanced around as if looking for something in the grayness. "I don't want Alex's best buddy Lucifer listening in. I get creeped out thinking he might be lurking in the shadows. Or in the tree."

"Good point." He took her hand. "We could recite the Our Father prayer. Do you know it?"

She nodded. "It's been a while, though."

"No worries. I'll lead. If you forget a word, you can echo."

"Sounds good."

Ben cleared his throat, and the two prayed.

"Our Father who art in heaven, hallowed be thy name. Thy kingdom come. Thy will be done on Earth as it is in heaven. Give us this day our daily bread, and forgive us our trespasses, as we forgive those who trespass against us, and lead us not into temptation, but deliver us from evil. For thine is the kingdom and the power, and the glory, forever and ever. Amen."

A moment of silence ensued before Iona whispered, "God, we really need you to answer that part of the prayer, 'on Earth as it is in heaven.' Right now Earth is a lot like it is in hell. At least what we've seen so far." She inhaled deeply and finished with, "Amen again."

Chapter Twenty-Two

Kat pushed the throttle to maximum. The sudden shift shoved her back against the pilot's chair. The shining portal drew closer at breakneck speed as did the rocky cliff behind it. No turning back now. It was do or die.

Light splashed and bathed the ship's interior. She zoomed through some kind of radiant channel. According to Trudy's description of what happened to her, the cruiser now flew toward the North Pole with portal partitions to the left and right and the Alaska tower site somewhere to the rear.

Kat turned the ship slowly to the left until the Alaska scene came into view, then straightened and headed toward it. Since darkness still covered the area and its ample supply of evergreen trees, the risk of crashing into one ran high.

She flipped the headlights on. Within seconds, she flew out over a snow-covered field. As expected, trees dotted the landscape, a few too close for comfort. After dodging a couple of evergreens, brushing against one of them and shaking snow loose from its laden boughs, she ascended above their tops and scanned the ground.

Below and to the left, the radiant portal engine shone brightly, shedding light on the nearby snow and trees. Far ahead, the tower's lights blinked, maybe three miles away, the top half shrouded by fleeing clouds, in sight only because of her bird's-eye view. If Trudy came through the portal on foot, she might not have been able to see it. She would be tromping through snowdrifts, blinded by the radiant portal wheel.

Kat turned the thermal sensor on and flew in a circle over the area. The dashboard viewer showed the portal wheel, so bright that it nearly overwhelmed everything else. If Trudy and Alex had stayed somewhere within the engine, it would be impossible to see them with the scanner, but since the partitions would block them if they tried to walk to the tower on the wheel, wouldn't they have to venture into the snow to make progress? So far, no other heat echoes reflected on the screen. They had had time to cover some ground, maybe a mile or more, but did they choose the right direction?

She turned toward the tower and flew slowly, glancing at the thermal sensor every few seconds.

The computer beeped. "Message received for Queen Laramel."

"What does it say?"

"It is a security verification. Someone is trying to access Queen Laramel's bank account."

"Does it tell you who the request came from? Or a user ID?"

"The queen's ID and password were entered correctly. The message is asking for you to verify the access since it originated from an unrecognized site."

"Unrecognized?" Kat drummed her fingers on the control panel. Ben knew the access codes, as did Iona. If one of them needed funds, how could she ignore the request? "Can you send a confirmation in my name?"

"Affirmative."

"Then send it."

"Confirmation sent."

An orange echo appeared, the right size for a human, but motionless and lying on the ground. With a swat at the controls, she sent the cruiser into a sharp dive. In a flurry of windblown snow, she landed, then slapped the button to open the side door. She hustled out and ran to the human form—someone lying face down, much larger than either Trudy or Alex, most likely a man, the hood of a cloak covering his head.

She turned him over and brushed snow from his face. "Leo!" She checked his pulse at his throat. Weak but steady. Grasping him under his shoulders, she slid him over the snow to the cruiser's door, then, calling on all her strength, hoisted him into the ship, rolled him to his back, and hopped inside.

After closing the door, she straddled his chest, a knee on each side, and patted his cheek. It felt like ice, and his bluish lips and pale face looked like a frozen mask. "Leo. Are you all right? Talk to me."

He blinked, then looked at her. "Kat?"

"Yes. You're in the angel cruiser. I found you in the snow."

He spoke slowly, as if coming out of a daze. "Yes, yes, I remember now. I was trying to get to the tower. I have to help Iona and Ben."

"I'll take you there, but you're in no shape to help anyone. If your soul detaches again, you'll die, and since we're on Earth, your soul will go straight to heaven."

"Or so one would hope." He narrowed his eyes, his voice clear and steady now. "Why are you on Earth? How did the cruiser get here?"

"I flew it through the portal to search for Trudy. It looks like she wrestled Alex into the portal to take her back to Earth. Good move because Alex is weaker here. She can't go into ghost mode. Anyway, I haven't seen any sign of them."

"No surprise that Trudy did that. She is the hero type." He smiled weakly. "Maybe trying to be a hero is contagious, but I'm afraid I was having delusions of grandeur—the valiant father battling a blizzard to help his little girl. In my mind, I knew I could find the right portal leading to her. Then I would leap through it and save the day." He sighed. "I suppose I didn't make it more than a mile, did I?"

"Maybe a little more. Pretty amazing, if you ask me. Brain injured and just a cloak to keep warm."

"A parka wasn't available at the time, but I wasn't thinking about the weather."

"No worries. I'll take you the rest of the way, but no hero stuff. Father or not, you can't rescue anyone if you're half dead."

"Understood." His eyes moved around, as if scanning the ship's interior. "How can you search for Trudy in these conditions?"

"Thermal scanner. I hope I don't find her face-planted in the snow like you were." Kat rose and extended a hand. "Want to try to get up? You'll get warm quicker if you move around."

"Yes, I would like that." He grasped her hand and, with her help, climbed to his feet. After blinking several times, he nodded toward the cockpit. "I would like to sit up front with you, if you don't mind."

"Not at all, but I want you to walk from the rear to the front three times. You need to get your blood circulating. You nearly froze to death."

"That's odd. I don't feel like I got that cold. Maybe my sensory—" He shivered, a slight tremble at first that strengthened to a hard shake. "Oh. This … this is … not good."

"Here." Kat grasped Leo's wrist and draped an arm around him. "Walk with me." She guided him down the aisle to the aft cabinet and then to the cockpit, trying to hug the shakes out of him as he staggered on quivering legs. After the third trip back and forth, he settled to a minor tremble and began walking on his own.

"Thank you, Kat. I'm feeling much better now."

"Good." When he seated himself safely in the copilot's chair, she took the pilot's seat and looked him over. "Your color's back. Rosy cheeks and all."

"Thank you again. You saved my life."

"A life very much worth saving." She engaged the lower thrusters and lifted off. "Let's go to the tower."

"Gladly, but now I feel like a spare tire that's gone flat. A hopeful automobile driver pulled me out of the trunk and found me to be useless, a huge disappointment." He shook his head sadly. "Some hero I am."

"Such a negative view of yourself." Kat pushed the throttle and flew slowly toward the tower, still glancing at the thermal scanner for any sign of Trudy. She reached over and set a hand on his shoulder. "But you're a hero to me, Leo."

He flapped his swollen lips. "Don't con me, warrior woman. I'm not half the man you are. I mean ... woman you are." He shook his head again. "Never mind. Don't listen to me. My brain is missing too many spark plug cables. But I still believe I can be of service to Iona. Perhaps a way to do that will come about."

"Fair enough. We'll check in with Jack at the tower, assuming he's still there. Maybe he'll have an update."

"Let's hope so."

Kat flew on while providing Leo with as much intel as possible. Some of it he knew, some he either didn't know or couldn't remember. Such was the state of his injured brain.

Not seeing any sign of Trudy, Kat descended between the tower and the outer edge of the portal engine. Jack sat on the portal-wheel floor, his crutches lying nearby. Austin stood next to him, staring at a portal partition. An unfamiliar man also stood on the portal floor, fidgeting as he cradled an orb of some kind in his gloved hands. A pile of parkas sat near the floor's edge, evidence of warmer air within the portal wheel's environment.

When Jack saw the cruiser, he grabbed his crutches and climbed to his feet. Kat landed, shut off the props, and opened the side door, then rose and turned toward Leo. "Are you coming?"

He looked at her, blinking. "Oh. Yes. Certainly." He rose slowly. "I apologize for my delayed responses."

"No problem." She extended a hand. "I'll help you out the door."

He strode past her, obviously trying to force steady steps. "I prefer to do it myself."

"Of course."

He hopped out of the cruiser. When he landed, he teetered to the side. Kat leaped to the ground and grabbed his arm, steadying him. "Are you all right?"

"I will be. The impact gave me a bit of a jolt."

"I'll stay with you until your head clears." They walked together to the portal wheel.

"Well," Jack said, leaning on his crutches, "what brings you two back from Viridi?"

Kat smirked. "The angel cruiser. Didn't you see it?"

"Smart aleck." He waved a hand. "Come on up. It's warmer here, about forty above zero instead of twenty below. Sweaters in Saskatchewan instead of parkas on Pluto."

Kat leaped up to the portal floor. "Been working on that quip for a while, I'll bet."

"Less than an hour. Not bad, I think."

"Not bad. Terrible is more like it." Kat reached a hand down to Leo. Austin joined her and helped Leo vault up to their level. When everyone but the older man had gathered in a huddle, Kat looked at Jack. "Let's get each other up to speed. First, who's the guy over there looking as nervous as a mouse at a cat conference?"

Jack chuckled. "Lemuel. He knows how to make this merry-go-round ... well ... go around. Apparently, Alex brought him here to do just that. He's been doing what we asked, but we shouldn't trust him. Word is that he's one of her influencers."

"Okay. Got it." During the next couple of minutes, Kat summarized all she knew about the happenings on Viridi, including her theory that Trudy forced Alex to return to Earth and the fact that neither of them showed up on the scanner.

When she finished, Jack looked out toward the snow-covered landscape. "I haven't seen either of them. Maybe they got lost."

"With Alex in the mix, almost anything is possible."

"Let me give you my news," Jack said, "then I'll take the cruiser out to search for Trudy. I'm not much use here other than being the muscle that makes sure Lemuel does his thing. Now that you're here, you can do that better than I can."

"Works for me. What've you got?"

He nodded toward the partition. Amorphous shadows blended with the orange glow, stirring in a mesmerizing soup as he spoke.

"This portal leads to a gray room with a table made from a tree stump. Ben and Iona have been in and out of there three times, and they left for the fourth time a few minutes ago. I assume they'll be back again. But Austin hasn't seen a bomb in the room, assuming they'll need one to destroy hell."

"Strange to the max," Kat said. "But I trust them. They know what they're doing."

Leo leaned closer to Jack. "Is someone able to go through this portal?"

"That's what it's there for," Jack said. "I assume you want to go."

"If I may. If there is a bomb in that room, I can sniff it out."

Jack gave his shoulders a light shrug. "But we don't know what's going on. Maybe Ben and Iona have already figured out exactly what to do, even if there is a bomb."

Leo spread his hands. "I'm no good to anyone here. Since one of you has to look for Trudy, one of you has to stay here as the muscle, and Austin is your eyes through the portal, you have the manpower you need. I would like to go to where Ben and Iona are. I know I could help … somehow."

Kat crossed her arms and looked Leo over. He seemed much steadier than he did earlier. And, besides, he was his own man. If he had even an atom of strength left, he would use it to help the cause in any way he could. "Okay, Leo. If you're set on going, I won't stand in your way."

"Good." He rubbed his hands together. "What do I do to get there? Just walk through?"

"No," Jack said. "This ridiculously big revolving door has to move. That's how Trudy got to Viridi, but I didn't see what she actually did, only that she walked with the movement of the partitions and out of sight." He nodded toward Lemuel. "Lem started it up with a controller called the symphony sphere, and then stopped it after about ten minutes. That's all I know. But we sent Ben and Iona on the wheel and stopped it after only a couple of minutes. We decided it probably doesn't need the full ten."

"How fast do I need to walk?" Leo asked.

"Not fast at all. Like a stroll in the park."

"I can do that." Leo hugged Jack, then Austin, and finally Kat, holding her for an extra moment as he whispered, "Thank you for rescuing me. For sixteen years of Iona's life, I wasn't a father to her. Now I have another chance." He drew away, took a deep breath, and squared his shoulders. "Let's fire it up."

"Coats on," Jack called. "Lem, we'll need another spin once we're back on ground level."

Lem frowned. "Whatever for?"

"Don't whine about getting cold again. It won't take any longer than it did last time."

"Oh, very well." Lem snatched up his parka, put it on, and stalked toward the edge of the floor.

Kat helped Jack put a parka on while Austin carried his over an arm. Once everyone but Leo had reached ground level, Jack twirled his finger in the air. "Make it spin."

Lem took his gloves off and pressed a button on the orb. A loud tone emanated from the tower and a light shot into the air. As he pressed more buttons, new tones rang out, and the partition began sweeping along the floor from right to left.

Leo walked in front of it at the same speed. He saluted and called out, "God help us all."

"A couple of minutes?" Kat asked as she sidled next to Jack.

He shrugged. "We were guessing."

"I'm just worried about Leo's stamina. A few minutes ago, he could barely walk from the cruiser's cockpit to the back wall."

Jack winced. "Yeah. Not good. Let's stop it at two minutes, and I can fly in the cruiser to see if he's gone. But we'll need Lemuel to play the right notes to stop it."

"I'll tell him." She searched the dim landscape for Lemuel, but he stood nowhere in sight. "Lemuel? Where are you?"

"He's a wimp about the cold," Jack said. "Maybe he took cover in the cruiser."

"Could be. I left the door open when I had to help Leo. Didn't think of it till now."

"Lem's an Alex supporter." Jack nodded toward a duffle bag on the ground. "Grab a gun and check on him."

Kat pushed the bag open. A semiautomatic rifle lay inside, a magazine already loaded. She snatched it, chambered a round, and hurried to the cruiser. The rifle aimed in front, she peeked through the open door from ground level. No one stood in sight. She vaulted aboard and looked around. The cruiser's mooring lights in the ceiling provided plenty of illumination to see into the cockpit and all around the seats—vacant.

The rear cabinet door burst open. Lem jumped out and aimed a handgun. "Drop it."

Kat set the rifle on the floor. "What do you want?"

"To fly away. I heard you tell Jack that Alexandria is back on Earth. If I stop the portal wheel, and Leo interferes with her plan, she will terminate me. I tried to take off, but the computer locked the controls."

Kat crossed her arms. "Yeah, the computer's pretty stubborn about not letting the ship get hijacked."

"Then it's a good thing I kept a gun hidden in my parka. I can make you fly the ship for me."

"Fat chance. You kill me, and then what? You'll still be stuck here. I'm the only one who can fly it."

"Or I could just wound you. That should work." He waved the gun. "Go to the cockpit, or you'll get a bullet in the kneecap to match Jack's."

Something moved outside the cruiser, barely visible through the open door. Maybe the wind. And if so, a sudden gust in Lemuel's cold-phobic face might give her a chance to attack.

"Okay. Okay." Kat backed toward the cockpit. With every step she took, Lemuel took his own step forward.

When he passed the side door, wind and snow blasted in. He turned toward the opening and pointed. "How do you close this—"

Something zinged in and stabbed him in the chest. His eyes rolled into the back of his head. He dropped the gun and crumpled in a heap.

Kat rushed to him. The tail of a crossbow bolt protruded from his ribs, the angle of the shaft upward toward his heart. She looked out the door.

Austin stood in the snow, a crossbow in hand. "Is he dead?"

Kat felt for Lemuel's pulse at his neck. A weak heartbeat thrummed against her fingers, but if the growing pool of blood under his body meant anything, he'd be dead soon. "He's bleeding out. Without Trudy, I don't think we can save him."

Austin walked closer to the door. "I wasn't trying for a kill shot. Just to wing him. A gust threw the bolt off course."

"I saw that, but we need him alive to stop the portal wheel." She searched his parka pockets and found the orb. She pulled it out and showed it to Austin. "Did you watch him closely enough to know how it works?"

He shook his head. "Sorry. I kept my eye on the portal walls while he did his thing."

"But you heard the notes that stop it, right?" Kat extended the orb through the open door toward Austin. "You're a musician. Can you use this ball to reproduce the notes?"

"*Was* a musician. It's been a few years. But I didn't pay much attention to the stopping notes. And, besides, Lem said the sphere is activated by his thumb print."

"That's not a huge obstacle." Kat grabbed Lemuel's wrist and stripped the glove off his hand. "I have a knife."

"Kind of extreme, unless he's dead."

Kat checked Lemuel's pulse again. No sign of life. "He's dead."

"Then he won't complain, but we still need the stopping notes."

"Maybe there's another way." Kat jumped out of the cruiser and joined Austin. "I know the notes that'll knock the portal wheel out permanently."

"But what if we need to open a portal later? Like to get Ben and Iona home?"

"Good question. I'm working on it." Holding the sphere in one hand, Kat grabbed Austin's arm with the other and walked with him back to the portal floor. Jack still stood in front of it, propped by crutches. "Listen," she said, raising her voice to overcome the gusting wind. "By my count, everyone but Ben and Iona are where they're supposed to be. Caligar's on Viridi. Trudy and Alex are on Earth. At least I hope they are."

Austin lifted a finger. "And Charlotte's on Earth. Inside her cloak. The one Leo was wearing. I heard her talking to him."

"Perfect, so all we have to do is get Ben and Iona home safely. In theory, we can disable the portal wheel with a series of musical notes the inventor of this monstrosity told us about. According to him, after the notes are played, the wheel will stop. The portals will stay open for one minute. After that, no one will be able to use them, which means we have to hope Leo will join Ben and Iona and bring them back before the minute is up."

"Oh, man," Jack said. "One minute? With Leo barely able to walk? That's going to take a miracle."

Kat sighed. "You're right. But it's all we've got."

"Okay." Austin extended a hand. "Give me the sphere and tell me the notes. It might take a lot of trial and error."

Kat rolled the sphere into his palm. "I'll get Lemuel's thumb."

Chapter Twenty-Three

Leo stared straight ahead as he walked on. His legs felt pretty strong, though weaker than when he first started this bizarre march. Good thing it would last only a couple of minutes. Any longer, and he might collapse.

The glow from the portal floor provided enough light to see several paces into the snowy landscape to the left, and the air within the compartment proved to be only moderately cold. The cloak would keep him warm. Yet, he had forgotten something. What could it be?

He clenched a fist. *Blast this brain injury!*

A cool gust brushed against his ears. That was it. The hood had fallen down. He raised the hood and spoke into the fibers. "I apologize, Charlotte. My brain is functioning at about two out of ten."

"No offense taken, Leo. I'm just glad to be with you on this journey. Your heart is a perfect ten out of ten, and I trust that will get you through."

"If my legs will hold up, maybe so. We'll see. Any idea how long it's been since we left?"

"About five minutes. Give or take a minute."

"Jack said a couple of minutes. To me, that means two, not five."

"I agree. I hope nothing's wrong."

"And I hope I'll know what to do when it stops. Just because Trudy figured it out, it doesn't mean that I can. She is as sharp as they come, and I am in an addled state."

"I will help you, Leo. Although my body is gone, my mind is intact."

"Good. Thank you."

After a few minutes of silent walking, Leo looked back. The glowing partition continued its quiet sweep at the same pace. "It must be closing in on ten minutes by now."

"Without a doubt. Something must've gone wrong."

"Or maybe it has stopped, and the continued movement of the portal is an illusion. Maybe I'm supposed to stop and let it overtake me."

"That's a possibility. I'm sure our allies wouldn't have forgotten to do their part."

"Okay. I'll give it a try. I'm nearly worn out." Leo halted. When the portal partition collided with him, he passed through and found himself facing the black wall on the other side. He still stood on the portal wheel floor on Earth, not in the gray room Austin described. "That didn't work." He accelerated, caught up with the wall, and, while still walking, set a hand on it—solid, no passing through from this direction.

He blinked. What could he do? His rattling cage of a brain couldn't come up with any options.

"Leo, can you get off the floor, jog quickly enough to pass the wall, and then jump back on?"

"I don't have much choice." Maintaining his forward pace, he angled to the edge, then hopped down to the snow. He sank into a drift until his feet struck solid ground. The impact sent a jolt up his spine and into his skull.

Wincing at the pain, he trudged out of the drift and jogged on icy ground, slipping at times as he tried to catch up with the partition. After about a minute, he passed it, climbed back onto the floor, and walked at his earlier pace.

Breathless, he spoke into the cloak. "Any ... other ... ideas?"

"Only to restate that something is terribly wrong. I can't imagine why they haven't stopped the wheel."

Well ahead, a human form came into view, blurry in the surrounding glow, though the increasing size made it clear that he or she was heading this way. "Someone's coming."

"Do you have a weapon?"

"Only my fists and feet. Teeth, if necessary. Last resort, though. I despise biting people."

Within seconds, the figure clarified—a woman, a familiar woman. "Trudy?"

"Leo?" She pushed something into her pocket and broke into a jog. When she met him, she spun and walked with him at his side. "Why are you walking on the portal floor?"

He jerked his thumb toward the partition behind him. "I'm trying to go there to help Ben and Iona, and I heard that it has to stop to send me through, but for some reason our allies back at the tower have not ended the musical-chairs melody, so to speak."

"Do you know what to do when it does stop?"

"No. I thought it might become evident."

"Not really. When the portal partition stops, you stop, and its glow will keep going for a few seconds and envelop you. Then the Alaska scene to our left will transform into the place the portal wall is supposed to send you. All you have to do is walk into the new scene, and you're there."

"Simple enough." He set a hand on his chest, trying to settle his racing heart. "But I'm afraid I'm nearly spent. It feels like my legs are growing numb. I might collapse at any moment."

"Let me help you." Trudy grasped his elbow and lifted as she walked. "Better?"

"Somewhat, but the best help would be to stop this blasted wheel."

"You're right. I'll run to the tower right through the partitions. That's where I was going anyway. I got delayed because I was with Alex, and she bolted into the snow. I couldn't find her anywhere."

"So she's in the wind? Literally?"

"Yeah. Bad news, I know. I got off for a while to look for her. I don't want that witch wandering free, even in the Alaskan wilderness."

"Bad news, indeed."

"But there's good news. Well, it can be good news, depending on how you look at it. Alex said if Iona destroys hell, Earth will be destroyed with it, so now Alex is trying to go back to Viridi to stay alive. And since she's an Owl, she'll be able to see through these portal walls and know where to be when it stops."

"That doesn't sound like good news at all." Leo puffed as he pumped an arm. "Are you sure you know the meaning of the words?"

"My point is that shaking Alex up gave us the intel we needed. And we already have you in position to warn Iona about Earth being destroyed if she blows up hell. You can stop her. She'll listen to you."

"Yes, I see. Our chance meeting is fortunate."

Trudy squeezed his elbow. "Nothing chance about it. Remember that."

"Yes, yes, you're right. And I'm glad I have a mission to accomplish instead of a vague notion that I can help Iona." Leo sighed. "I only wish the wily witch wouldn't be able to escape the fate she deserves."

"I agree, but Caligar can handle her. Ben talked to him about what to do if she tries to become a permanent resident of Viridi, but I shouldn't say anything more about that. Don't want to jinx it." Trudy withdrew a creased page from her pocket and began unfolding it. "Check this out. Alex gave me something that'll help me stop the portal wheel."

Leo shook his head. "No need for me to see it. You should go. Now."

"You're right." Trudy released Leo's elbow. "Triple time. Somehow I'll get it done."

"Thank you."

She kissed him on the cheek, turned toward the partition, and ran through it. When she disappeared, Leo scanned the wintry world to his left. Alex lurked somewhere, and that couldn't be good. She could hop back on the turntable anywhere she pleased and avoid detection. Maybe she already had. No wonder Trudy didn't want to explain Ben's plot with Caligar. She might be listening.

"Trudy will arrive quickly," Charlotte said. "She is young and athletic."

"True." Leo marched on. A wave of dizziness washed in, and all feeling in his legs washed out. The numb limbs moved on their own, as if they were no longer attached to his nervous system. If one of his remaining soul attachments had snapped, he might die soon. Only a little time left. "Charlotte," he whispered, gasping, "I need to tell you something."

"Say whatever you need to say."

"I ... I love you. I always have. I always will. All those years, I missed you so much."

"Oh, Leo. I love you, too. And this time, I will stay with you to the end. I promise."

"Till death do us part?"

A laugh flavored her reply. "I'm already dead, Leo. It seems that even death can't keep us apart."

"Maybe so. Maybe so." Leo trudged on. It seemed that in mere moments, they would find out if her words would come true.

When the grayness cleared, Ben pushed a hand into his pocket and started the stopwatch. He stood with Iona in a yard that faced a humble cottage home. Enclosed by a wooden fence with a few missing boards and surrounded by fields populated by withered cornstalks and weed-infested pastures, the land appeared to be an abandoned farm.

"Ben?" Iona's voice quavered. "This is my home."

He looked at her. Still holding his hand, she stared at the front of the house. "Your home?" he repeated. "Where you lived with your adoptive parents?"

She nodded. "Why would the portal take us here? No evil is going on, at least not since the so-called angel killed my parents."

Ben pondered her words. So far, they had traveled to places where evil flourished, where despicable excuses for human beings oppressed innocent people. And at each location, he and Iona had been able to put a stop to the practices, at least temporarily. If Satan were really in charge of this series of quests, he wouldn't want to lose those battles. Maybe that meant God was really in control of where they were going, and Satan might have no idea what was happening beyond the planting of seeds and the collecting of fruit. But why Iona's farm home? That didn't make sense. "Can you tell where the seed's supposed to be planted?"

"I don't sense anything yet." She walked slowly past an open gate and climbed two stairs to the house's wraparound front porch. To the right, a swing hung from a pair of chains and swayed lazily in the soft breeze as leaves tumbled across the porch floor as if swept by an invisible broom.

Ahead, the front door stood ajar. She pushed it fully open and peered inside. "Everything's the same. Like no one's been here since I left." She waved a beckoning hand. "Come on. I'll show you my room."

Ben followed her inside to a living/family area with a worn green sofa and two straight-backed wooden chairs with upholstered seats. A small puddle of water lay on the varnished wood floor in front of one of the chairs, maybe from a roof leak. He inhaled through his nose. Mildew had set in. How long ago seemed impossible to know.

Iona led Ben to a bedroom to the right. She sat on a single bed, the mattress still dressed with white sheets and a pink blanket. "This is where I slept." She pointed across the room. "We put Little Brother's crib against that wall. It was my job to take care of him most of the time, especially at night so Papa could sleep. Mama said to bring Little Brother to her if he got too fussy. Since he was sick most of the time, he got fussy a lot." She let out a deep sigh. "It was hard sometimes, especially if I had to clean the stalls that day or hoe the fields. I didn't get much sleep when he fussed."

"You had a lot of adult responsibilities."

She nodded, a sad sort of smile inching across her face. "Especially after my parents died. I had to do everything."

"That must've been awful."

"It was. That's why I decided to sell the farm and go to the temple. I couldn't handle it."

"No wonder." Ben scanned the room. Peeling plaster and corner cobwebs broke the monotony of dull walls, as did the few thumbtacks that held only torn scraps of paper. He pointed at one of the scraps. "Did you have a photo there? A poster?"

"Um …" Iona averted her eyes. "A photo of me holding Little Brother in my lap. Mama tore it down after he died. Same with the others. She didn't want the memories."

"What about other decorations? Drawings? Birthday cards? Paper dolls? Pretty things girls like to look at?"

She shook her head, her eyes focused on the floor. "I never had time for anything like that, not with chores and taking care of Little Brother. At the end of the day, I always collapsed into bed, too exhausted for anything else."

"Only to take care of your brother during the night."

She brushed a tear from her cheek and nodded, saying nothing.

Ben eyed her forlorn posture—head low, shoulders drooped. So sad. Despondent. Was she ever allowed just to be a little girl? To climb trees, roll down hills, make mud pies? Did she blossom from frilly dresses to soldier camo through natural maturing? Or did she escape to become a warrior out of brutal necessity?

He sat on the bed next to her. "How about if we lighten the mood? What fond memories of this place can you tell me about?"

After brushing another tear, she looked at him, a tremulous smile emerging. "My tire swing." She leaped up and scurried from the bedroom. "C'mon. It's out back."

Ben rose and followed. A screen door at the rear of the house banged open, then swung shut. He passed through a small kitchen and found the door, Iona visible through the screen. She dumped water from a tire that hung by a rope attached to the limb of a huge oak about thirty paces away. She pushed her legs through the hole, her impish grin and bright eyes making her look about twelve years old, the same age she appeared to be the day they first met.

As Iona pumped her legs to make the tire sway, Ben hurried to her. "Want me to push you?"

She paused and looked at him, a hand on each side of the tire. "Um ... sure."

He grasped the rope. "Hasn't anyone pushed you before?"

"My friends a few times. I usually swung myself."

Ben studied the frayed rope and triple knots at both ends of the line. "Who hung the tire?"

"I did. Well, Lynette and Timmy helped some. You know, the kids who died."

"Yeah. I'm so sorry. Did you have anyone left to play with?"

"We never played much. Sometimes hide and seek. Freeze tag. Stuff like that. Helped each other with chores mostly." She shrugged. "After they died, I was alone. No friends, I mean. That's when I started learning how to shoot, first with a crossbow, then with guns."

Iona's words sent a spike through Ben's heart. He had to halt the conversation. "Time for a swing." He set his hands at the back of the tire and gave it a hefty shove.

Iona and the tire shot out in a high arc. As she let out a delighted squeal, it swung back. Ben pushed it again, even higher this time. Iona giggled like a little girl, maybe the happiest she had been in years.

After the fourth swing, Ben grabbed the tire and gave it a spin. The tire twirled, sending Iona's hair into a frenzy. She whooped and laughed, then called out, "You'd better stop me. I'm getting dizzy."

When Ben reached for the tire, the rope snapped. The tire flew on, hit the ground, and rolled with Iona still in it. After three or four rotations, she squeezed out and tumbled prostrate into a grassy area.

As she pushed up to hands and knees, Ben ran to her and knelt at her side, stifling a laugh. "Are you all right?"

She grasped a handful of grass and threw it in his face. The blades flew into his mouth and eyes. As he peeled grass from his tongue, she grinned. "Yeah, I feel great."

Ben wrapped his arms around her and wrestled her back to the ground. They tickled each other and laughed until their sides ached. Then they rolled to their backs and looked up at the clear blue sky. She slid her hand into his and turned her head toward him. "I think that's the most fun I've had in my whole life."

He smiled, his heart feeling like it might burst with joy. "Same. At least since I was a kid."

She gazed at him with a big smile of her own. Then, during the quiet moment, her smile wilted, and her eyes began sparkling with tears.

"Is something wrong?" Ben asked.

"Well …" She propped her head with a hand, her elbow on the ground. "Kat told me why you and she never had children, and it's really tragic because you always wanted to be a father."

He nodded. "That's true. I always have."

"Well, you would make a fantastic dad. I know you would. I'm so sorry it never happened. Really, really sorry."

Ben's throat narrowed. He swallowed to relieve the pressure. "Thank you for saying so."

"You're more than welcome." She rose to a sitting position and crossed her legs. "I guess all good times must come to an end. I have to find the place to plant the seed."

Ben rose as well and faced her. Her serious aspect said so much. Her brief transformation to little-girl mode had ended. It was time once again to be a warrior. "Any sensations?"

"I feel something." Her brow inched down as she swiveled her head. She leaned to the side and touched the spot where she had plucked grass earlier. "See how this grass is still kind of green and the rest is brown for the winter?"

Ben nodded. "It's a different variety, as if someone sodded that patch."

She grabbed two handfuls and pulled, but only the tops of the blades gave way. "Maybe so, but it's rooted now."

"Is that where the feeling's coming from?"

Her expression turned forlorn. "Yes. Sadness. Disappointment. Heartbreak."

"Let's check a bit deeper." Ben withdrew his knife and plunged the blade through the grass. It penetrated easily. "The soil's soft. Maybe it's been dug up before."

She winced. "The feeling's stronger than ever. I think I should plant the seed here."

He twisted the blade and drew it out. "Now there's a hole to plant it in."

She shifted to her knees, pulled the black seed from her pocket, and dropped it into the hole.

Ben cut into the surrounding soil and covered the seed. "Let's give it plenty of room." He and Iona rose to their feet and backed away.

Within seconds, a black shoot sprouted from the ground, already covered with rough bark that looked like wrinkled charcoal. It grew at the usual hyper-fast rate, shooting out thick roots that burst through the ground with knobby protrusions. Dirty glass bottles and bent cans erupted with the roiling earth, as if a dump site were vomiting its contents.

When the tree finished growing, it stood only about twenty feet tall, and the girth of spindly leafless branches spread out only fifteen feet or so, every inch of bark as black as it could be. Yet, no fruit had formed, and the branches seemed incapable of supporting any. No icicle-shooting flowers or fire-breathing dragons or poison-peddling children anywhere in sight.

Iona pinched the end of a low branch and broke it off. "If this were any other tree, I'd think it was dead. It's as brittle as onion skin."

"Then we have to wait." Ben fished the stopwatch out. "Twenty minutes left. I guess time slipped away from us."

"That's all right. It was fun."

"Definitely."

"What's this?" Iona strode to the base of the trunk and knelt. She brushed dirt away from the top of what appeared to be an old, rusted toolbox. "Papa used to bury trash in the yard, so I wasn't surprised to see all that junk, but this is weird." She shook a padlock dangling at the box's front, but it wouldn't open. "Why would he bury a locked box?"

Ben withdrew the gun from his waistband. "Scoot back. I'll open it."

When Iona slid away on her knees, Ben stooped close and shot the lock. The bullet shattered it, and the lid flew open. A file folder with a couple of sheets of paper lay within, curled to fit inside. He pulled the file out, revealing a yellowed piece of paper underneath that looked like an article cut out of a newspaper.

Ignoring the paper for the moment, he sat on the ground next to the box and opened the folder. A headshot photo of a male teenager had been clipped to the top of the page. As he read the title and first paragraph, he summarized it for Iona. "It's a county sheriff's report on the death of Timothy Floyd." He showed Iona the photo.

"Yep. That's Timmy." She sat next to him. "Let's hear it."

"I'll jump straight to the conclusion." He read the report summary at the bottom out loud. "Although Timothy was only fourteen years old, he drove the family car for reasons unknown. When he came to a hilly road, he lost control, and the car plunged into a ravine. The medical examiner was unable to determine if he died immediately upon impact or because of the ensuing fire, but his body was burned beyond recognition. The examiner used dental records to identify him. Leland Martin, the investigating detective, suspected suicide, but Sheriff Niemann overruled his findings and concluded that mechanical failure caused the accident."

Ben looked up from the page. "How could they possibly determine that it was mechanical failure after a crash and a fire?"

Iona cocked her head. "And why would that folder be locked in a box here instead of filed at the station?"

"Not sure." Ben scanned the top of the page. "It has a stamp that looks like the sheriff office's seal—an original, not a copy. Someone took it from the office." He turned to the next page. "The second sheet is a medical examiner's report about an unnamed boy born to the Horace Macklin family."

"That's Papa."

"I know. So the unnamed boy is—"

"Little Brother. I didn't know they ever did an autopsy."

Ben searched the page for the authorization. "Requested by Leland Martin."

"The detective who suspected suicide in Timmy's crash."

"Right." Ben scanned down to the conclusion and read it silently. The boy had been poisoned over a span of several weeks, and DNA evidence suggested that Horace Macklin was not the boy's father. His mother conceived him with a different man.

Ben's face flamed with heat. Obviously Iona had no clue about this report. What had Horace Macklin done? Did he poison Little Brother as revenge over his wife's infidelity? Did he also steal this file? If so, why hadn't he simply burned it? Could these reports be souvenirs? Reminder tokens of twisted evil for the blackest of hearts?

"C'mon, Ben. Spit it out. What did the examiner find?"

"Just a second." He plucked the newspaper article from the box. Underneath lay a few photos scattered about. He could check those later. He read the article's headline—"Sheriff Detective Murder Still Unsolved." Stifling a gulp, he searched the article for the detective's name, already knowing what it would be. Yes, Detective Leland Martin was murdered a few weeks after the death of Iona's brother. And only one way all of this could have been tucked away from scrutiny. The sheriff was complicit. But why?

Iona gasped.

Ben looked up from the article. She held one of the photos, staring at it with her mouth open. She ripped it in half, threw it at the box, and covered her face. "No, no, no!"

Breathless, Ben set a hand on her shoulder. "What's in the photo?"

She lowered her hands and looked at him, tears streaming. "Timmy. He's ... he's ..." She shook her head. "I can't say it." She covered her face again and sobbed.

Ben laid the folder down and scooted on his knees to the photo. He picked up the top half. It showed Timmy, Horace, and an older man from the waist up, all shirtless and smiling, though Timmy's smile seemed forced. Ben spotted the bottom half lying face down nearby. Imagining what could've made Iona break down was enough. No need to look. It was all coming together—what Horace had done to Timmy. And the older man, likely the sheriff, had taken part.

When he turned back to Iona, she held the sheriff's folder open on her lap. As she read, her eyes widened, and her mouth dropped open again.

He shuffled toward her on his knees. "Iona, that autopsy report is—"

"No!" Her cheeks as red as fire, she threw the folder on the ground and shouted, "It can't be true!"

He reached for her, but she slapped his hand. "Get away from me!" She shot to her feet and ran toward a fenced pasture, screaming a wordless wail. She threw open a gate and stopped, staring at the field of grass, pulling her hair as she breathed in chaotic spasms. The betrayal she felt had to be tearing her heart to shreds.

Ben leaped up and jogged after her, his sore foot's bandage finally giving way and hampering his pace. He slowed to a stop about ten paces from her and checked the watch again. Only eight minutes left. He studied her posture. With her back to him, her fists tight at her sides, she was probably battling another screaming eruption. He called in a calm tone, "Iona."

She spun toward him, her eyes red and her cheeks still aflame. She swallowed and answered with a squeaky, "What?"

"Less than eight minutes left. We need to go soon."

Her voice dropped to a near whisper. "But there's ... there's no fruit."

Ben glanced back at the tree. As she had said, the tree had not yet borne any visible fruit. At that moment, Azrael's words returned to mind. *The deadliest fruit is borne of hidden poison, for it disguises itself as revelation.*

He pondered the words. With the other trees, the danger was obvious—icicle spears, dragon fire, and a toxic touch, but this apparently dead tree bore nothing at all except uprooted secrets in an old box. Yet, they were toxic all the same. Revelation. Betrayal, the deadliest of all poisons.

Now the insidious nature of this tree had come to light. It revealed her adoptive father's betrayal, and she consumed it. The poison had infected her heart. Maybe returning to the table would free her from its clutches. "Iona, the tree did bear fruit. We should collect it and go back to the Oculus Gate. You still have to finish your quest."

Her fists again tight, Iona leaned forward and shouted, "I don't *want* to destroy hell. Papa deserves to be there. He's the evilest person who ever lived. I hope he suffers forever. Longer than forever. And those other people. The traffickers. The baby killers. The researchers. I hope they all go to hell and stay there forever."

Ben gazed at her furious pose. She was right. And now it was clear why God sent them here. He wanted Iona to believe that he was a perfect judge, and he wanted this earthly surrogate father to reflect his love instead of his wrathful judgment.

"Iona," Ben said softly. "What about Leo?"

Her fists loosened as she looked at the ground. "I ..." She swallowed and continued her downward stare. "I don't know what to do about Leo. Even if I did destroy hell, Alex might change her mind about trying to heal him. We wouldn't have any leverage left to make her do it. So it won't matter. Nothing matters. It's all hopeless."

Ben bit his lip. The poison of treachery had crushed her spirit, obliterated every ounce of resolve. He cast a quick prayer to heaven. *Lord, what should I do?* But no time remained to wait for an answer. The only idea that came to mind was to go for broke. "Iona."

She tightened her fists again and stamped a foot as she glared at him. "I told you to get away from me. Everyone's corrupt. Everyone lies. Everyone—" A new sob throttled her voice. "I can't trust anyone."

The urge to say "You can trust me" seemed overwhelming, but they were just words. What could he do to *show* her light in the midst of her darkness?

Iona opened her mouth to speak again, but a spasm rocked her body. She fell to her knees and stared at Ben, her eyes wide with terror. Then she toppled to the side.

Ben rushed to her, dropped to his knees, and gathered her into his arms. As he cradled her, she breathed in chaotic gasps, her eyes tightly shut. Dark, throbbing raised lines ran along her face, like veins pulsing with black blood. "Iona! Can you hear me?"

She twitched as if ready to erupt in convulsions. He held her closer in a tight embrace. That calmed her down, but might another spasm come soon? This poison had not only infected her heart, but also had coursed throughout her body. What could he do to stem this septic flood?

As if answering his question, Azrael's second truth echoed in his mind. *A father's betrayal is the source of that poison, and only a father's sacrifice can heal a heart that has been infected by it.*

He shouted toward the sky, "But I'm not her father. How can I sacrifice for her?"

No answer came except his own words returning to mind, moments before they prayed.

We shouldn't go on the fourth quest thinking we're invincible just because we survived the other three without too much trouble.

And now the fourth tree proved the prophecy. They were far from invincible, and they needed help. Trying to calm himself, he looked into the sky again and spoke as clearly as his quaking body could manage. "God, I don't know what to do. Iona's been infected by the poison of betrayal. How can I heal her with a sacrifice if I'm not her father?"

Again he waited for an answer, but only a quiet whisper entered his ears, a light breeze brushing the nearby trees. Then another whisper blended in, almost too quiet to hear. "Ben?"

"Iona?" He looked at her ashen face. The dark lines still pulsed across her cheeks and forehead. "Can you hear me now?"

"Yes." She blinked, as if just waking up. "Are we back at the Gate?"

Squelching a sob, he held her as close as he could. "No. We're still at your farmhouse."

She winced. "Why can't I move anything? My legs. My arms."

"Poison. From the tree. Too much to explain. But I have to find a way to heal you. Azrael said a father has to sacrifice for you to heal a father's treachery."

As she gazed at him, she licked her dry lips. "You ... you already have."

"Sacrificed for you?"

She nodded.

"But I'm not your father."

"You rescued me ... from a dragon."

"The tree? I just threw a grenade in its mouth. That wasn't much."

Her face tightened, the dark veins swelling. "You took ... a bullet for me."

"A minor wound. Not much of a sacrifice at all. You're the one who put those vermin down."

His second denial seemed to expand the veins further, as if reflecting her disappointment in his answer.

After a strained swallow, her voice strengthened. "You went to hell for me."

Her words sank in. Warmth ran along his skin and penetrated his heart. She was right. He couldn't deny it. And he shouldn't deny it. He did willingly jump into hell to save her. "Yes, Iona. And I'd do it all over again. In a heartbeat."

"I ... I know you would." The veins turned gray and receded. "That's what fathers do."

"But I'm not your—"

She pressed her finger against his lips. "Shhh, shhh."

"You can move your arms now?"

She nodded. "Barely. My legs won't budge, though."

"Then I'll carry you." With Iona still in his arms, Ben rose to his feet. "I'm guessing we have less than two minutes left."

"What about the fruit? I can't make a decision about destroying hell without it."

Ben carried her toward the tree. "It's the box. The stuff that was in it, I mean."

"The papers and photos?" As she blinked again, the dark veins shrank further and began receding. "That's weird."

When they arrived, Ben set her on the ground and checked the stopwatch. "Fifteen seconds left." He grabbed the folder and photos, stuffed them into the box, and closed the lid.

"I'll carry it." Iona reached for the box. "Put it in my lap. It's my burden to bear."

"Okay. For now." When he set the box in her lap and scooped her up again, their surroundings fractured into thousands of pieces, like a jigsaw puzzle breaking apart. Within seconds, the grayness returned. He stood next to the table between two of the chairs. The flickering candles had dwindled to stubs, barely able to cast light beyond the empty backpack on the table. Soon, the room would be too dark to see anything.

Ben set Iona in one of the chairs, took the box from her, and thumped it onto the table.

"How are we going to get the fruit into that little hole?" Iona asked.

"Good question." Ben eyed the box and the hole. "Wadding every page and photo won't compress the stuff nearly enough to fit."

She scowled, her face nearly clear of the dark veins. "Then burn it. Burn it all. We'll cram the ashes into the hole."

Ben picked up one of the candles and opened the box. "Are you sure?"

"Positive. I know that sheriff. The angels killed him a couple of weeks before I left for the temple. The dead are dead, and the guilty are in hell. If Mama went there, too, that's ..." Her words pitched higher. "That's up to God." After a tight swallow, her voice steadied. "I want her reputation to rest in peace."

"I understand." Ben lifted a page and lit the bottom corner with the candle. The flame crawled up the paper, growing as it spread. When he dropped it into the box and put the candle back in place, he and Iona watched the contents burn. Sizzles and pops erupted, and sparks infused the rising smoke in a swirling dance, as if celebrating the destruction of the foul contents.

Once everything had burned, Ben dumped the ashes onto the table's surface. "They're too hot to touch. We'll have to wait a few minutes."

"I'll probably need those minutes." Still sitting in the chair, Iona massaged her thighs. "They're tingling now. I think that's a good sign."

"I hope so." Ben crouched next to her and looked her in the eye. "In the meantime, have you made a decision? Are you going to try to destroy hell?"

Chapter Twenty-Four

With a felt-tip marker in hand, Kat stood close to Austin as he cradled the sphere on his palm, his other hand pinching Lem's severed thumb. It had taken way too long to cut it off and clean the blood while she and Austin took shelter in the cruiser. The slightest bit of blood on the print kept the sphere from recognizing it.

Austin used the thumb to press a button, one of the few on this section of the sphere Kat hadn't yet marked with an X. The tower emitted a new tone, a shrill, high-pitched note.

He nodded. "I think that's it. F-seven."

"Finally." Kat wrote "F7" on the button, blotting out the 12.58 that had already been printed there, presumably by Harrid. To this point, she and Austin hadn't been able to figure out what those numbers stood for, but they probably helped Lemuel know what to do. Too late to ask him. "Okay, now we need G-one. It's real low, right?"

"Right. The lower notes are on the other side." Austin rolled the orb over and pressed a button with the thumb. The tower's note shifted to a rumbling bass tone that sent vibrations into the ground and Kat's numbed feet. He shook his head. "B-one, I think."

"Got it." She marked that button with the pen.

"I'd better go," Jack said. "Now that you're not cutting body parts in the cruiser, I should fly to check on Leo."

Kat looked up at the sky. Clouds raced away, leaving only a smattering of snowflakes swirling in the air. "Good idea. I unlocked it with my voice. It should let you—"

"Someone's coming," Austin said. "On the portal wheel. A woman."

Kat swiveled that way. The woman sprinted toward them on the portal floor, now about a hundred yards away, her features washed out by the radiance.

"It's Trudy," Austin said.

Jack whistled. "She's flying like a bat out of ... well, you get the picture."

A few seconds later, Trudy leaped off the portal floor and broke into their huddle, gasping for breath. "I saw ... Leo. ... He needs help. ... We have ... to stop ... the portal wheel."

Jack shoved her arm. "Right, genius. That's exactly what we've been trying to do."

"Stuff it, Jack. If Leo doesn't make it, the whole world's a goner."

"The whole world? You mean Earth?"

"I'll explain later." Trudy glanced around. "Where's Lemuel?"

"Dead." Austin showed her the symphony sphere. "We have the device that stops the engine."

"But Lemuel knows the notes to stop it. How can you—"

"I know other notes that'll work," Kat said, "but we're guessing which buttons to push. And we're not even sure we're getting them right. We're relying on Austin's ear."

Shivering, Trudy pulled a wrinkled sheet of paper from her pocket and smoothed it out on Kat's back. "What note do you need?"

"G-one."

While Jack shed his parka, Trudy's eyes darted back and forth as she scanned the page. "G-one ... G-one ... Frequency forty-nine hertz ... wavelength ..." She thumped the page with a finger, still on Kat's back. "That button should be marked seven oh four, the note's wavelength in centimeters."

Austin rolled the sphere and set a severed thumb on the button. "Got it."

Trudy grimaced. "Is that Lemuel's?"

"What's wrong, Doctor?" Jack asked as he draped his parka over her while balancing on a crutch. "Queasy if you don't do the surgery yourself?"

"Get a life, Jack. We have a planet to save."

"Copy that, Sis." He crutched toward the cruiser. "Good thing the storm's clearing. Search and rescue in a blizzard would be pretty hopeless."

Trudy nodded at Austin. "Go ahead."

He pressed the button with the thumb. Another low note boomed from the tower. "Yeah. Pretty sure that's G-one. But I have to play the first note again to put them in the right order. I played a different one in between when we were guessing."

"Okay. Do it. Then we'll play the next note right after."

"And it's the last one," Kat said. "B-eight. Start looking it up."

Austin pushed the first note with Lem's thumb. "B-eight will be an ear splitter."

As the F7 sounded, the cruiser lifted off with Jack at the helm. Kat imagined him searching for Leo, probably by sight rather than the thermal scanner. No way would his echo show up from the portal engine floor, whether sprawled in an unconscious state or still walking.

When Austin played the G1, Kat's image of Leo hobbled on, barely able to stay in front of the portal wall. Fortunately, in a few seconds, he could finally stop, but did he know he had only one minute to get through the portal before the wheel would die for good?

The B8 note split the air, a high-pitched squeal. Kat covered her ears and continued focusing on her image of Leo. No, he didn't know about the one-minute limit. He left when Lemuel was still alive, before they decided to use the kill-switch notes. And now Jack was gone. He couldn't relay the message to Leo.

Kat heaved a long sigh, sending a jet of vapor into the wind. No use telling Trudy or Austin about her worries. Only God could help Leo now.

Leo walked on, his legs numb, though sharp pain knifed up from them into his hips and back. Limping didn't help at all. Both sides hurt equally. It would take a miracle to continue more than a few seconds longer.

"Leo," Charlotte said from the cloak's hood. "You can do it. One step at a time. Listen to my beat. Step ... step ... step."

Leo clumped a foot down with each of her commands. Her steady voice helped, but it couldn't last.

A knee buckled. He stumbled forward and smacked his cheek on the floor. He twisted his neck to see the portal partition. In two seconds, it would overtake him. When it drew within inches of his body, it suddenly stopped. The wall's radiance expanded and flowed over him, warming his skin and blinding his eyes.

When his vision cleared, he looked out over what used to be the dark Alaskan landscape. A circular wooden table with a tree growing out of the center stood in the midst of grayness—nothing but a sea of slate all around.

"What happened, Leo?" Charlotte asked. "Are you all right?"

"I'm still alive, if that's what you mean." He pushed against the floor and rose to his hands and knees, every muscle and sinew screaming with pain. "But I feel terrible."

"The portal wheel stopped. Did it work?"

"You're a Reaper. Can't you see from the cloak?"

"In a limited way. All I see is a bright glow."

"My own eyes might be deceiving me, but I see a table and three chairs in a gray room. But I don't see Ben or Iona."

A man walked into the room and set a redheaded girl on one of the chairs. She held a rectangular object in her lap, maybe a toolbox. She had to be Iona, and the man who set her there was likely Ben.

"Iona," Leo called. "Ben. Can you help a wounded warrior get to one of those chairs?"

They appeared to be carrying on a conversation, inaudible from where he perched and oblivious to his call. He probably had to get off the portal wheel to open an audio channel, or whatever Harrid the ghostly geek would've labeled it. "I see Ben and Iona, but they can't hear me. I'm going to try to walk to them. Or maybe crawl."

"You're doing so well," Charlotte said. "Do you need me to talk you through it again?"

"No. I can manage." Leo crawled toward the edge of the portal floor, slowly, painfully. His head pounded, and dark streaks crossed his vision. Were his soul's final attachments to his brain ready to snap? It seemed so. He already felt like an unmoored ship drifting out to sea, burning and sinking into the deep.

Ahead, the plane separating him from Ben and Iona lay only a few feet away. It shimmered like wrinkled plastic wrap, and static lines rippled across the scene. Was the portal closing?

Summoning his last grain of strength, he threw himself toward the room. When he struck the portal plane, an electric shock sizzled through his body, then he dropped, and blackness filled his mind.

Alexandria walked in reverse in front of a portal partition and peered through it with her enhanced vision. Although only one eye worked as well as it should, it would be sufficient. On the other side, Caligar stood among the tower debris staring straight back in her direction, though he certainly couldn't see her.

Benjamin had probably stationed the big oaf there as a guard in case a certain Queen of Hell returned, knowing that Caligar's size would give him a physical advantage that could overcome her martial arts skills. True. But her ability to switch to ghost mode immediately upon arrival would make her impossible to catch.

She touched the broken end of the arrow still protruding from her abdomen, another reason to transform into ghost mode right away. She withdrew the audio recorder from her pocket. It was small enough to quickly transfer with her to ghost mode and back. No worries about that.

Only one worry persisted. At any moment, Iona might finish her quest and unwittingly destroy Earth. She had certainly spent more than enough time on the quest, which meant that she might have failed and could be dead. Or Benjamin, being the principled purist that he was, might very well have talked her out of completing it.

Either way, Earth was still doomed. Harrid's mirror portal on Viridi would see to that, and activating it as soon as possible made sense. Why wait for the impetuous redheaded brat and her holier-than-thou guardian? Especially since the guardian had proved himself to be smarter than most. He might find a way to foil the entire plan.

The portal wheel stopped. Alexandria stood close to it and let the expanding glow wash over her. A moment later, she turned toward the former Alaska scene. As before, Caligar stood close to the portal wall, but he still seemed unaware of her presence. That would change in the blink of an eye.

She stepped off the portal wheel and into the dim light of Viridi. The moment Caligar saw her, he charged. She dodged a split second before his meaty hand could grab her throat and let him stumble past as she began her transformation to ghost mode. He stopped short of the portal, snorting like a bull. "I will destroy you, witch."

When her transformation finished, she hummed through a laugh. "Caligar, why the incensed hatred? I am your new roommate, so to speak. I plan to live on this planet for the rest of my days and then forever. I think a peace treaty is in order."

He jabbed a finger at her. "You killed my precious daughter. I will never be at peace with you."

Alexandria feigned a sympathetic sigh. "Yes, I can understand. No decent father would make a truce with his daughter's killer, but I know something you don't. Lacinda is alive."

He gasped. "What? How can that be true? I was told that you—"

"Yes, yes, I know. But I will prove it to you." She turned the audio recorder on and displayed it in her palm.

Lacinda spoke through its tiny speaker. "Father. I am on Earth. Alive. Someone put me on a … a device? He called it a portal wheel. I am in Alaska, but I am warm enough. And safe. For now."

Alexandria switched off the playback. More of the recording remained to be played, but that would have to wait for Caligar's obvious question. Even this towering ignoramus would think of it.

Caligar stared at the recorder. "How can I be sure that the voice is really Lacinda's? I was told that you mimicked her voice through my android. I don't want to be fooled again."

"I anticipated your question and asked her to say something I couldn't possibly know." Alexandria switched the recorder back on.

"I could speak to him in our native tongue."

Alexandria's voice followed, quieter, as if recorded from farther away. "No, I want to understand what you're saying."

"Very well." After a short pause, Lacinda's voice continued. "Father, I know you remember the day when I was on a hunting … expedition, I think is the right word. I broke my foot and—"

"Stop." Caligar raised a hand. "I don't want to hear anything more."

Alexandria turned the recorder off. "Why not? You do remember the event she's describing, don't you?"

"I remember, but you could have learned about it while she was your prisoner." Caligar narrowed his eyes in a skeptical manner. "You had the opportunity to prove your claim by allowing Lacinda to speak our language, but you avoided doing so, giving me sufficient reason to doubt your words."

Alexandria pursed her lips. This giant was smarter than she had realized. "Sufficient reason? Are you saying you *don't* doubt my word in spite of the lack of proof? You believe Lacinda is alive?"

Caligar nodded. "I do believe you. I can feel it."

"Ah. A father's intuition is powerful." She slid the recorder back into her pocket. "If you want me to restore Lacinda to you, I demand a peace treaty that gives me half of Viridi. You will keep the other half. But I need assurances that I can trust you to keep your side of the bargain."

"It is said in your world that a verbal contract and a handshake were once an iron-clad contract, though that is true no longer. Here, we have a similar solemn vow, and its force remains intact." He withdrew a knife from his belt, pulled his braid to the front, and sliced it off at the neckline. "The most solemn vow I can make is to cut off my braid and give it to you with a handshake. That binds me to my word forever. Will you accept that?"

Alexandria looked Caligar in the eye. No sign of deception. This quaint tradition meant a lot to him, and of course he wanted his daughter back. "I will accept it, but I also need access to your mirror portal immediately."

"To contact the person holding Lacinda, to tell him to send her through the portal?"

"Yes, of course. I'm not going to risk going back to Earth myself to tell him."

"Very well." Caligar extended his hand, the braid held in his palm by his thumb. "I agree to your terms."

Alexandria returned to physical mode and shook his hand. "May the peace between us last for many years to come."

Iona nodded toward the pile of ashes. "I want to see the bomb no matter what I decide to do. We've come this far. Let's see what the fruit does."

"Fair enough." Ben used the empty backpack to sweep the still-hot ashes into the hole in the tree trunk. The three colors drained from the network of veins on the table's surface and flowed into the same hole. Then blackness oozed into the trunk and filled the bark, making it look like charcoal.

Like oily blood, the fruit's juices crawled up the trunk in forking arteries that threaded into the branches. The shimmering leaves darkened, as if a shadow had cast a pall of gloom over the once-radiant tree. The leaves crinkled and dropped to the table, first one by one, then by the dozens in a raining cascade of lifeless black ashes that dissolved on impact. In less than a minute, only a charcoal skeleton remained, its spindly arms void of any life. Yet, the candles burned on, less than an inch of wax remaining in each.

A loud click sounded, then a hum. A door slid open in the trunk where they had found the stopwatch, revealing a cone-shaped object that looked a lot like the cap for the Liberty missile.

Ben reached into the shaft and slid the cap out onto the table. Diode lights blinked all across the metallic surface—blue, red, and yellow. The hum seemed to originate from the bomb itself, apparently a sign that it had been fully fueled by the fruit and now sat armed and ready. "The bomb, I assume."

"Definitely." Iona pointed. "And it has blue, green, and red buttons. Just like on Liberty."

"So you push blue first, then green, then red."

"Right." Iona gazed at Ben, her brow deeply knitted. "But I'm still not sure what to do. I think—"

Something sizzled. A man flew into the room, thudded onto the floor, and rolled to the base of the table face down, groaning. Charlotte's cloak covered his body from head to thighs.

"Leo!" Iona tried to push herself off her chair, but Ben stopped her.

"I'll take care of him." He looked in the direction Leo had come from. A window flickered, then disappeared. The portal that brought him to the Oculus Gate had come and gone in a flash. He crouched at Leo's side and hoisted him into one of the chairs.

Leo sat in a woozy sway, his eyes blinking as he looked at them. "Iona? Ben?"

"Yes," Iona said, reaching a hand toward him. "How did you get here?"

Ben pushed her chair arm-to-arm with his, allowing them to hold hands.

"The tale is far too long to tell," Leo said. "The important fact is that I made it."

Ben looked into Leo's eyes. They seemed relatively clear. "So you were *trying* to get here?"

"Yes. That much I know." He scratched his head through his dense, ragged mane. "What I don't remember is why. Only a vague notion that I have to help you two somehow."

Iona pushed hair from his forehead and massaged his scalp. "Your soul connections, right? You have to rest. We don't want them to break."

"What good are they if I can't remember why I came here? I know it was something critical."

"Let's review," Ben said as he pulled the third chair close. "I'll summarize what's going on here. Maybe that'll trigger your memory."

"Yes. Yes. That might help."

Ben began relating the tale. Not knowing how much time they had, he couldn't guess how quickly to tell it, but when Iona broke in at several points to add details, he went with the flow and included as much as he could remember, including how the bomb worked, its limited physical explosiveness and realm-destroying impact, Iona's ghost-mode protection from it, and the Oculus Gate's impermeability, as well as the fact that the detonation would send everyone back where they came from.

When Ben finished, Leo set his hands over his ears. "I think you filled my brain to capacity. The information is leaking." When he lowered his hands, blood covered his fingers. He blinked at the sight. "Well, that's a bad sign."

"Leo!" Iona touched his earlobe. "Blood's oozing out. Not a lot, but any at all can't be good."

"Then we have to move along," Leo said.

"Right. The sooner I do this, the sooner we can get you back to Trudy to see what she can do to help you. Alex is probably gone for good."

"True, but no more talk about that. How are your legs feeling?"

"Better." She pushed on the chair arms, rose to her feet, and shifted her hands to the tabletop to keep her balance. "See? I can stand."

Leo narrowed his eyes. "Pretty wobbly, I think."

"But they're getting stronger all the time. I'll practice going to ghost mode. By the time I get the transformation down to five seconds, I'm sure I'll be able to carry the bomb into hell."

"What's your fastest time so far? An estimate."

"Um ... maybe twenty seconds. But I never concentrated on speed. On Earth, I couldn't safely transform without shooting into the sky. But I can find out real quick if I'm safe here." With the bomb on the table in front of her, she closed her eyes. "Transforming now."

"Wait." Ben whipped out the stopwatch and pressed the start button. "Go."

She scrunched her brow. Her hands and arms faded, then her torso and legs with no sign of a force lifting her into the air. Finally, her head joined the rest of her body, all semitransparent. "Done."

Ben stopped the watch and looked at it. "Twenty-four seconds. Way too slow."

Her head turned opaque, her expression frustrated. "I can do it faster. I just need more practice." When the rest of her body returned to normal, she sighed. "But do we have enough time?"

"We'll take the time. Just keep practicing."

"Will do." She took the stopwatch from Ben. "I'll time myself. The watch is small enough to transform with me."

While Iona practiced, Leo tugged on Ben's sleeve and drew him close. He pulled his hood up as if it might help shield his whisper. "Are you thinking what I'm thinking?"

Ben whispered as well. "That we can't let Iona take the bomb into hell no matter how much she practices?"

"Exactly. I'm glad we're on the same wavelength. Even if she practices herself down to one second, it's too dangerous, especially in her weakened state. I don't want her risking her life to save mine."

"Or mine. I've been opposed to destroying hell from the beginning, but I don't know what options we have. We agreed that God could create hell again if he wanted to, but that seemed like a lame dodge to me."

"True, but considering the alternative, that you and Iona would be trapped here for eternity, maybe I could test how lame the dodge really is. I could take the bomb into hell and beg God to strike me down if I shouldn't ..." Leo blinked. "Charlotte?"

Ben drew his head back. "Charlotte? Is she here?"

Leo tapped a finger on the hood. "In the cloak. I had forgotten until I pulled the hood up. She speaks to me through it."

"Yes, I've experienced that."

"What, Charlotte?" After listening quietly for a moment, Leo groaned. "Oh, right. I remember now. I can't believe I forgot."

"Remember what?" Ben asked.

"The critical reason I came. The trees you planted tied hell and Earth together. If you destroy hell, you'll destroy Earth with it. It seems that Alex spilled the information when Trudy forced her back to Earth. Alex doesn't want to be a mouse caught in her own trap."

Ben felt his mouth drop open. Now everything was beginning to make sense. The soils of suffering were the closest places to hell on Earth, the borders of each realm where the greatest evils in the world took place. And Alex knew he would go with her to help her and keep her safe from tree to tree. He pounded a fist on the table. "Satan and Alex knew all along what planting the trees would do. This changes everything."

"Then what do we do?" Leo asked.

"We have one option left. Detonate the bomb here. It will destroy only this realm, the Oculus Gate. Since these walls are impervious to the blast, no other realms would be harmed. The person holding the bomb would die, but the other two would escape. In theory, anyway. Satan told us that when the bomb detonates, we would be automatically transported to the point where we entered."

Leo stroked his chin. "I see. Like the proverbial grenade in a foxhole. One person dives over it, and the others are protected, though the diver is obliterated."

"Exactly. And an angel told us that Satan was bound to the truth. He wasn't lying about anything he told us."

"Easy decision, then. I will detonate the bomb here while you and Iona escape to Alaska. It is better that I sacrifice myself than for either of you. I'm dying anyway." Leo touched his ear and showed Ben the fresh blood on his finger. "I'm not going to last much longer."

"With rest and Trudy's expertise, you'll be all right. And you're Iona's father. She needs a real father who'll love her. Not like that scoundrel who adopted her."

Leo's shoulders sagged. "Yes, that part of the story was the saddest of all, but you can be a father to her. Only a blind man wouldn't notice how much you love her."

"I don't deny that I love her, but remember the part of my story about a father sacrificing for her to heal her? Apparently, it worked with me being the sacrifice, so I should be the one to finish my sacrifice so she can be healed completely. You saw for yourself that she still has a ways to go."

"And my sacrifice would likely do the same." Leo blew a sigh. "Listen, Ben, we could argue this forever. We'll settle this the way your commander and the doctor did. We'll flip a coin."

Ben squinted. "A coin toss to decide who lives or dies?"

"Is that method good enough for your commander, but not good enough for you?"

Ben again looked at Iona and counted the seconds of her latest try. She was getting faster, maybe seven seconds now. Once she made the five-second goal, she would insist on being the one to detonate the bomb. Since she had the power to elude them, it might be impossible to stop her.

"Okay," Ben said with a sigh. "Do you have a coin?"

"I do." Leo fished a quarter out of his pocket and balanced it on his thumb and forefinger. "Call it." He flipped the quarter into the air.

"Tails," Ben said as he watched the coin's flight.

The quarter clinked to the floor, the tails side showing. "Tails it is, Ben. You win, in a manner of speaking."

Ben's throat narrowed. He had won the privilege to sacrifice himself for Leo and Iona, just as Chantal sacrificed herself to rid the world of the so-called angels. The cost would be high. Kat would miss him, but she would understand. She had Jack and Trudy to—

"What are you two doing?" Iona asked, her eyes narrowed to slits. "What are you up to?"

Leo snatched the coin from the floor. "Making a decision between gentlemen."

"What decision? What are you trying to hide from me?"

"Hide from you? Have you been a cabalist for so long that you don't trust us?"

She blinked. "Cabalist? What the heck is a cabalist?"

"Someone who is skilled in esoteric matters, as you were as an angel aide. You lost trust in them because of their treachery, and now you're a skeptic. It stands to reason that you—"

"You're dodging my question. The only reason to flip a coin is to …" Iona's eyes widened. "Oh, no you're not. This is no time for chivalry." She prodded her chest with a thumb. "*I'm* the one going to hell. Neither of you can transform at all, and I've got it down to seven seconds. I'm almost there."

Ben shook his head. "Not good enough. Besides, I just learned from Leo that destroying hell will destroy Earth with it." He picked up the bomb. "Leo can explain all that, but I'm setting it off here in this room to destroy the Oculus Gate. You and Leo will go back to Alaska."

"What?" Iona said in a near shriek. "Ben. No. You'll die." She looked at Leo. "Tell him. I'm the one who has to do it. Like I said, I'm down to seven seconds. Don't let him go all hero on us."

"Well …" Leo rolled his eyes upward as if trying to look at his cloak's hood. "Yes, Charlotte? … Oh. … Really? That bad?" He let out another sigh and gazed at Iona. "My dear daughter …" He caressed her cheek with a finger. "I love you so much."

Tears sparkled in her eyes. "And I love you, Leo, but we have to—"

"Charlotte says you can hear her. She has something to say to you."

"Okay." Iona sniffed. "Go ahead, Charlie."

As she stared at Leo, she cocked her head, apparently listening to a voice only a Reaper could hear. "Yes, I understand. But—" As she continued listening, tears dripped down her cheeks as her voice pitched into a wail. "No, Charlie. No. I can't let him."

Leo drew his arms out of the cloak sleeves but left the hood over his head. "I'm ready."

"Ready for what?" Ben asked.

Iona spun toward Ben. "Don't let him. He's going to—"

"Hush, Iona." Leo lunged at Ben, swiped the bomb from him, and pushed the first two buttons in order. "Run for cover!" He held the bomb close to his chest with both arms, a finger over the red button. "Now!"

Ben grabbed Leo's wrist, but he jerked away. "I won the toss," Ben growled. "We had a deal."

"I'm changing the deal. You have five seconds to save Iona." Leo pushed the red button. "Go!"

Chapter Twenty-Five

Ben reached for Iona, but she dodged and snatched Leo's cloak, falling as her legs buckled and gave way. Ben scooped her up cloak and all and leaped into a headlong dive. An explosion rocked the room. In an instant, darkness shrouded everything. Clutching Iona with both arms, Ben flew through the air. They landed on their sides, both grunting on impact, then slid across a smooth surface and into something soft and cold.

Iona rolled away from Ben and struggled to her feet. She stood next to him, barely visible in the dimness as she held Charlotte's cloak over an arm. A hard shiver fractured her words. "Are you … all right?"

"I think so." She leaned over, grasped his wrist, and pulled him to his feet. A moonlit sky painted their shadows on the surrounding snow, and a few evergreen trees dotted the white landscape. "Are you?"

"No." A stiff breeze whisked through the trees, the only sound other than Iona's tortured voice. "I mean, my legs got better for some reason, but … but my heart hurts. My father …" She broke into a sob. "He's … he's dead, Ben. I didn't even … get to say goodbye."

He grasped her wrist and drew her into his embrace. "Iona, I'm so—"

She pulled free and stepped back. "I … um … I have to put Charlie's cloak on. It's cold."

"Yeah. Sure. Good idea." While Iona pushed her arms through the sleeves, Ben shivered hard. Her rejection of his touch injected as much cold as did the wind. But he couldn't think about himself, not when she was hurting so much. He pivoted in place, searching for a dense group of trees or maybe a building, but nothing lay in sight. "We need to find shelter. Fast."

"Maybe so." The stiffening wind seemed to swallow her ravaged voice. "But I don't really care if I freeze to death."

"Iona …" The urge to reach for her again seemed overwhelming, but he resisted. "Leo was a great man. One of the best I have ever known." Ben searched the heavens for the evil eye in the sky, but it was gone, completely vanished. Now only the normal stars cast their light from above. "And look," he said, pointing. "The Oculus Gate is gone. Forever. We never have to worry about aliens or any other cosmic intruders again. Leo did that for us. For everyone. He and Chantal are probably the greatest heroes the world has ever known." He shifted his pointing finger toward her. "And that hero gave his life for you more than for anyone else. Your father wants you to live."

She lowered her head. "I know." After a few seconds of silence, she looked at him again, a tight hand clutching her shirt at her chest. "But it hurts so much to live. I feel like roadkill. Squashed. Vulture bait."

Ben blew a vapor-filled sigh into the frigid air. "I understand. I felt the same way when I thought Kat had died. Sometimes I could barely take a breath."

"Right. It's … it's crushing. Like my heart is pressing on my lungs." She lowered her head again. "Like I'm back in hell."

"I know the feeling well." Ben scanned the sky. A strobing light pierced the darkness, drawing closer, flying maybe two miles away and about a hundred feet in the air. "I see a light. Looks like it's heading in our direction."

Iona looked up. "It is, but that doesn't mean the pilot will see us."

"No flashlights. All we have is our handguns. Let's rapid-fire both at the same time." Ben drew his gun from his waistband. "Ready?"

She chambered a round in her gun. "Ready." Her voice carried a lot less fire than usual.

"On three. Perpendicular to the craft's direction across the front. One … two … three!" Ben and Iona fired shot after shot until their magazines emptied. The wind seemed to swallow the bangs, reducing them to muffled pops. The pilot probably didn't hear them at all.

Still, the craft drew even closer, accelerating and descending as its beacon split into twin headlights. The hum of whipping rotors competed with the whistling wind.

"It's the angel cruiser!" Iona shouted.

Now only a foot or so above the ground, the landing propellers blasted fallen snow in every direction. Ben tried to look through the windshield to see who piloted the ship, but the flying flakes blocked his view. "Can you tell who the pilot is? If it's Alex, we could be in trouble. Our ammo's gone."

"No." Iona shielded her eyes with an arm as she blinked. "Too much snow."

A gust made the runners hit the ground with a sideways lurch that sent the cruiser barreling toward them in an icy slide. He grabbed her around the shoulders and flexed to dive, but it skidded to a stop, the passenger door only a few feet away. The door slid open, revealing the well-lit interior with seats in view, but no passengers.

Ben limped to the opening with Iona at his hip and peered inside. Jack crutched closer from the cockpit, a huge smile on his face. "Well, look what I found on my hunting expedition. A frozen kids' treat. Grape, judging by the purple color." He looked past Ben. "And a strawberry one." He frowned, though a hint of a smile broke the façade. "Put your hood up, girl, or you'll catch pneumonia."

Ben stepped to the side and boosted Iona as she hopped up to the interior floor, her hood down, as Jack had mentioned, snow speckling her fiery hair. She turned and extended a hand. Ben grabbed it and hauled himself in with her help. "Thanks, Jack. You're a godsend. Literally."

Jack pressed the control button, closing the door. "I was on a mission to find Leo and saw you two on the thermal scanner, too small for polar bears. Thought maybe you were lost penguins wandering at the wrong pole. Anyway, I heard a barrage of gunshots and guessed that penguins didn't pack heat so I checked it out." Grinning, he pulled Iona's hood up for her. "Penguins packing heat. Get it? Cold and heat?"

Iona stared at him blankly. "I get it."

"She's hurting, Jack." Pain roaring back into his wrist and foot, Ben limped to the front row of passenger seats and sat heavily on the window side, leaving the aisle seat open for Iona. She took the seat on the other side of the aisle, her head low and the hood shielding a view of her face.

Ben stared at the empty seat. The gap felt as empty as the hole in his heart. Leo's death and Iona's grief had dredged a gorge between them.

Jack crutched to the cockpit, settled into the pilot's seat, and swiveled it toward them. "Obviously something's hit you two like a freight train. What happened?"

Ben cleared his throat to keep his voice steady. "Leo's dead."

"Oh." Jack drew his head back. "Oh, wow. That's terrible."

"He gave his life to save us and probably everyone else on the planet." He nodded toward the front. "Let's head to the tower. We'll tell our story on the way. And since the cruiser's here, I assume Kat's there."

"She is. She had Harrid's key to shut the portal wheel down." Jack swiveled to the front, piloted the cruiser into the air, and accelerated into the night. "And Trudy forced Alex through the portal to Earth to make her vulnerable to her own Earth-destruction plans, and we suspect that she might have gone back to Viridi through the portal wheel." He craned his neck and looked at Ben. "Any word on that? Kat said Alex might have a backup plan to blast Earth out of existence."

"If Alex is on Viridi, she'll probably try to get access to Caligar's mirror portal to contact the Arctic tower network, but now that the Oculus Gate is gone, her plans are toast."

"Gone? Really?" Jack whistled. "How'd that happen?"

"Lots to tell." As they zoomed along, Ben gave Jack a summary of the harrowing quest with Iona. Since she stayed quiet, he left out some of the details. No need to mention her adoptive father's despicable acts.

Jack told of Lemuel's treachery, Kat's and Trudy's combined efforts to vaporize the portal wheel, and Austin's crucial help seeing through the portal walls.

While Jack talked, Iona sat quietly, staring at her lap while stifling sobs. Ben ached to try to hold her again. She had lost her father, a sacrificial warrior, a hero. She needed comfort, but she had made it clear that she wanted to be alone.

As he watched her grief, new warmth coursed through his body. His own grief rushed in like a cascading avalanche. He sucked in a breath, trying to squelch the upwelling sobs, but one broke through, then another, then another. Bitter tears flowed. It seemed that the losses of great men and women along with the release of years of pressure had burst a dam. He wept openly.

Iona rose from her seat, sat next to him, and curled her arm around his. They both shook as they wrapped their arms around each other and cried.

Jack cleared his throat. "I'll tell you the rest of the story later."

After a few minutes, he pointed forward. "Tower's in sight. And a fire I built. Who knew that giants from Viridi would burn so well?"

Ben sniffed and brushed tears from his cheeks as he drew his arms back from Iona. "Pretty morbid, but you do what you have to do."

"Waste not, want not." Jack slowed the cruiser and descended. "We'll be on the ground in a minute."

"Ben," Iona said, her voice steadier now, "I've been talking to Charlie."

He looked into her bloodshot eyes. "In your cloak?"

"Right. Back in the Oculus Gate room, she and I had an idea, and it worked. When Leo pushed the first two buttons, it was obvious no one could stop him, so she reached into his brain and started breaking his soul's connections, and I was ready to grab the cloak. Anyway, the moment he pushed the red button, Charlie pulled his soul into the cloak. He's inside. Kind of confused, but he's all right. Getting more lucid every minute."

Ben tightened his arm around hers. "Tell him that I think he's amazing. A true hero. And I'll make sure the world learns what he did. We'll erect a monument somewhere. Maybe create a Huntsman Hall of Fame."

Iona smiled. "I'll tell him. He'll be all humble about it, but I'm sure he'll like it."

"I agree."

"And you know who else is in the cloak? The Harrids. Charlie captured them. No wandering forever on Viridi for those two."

"She had a cloak? I guess it was a soulish one that worked just as well."

"Right." Iona breathed a satisfied sigh. "We're almost there, getting everyone where they're supposed to be. But if Alex went to Viridi, we might never know how Caligar handles her."

"True. But she didn't destroy Earth. So far, so good."

When they landed, Jack swiveled toward them in his chair. "Go on ahead. I'll come behind you. Still pretty slow on these crutches." He pushed the control panel button that opened the side door. "See you in a minute."

"Take your time." Ben rose with Iona. The two walked to the door and hopped to the ground. A fire blazed directly ahead, Kat, Trudy, and Austin standing close to it, warming their hands.

When Kat saw Ben, she ran to him and threw her arms around him. After a warm hug and a fervent kiss, she drew back. "You survived!"

He ran a hand through her windblown hair. "Yeah. Long story. Let's head home, and I'll tell you every gory detail."

"I can't wait. I noticed that the Oculus Gate is gone." Kat kissed Iona on the forehead. "I was worried that you were following a little too closely in Chantal's footsteps."

Iona offered a tremulous smile. "Yeah. I'm still wondering if I should've been the one to give my life." She walked toward the fire. "Anyway, I need to do something important. You might want to watch."

Hand in hand, Ben and Kat followed Iona, and they gathered around the fire with Trudy and Austin, then Jack as he crutched to join them. After everyone exchanged hugs and a few words of greeting, Iona took her cloak off. "I said my goodbyes. It's time for everyone to go home." She threw the cloak into the fire.

As the material crackled at the top of the heap, Iona took Ben's hand and gazed at the flames. Soon, two figures rose and swirled within the rising smoke. They broke free from the plumes and streamed to Iona, the faces of Charlotte and Leo clarifying in the misty forms. Smiling, they twirled around Iona's head, and the smiles seemed to infuse her with a smile of her own. Then she laughed and called out, "Goodbye, Leo. Goodbye, Charlie. Thank you for loving me so much. I love you both, and I'll never forget you."

As the others waved, the two souls shot into the sky in a sparkling jet, like a streaking meteor with twin tails. Seconds later, they vanished.

"Gone to heaven," Ben said, his voice breaking. "Joy forever."

Trudy nudged Iona with an elbow. "What made you laugh?"

"Something Leo said." Iona's grin widened. "I'm a heaven-bound huntsman. Thank you for restoring my soul, my carrot-topped cabalist."

Jack narrowed his eyes. "What's a cabalist?"

"Stumped?" Trudy prodded his arm with a finger. "The cruiser computer has a dictionary. I'll teach you how to use it. Eighth-grade vocabulary words can be a challenge."

"Let's also look up nag. Or maybe just find a mirror for you to look at."

"Hush." Iona squinted at the fire. "I see the Harrids. They're rising from the cloak."

"Where?" Ben asked, blinking at the smoke. "I don't see them. Because I'm not a Reaper?"

"I guess so. Maybe Charlie somehow made herself and Leo visible to everyone. Anyway, the Harrids are gone now. They suddenly disappeared."

"To heaven? Hell?"

Iona shrugged. "No way to know. I'm not even going to think about it."

After packing what little they had brought, they boarded the cruiser, Kat again at the controls and Jack in the copilot's chair. As they flew toward home, everyone told their stories, though Iona added only a little to Ben's account as she sat next to him, holding his hand. The devastating grief would probably overwhelm her for a long time to come.

They landed in the temple parking lot, and Ben led the procession down the corridor toward the basement vault, Jack again on crutches at the back of the line. Since the burning of the rebel base, the vault remained as the only home they had, at least for now.

At the end of the hall, the vault door stood open. Ben raised a fist, signaling a halt. Kat sidled to him and whispered, "Alex?"

"Maybe, but getting here from Alaska isn't easy. No air transport."

"From Viridi is even harder."

Ben shook his head. "I refuse to believe that Caligar let her use his mirror portal. She always has leverage, but no amount of leverage could be enough to convince him."

"I know you forgave him, Ben, and I heard that little speech he gave while we were waiting out the storm, but his throwing you into hell still sticks in my craw."

"Yeah, I get that, but ..." Ben closed his mouth tightly. No use trying to defend Caligar. Kat's doubts were reasonable, and she always had a passion for defending her husband. "You've got a point."

Trudy joined them. "We don't have any weapons, but we have numbers. I'm sure we can take her."

"I'm telling you, it's not her." Ben strode to the opening and looked inside. A man sat in the desk's swivel chair, leaning back casually and watching the door. He seemed familiar, but his identity failed to register.

When he saw Ben, he rose to his feet. "Ah! I'm glad to see you, Benjamin." His face glowed with an unearthly radiance.

"Zachariel?"

"Yes, of course." As the others gathered behind Ben, Zachariel jerked a thumb toward his back. "I assume you didn't recognize me because of my lack of wings. I have no need of them for this assignment, so I retracted them." He waved a hand. "Everyone come closer. I have something important to tell you."

Ben and the others formed a semicircle in front of Zachariel, their backs to the door. "What's going on?" Ben asked.

"Quite a lot." Zachariel set a hand over his heart. "First, it is my honor to tell you that the Almighty is pleased with you to the fullest. All of you. This team of warriors is among the best he has ever called to do his will."

Ben bowed his head. "Thank you. I'm sure we're all grateful for those kind words."

"They are well deserved." Zachariel raised a pair of fingers. "Second, Leo and Charlotte are both in heaven, and they are enjoying the pure bliss of God's presence. Leo, in particular, is ecstatic. He said that he hopes all of you will join him soon, but not too soon. He wouldn't want anyone to meet, as he put it, a premature passing."

Ben glanced at Iona. Her smile seemed to brighten the entire room.

"And third ..." Zachariel gestured toward the open door. "You might be wondering why you found the vault unsecured. When a bullet put the wall monitor out of commission, the computer automatically called for a repair technician. Of course, the technician, an elderly woman of great patience and skill, could not enter because of the locks, so God granted me the opportunity to let her in. I had been praying for the freedom to help you again, but until that time, God always said no, that you had everything under control. That's why I was delighted that I could do this small favor."

"Why was the repair important?" Kat asked. "It could've waited till we got home. It's not a high priority."

"Oh, but it is. I hoped to provide a dazzling display of an event that you know nothing about. You see, Caligar transmitted a message from Viridi for the destruction of the Oculus Gate, and the vault computer captured it. I trust that someone here can show it on your newly repaired screen."

"I can do it." Kat sat in the swivel chair and rolled it to the desktop computer. When she clicked on a few keys, the huge wall display flashed to life and showed her keystrokes as she continued typing. "Found the message. Two seconds."

A video played. Caligar stood in front of the portal at his demolished tower. Apparently, he had placed a camera close enough to record his activities. A few rainwater puddles lay here and there. Another storm had recently blown through.

A few seconds later, Alex appeared from the portal and walked toward him. Caligar lunged, but she dodged and began turning semitransparent. When he spun back, he shouted, "I will destroy you, witch."

At that point, they conversed too quietly to hear, but Alex's voice came through loud and clear when she said, "Lacinda is alive."

Iona gasped. "No. She's dead. When Alex told me so, the mirror said she was telling the truth."

"And Caligar has the mirror," Ben said. "Right?"

Iona nodded. "I explained how it works. He knows she's lying."

On the display, Alex displayed a small device in her hand. Lacinda's voice seemed to come from it, though her words were too quiet to hear.

"Alex is an expert at mimicking," Iona said. "She's trying to fool Caligar. That's her talking, not Lacinda."

The Viridi conversation continued. "If you want me to restore Lacinda to you," Alex said, "I demand a peace treaty that gives me half of Viridi."

Again the following words fell by the wayside, too quiet to hear. After a few seconds, Caligar pulled a knife from his belt and cut his braid off.

Ben nodded. "That's part of the solemn vow he told us about."

On the screen, Caligar extended his hand, the braid secured in his palm as his voice boomed. "I agree to your terms."

Alex's wounds returned, a sign that she had gone physical again.

"Something's glimmering in his hand," Iona said. "Behind his braid. I wonder if Alex can see it. Her wounded eye might not pick it up."

Alex shook Caligar's hand. "May the peace between us last for many years to come."

"All will have greater peace now." Caligar yanked the braid from the clasped hands, keeping his hold on Alex. "Go to hell, you monster."

Alex jerked back, but Caligar hung on. As she cried out in a raging wail, her leather-jacketed body elongated into a black ribbon. He opened his hand, revealing the mirror. The surface slurped her in like a dark pasta noodle. Within seconds, she was gone.

Caligar looked at the mirror for a moment, then slammed it down. With a heavy stomp, he crushed it and ground it into the dirt. His head low and his shoulders sagging, he trudged down to the ledge and knelt close to the camera, his face nearly filling the screen.

"Benjamin ..." A huge tear dripped down his cheek. "Your plan worked as expected. Winella sang *the Eternity Psalm* to activate the mirror. Winella and Bazrah have been concealing themselves in the tunnel in case the psalm's effect on the mirror elapsed and I needed Winella to sing it again. What you cannot know is that the mirror revealed that Alex was telling the truth. Somehow Lacinda is still alive. I could not discern if the voice Alex played was really Lacinda's, but the statement that Lacinda is alive was clearly true. Yet, I carried out our plan and sent Alex to her doom, which I verified by watching her splash into the Lake of Fire."

Caligar's voice cracked. "Benjamin, I have atoned for my sins against you. I rejected the temptation to trust Alex as a way to save my beloved daughter, realizing that she would use my mirror portal to bring harm to you. I could not allow that, even at the terrible price of losing Lacinda once again. I chose to trust you and God instead." More tears coursed down his cheeks. "Benjamin, I beg of you, please do all you can to find Lacinda. If you do find her, and even if you are unable to send her back to me, at least she will be safe. I hope you will be able to somehow let me know. Then I can be at peace." He heaved a sigh and reached a hand toward the camera. "Now I must hurry to the mesa and send this message to you before—"

"Father?"

Caligar shifted on his knees and looked behind him. A tall girl wearing prairie-style leather stood a few steps away, a long dark braid draped over her front. "Father, am I dreaming?"

"Lacinda!" He climbed to his feet, stumbling at first before leaping to her. He gathered her into his huge arms and held her close. "No, no, my dear daughter. You are not dreaming."

Winella and Bazrah ran out of the tunnel and joined them in a family hug, both squealing with delight.

Iona slid her hand into Ben's and held it tightly as she gave it three squeezes. He returned four and smiled. How could it get any better than this?

When Caligar drew back, breaking the huddle, Lacinda nodded toward the camera. "I was wondering if I was dreaming because you were speaking English to someone I cannot see. I decided to speak in the same manner."

"I will explain later." He grasped her shoulders and crouched to look at her eye to eye. "I heard you were dead. How did you survive? How did you get here?"

She blinked. "It was so strange. Somehow I awakened in a forest with an angel named Azrael standing over me. He said that my soul stayed in my body because hell is not meant for those from Viridi. He decided to restore my life because the only way I could leave hell would be if I were alive. Then he flew with me in his arms to a cold place, and he left me on a strange glowing floor. He told me to wait, and I would see my murderer, but to stay out of her sight until I could secretly follow her through a ..." She cocked her head. "A portal?"

"Yes," Caligar said. "A portal. Go on."

"When she went through, I pushed my head into the portal and waited a moment until she was in conversation with you, then I passed the rest of the way through and hid behind a boulder, watching, certain that I had to be dreaming because of the way she disappeared. Then I watched you come down to this ledge, and I followed."

Caligar embraced her again. "I will return in a moment." He hustled back to the camera. "Benjamin, I need not tell you what transpired. You have seen it for yourself. Now I must hurry to send this message to you. Thank you for trusting in me, my friend, though I did not deserve it."

The screen went blank, and everyone stood in silence. After a few seconds, Jack began a slow clap. The others joined in, and the clapping accelerated. Jack let out a whoop, and everyone hugged each other until there was no one left to hug.

When the celebration ended, Zachariel breathed a satisfied sigh. "It is so good to see this result. You have all suffered greatly, and it is time to heal."

"Is there anything left for us to do?" Ben asked.

"Not much. Four trees need to be cut down and their fruit burned. A few people still have Refectors possessing them, but without a leader, they are relatively harmless. You can collect them in time. And the governments of the world need to be restored to prevent chaos."

Jack flapped his lips. "Not much. Just destroy the fruits of evil and bring about world peace."

Zachariel laughed. "Whether or not you will be involved in that process is up to you. Feel free to rest and heal, both in body and in spirit. You deserve it." Wings appeared behind him, and he flew toward the door. "Farewell, my friends. I will see you again in heaven someday."

When he left, Ben extended his arms. Everyone joined in a huddle and embraced in a group hug. He looked at each tired face in turn. Tired, yes. But their smiles proved that all the suffering was worth it. "We are an amazing team. Every one of us has done his or her part to save this world, and for that you should all be proud."

Jack called out, "Hear, hear! You're right about that. The best team on the planet."

Ben smiled. "Yes, a team, but more than a team. We're a family. We're not all named Garrison, but we're still a family. Me, Kat, Jack, Trudy, Leo, Charlotte." He looked at Austin. "And you?"

Austin drew his hood back and smiled. "Yeah. I'm in. I'm still adjusting to being out of hell, but yeah. This family is a blast. Literally."

"Glad to have you aboard." Ben looked at Iona. "And how about you?"

She beamed, her wide smile and eyes highlighting her freckled glow. "Definitely. I can't consider myself part of the Horace Macklin family anymore. That part of my life is gone forever."

"Cut the schmaltz," Trudy said, rolling her eyes. "Finish your speech and let's find some food. I'm starved."

"Hear, hear!" Jack said again. "I mean, I'm all for feel-good speeches, but we haven't had a decent meal in I don't know how long."

"All right, all right." As the group uncoupled, Ben kept a hand on Iona. He bent over and looked into her eyes. "Welcome to the family."

She leaped into his arms, and they hugged again. As he pivoted slowly with her, Kat watched and brushed a tear from her cheek.

Iona whispered into Ben's ear. "My name is Iona Garrison, daughter of Ben and Kat Garrison. Niece of Jack and Trudy Garrison. Our family cornered the fake angels so Chantal could blow them up, you ... Dad ... jumped into hell itself to rescue me, and you outfoxed Alex to save the world. Hardly anyone will ever know what a hero you are." She tightened her hold and kissed his cheek. "But I'll know. And I'll never forget."

Ben swallowed back an emerging sob. His voice shaking, he whispered in return, "That's all I need, Iona. That's all I need."

Made in the USA
Columbia, SC
08 February 2023